2009

EXILES

EXILES

ELLIOT

KRIEGER

Published by
Soho Press, Inc.
853 Broadway
New York, NY 10003

Library of Congress Cataloging-in-Publication Data

Krieger, Elliot.
Exiles / Elliot Krieger.
p. cm.
ISBN 978-1-56947-589-8
1. Student movements—Fiction. 2. Americans—Sweden—Fiction.
3. Sweden—Fiction. 4. Nineteen sixties—Fiction. I. Title.

PS3611.R5435E95 2009
813'.6—dc22
2009010631

10 9 8 7 6 5 4 3 2 1

In memory of my parents, Sidney and Ruth Krieger

Flashing for the warriors whose strength is not to fight
Flashing for the refugees on the unarmed road of flight
. . . We gazed upon the chimes of freedom flashing.

—Bob Dylan, "Chimes of Freedom"

FEBRUARY

1970

1

One of the pleasures of a railroad journey is the illusion that the landscape is passing by, though in fact, as you are reminded when you catch a glimpse of cars idling at a gated crossing or passengers on a platform waiting for the local or a group of children waving and tossing stones from an embankment, you are the one in motion while the landscape is fixed in its place and undisturbed by your passage. On a long enough journey, the view from the window becomes a narrative, but with no beginning and no end, just a continuously receding strip of a world that can be, for the traveler, a way to translate space into time, as what's left behind vanishes not only into the distance but also into the past.

Spiegel had been traveling for more than three days. He had crossed the ocean, been whisked by cab through the evening rush in the amber light of the city of Paris, had struggled with his heavy bags and his rudimentary French as he plunged his way through the Gare du Nord barely in time to catch the North Star, which carried him across the plains of Belgium and the dark flatlands of Germany, up through the night into Denmark's little mitten, and, with ferry crossings, at last into the forests of Sweden. He rustled the leaves of his railroad ticket, smearing the ink onto his fingertips. After a turbulent, restless night in the *couchette*, he had idled away the morning and afternoon contemplating the monotonous stretches of frozen lakes and snow-dusted pines until the gray sky gave way to black. When Spiegel looked out the window at the winter night, he saw only his own pale reflection staring back, as if, ghostly, a disembodied portion of himself had been brought along on the journey to act as a guardian.

In Stockholm he transferred to the local for the final leg, or toe perhaps, of his travels—an hour's ride north to the small city of Uppsala. He liked that name. It was one of the few words in Swedish he was sure that he could pronounce. Uppsala—what could go wrong in such a place? For the fortunate citizens of Uppsala, wouldn't life be a matter of constant good cheer, self-improvement, and civic boosterism? Uppsala, he thought, where Swedes go to get high. He knew nothing about the city.

Spiegel's knees seemed to quiver as he walked along the open platform toward the small Uppsala station, as if he had forgotten how to walk on a solid footing. The train had pulled away, leaving behind an emptiness, a vacuum. The air seemed extraordinarily cold, the night quiet. The few noises from the station house, the rail yards, the adjacent parking lot seemed to Spiegel's ears, after the unabated roar of steel on steel, like mere whispers. He was surprised, too, by the pervasive darkness. The platform clocks said it was a few minutes past six, but the sky was black as carbon and the air seemed icy and almost palpable. Spiegel's breath didn't leave the kind of foggy smoke that he remembered from cold winter nights in America but a more fragmented kind of ice-mist, as if the air were so still and dry that the moisture from his lips exploded immediately on exhale into a crystalline vapor, and then disappeared.

No one but railroad workers, slapping their hands to startle the cold, stood on the platform. Spiegel could see a few people, their faces mummified in thick wool scarves and downy caps, inside the station house, tapping the frosty glass, swirling their gloves against the panes in big circles to wipe lopsided portholes through which they could survey the platform. The row of faces, each peering through its own island of cleared glass, looked to Spiegel like a comic strip. He scanned the panels. How could he recognize anyone? There was nothing to see but fabric and eyes. Sweden, he thought, is a land without features. So far, everyone here looks alike—they look like no one.

He shouldered his backpack and lugged his duffel bag into the station. The ticket windows were closed. There was a little snack bar, called a kiosk, that seemed to sell only strange tubes of what seemed to be processed cheese. Spiegel bought a tube because he needed the change. He squeezed a bit of the contents, which looked like beige plastic flecked with some kind of spackling, onto his fingertip. It tasted, well, not so bad—like an especially pungent Velveeta. Spiegel was glad, though, that he couldn't read the label. Maybe, after all, he had purchased some sort of skin ointment or welding glue?

He found the telephones, and found them to be confusing. A big red button at the center of the dial had some words in Swedish and a weird icon of a person in great distress—sort of like a little sketch of Munch's *Scream*. What if I push it? Spiegel wondered. Will it connect me directly to the art museum? He fumbled in his pocket for some kroner and for the slip of paper on which he had scribbled the number that he needed.

And then he felt a hand on his shoulder. He turned.

"Lenny? Yes, it's you. Sorry I'm late. I wasn't sure you'd be on this train. Welcome to Sweden. I recognized you right away."

He recognized the girl right away, too. He had observed her often back in the States. He had seen her chatting with friends in the cafeteria, handing out leaflets on the green, speaking at a rally, studying, or seeming to, at a carrel in the library. She had never noticed him, he knew, but that was all right. He was content, or at least resigned, back in those days, to admire her from afar. He was new on the campus, trying to get back into the groove of academic life after a rocky start at one of the state schools. He had spent most of his first semester wishing that he had the courage to talk to that lovely girl with the pigtails and the almond eyes. Only later did he learn her name, Tracy Green. By that time, she had gone underground.

"You're Tracy?" She nodded, smiled. He reached to shake her hand, but she spread her arms wide and pulled Spiegel to her in a tight embrace. He reached his arms around her, and the nylon of their down jackets scratched and whistled.

"It's good to see you. We've missed you," she said.

"Missed me? You've never really met me."

"We've missed America, and everyone back there. Iris has been in touch with us. She's told us all about you, and about everything you did for us. Just hearing her voice—"

"You've called her? She never told me."

"Not often. It's risky, and too expensive. Look." She broke the embrace, pointed to the bank of phones. "Twenty-five kroner just for a local call. Just because the phone system is owned by the state doesn't mean it's cheap. Everything here is taxed phenomenally. Fuel tax, food tax, liquor tax. Water tax every time you flush the toilet. Clean-air tax every time you open the window."

"Complaining about taxes, you sound like a capitalist."

"All the categories are different here," she said. "You'll see."

"I don't know. So far things look pretty good. Clean, at least."

"Yeah. Everything's clean. Come on." She hoisted his duffel bag.

Tracy's little, but strong, Spiegel thought. He had been shouldering his pack for three days, and his arms felt as if they were about to pop from the sockets. Maybe it was his crazy night in the *couchette* on the train—a compartment with six beds that popped from the wall like venetian blinds, and not enough room, once you're zipped inside your slot, for even a big dream.

"How far is it?" Spiegel asked.

"It's right here."

"You live in the station? I didn't know housing was that tight."

Tracy looked at Spiegel and smiled. She liked his sense of humor already. "I've got a car," she said. "See?"

Tracy's Beetle was parked in a far corner of the nearly empty lot, under a street lamp that cast a weird sodium glow like rust. The car looked battered. The front fender sagged, and a tattered sticker with two raised fists and some words that Spiegel couldn't discern was fixed to the rear bumper, like some sort of bandage.

"How'd you get a car here?" Spiegel asked. "You didn't have it shipped?"

"No, that would be way too expensive. We can't really afford Rosa, either."

"Rosa?"

"You're in her. Rosa the Red. She's kind of owned by the whole community, but we get to keep her."

"Like a dog that followed you home from school?"

"Yeah, we like strays."

As with most VWs Spiegel had known, the front seat had become an all-purpose receptacle, filled with books, leaflets, crushed cigarette cartons, unmatched gloves, soda cans, and a box or two crammed with records, wrenches, and spare auto parts. He scrunched his knees in and wiped the window with his wrist. He thought he would get a look around the town while they drove to Tracy's place, but it was hard to keep the windshield clear of frost. The heat roared, and, in the confined space, the moisture from their breath and their bodies kept the glass in a steady soak. So Spiegel's first view of Uppsala was like a series of snapshots taken through a mist—a glimpse of a row of neat, amber-colored town houses as Tracy wheeled around a corner; a triplet of low-arched bridges crossing an ice-blocked river; a warren of narrow cobblestone streets that cut like a maze through the high embankments of fresh snow; Gothic brick buildings whose white spires gleamed in the moonlight like ivory.

"We live here," Tracy said, as she turned into an alley between two tiny shops, closed for the night. All that Spiegel could see at first was a little sign that read TOBAK. That one, he could figure out. "Hey, I'm learning Swedish already," he said to Tracy. "It's a tobacco store."

"You're a natural linguist," she said.

Behind the shop, at the back of the alley, stood a two-story house with tall bay windows framed by wrought-iron filigree. Gingerbread trim ran the length of the steeply pitched roofline. It's like a dollhouse, Spiegel thought. He expected to see, poking above the roofline, a brick chimney with a little curlicue of gray smoke twisting into the sky, like a child's drawing of home.

"How did you find this place?" Spiegel said.

"There are a lot of one-way streets in the Old City. But we're really not that far from the train station. I'll show you how to walk there, in the morning."

"No, I mean—

"Oh. Find it? There's a list of available housing. The city council runs it in the paper. But to get a good place, you have to be lucky. You like it? "

"It's like a postcard of Europe. It's where I imagined you should be living. Artists in a garret, philosophers in a salon—"

"Trolls in a hut."

"No, I think your house is perfect," Spiegel said. "America's full of places that look like this, but they're all pseudo. You've got the real thing."

"Funny, but this place came cheap," Tracy said. "Around here, people don't really like old houses. Most Swedes want something new, up to the minute. They let the older houses fall apart, and then rent them to students, or worse."

"What's worse than students?"

"Us. Foreigners."

Spiegel hauled his bags out of the backseat as Tracy brushed some snow off the stone doorstep.

"I think I could get to like living in this kind of place," Spiegel said.

"Well, don't get too used to it. Where you're going to be living, it's brand new. In fact, they're still building it."

"Yeah, the university set something up," Spiegel said. "A place called Flogsta."

"You'll dig it," Tracy said. "But it's kind of far out."

"I like far-out."

"I mean far out of town," she said, fumbling with a key. "Here we go."

Tracy opened the front door, and they stepped into a small vestibule. On a closer look—or maybe because he had been clued in—Spiegel could see the evidence of shabbiness. The carpet was frayed, the plaster on the walls was spidered, there was a faint odor of must and rot, perhaps rising from beneath the floorboards. At the doorway stood several precarious stacks of magazines and newspapers, set out for some indeterminate collection. Tracy fumbled with a big silver skeleton key.

"Here, get the handle, would you," she said. "I don't know why he locks the inside door."

Spiegel slipped his bag off his shoulder and worked the door handle, a large lever, made of nickel probably, and rubbed smooth by years of use.

"We're here," Tracy called as they entered. "I found him." She pushed open the door.

"This place is great," Spiegel said. The apartment had everything you could want: good floors, high ceilings, huge windows almost two stories tall. The furnishings were spartan, even by student standards: some orange-crate coffee tables and bare-board bookshelves and spice racks, a couple of beanbag chairs, a frayed oval rug on the floor. Against the far wall sat an overstuffed, scratchy-looking couch. Scattered about the room were stacks of pamphlets, drafts of petitions, leaflets and colorful brochures for the National Liberation Front, the PLO, the Sandinistas, the Venceremos, the Black Panthers, the Red Army. It looked like a recruiting station for the Third World.

Tacked onto the walls were great posters, colorful and tattered—some in Swedish, some in English, some apparently in Chinese, all urging the workers to rise as one and fight the oppressors, to lift up their arms against colonial aggression, to remain valiant in the struggle to return the land to the people. There were enormous pictures of peasants bearing arms, climbing mountains, digging irrigation trenches, their faces radiant and determined, fixed on some distant point so that in effect the viewer was not drawn in but encouraged to turn away from the poster, to focus attention on the work remaining to be done in the material world.

"You'd never see those back in the States. We got them from the People's Republic," said a fellow as he stepped in from the kitchen, drying a coffee mug with a dish towel. "Do you like them?"

"Sure," Spiegel said. "Screeds against injustice is my favorite form of art. I call it Oppressionism."

"This is Lenny Spiegel," Tracy said. "And you must know who this is," she added, turning to Spiegel.

"You're Brian Aaronson."

"Come here, man. It's great to see you at last," Aaronson said.

"We've heard so much about you from Iris. About all you've done already."

"It wasn't so much. I was just in the right place at the right time—"

"But this. Coming all the way here. Lots of people say, yeah, I'm going to do something, to help you guys in Sweden. And then they forget, or they cut us a check and that's it. Their conscience is clear. They've paid their debt. But you—well, you're here. That says it all."

"Thanks, man," Spiegel said. "Those are good words to hear." Spiegel held out his hand, palm open and fist up, for a soul handshake, but Aaronson took him by the shoulders and pulled him close, chest to chest, for a brotherly embrace.

"We're going to end this fucking war," Aaronson said.

Spiegel laughed. "I don't know about ending the war. That's a lot to put on one guy's ticket. But I came here to help your community, maybe to bring some of you guys home."

"It's the same thing," Aaronson said. "We're not coming home until the war is over. But you can bring our message home."

"And tell us everything that's going on back in the States," Tracy put in. "We hear so little—and even then I don't think we get the whole story. Everyone's worried, whenever they talk to us, about being taped or tapped. And I'm not even sure that the mail's secure."

"Definitely, I'll fill you in," Spiegel said. "There's a lot to tell."

"But first," Tracy said, "let me get a good look at you two guys together. Stand side by side. No, back-to-back."

They complied, like schoolboys told to line up for recess, awkward, impatient, maybe slightly annoyed to be placed under scrutiny.

"It's weird," Tracy said. "To think, you two guys must have crossed paths all the time back in school, but you never met. You had to travel halfway around the world for your lives to converge. So I guess I'm the first one to see you actually together."

Tracy compared them as if she were examining some rare biological specimens. She moved close, leaned back a little, slowly walked around Spiegel and Aaronson to see them from every angle. At first, she was disappointed. The resemblance was not immediately obvious, for Spiegel's hair was a tangle of unruly brown corkscrews and his smile was obscured by a shaggy auburn beard while Aaronson was clean-shaven, his hair neatly cropped. But as she adjusted her focus, Tracy could see why so many people had mistaken one for the other. They had the exact same facial structure: angular, slightly lantern-jawed, thick eyebrows, intense blue eyes. More remarkably, they carried themselves the same way, leaning slightly forward, as if always in a rush, a tangle of nerves and impatience. They had the same mannerisms, too—fidgety hands, feet tapping to some mad internal rhythm—and, evidently, the same taste in clothes, or the same budget. They each wore jeans, flannel shirts, and thick-soled work boots. They could be brothers. They could be twins.

"I understand it now. It must be weird for you guys, to look at each other," Tracy said.

"I don't know," Spiegel said. "I'm not sure I see the resemblance."

"That's because you didn't see him before he cut his hair," Tracy said. "I'm looking at you, and I see Aaronson, the way he looked six months ago."

"You have to get beyond the hair, man," Aaronson said. "Hair's just superficial."

"Is that why you cut yours?" Spiegel asked. "To try to get down to the bare essence?"

Aaronson laughed. "It's nothing like that," he said. "Long hair made me stand out too much. It marks you right away as an American."

"What are you trying to do then? Blend in? Become a Swede?"

"In six months, you'll need subtitles to understand me."

"Say something, then," Spiegel said.

"*Da ringer jåg på torsdag kväll.*"

"What did he say?"

"He said, 'I'll call you up on Thursday night,'" Tracy said. "He just memorized it because it sounds so Swedish. Whenever people ask him to say something, that's what he comes out with. It's the only thing he can say."

"How about you, Tracy?"

"*Nej, tack*. That means, no thanks. That's what you say when they offer to put ketchup on your hot dog at the kiosk."

"I'm thinking I might want to learn a little of the language, too, while I'm here," Spiegel said.

"You should," Tracy said. "Anyone on a student visa can sign up for a Swedish class, and they teach you for free."

"Are you guys in the class?"

"Well," Aaronson said. "Right now I'm concentrating on my political work."

"We're involved with a group of deserters, here in Uppsala," Tracy said.

"I'm kind of their representative," Aaronson said. "I go before municipal boards and hearing officers, helping guys apply for permits and vouchers, housing allowances, food and welfare certificates . . ."

"They give out all that stuff, to the deserters?" Spiegel said. "Sounds like an American here has got it made."

"No American has it made. We're at their mercy, and they know it. We can't leave, obviously, until there's a general amnesty. Sweden's like a big prison, a prison without bars. And I'm like the trusty, the guy who asks the warden for a bigger ration of bread."

"That's not true," Tracy said. "You've become the real leader. Without you, there would be no movement in Uppsala."

"Iris says you were a leader back in the States, too," Spiegel said.

"Not really," Aaronson said, shaking his head. He sat down in the beanbag chair. "I just got sucked into the role. I must have been crazy. My nerves were like live wires. I'd been strung out all summer trying organize the cafeteria workers at the student union. You heard about that?"

"Yeah, Iris told me. The movement that went nowhere. In fact, the workers voted to decertify."

"Right. I felt useless, wasted. Guys in the movement were

ignoring me, like anything I touched would turn to poison. I felt I had to do something dramatic to prove myself, to prove my worth."

"So you busted up the draft office just to prove yourself? People back on campus, guys like Brewer, always said it was a carefully executed plot."

"No, it was an impulse," Aaronson said. He laughed again. "I never expected it to lead to this, though: life in exile for me, for Tracy, now for you, too. I never thought one crazy act could change the course of so many people's lives."

"No, me neither," Spiegel said. "I never even thought I would be drawn into the movement. I had a low draft number, and I was basically nonpolitical. But I guess I learned that you can't really run away from history, or at least from your own role in it. Iris taught me that we all bear some responsibility for the sins of our parents, and for the crimes committed in our name."

"You mean the war," Tracy said.

"That, and everything," Spiegel said. "It's all connected. One thing leads to another. If you hadn't smashed up the draft board, I wouldn't be here."

For Aaronson's attack on the draft board, and its aftermath, had set off the most amazing, and unsettling, series of events in Spiegel's life, a chain reaction of mistakes, misperceptions, and deceptions that had nearly gotten Spiegel killed, but that eventually, he would come to realize, had saved his life and brought him here, at last, to Aaronson's door.

Spiegel had enrolled in the state university hoping to get his wayward academic career, which during two hazy years at one of the downstate colleges had been devoted primarily to cigarettes and other combustibles, back on track. He thought that he could make a fresh start, that he could blend into the background on a big campus in a big city. He took an apartment, alone, in a little carriage house behind a shabby Victorian on a quiet side street, and he determined to devote himself to his studies, English, with the thought of pre-law. He staked out a carrel in the library, and through the fall tried to concentrate on schoolwork, which he found to be surprisingly easy. His mind clear of intoxicants, his life devoid of friends and other distractions, he became a reasonably good student, for the first time since grade school, since he had discovered the vices of sex and rock 'n' roll.

But later in the semester, with the first snows, things began to get weird. Spiegel wondered if his mind was shot. He wondered if it were the long-term effects of some of the exotic chemicals he had ingested downstate, maybe some peculiar time-release psychic multivitamin that had been cooked up in one of the pharmolabs in Brooklyn where he and his pals used to send out for supplies. He couldn't quite explain it, but it was as if he were leading a double life. People he didn't know would greet him, make strange comments to him in passing that they expected him to comprehend, even leave cryptic messages on his windshield, drop things off at his library desk. What was happening? When he wasn't in his own life, whose was he in?

Until eventually, he thought, maybe he should follow the path, the paper trail, and see where it led him, track down the source of one of the messages and see if he could discover the origin of this force that had threatened to unsettle his life. One day a cute girl he had been eyeing in the library left a stack of flyers beside his book bag. Maybe she had left them for him, maybe for someone else, maybe inadvertently. But Spiegel decided to take the flyers, hang on to them, and see what developed. Would the girl come back in search of them? The leaflets announced a rally to be held at a downtown square later in the week—Students and Workers United Against the War. Spiegel hadn't thought much about the war. His draft number was hopeful, and even if he were called for a physical he was confident that if he smoked hard enough and dieted ruthlessly he could probably incapacitate himself sufficiently to fool an army doctor. But he thought, well, maybe he should go to this rally, just to see.

He never got to go. Two days after he took the leaflets, a platoon of armed cops stormed his apartment. He had been in the shower. He saw the flashing lights, heard the sirens, heard everyone hollering and banging on the door. He was sure his place was on fire, so he grabbed a towel, slipped out of a window, slid down a porch railing, and landed hard in a snowbank. Immediately, a swarm of cops was on him, swinging their batons, mashing his face into the snow, pinning his arms back, snapping plastic cuffs around his wrists, yelling. The lights were blinding him, TV cameras were in his face, he was freezing, terrified, and in agony from the beating and from the fall. Someone hauled him up by the shoulder, shoved him toward a police car. Someone else yelled for a stretcher, an ambulance. A reporter shoved a microphone at him and screamed out questions that made no sense: Were you acting alone, or on orders? Was your group responsible for the bomb in Syracuse? Were you making a statement or—

That was the last Spiegel heard, the last he could remember. He was shoved into a squad car. Someone threw a greatcoat over him. He hugged the scratchy warmth to his face and collapsed sideways onto the seat as the sirens wailed off into the night.

He awoke the next morning in a hospital bed. His right leg was in traction, his left arm in a cast. A thick bandage covered his right eye. His tongue felt dull and waxy, his skin hot. He felt a sharp pain in his neck as he turned his head to look around. Gray snow streaked the tall windows. In a wooden chair by the door sat a uniformed policeman, nodding into sleep. At first Spiegel thought, how nice, they've sent an officer to protect me. Then it came back to him—the cops bursting into his apartment, crashing through the door, surrounding him in their vicious huddle, on him like dogs on a bone, the nightsticks going up and down, up and down—and he broke into a sweat. Nausea passed through him like a tide, and he thought, how do I get out? Where do I go? He couldn't move, even to reach the call button.

And then he heard an argument in the hall. The cop at the door was awake, standing, barring the entryway with his fat blue bulk. Beyond him, her face crowned by a halo of light cast by a globe in the hallway, stood a woman, tall, beautiful, her hair a dark cascade of ringlets that fell to her shoulders. She was talking at the cop, not yelling exactly, but speaking forcefully, aggressively: "You've got to let me in . . . right to counsel . . . see my client . . ."

Perhaps I'm dreaming, Spiegel thought, and if I close my eyes,

I will wake up in my own bed, free of pain. He tried to will himself deeper into sleep, to a depth beyond dreams. And perhaps he succeeded, because when he opened his eyes again the room was quiet, the arguments had ceased. The shades had been drawn, which tinted the room with a faint wash of gray shadow. The policeman was no longer in the doorway. Standing over his bed, looking down at him with a strange mixture of solicitude and disquiet, was the lovely woman he had seen in the hallway. He had seen her before, of course, on campus, at the library. She was the one who had left the leaflets on his desk. Her name was Iris.

"And who the hell," she said, "are you?"

He found that, with great concentration and care, he could manage to speak. He told her his name.

"Listen, I thought . . . Jesus," Iris said. "I mean, do you know why you're here?"

"A bunch of cops," he looked around to make sure that they were alone, "beat the shit out of me."

"They booked you, too."

"For what? Resisting arrest?"

"They think you smashed up the draft board."

"They what?" Spiegel said. "Why would I do that? I'm going to be four-F."

"They thought you were someone else. The thing is, and I think I can tell this, even with that stuff wrapped half around your skull, you look just like this other guy."

"Like who?" Spiegel was having trouble focusing. Maybe they had given him some drugs. Maybe he needed some. "Are you a nurse?" he said.

"I'm a lawyer. Well, a law student, actually. But, as they say, you don't need a weatherman . . . I mean, you've been screwed. And we've got to figure how to get you out of here."

It was clear right away to Iris—Iris Mandel—that the cops had arrested the wrong guy. She knew, through a series of frantic, heavily coded calls from her best friend, Tracy, that Aaronson had trashed the downtown draft board and then crossed the bridge to Canada. Tracy had followed with a trunkful of Aaronson's clothes and books. Their plan was to head for Toronto and try to put together enough gas money to go west. They had friends who owned a bookstore in Vancouver.

But meanwhile the cops, acting on some bad information supplied by a mole the dean must have placed among the student left—they would have to get to the root of that one, unearth the bastard—had learned almost immediately that it was Aaronson who had trashed the draft board, and they got a federal warrant for his arrest. But then, with typical pig ineptitude, using a photo ID supplied by stoolies from the university registrar, they went off and nailed the wrong guy, Aaronson's exact look-alike, his double.

Iris looked closely at Spiegel. Yes, anyone could mistake him for Aaronson. Perhaps, in the past, she had done so herself. "Don't worry," she said. "I can get you off."

She did, and it was terribly embarrassing for the feds and the police. Once they realized that they had the wrong guy, they threatened to book Spiegel anyway, on the theory that, as an out-of-state student enrolled at the university, even if he hadn't ripped up the draft board he was probably violating some sort of federal law: conspiracy? Unlawful assembly? Flight to avoid arrest? Who cares. But no, Spiegel was clean, anonymous, uninteresting—until, at Iris's urging, he threatened to sue for false arrest, police brutality, violation of his rights to due process and protection against unreasonable search and seizure, the works. Then, he got really interesting, and the feds suggested that he had conked two of the city cops; they had it on video from one of the TV stations (how they had gotten the video without a subpoena would be a damn good question, Iris realized), and if Spiegel so much as filed a motion for discovery in regard to any civil suit, they warned, the criminal case against him might find its way directly to the next session of the federal grand jury.

Fuck them, Iris counseled. She was beginning to like Spiegel. True, he had no political history and he showed serious tendencies toward bourgeois individualism. She would have a lot of education to take on with this guy, a real project. But still—he was cute. And he was courageous. He'd fought those pigs, he held out, wouldn't tell them a goddamn thing about who really hit up the draft board, what he knew about Aaronson's where-abouts—which was, frankly, nothing, although the feds didn't believe that—how he came to have in his possession numerous documents that advocated the overthrow of the United States government, anything. How had he gotten those leaflets?

"You gave them to me," Spiegel told her. "Of course you don't remember." Now he understood that she had mistaken him for Aaronson when she left the stack of flyers on his library desk. He never told her why he had held onto them, that he had hoped the flyers would bring them together.

Iris took Spiegel on as her protégé, bringing him with her to meetings, introducing him to others in the movement. She had tons of work to do for Students and Workers United, especially with Aaronson and Tracy gone. Iris worried about them, but she had no way to reach them directly. She got an unsigned card from them occasionally and once a hurried, whispered phone call from Tracy that woke her toward dawn. They were in Montreal, where a separatist printer was going to run them fake passports, and a shadowy internationalist organization had fronted Aaronson the money for passage to Sweden. Canada was okay, apparently, for the garden-variety draft evader, but for more serious activists, resisters, deserters, felons on the run like Aaronson, it was dangerous ground. If found out, he could be held and deported. They had to travel farther, to get beyond the reach of America's tiger claws. Iris wished Tracy good luck, and went back to sleep in tears.

She didn't hear from Tracy and Aaronson again for weeks, when Iris got a three-page letter from Uppsala. In Sweden, they were out of danger, for Sweden, alone among the European nations, would not extradite political refugees, and was, as a result, a haven for leftists, rightists, nationalists, and extrem-ists of every hue. But few Americans had settled in Uppsala. Uppsala was a university town, and for the deserters, most of them high-school dropouts whose reading consisted of car manuals, diner menus, and comic books, a university was more exotic and more frightening than an Asian jungle flushed with fire. Most of the deserters huddled in Stockholm, which afforded them a degree of anonymity and where hashish and other items of contraband were in ready supply in the dark alleys behind the railroad yards. But as the American community continued to grow, as more and more soldiers threw down their arms and went over the wall, the deserters found themselves the objects of scrutiny, wrath, and occasional harassment. Some right-wing politicians had begun to campaign against the American invasion, which they believed would strain the Swedish economy and corrupt the morals of the nation's youth.

Because Stockholm had become so hot, a stewpot of anti-American rhetoric and of jingoistic backlash, the movement decided that the next wave of deserters should be settled in the outlying cities. Aaronson agreed to establish a new settlement in Uppsala. His job was to keep the chapter in the news so as to draw some of the heat, and some of the American population, away from Stockholm. What irony, he wrote to Iris. I have become like an army recruiting station, but in reverse. We end up by becoming that which we destroy. He wondered if, after all, he and Tracy might have been better off staying home and making a stand, enduring a huge political trial and, at the end, at worst, a stint in federal prison, where Aaronson could organize and Tracy could maybe write a book.

Iris wrote back, through a safe drop-box number in Paris where a French student leftist group picked up sensitive mail and distributed it by private courier throughout the Baltics, and she told them about Spiegel. They had never met him, but now they would understand: why the flyers Iris thought she had delivered to Aaronson never arrived, why so many people during Aaronson's last days on campus had thought they had seen him in places he hadn't been. Iris described how Spiegel had been arrested in Aaronson's stead—they had heard something about that, but never understood how the cops could have made such a mistake—and how she had gotten him off, and gotten to know him, in fact to like him and to trust him, had brought him into Students and Workers United, introduced him to the leaders, to Brewer and the others.

She didn't tell Tracy in her letter, but she and Spiegel were

living together. They tried to keep their relationship in the
shadows because the high priests of the movement preached that
love was a bourgeois concept, a form of ownership, a relic of
the colonial and imperialist ideology. Love, as Brewer had once
argued during a self-study seminar, was the most powerful of the
opiates, much more seductive than religion had been to Marx's
generation.

So no one in the movement actually dated. They danced,
drank, smoked dope, sometimes went out to hear a band or to
see a movie, but never as couples, always in a small group, three
at the least, "two students and a worker," someone once joked.
When Iris learned about Tracy and Aaronson, not just that Tracy
had followed Aaronson to Canada, but that she had moved in
with him, fallen in love with him, linked her life and her fate to
his, Iris was, she had to admit to herself, puzzled and hurt, as
if she had been taken advantage of, as if there were a big party
going on down the block and she had not been invited, or worse,
had never even known of the goings-on until she came upon the
soggy streamers and the flat balloons strewn about the yard and
sidewalk the next morning.

Iris wondered, though, how much Brewer had heard about
her and Spiegel when he made his suggestion that Spiegel be
dispatched as a liaison to Sweden. It was during one of the weekly
cell meetings, a dozen students crowded into Brewer's tiny apartment: lights dim, shades drawn, radiators coughing steam and
heating the room to a fizz. Since Aaronson's departure, Brewer
had assumed the leadership of Students and Workers United,
and his goal, he said, in the aftermath of the great cafeteria-work-
er fiasco, was to build solidarity with the international brigades.
He argued that Spiegel would be the perfect delegate to send
abroad because he was new to the movement and unknown to the
spooks and the feds. Besides, Brewer said, while the case against
Spiegel was still hot, it would be better, safer, to clear Spiegel out
of the country and let the city cops forget all about him, let the
story of his arrest blur in memory, fade off the screen.

"What do you think about that?" someone asked Spiegel, and
he said, truthfully, that he had received his political education

from the blunt edge of the nightstick, that he understood from experience the oppressive power of the pig establishment, and that he would be willing to put his life on the line to advance the cause of liberation and worker solidarity. Brewer smiled, and everyone in the room stubbed out their cigarettes, whistled and cheered, all except Iris, who, as she locked eyes with Brewer, tried to sort through her mixed feelings of pride and sorrow, her willingness to sacrifice love on the altar of politics and her fear that she had been abandoned and betrayed.

Over the next weeks, it was arranged that the SWU would finance Spiegel's journey, using money raised for the Aaronson defense fund. As a cover, Spiegel was enrolled through the little-known state university year abroad program (SUYAP) as an exchange student at Uppsala University. That way, he'd told Iris, he wouldn't even lose credits during the spring semester. Yeah, Iris said, you can build a dictatorship of the proletariat and build up your résumé for law school, at the same time. That's not what I meant, Spiegel said. All I meant is, when all this is over, I can come back here and be with you again. So Iris was sorry to have snapped at Spiegel, to have distrusted him. Perhaps he had, in part, taken on this mission to prove his loyalty and to test his valor, like a knight embarking on a quest. It would be hard to let him go.

"It's a hell of a story," Aaronson said to Spiegel, "all that happened to you—and all because you look like me, they say. But I'm glad it happened. If the cops hadn't grabbed you when they did, they would have come looking for me, and for Tracy. Whether you know it or not, you gave us just the time we needed to get across the border and go underground."

"Even though it probably turned out to be a pretty bad trip for you," Tracy added.

"Yeah, at first. But some good things came out of it, too," Spiegel said. "If the cops hadn't busted me, I never would have met Iris."

"We miss her," Tracy said. "Tell us about her. Tell us everything you know about the States."

They spent rest of the evening talking, drinking tea, and eating what Spiegel would describe as weird stuff from cans, pastes and jellies of various sorts spread onto crunchy rye crackers. Swedish sandwiches, Tracy said. When they finished eating, Tracy collected the cups and dishes and swirled them clean with a long brush she had hung from a hook by the stainless-steel sink. Spiegel felt physically tired but mentally alert, as if he had reached a plateau above the need for sleep. His ears were still ringing from the hours on the train, and he thought he would try to stay awake for a while longer to luxuriate in the silence of the night.

Aaronson snuffed out a smoldering cigarette in a glass tray. "We'll move you into your own place tomorrow," he said. "Give you a little while to settle in. In a week or so, I'll have somebody contact you."

"Whatever you want," Spiegel said. "That's why I came. I mean, I'm not here for the classes or anything. I could start working with you right away—"

"No," Aaronson interrupted. "We'll have to take it a step at a time. The best thing would be for you to separate from us, get going in your own life here and your own routines. Make it look as if you're just a regular exchange student. Don't make it so obvious that you came here for us."

"Yeah, but I don't want to just sit around learning about cheese sandwiches. I want to do what I can to help end the war."

"Well, that's not going to happen overnight," Aaronson said. "I'm telling you. First, get your feet on the ground. Sign up for classes. Get to know the lay of the land. The people here are really uptight, cautious, and they won't take you into their confidence right away."

"I've heard that about Swedes. It's almost a cliché."

"I'm not talking just about the Swedes, though. I mean the Americans, too. A lot of them have been burned by strangers. They've learned to trust nobody. Especially people who haven't been tried by fire."

"So what are you saying? That you're planning to test me?"

"No," Aaronson said. "We're just going to give you a little

time and space. We want you to learn the rules of the game before we put you on the field."

"You okay with that, Lenny?" Tracy asked. "We thought you'd be better off living in your own place. This flat can get crowded, especially when people drop in on ARMS business."

"On what business?" Spiegel asked.

"ARMS. That's our group, American Resisters Movement— Sweden. We'll hook you up with the organization, when the time comes," Tracy said.

"Sure, okay," Spiegel said. "But can't I do something for you guys in the meantime? Run the mimeo or send out pledge cards? Organize a fast or a sit-in?"

"We've got stuff in mind for you," Aaronson said. "But you have to do things on our terms. Nothing rash, nothing crazy. Our relation with the Uppsala city council is really tenuous, and we don't want to do anything to jeopardize our residence status."

So Spiegel let it rest.

"It's late," Tracy said, drying her hands with a terrycloth towel. "I'll get the mattress."

Because of the high ceilings, the apartment seemed to be large. But once you tried to find a place to lie down for a night's sleep, it became obvious that the sense of space was an illusion. There would be plenty of room if you could sleep standing upright. Everywhere Spiegel looked he saw a corner, a doorway, a closet, or some other immobile obstruction that would prevent him from spreading out his gear on the floor.

"I can sleep on the couch," Spiegel said. "It's only for a night."

"No, we can roll this out here," Tracy said. She unfurled a thin cotton mattress, more like a coverlet, and she and Aaronson made up a small bed for Spiegel beneath the bay windows. Lying on his back he could watch the snow crystals drift past the street lamp and disappear into the black sky.

Tracy cleared a bookshelf so that Spiegel could have space to lay out a change of clothes. She watched as he unpacked.

"You didn't bring a lot, for a six-month stay," she said.

"I figure I can get the stuff I need here," Spiegel said. "They have stores in Sweden, don't they?"

"Sure," Tracy said. "But everything's so expensive. You'll wish you'd brought more with you."

"I couldn't carry any more. But somehow, I ended up with this." He handed her a pamphlet.

"That's from the Universal Peace Church, isn't it?" Aaronson said. "Let me see it."

"Did you think it was antiwar?" Tracy asked Spiegel.

"No, it's just—I've got to tell you. I had a strange encounter."

"Those guys are strange," Aaronson said. "They seem to live in the airports and train stations. I think they're spreading all over Europe, like a virus or a rash."

"Yeah, their church is based in Denmark," Tracy said. "Isn't that right?"

Aaronson nodded.

"A bunch of them got on the train with me, in Paris," Spiegel said. "They wandered up and down the aisles all afternoon. In the evening, one of them came into the compartment where I'd been riding."

"I would have moved out. I'd rather sleep sitting up in the café car."

"I was hoping he didn't speak English, but, my luck, he was an American, a big guy, with eyes the color of steel and a jagged scar sliced across his jaw. He was the kind of guy you used to try to get away from in gym class. He'd slam the basketball into your face, just for the hell of it."

"I don't know. Girls' gym was different."

"So this guy sits across from me and stares at me. It's a little creepy; it's going to be a long journey."

"You should have split."

"I tried to ignore him. But he leans forward, fixes me in his mad-man gaze, tells me that the church has changed his life and that it will change mine. Then he shows me this pamphlet. He says the book gives him strength and power, the power to bend my will to his command. He says there is nothing I can do to escape from his control, that he is going to bring me with him to the elders of his church and I will submit to their authority. That's where I should have told him to knock it off, I'm not interested."

"But instead . . ."

"I let him go on. He said the only way I could free myself would be to buy the book from him. Then, I would have the power at my own command."

"So the whole thing is like a big sales pitch," Tracy said.

"Sort of. We sat there, in a showdown. I told him that if he was so powerful, let's see if he can make me buy the book. He couldn't think of anything to say or do. Nothing had prepared him for this. He just sat there grinding his molars. Finally, he says, 'I'll do anything to make you read this book.' 'Fine,' I said. 'Just give it to me.' At that point, like he's acting on cue, he leans toward me, puts his face right in front of mine, and says, 'I'm taking you to our church.' And I say, 'You are?' He nods. So I say, 'I'm taking your book and throwing it out that fucking window.' I reach and grab for the book—of course, the window's closed—when he jumps on me and tries to pin my arm back. I hit him as hard as I can across the chest, and then another shot, to the side of the head. The book goes flying, and we both tumble to the floor. I'm trying to get some leverage so I can pin him, working my knee into his chest, but it's a tight space between the seats. And the next thing I know, someone's pulling me up, by the armpits.

"*Was gehen sie hier?* someone's saying, or something like that. It's the conductor, big German guy, in a uniform. He has a dark walrus mustache and a huge beer gut. He doesn't speak a bit of English, which seems odd in his profession. Two other guys from the church come in and try to calm everyone down, telling the conductor, *der est nicht, nicht*—nothing, nothing, I guess. *Nein, nein* the conductor's saying, and he wants to see everyone's passport."

"You know, you probably should have flown right to Stockholm," Tracy said. "At least they couldn't throw you off a plane."

"Well, no one threw us off, but we did show the guy our passports. Then he took the believers out, to another car I guess. I never saw them again."

"So how'd you get the book?"

"It's weird. I woke up in the morning, just before the train got to the ferry, and the book—it was in my pack. Maybe my pal slipped it there, or one of his partners did, on the way out. Like the tooth fairy."

"So now you've got the power," Aaronson said.

"Well, only if he reads the book," Tracy said. "And masters its teachings."

"And that's the funny thing," Spiegel said. "After all that, he must have slipped me the wrong book. Except for the cover, this one's all in Danish, or Swedish. Can you tell?"

Tracy opened the pamphlet, and leafed through the pages, cheap ink poorly printed on coarse paper. "Danish, Swedish, gibberish—who cares. Let me know when you're planning to convert, and I'll get someone to translate this."

"Sure," Spiegel said. "I'll call you up on Thursday night."

They all laughed.

"Well, what did you think about his story?" Aaronson asked Tracy as she stepped through the beaded curtain that separated their bedroom from the living room. Tracy sat on the bed, folding her legs beneath her, Indian-style. She ran a comb through her thick hair.

"I think he's lucky that he got here," she said. "He's lucky they didn't arrest him and fuck up the whole thing."

"I mean," Aaronson said in a whisper, "do you think he was followed?"

"Yes, I do," Tracy said. "Someone spotted him in Paris. Someone must have been watching, at the Gare du Nord. They were watching for you, and they wanted to provoke you and take you into custody. The conductor was probably in on it, too. But when he saw Lenny's passport, he let the matter drop."

"And do you think . . . "

"Of course. They thought Lenny was you."

"Well, that's all right, then," Aaronson said. "Let's not forget why we brought him here."

"For his good looks, right?"

Aaronson moved closer to Tracy. She set her hand on his thigh. He was smoking a thin joint. As he held in the smoke, he offered the joint to Tracy. She shook her head no.

"What we have to do," Aaronson said softly, "is watch him for a few days before we fill him in on our plans."

"He must have some idea. Iris must have talked to him," Tracy said.

"Maybe. But it makes me nervous, how he managed to get into a scrape before he even got to Uppsala. We need someone who can stay out of trouble. I want to make sure that he's clean, and that I can trust him."

"Trust him," Tracy said. "With what?"

Aaronson laughed. "With you."

"Sure," Tracy said. "We'll see," and she moved closer to Aaronson and let her breasts dangle in the chilly air, her nipples brushing against his cheeks, his lips, until at last he opened his mouth, and, as a cloud of sweet smoke rose slowly toward the ceiling, he pressed his tongue against her cool flesh.

Spiegel lay on his mattress for a long time, trying to fall asleep, trying to blot from his mind the thin squeaks of pleasure he could hear from the adjacent room. From time to time he would get up and look out the window at the quiet street. Large flakes of snow were falling, and some landed on the window ledge.

He wondered if he had been a fool. He should have thrown the pamphlet away before arriving in Uppsala, or he could have said he had picked up the book in the station, and let it go at that. He had begun to realize, though, as he told the story and as he watched Tracy and Aaronson, their expressions so rapt and intense, interested beyond the normal degree of polite attention, that his encounter on the train was more than happenstance, that the actions of the proselytes of the church held some significance that Tracy and Aaronson had decided, for the moment, to keep to themselves. Perhaps the encounter had been a test. If so, had he passed?

2

As a child growing up in the suburbs of Washington, Spiegel felt as if he had been groomed, bred, perhaps destined someday to take his place among the gray-suited, fedora-topped herds of men who migrated each morning into the city and returned home in the evenings, haggard and weary, their briefcases bulging with typescripts and carbons, the *Post* or the *Star* folded neatly and wedged under the arm. His father was one of these men: vanished before daybreak, a stern and silent presence at home, whose weekend pleasures consisted of guiding the power mower in geometric patterns through the patch of yard and then implanting himself, recumbent, before the flickering light of the television. When he was young, Spiegel knew nothing about his father's work except that he worked for "the government." As he got older, he learned a little more, but not much. He learned to say, when pressed for specifics, that his father was in the "foreign service," and after he had learned that his father was an expert on languages and codes he would say, dismissively, a sort of in-joke among his jaded friends whose fathers were judges, undersecretaries, and senior staff aides, that his father was a "crypto-bureaucrat." At that time he knew only that his father wrote papers and reports that required at first a great deal of research and time away from home at nights and on weekends and, later, when Spiegel was in high school, an ever-increasing amount of travel overseas. Spiegel, immersed in the pressures and passions of his own life, thought little about his father's absences and his mother's consequent long engagements with bridge, tennis, cigarettes, gin, and dinners at the club. Her marriage, her life, was coming apart, and Spiegel's mind was thankfully—or perhaps necessarily—elsewhere.

He went off to college set on learning the rudiments of knowledge and behavior that would earn him a station at the entryway to his father's world. Barely a month into his freshman year, that world changed forever when his father announced, in a telegram, one of his favorite modes of communication, that Spiegel's mother had been diagnosed with cancer, whose symptoms of pallor and emaciation she had evidently masked, or concealed even from herself, so successfully that, without medical detection, the disease had more or less consumed her unhindered and at leisure while she had fixed a lipstick smile on her pain-wracked face and dealt innumerable hands of cards. Spiegel went home anticipating a tearful, reconciliatory visit, but his mother, numbed beneath sedatives and enmeshed in the strands of clear plastic tubing that dripped the final spirits of life into her veins, had drifted out to the sea beyond the horizon of the conscious world. Shortly after she died, Spiegel's father put in for a transfer to the directorate of operations, and while Spiegel was studying for final exams his father sold the house in Silver Spring and disembarked for a post in Africa. Spiegel took refuge in his work, determined to focus on his studies and, through excellence and achievement, to fill the void left by his mother's death and his father's absence.

And then—the sixties hit Spiegel like a wave and knocked him over. Anything that came along, he inhaled, ingested, and, at last, injected. And that's as far as Spiegel got. A dizzying acid trip, which left him lying naked in January on a cot in the unheated attic of a downtown crash pad, pulling his hair out by the roots and sobbing, afraid of death and afraid to go on living, shook him so deeply that he left school in the middle of the semester, with all the belongings he would need stuffed into paper bags piled onto the seat beside him on the Greyhound. By that time, he knew almost no one in the college, anyway. One after another, his friends had dropped out and disappeared into the warrens of lower Manhattan, the remote hilltop villages of the Adirondacks, or the sun-bleached cities of the Far West. He set out to join some of them in a commune on an abandoned Ohio beet farm, where the barn had been converted into a Shinto temple.

He thought it would be the perfect place to strain the acid out of his skin, his veins. The life was quiet, regimented, pacific. Everyone shared in the cooking, cleaning, farming, and decision-making. Each evening, they gathered for a community meeting, at which they would discuss such issues as whether to replace the oil furnace, when to plant the rye, whether it would be morally correct to raise worms for bait. Spiegel hated every minute of this life. He was not designed to till the soil. At the end of each day, his back was killing him and his mind was numbed. If man must live by the sweat of his brow, what is man to do with his eyeglasses? Spiegel wondered. His were so covered with salt streaks by late afternoon that he couldn't see to plant straight, and he was quite as likely to chop up a potato patch or a corn row as to hoe out any weeds. Besides, his draft situation was a bit tenuous, and "agrarian worker" was not an acceptable deferment. So one morning in August he turned in his bandanna, said his last devotions to the Buddha, stuffed what he could seem to recall as his former belongings into some bags that had been set aside for recycling, and headed east along the lakeshore to the university, with every intention of staying clean, making good.

But meeting Iris had changed everything. She enlisted him in her own troops, fighting the war against the war, and for this Spiegel was entirely unprepared. Although the first tidal wave of the sixties, the acid revolution, had knocked him off his feet and sent him into retreat on the Shinto farm, he had till then successfully sheltered himself from the buffeting winds of the next great storm. The fury that hit the American campuses as Johnson and McNamara built the war machine into an unimaginable monstrosity, the firestorm after the police clubbed their way through the peaceful protesters in Chicago, he had missed all of this, digging in the cornfields. He was astonished by the fervor, and even the sophistication, of the organized student left—if *organized* was the word, for at times it seemed a most disorganized, anarchic gathering of tribes, a giant beehive full of buzzing, in which everyone zipped back and forth, this way and that, from meeting to seminar to self-study to rally to picket to who knows what, never stopping for a moment, never listening or absorbing or learning, for who had time for reflection with war in the air?

Once Spiegel moved in with Iris, he found himself caught up in the same vortex. He felt as if he had been lifted from the earth, like a leaf in a storm, and he didn't mind, so long as he could be near Iris. In the mornings, she took him along with her to the factory gates where she sold copies of the *Workers World*, then to the Students United steering committee where he would listen as the brain trust of the movement planned tactics and strategy, and later to one of the dingy bars near the Black Rock Canal where they would talk, late into the night, always with a group, mostly students and a ragged few recruited from the nearby battery factory, the token worker who had little to say while he sucked on a longneck but whose occasional pronouncements about how the work at Trico was just fucking boring were met with such awe and astonishment that you would think you had heard an oracular utterance direct from the fount of Marx or Marcuse. Finally, they would go back to Iris's apartment, where at last Spiegel could be alone with her, touching her and tasting her and breathing in her smoky scent, and all of the indoctrination, all of his nascent interest in the culture of the proletariat, was blown away like dust in the wind.

When Brewer proposed that Spiegel be dispatched as the Students United official emissary to Sweden, Spiegel was, at first, angry and a little bit hurt. He wished that Iris had protested, said she wanted him to stay. Instead, she agreed with Brewer that it would be prudent to move Spiegel out of the vicinity until the tempest over the mistaken arrest had been forgotten. And Spiegel sensed that Iris had other reasons as well. Apparently, he had to prove himself in some way, maybe not to her, but to Brewer and the others, who distrusted him for having been off digging earthworms while the student vanguard was fighting on the ramparts, breaking storefront windows on Main Street, and tossing hissing tear-gas canisters back at the plastic-visored police. Spiegel's movement credentials were dubious. He was considered a hero for his role in the botched arrest. He had become known as the one who took the heat and allowed Aaronson enough time to cross the border. But he was an inadvertent hero at best, the beneficiary of misfortune, like a hapless war veteran who has earned his decorations through the bad luck of having been shot. Fate had come knocking at Spiegel's door, in the guise of a riot cop without a warrant, and he'd happened to be standing in the line of fire.

His trip to Sweden was, he now realized, Iris's attempt to close the circle of fate, by presenting him to Tracy and Aaronson. They would see him and they would understand all that had taken place back in the States while they had made their surreptitious way across the border. But what was expected of him in Sweden? Tracy had evidently told Iris that there was vital work to be done and that the community of deserters needed the help of an American who was able to travel. Spiegel was willing, but so far he had been kept in the dark. He was beginning to wonder if it would have been better to stay with Iris and prove himself to her in some other way. Perhaps it had been a mistake to come to Uppsala.

He began to wonder if he was really needed. Tracy and Aaronson, though friendly enough, had been rather circuitous and evasive when he tried to find out what it was that they wanted of him. He did like them both, though, right away. Spiegel had expected, after all he had heard about him, that he would be intimidated by Aaronson. Back home, Aaronson was spoken of as if he were some mythic figure, a courageous revolutionary who had struck a blow at the war machine and then been chased by the furies into exile. Spiegel had pictured Aaronson off in the Arctic, like Thor returned to Valhalla, a hero bitter in defeat, tending some eternal flame of revenge. But Aaronson had turned out to be much more self-effacing and approachable than Spiegel expected. Aaronson scoffed at the idea that he had been a hero and was an inspiration, and he spent much of the evening talking about all the things that he missed from America—the all-rock radio stations, the movie theaters with stale popcorn and sticky puddles of soda on the floor, the greasy cafeteria fries and thick white mugs of bitter coffee, the fumes of the big cars and of American cigarettes, the boisterous camaraderie on the quad between classes and in the student union at noon and around the basketball court on a Saturday morning—rather than about the wayward course that had brought him to Uppsala and the political realities and ideological commitments that kept him there, a prisoner of history, a victim not so much of his beliefs as of his impulses and his passions.

The next morning, Aaronson slept late while Tracy left early to pick up some flyers from a print shop. Spiegel wondered why she hadn't woken him or stayed a little later and offered him a ride. Though Tracy had been helpful, even solicitous, when she met him at the station, Spiegel was beginning to suspect that she had not been altogether straightforward with him, either. Clearly, she wanted him out of the apartment as soon as possible, and she didn't want to be seen driving him through the city. Was he being watched by someone? Or was she? Spiegel had no idea.

It was only a short walk to the bus terminal. Spiegel found that the air, stinging with cold, sharpened his mind. He walked down an alley where the snow had been cleared, exposing an uneven cobblestone footing treacherous with hard black ice. The alley opened onto a small park where a narrow pathway had been cut through fresh snow that looked like grains of sugar but that had frozen as hard as rock. Crossing the park, Spiegel could pick up the scent of balsam mixed with the oily fumes of burning diesel rising from the buses idling at the terminal. Vaporous clouds spilled from the buses and hovered on the walkways like ground fog, filling the little square with thick spoors of white smoke. The small gabled shop buildings with their shutters fastened against the cold, the filigreed lampposts, the scrawny urban pines rimed with ice, all were shrouded and obscured, as if the whole square had been packed in cotton wool, like a delicate gift. Spiegel stood for a moment in the hazy, refractive light before extracting the correct change and boarding the bus that would take him out to Flogsta.

As the Flogsta bus meandered along the river, then climbed the gentle hill beside the Gothic towers of the university and out past the last brick rows of a public-housing project—bland and ugly as any of its American counterparts but without the apparent threat of a dangerous undertow of crime and violence—Spiegel got a sense of the true dimensions of Uppsala. It was a tiny city surrounded by fields and farmland, an oasis of learning set in a desert of snow-covered plains. The city gave way at its perimeter not to suburban development or industrial strip but to a great nothingness, a virgin wasteland that seemed vast and almost featureless. Spiegel had been familiar with the open spaces of the Midwest, but something about the fields around Uppsala disturbed him in a way he had never known back in Ohio. There was something nightmarish about the subtle undulations of white ground, ruptured by a few knobs and hills that broke through the snowy monotony with clusters of scrub pine and clearings of mud.

The bus route ended at the foot of a narrow path scraped clear of snow. A few young people, university students apparently, book bags and satchels slung over their shoulders, waited to board the bus, which would complete its turnaround and take them back toward town, toward the school. Spiegel was the last outbound passenger. He dragged his duffel down the steps, hoisted his backpack onto his shoulder, and set off on the pathway up the hill to the Flogsta complex.

Tracy had told him a little about Flogsta. It was, someday, to become the center of a small satellite campus. So far, though, it was just a cluster of buildings amid the rock and rubble of a construction site. Few Uppsala students had chosen to live here. It was too remote, too far from the campus and the shops and social haunts of the town, so only the late registrants and the exchange students found themselves assigned housing up on the hill. Spiegel didn't mind. He was glad that the university exchange program had reserved a room for him. He would arrange payment terms once he was enrolled in school. Maybe, he figured, he could draw that process out as long as possible and squeeze in a few weeks rent free, before anyone knew he had arrived.

The Flogsta dorms were an architectural desecration, six towers rising from a barren patch of land that had been roughly cleared of brush at the top of the windswept hill. The hilltop offered a vista of the surrounding woods and fields, but the effect was diminished by the oppressive closeness of the buildings. Spiegel felt both claustrophobic and isolated, as if the world were crowding in on him, yet he was all alone. Perhaps it was all the traveling he'd done and the disorientation caused by the many time changes, but for a moment he felt as if the whole journey had been a mistake, an act of self-aggrandizement. Maybe it's the latitude, Spiegel thought. Can that have the same effect as altitude on the mind?

He had been assigned to building five. None of the buildings had names, although someday, no doubt, each would bear the moniker of a famous Swedish botanist or the like. Building five was still under construction. The small lobby was being used as a storage shed for tools and ladders. The work crews had left buckets and trowels in a corner by the stairway. There was no functioning elevator. Spiegel climbed to his suite on the third floor.

As it had been explained to him, each student had a bedroom and private bathroom, and each hallway shared a small communal kitchen. The arrangement promised the advantages of both the privacy of an apartment and the sociability of an American-style student dorm. He liked the prospect of meeting Swedish students, although he didn't imagine that he would become terribly involved in the life of the university: cheering the bobsled team, getting drunk on reindeer punch, whatever Swedish students did. No, he knew he had to concentrate on his work, and he had to find out, as soon as possible, what his work was meant to be.

The room he had been assigned was better than he had hoped. At least the interior had been completed, even if the exterior of the building was decked in construction scaffolding. The room was fitted with a good desk, a comfortable platform bed, built-in shelves, and a solid chair made from attractive white birch. The bathroom, tiny and clean, had an ingenious shower arrangement. The floor was sloped toward a drain and, by drawing a curtain along a small ceiling track, you could transform a corner of the bathroom into a shower stall. The whole place seemed designed with great intelligence and efficiency. It will be like living inside of a machine, Spiegel thought, with some relief. For, after his arrival at Flogsta, in which he was impressed by the general state of disarray, it was nice to see that his own small place was well-suited to his needs. He resolved to figure out, in the afternoon, exactly what he would have to buy to furnish the room—a clock? a desk lamp? a wastebasket?—and to catch the bus back to town to shop.

He had brought no cooking supplies or equipment. Before leaving the States, he had thought that he would eat out most of the time. He barely knew anything about cooking. But Tracy had mentioned how expensive it was to eat out in Sweden. Restaurants were heavily taxed, and even the students, denizens of bars and coffee shops back home, rarely went out except for a draft beer in a student pub. From his window, Spiegel could see one of those little kiosks he had noticed in town. Apparently, in accordance with some Swedish law, the kiosks sold only food in cans and tubes. (Grilled hot dogs counted as a tube.) Other than that, there were no restaurants anywhere near the Flogsta complex. He hadn't anticipated living in such isolation. He walked down the hallway to check out the kitchen.

Like the bedroom, it was clean, compact, and well designed, much nicer than anything he had known in any student housing in America. There was plenty of counter space, good wide steel sinks with strong water pressure, two four-burner electric stoves, a spacious refrigerator built into a recessed wall. The cabinets were an attractive wood laminate. Spiegel reached to open one of them. He was hungry and hoped that perhaps the communal living extended to cereal packs, as well. Four of the cabinets were locked. One was bare; his, he assumed. Maybe, he figured, he could raid the refrigerator and replace what he took later, after he'd had a chance to shop.

Scanning the refrigerator, however, was like trying to read a book written in an unknown language. The contents were, recognizably, food, just as a foreign language is made up of what are recognizable as words, but what did the words mean? He saw many jars with what seemed to be pastes and crushed berries and creams, some carafes of pale liquids that reminded him of vitamin elixirs, a few slabs of cheese sliced into unrecognizable dimensions, and more of the ubiquitous tubes, many of which bore pictures of smiling, bright-blond children. Were these tubes of toothpaste? Spiegel took one, and squeezed a dab onto his fingertip. Out came a dollop of reddish-orange gel. Maybe hair cream? But why would it be kept in a refrigerator? He lifted his finger to his nose, and caught a whiff of fish, just as he was startled by the noise of someone entering the room.

"*Hej*," a voice behind him said.

Spiegel quickly lapped up the gel. He almost gagged from the intense, salty taste. What had he eaten? Some horrible cooking infusion meant to be used in microdot proportions? He turned quickly, embarrassed, trying to hide both his guilt and his revulsion.

"Hey," he said. Standing before him was a willowy girl wearing tan chinos and a skintight olive T-shirt. Her straight blond hair, parted perfectly, hung to her shoulders, and framed her lovely face, her clear and perfect skin, her delicate cheekbones.

"I'm sorry. I don't speak Swedish," Spiegel said.

"That's cool. I'm American, too."

"American? You're kidding."

"What's that there?"

He was still holding the tube in his hand. He quickly twisted the cap shut. "I don't have a clue," Spiegel said, truthfully.

"I wouldn't touch their food."

"Socialism doesn't apply to refrigerator shelves, then?" Spiegel said.

"No, not that. I mean, I wouldn't touch it with a ten-foot pole. Unless you like crushed fish-egg paste."

"I could develop a taste for it. If I were stranded on an ice floe."

"I'm Melissa," she said. She held her hand out to Spiegel.

"Lenny Spiegel. I guess we're neighbors."

"Are you from California, too?"

"No, I mean I've got a room on this floor."

"Yeah, I heard another American was joining us."

"There's others?"

Melissa put on water for a pot of coffee. "UCLA has an exchange program," she explained. "Although I guess it's not really an exchange because we don't get anything back. We just send our students to Uppsala. I'll get a year's credits and, how do they put it in the brochure? The life experience of living abroad. What about you?"

"Well, I'm from the East," Spiegel said.

"I could tell that," Melissa said.

"How could you?"

"I mean, your clothes, all that flannel and khaki. And your hair. And even the way you talk. At first, I thought maybe you were one of the soldiers."

"You mean the deserters? Why would you think that?"

"There are more moving to Uppsala all the time. Some want to enroll in the college, but I don't know."

"What don't you know?" Spiegel asked.

"It's hard for them. They don't seem to fit in. You'll see. This place is very closed-minded."

Melissa had been living in Flogsta for a few weeks. She was one of the pioneers of the complex, an early settler. She had arrived even before the kitchen was completed, and during her first few days in Sweden she'd had to subsist on cold cereal and sandwiches. She had enrolled right away in the language course and was already picking up the rudiments. But it was hard to learn the language, she said, because everyone, once they learned she was American, wanted to speak to her in English.

"We'd be better off, you know, in France," she said. "I had a girlfriend there, on an exchange program in Dijon. She said that everyone there hates English, so you learn to speak French really quick."

"Why don't you just pretend to be Swedish, but kind of shy, or dumb?"

"People do think I'm Swedish, at first," Melissa said. "Actually, I'm Irish. But there was some kind of Viking invasion back there in history, you know? What about you?"

"Yeah, I thought you were Swedish."

"No, I mean, what are you?"

"I'm Jewish. I don't think the Vikings invaded the shtetls."

"So I guess you're not here to find your roots or anything. Most of the California kids, that's why they come. That, or they're nuts about Bergman films. They expect to meet death on a beach and play chess or something. But there are no beaches here, not like we have back home."

"And no death, either?"

"No, there's probably that," Melissa said.

"But that's not why you're here," Spiegel said.

Melissa laughed. "To play chess with death?"

"To find your roots."

"No, I'm doing theater."

"All the way to Sweden for that?" Spiegel said. "I'd have thought UCLA was the place."

"I'm not into Hollywood shit," Melissa said.

Suddenly, Spiegel felt better about her. Maybe she wasn't as simple as she had appeared, or pretended, to be.

"What about you," she said. "Why'd you come all this way? You trying to get out of the war?"

"No. My draft number's good. I'll probably never be called."

"So why Sweden?"

"You know, the life experience of living abroad."

"But the only people you've met here, so far, are your fellow Americans."

"Well, yes. How did you know?"

"This is Flogsta. Port of last resort. It's all foreigners."

"There's Swedes on this floor," Spiegel said. "I can smell their fish eggs."

"But the Swedes—they keep to themselves. And they don't even say that much to each other. They're not like American students. They take one course a term, and they really have to focus on that subject. So all I'm doing this term is acting. What's yours going to be?"

"I thought I'd do the language class."

"*Svenska for invandrare*. Do you know what it means?"

"Swedish for invaders?"

Melissa laughed. "Close. Swedish for immigrants. But that

class is run by the government. You'll have to register for university classes, too."

"I haven't done that yet."

"Your exchange program probably registered for you."

"No, it's a really new program, and they set it up in a half-assed way," Spiegel said. "The adviser's back in Albany. He's supposed to come here in the spring to check on things, but I think it's just a huge scam so he can travel."

"I've got to run to rehearsal," Melissa said, finishing her coffee. "But I can give you the name of the guy who runs the California program. Maybe he can get you registered."

"I don't know . . ."

"Come on, I've got his name in a notebook in my room."

She gave the coffee cup a quick swirl and dumped it into the sudsy sink. Spiegel followed her down the hall. She walked fast, and looked great from behind. She's used to this, Spiegel thought. She's used to being admired and obeyed, and she expects no less. Watch out, he told himself. She hasn't come all the way to Uppsala to wrap her long legs around the likes of Lenny Spiegel.

Melissa's room was decorated like a spread from a special psychedelia issue of *House Beautiful*: framed Escher prints and Peter Max posters, Asian wall hangings, plush chairs upholstered in black-and-white op-art patterns, and a bright orange rya rug with shag thick as ropes.

"Does the Museum of Modern Art know you took all this stuff?" Spiegel said, as he examined a double-exposed photograph of a Botticelli Venus emerging from a Venus flytrap. *Which One Am I?* the legend beneath it read.

"I shipped a lot of stuff ahead," Melissa said. "I like to have a nice environment around me when I work."

"You're a collector."

"Of photos? My dad is. He gets a lot of stuff from, you know, his clients." She was fumbling with the lock on a steel filing cabinet.

"He's a lawyer?"

"No, a philosophy professor."

"Your dad?"

"The adviser. From the California program. Here it is. I wrote his number on my script." She pulled a folder from the cabinet, and a tore off a scrap of paper with a phone number. "My dad's an agent, sort of a talent agent I guess you'd say."

"Movies?"

"Clubs, more. He had a club in New York. That's where I was born. But something went wrong, he's never exactly told us, and he lost it. One day, I was, like, in seventh grade, and I came home from school—I was staying late for cheerleading, if you can believe that—and when I got home my mom was packing. She said we were leaving that night. My dad drove us to Newark, the airport, and my mom and me flew to LA and stayed for a week in this little motel on the strip. I loved it. We had a pool. My dad came and joined us. He drove out, in this little Studebaker he had. I didn't go back to school until the fall."

"It was probably Mafia," Spiegel said. "They wanted a cut. He must have clipped them or didn't pay for protection or something."

"It could be, but it worked out okay. We liked LA right away. My dad knew some people there, he had contacts, and he got into booking, you know, small acts at first, nothing you would have heard of, back then. But eventually he got some bigger names, like I think he helped Nat Cole when he came out west, or maybe it was Johnny Mathis? We always had interesting people coming by our place."

"The motel?"

"No. By then, Bel Air. That's where we live."

"I don't know LA," Spiegel said, "but your dad must have done all right."

"Yeah, but I don't want that kind of life. I want to do something creative. I don't care about money."

Sure, to hell with it, Spiegel thought. You don't have to think about money because you've got all you need. He looked out the window. The day was bright and clear, but Melissa's room was cast into shadow by two Flogsta towers, flat and dull, like huge credit cards jammed into the earth. A margin of white light separated the towers, a thin slat through which Spiegel could discern in the distance a narrow vista of fields and snow.

"And what about this stuff," he said, tapping the cover of a glass display case resting on brackets at the head of Melissa's bed. Inside the case were slender whips, a long-bladed knife with a handle of dark bone, and a small silver pistol.

"I need those," Melissa said.

"Your dad must have some far-out clients."

"No, those are mine. They're for classes."

"I thought you were taking acting, not S and M."

"I am." She stood her ground, folded her arms across her chest, as if to tell him: Don't push too hard.

"You are what? Taking S and M?"

"Acting."

"Someone wants to cast you in a nice Swedish movie, I bet. Look, Melissa, I don't really know you, but—be careful. Not every Swede behind a camera is Ingmar Bergman."

"These are for acting classes. Props." She went to the display case and picked up one of the whips. "This is a riding whip," Melissa said. "Didn't you ever read *Miss Julie*?"

"No, I'm pre-law."

"It's Naturalism, and all that. It begins with a cook onstage, alone, for about five minutes, frying up some kidneys in a real kitchen. So it feels like you're really in a country kitchen on a Swedish estate at the turn of the century."

"And you're the cook."

"I'm reading for the part of Julie. I have to learn to use the whip."

"Does she ride?"

"No, she snaps it at her lover. To make him jump. Want me to show you?"

"I'll pass."

"It's a great part. She's a rich girl who falls for a poor boy, her father's groom. She's a tyrant. She has power over men." She suddenly raised her hand high, snapped her wrist, and cracked the whip against the floor.

"Yeah, she's a man-eater," Melissa said, fumbling through the loose pages of her script. "Listen: 'Oh, how I should like to see your blood and your brains on a chopping-block! I'd like to see the whole of your sex swimming like that in a sea of blood. I think I could drink out of your skull, bathe my feet in your broken breast, and eat your heart roasted whole.' "

"You'll have to learn to use more than the whip to play that part," Spiegel said.

"Well, those are just words." Melissa put the whip back in the case. "As it turns out, she doesn't do any of that shit. She lets the groom fuck her and then, when her father returns to the estate, she kills herself out of shame."

"The gun?" Spiegel asked.

"No, that's *Hedda Gabler*. This." Melissa picked up the long steel blade. "A razor. Jean, the groom, puts her in a trance, and Julie slices open her own throat."

"So she wasn't so strong after all," Spiegel said.

"Yes she was. I think you have to be strong to make such a powerful exit."

"I don't believe that," Spiegel said. "I think the stronger person is the one who, you know, stays on the stage."

"To do what? Bury the corpses? Turn off the lights?"

"Exits are cheap, and easy," Spiegel said.

"Are they always? Even when the world you're leaving is—intolerable? Immoral? Even when there's no turning back?" She looked at him, to see if her words had registered, to see if he understood exactly what she meant. "You'll see," she said. "Sweden is like a big stage. A land of exits." And with that, she made her own.

Later in the day, Spiegel thought about what Melissa had said as he sat by the window in his room. His view was to the west, away from the town. Looking into the fading light, he could see a few lonely farmhouses and a railroad track crossing a snowy field, like a seam. He crumpled the scrap of paper Melissa had given him and tossed it into the trash.

3

"De här ar Fröken *Fält,"* said the teacher.

Spiegel had been attending Swedish class for a week now, so he understood: Here is Miss Felt. The teacher, a rail-thin, stone-serious woman in her mid-twenties whose blond hair was cropped so short that it looked to Spiegel as if she were wearing a yellow bathing cap, placed the flat little cutout figure of a girl onto the display board. *Fröken Fält.* It amused Spiegel that the display board was covered in felt; a felt board they used to call these things when he was in kindergarten. He wondered if anyone else in the class would get the pun.

Spiegel was in a somewhat honored—or at least privileged—position in the class, for he was the only one whose native language was English, and English was the coin of the realm. No one's ability in Swedish had advanced beyond the primitive stage of answering the phone and ordering a sandwich. So the closest thing to a common language was English. The Mexican world wanderer was nearly fluent, the Biafran refugee spoke good if rather bookish English, the two Guatemalan freedom fighters spoke broken English filled with idioms gleaned from television. Others spoke little or no English: the two furtive Kurdish nationalists, the diligent Polish agricultural exchange student, the Moroccan with his furrowed brow couldn't speak a word, and as a result they were cut off from the occasional cafeteria, hallway, and even classroom banter. But Spiegel knew that while he and his friends traded their jokes in English, the noninitiates would forge ahead into the strange new world of the Swedish language.

Until coming to Sweden, he had thought that Vietnam was the only war in the world. Now he was learning about wars he had never heard of, some of them fought in countries he had never heard of. Where was Kurdistan, he wondered, and who knew there was a battle for independence raging there fierce enough to send refugees in truck caravans across the whole length of Europe to seek sanctuary in the glacial north? He had heard of Biafra and Guatemala and their Bosch-like scenes of death, destruction, and famine, but he had never realized how deeply war had permeated the colorful fabric of life in these tiny countries. In the Third World, there were no deferments or draft lotteries. Everyone had to choose a side, and those who chose ineptly, that is, who backed the loser, paid with their lives.

Most of the refugees, Spiegel noticed, had about them a look of perpetual astonishment. It was as if the jets that lifted them to this safe haven were more like rocket ships that had blasted them to another planet, for Sweden had not come to them first through the filtering lens of Bergman or through the highbrow porn that showed up in cinemas near American college campuses. To them, everything here—the hibernal climate, the culture that was so tolerant in the abstract yet insular in its particulars, the buildings so effectively sealed against the elements, the weight of heavy wool on the body, the monotony of white skies and spindly trees, the birdlike swoops of the spoken language, the innumerate variations on straight blond hair—was an awakening, a challenge, almost an assault on the memory of all they had left behind. They must have wondered at times whether they should have made their own pact with death, whether dying at home might have been preferable to eternal exile in this prison of darkness and snow.

Spiegel had struck up a friendship with a Portuguese war resister, Jorge Ramos. Unlike the other refugees, Jorge had learned to luxuriate in his exile. So far as Spiegel was aware, Jorge had never seen war firsthand. He had fled to Sweden, he told Spiegel, so that he would not have to fight in the African wars. That was another conflict that had gone completely unnoticed, so far as Spiegel could tell, by the American left. From what he knew, Portugal had vaguely bumped into Africa when Henry the Navigator tried to send his ships round the Cape of Good Hope back in—when the hell was it?—the fifteenth century? And then they made that terrible mistake, allowing the pope to divide the New World, and they wound up with Brazil while ceding rights to the rest of South America and all of the north. If they had cut the cake the other way, maybe the Portuguese army would be fighting colonial wars in—who knows? Alaska or the Yukon, trying to suppress the Inuit. They could be running a puppet government out on the Great Plains. But instead, Portugal was stuck with the remote African states, great savannahs filled with zebra and wildebeest and huge mines gorged with copper and diamonds, Spiegel imagined, and they had been fighting for most of the century to hang on to these last possessions, the remnants of empire. It seemed to Spiegel that the African wars must be horrible and savage beyond anything the American troops encountered in Asia. And what chance of victory, he wondered, could the Portuguese soldiers have, a little spit of a country known more for wine and cork than for guns and guided missiles?

Jorge knew that Portugal had no chance at all. He had not seen the war, but he had seen its effects, he had seen what it had done to his brother. Jorge was a son of the sophisticated urban bourgeoisie; his father was in furs and leather, importing the raw materials, exporting finished coats and wraps to the best shops on Savile Row, and Jorge's brother had been educated at a top military boarding school. On graduation, he was commissioned, and they flew him down to Mozambique, where he joined an antiguerilla platoon. They roamed the countryside in a fleet of Jeeps, stopping at little dusty villages suspected of collaboration. They would ferret out the village chief and chain him to a stake in the market square. As the chief baked to death in the midday sun, the soldiers would go through the population, men, women, children, no order, just random intimidation, until someone talked, told them who the rebel leaders were, where they stored the arms, where the troops were hiding. Then the soldiers would burn the village to a cinder and leave.

One evening on patrol, as he rounded a hill and walked

through the small clearing heading back toward the camp, he was ambushed by a band of rebels. One held a rifle to his throat while the others stripped him of his gun, his magazine, his shoes. They tied him by the waist to a thorn tree. They made him raise his arms straight up over his head and they tied his hands, by the wrists, to the trunk of the tree. A firing squad assembled. As they took aim at his heart, the leader of the rebel band, who wore a brightly checkered scarf wrapped around his face so that he peered out only through a little slit in the fabric, stepped forward and, with two quick blows of his machete, sliced off Jorge's brother's hands.

Jorge had told Spiegel that his brother, before the war, had been known as one of the best young guitar players in Lisbon, a passionate devotee of traditional Portuguese fado music, with occasional excursions into Spanish flamenco, which he considered a bastardized form of the only true guitar music, and even more rarely into classical compositions—Bach, de Falla, and so on—which he considered to be a technical challenge but, after all, soulless. Jorge had no interest in traditional music of any sort, but when his brother came back from Africa with his arms swaddled in dressings, Jorge took up the guitar in his brother's honor, in memory of his brother's lost hands, and he became a more than competent interpreter of British pop, his great passion. He loved everything British—not just the music but the whole culture of England: the Carnaby Street clothes, the sculpted hair, the Cockney and Liverpudlian accents, the discotheque scene, the girls in their minis, and most of all the music. Jorge loved to point out that in English his name would be George, hence, his favorite Beatle, his idol, was the lead guitarist, George Harrison.

Against his father's wishes, Jorge vowed that he would never fight in Africa, or anywhere else. When he graduated from secondary school, not the military boarding school that his brother had attended, but a fine preparatory school in Lisbon favored by the ambassadorial set, he left for London, ostensibly on business for his father's firm. He bought a whole wardrobe on Carnaby, packed it into two large steamers, and set out for Sweden. He had spent the summer in Stockholm, during which time he had concentrated not so much on learning the language as on learning the people, specifically the "birds," as he called them. He had met a Swedish *flicka*, a university student who was working a summer job as a cocktail waitress in a hotel disco bar, and, in the fall, after an ardent courtship, Jorge moved back with her to Uppsala and into her suite in Flogsta. They had vague plans to marry sometime after she—her name was Lisbet—graduated. Meanwhile, Jorge had agreed to make an effort to learn her language.

Spiegel noticed, however, that most of Jorge's classroom efforts were devoted to practicing his English, a much more important language, to his mind, than Swedish could ever be. It seemed that Jorge could not comprehend—or at least could not acknowledge—that the course his life had taken might mean that he would be living among Swedes, and that they might tolerate speaking English with a tourist or a student, but a permanent resident, a foreigner married to a Swedish woman, would have to learn the language and the ways of the country or else always be considered an alien, an *invandrare*.

"*Har ni någon ost?*"

"*Ja, det har vi.*"

Do you have cheese?

Yes, we have some.

Spiegel was restless. So was Jorge. It did feel rather ridiculous to be moving along on such a rudimentary level. The class was at once both more intense and more banal than any other language class he had ever taken. The teacher could never discuss or explain the language and its nuances, for there was no common tongue in which she could do so. There was no gossip, no banter. The class was never interrupted for bulletins or announcements. Karin was all business, and her business was Swedish. How can she stand it, Spiegel thought, day after day, speaking to us in slow motion, her lips stretching to accentuate each inflection, as we stare at her in wonder, so helpless and dependent? Our clumsy attempts to mime her inflections must sound to her like a travesty, a parody of her speech. How can she stand us?

Bra, Karin said. *Det går bra.*

Bra, the Swedish word for good. Spiegel wondered who else got the joke, and even if it was a joke.

Vill ni ha någon ost? Would you like some cheese?

Bara bra, said Karin. Very good.

Spiegel felt a nudge, a kick at his ankle. Jorge was passing him a little folded note, as if they were kids in first grade. Well, it looked like first grade: the felt board with its cutout figures of a happy blond family, the alphabet cards festooning the room, essentially the same as the English alphabet except for those pockmarked vowels wearing the caps and goggles over their heads and for the disturbing absence of the W, whose vacancy was felt disproportionately, like a missing or chipped tooth whose gap is continually prodded by the restless tongue.

Jorge's note said: *Karin wears a bara bra*. Spiegel dropped his face into his folded hands, trying to smother a laugh. It was all so stupid, so juvenile, yet something about the atmosphere of this class made juvenile behavior permissible, even appropriate.

Jorge took a long drag on a Players, then stabbed it out on the rim of his saucer. Jorge, Spiegel, and some of the other students had adjourned for coffee to the little canteen in the basement of the school. Here, Spiegel thought, we speak *English*. He and Jorge, because of their fluency, found themselves at the center of a cluster of acolytes whose proximity to the nucleus was determined, more or less, by their ability to speak the language. Lonesome for their obscure or distant native tongues, unable yet to hear in the rise and fall of Swedish the crystalline ring of a recognizable grammar, they were drawn to the hum of spoken English as if the very utterance of the words gave off a small, sustaining warmth. Beyond the periphery of the conversation, in the farther margins of the room, sat the few isolates for whom even English was exotic and unknown. Pale, impoverished, they hunched over their books with a determination fired by the white flame of their isolation.

"Don't you think," Spiegel said, "that it might be worth it—I mean for you—to pay attention? I mean, you've got to learn the language someday."

"I learn better when I don't pay attention," Jorge said. "I'm left-handed."

"*La siniestra*," said Luis, the Mexican.

"Blimey, will you speak English," said Jorge.

"It is English," Spiegel said. "*Sinister.* It mean, like, strange, and maybe a little evil."

"Well in Spanish, it means the left hand. It's a Spanish word, too," Luis said.

"What's that got to do with paying attention, I want to know," Spiegel said.

"It's like this," said Jorge. He took a good long sip of his coffee. "You learn language with the left half of your brain. True?"

"I don't know."

"Yes, it's true. Believe me. Now your left brain controls your right hand, and, how do you say it? Vice verse?"

"Vice versa, yes."

"Okay. I'm left-handed. I write, I scribble, I do everything I can to keep my right brain busy during the class, you see. This way, my left brain is totally free to learn the language. That's why I'm good in languages. All left-handers are."

Spiegel picked up a pencil. "See this?" he said. Jorge and Luis nodded.

"*Sí*," Luis said.

"*Sí*. This," said Spiegel. He began to scribble on the cover of his notebook, circles and spirals, meaningless doodles. "I'm right-handed, so I'm using the left side of my brain now, yes?"

"Yes, the language side," Jorge said.

"So how do you know I'm not developing it? You know, strengthening it, like an exercise. Maybe the more I use this part of the brain, the stronger it gets. More blood flows to it or something. And if I just doodle and doodle through the whole language class, like, in no time at all I'll be out in a restaurant with Karin ordering—a cheese sandwich."

"*Smörgås med ost!*" Luis said.

"And undoing her bara bra," said Jorge.

"And what?"

It was Melissa. "Hey, sit down with us," Spiegel said. It was the first time he had run into her in the classroom building. Classes were scheduled so that only one group used the small canteen at a time. A two-week veteran, Melissa was in a higher learning group, already conversing about the postal service and the weather, advanced stuff.

Spiegel hadn't seen Melissa much all week at Flogsta. Because of her rehearsals, she was rarely home in the evenings. But Spiegel also noticed that they didn't go out of their way to seek each other's company. It almost seemed as if they were making a conscious effort to avoid each other, to keep at a slight remove. No doubt Spiegel was attracted to her, or could be if he would let himself, but there was something dangerous, devouring about her that put him on his guard. She must have felt that there was something slightly off-putting about him, too. Perhaps she still suspected that he was a deserter who was not owning up to his reasons for coming to Uppsala. Or perhaps she felt that an attraction to Spiegel would constitute a kind of transgression, almost like an incest violation— for as two Americans in the same dorm complex, weren't they in fact almost like siblings in a nuclear family extempore? It would be better if, having resisted the first impulse of sexual attraction, they could regard each other from a distance, like friendly if slightly suspicious allies who had not so long ago been antagonists in a war.

"Welcome to Swedish for Invaders," Melissa said to Spiegel. "I thought maybe you weren't going to sign up."

"Invaders?" Luis said.

"It's her little pun on *invandrare*," Spiegel explained. "Immigrants."

"I think it means in-wanderers. People who wandered in," Luis said.

"How do you like the class," Melissa asked Spiegel.

"*Det går bra*," he said. "*Bara bra.*"

"Yeah, that's a good phrase. You'd be surprised how much conversation that will carry you through."

"Sure, that and *vackra svenska flicka*," Spiegel said.

"Pretty Swedish girl," Luis intoned.

"How are things going for you," Spiegel asked Melissa. "Cracking the whip?"

"The whip?" Luis said.

"Don't I wish. So far, all I'm doing is dancing with the peasants. We do a chorus while Julie and Jean go into his chambers for a tryst."

"I'm sure you'll get a chance to—what was the phrase? Bathe your feet in his broken breast?"

"I've got to do something to get the director to notice me," she said.

"Like learn Swedish?"

"That doesn't matter. He's Australian."

"Well, I wouldn't worry about it. He'll notice you. You just have to make the most of your opportunities, right?"

"Absolutely. Look, I've got to run, as per usual. Catch you later?"

And she was off. Spiegel couldn't help but admire her, as she left: her shape, her bearing, the way she seemed to pass through the room in one fluid motion, like a leaf borne downstream on a swift current. Heads turned to look at her. Spiegel was flattered, and a little self-conscious, to have been singled out by Melissa, the object of her attention and her solicitude. Luis finished his rye toast in silence, his face still warmed by the glow from her presence.

It was almost time to head upstairs for the afternoon class. Spiegel was about to turn to Jorge to see if he had finished his coffee when he was startled by a low moan, a whimper.

"You okay?" Spiegel said. Jorge looked to be in great pain. He held his hand to his gut, and leaned over the table. His face looked pinched, and a little flushed. He bit his lower lip until the skin turned white, as he uttered a soft, almost canine lament.

"Oo, oo," he said.

"Jorge, man, what is it?"

"*Que tienes?*" said Luis.

"You all right?"

"That bird," Jorge said. "That bird."

"Melissa?"

"The one with the whips!"

"It's for a play she's in."

"You had not told me that you knew that bird," Jorge said. "The one who will dance with the peasants."

"I'm sorry, I—"

"If I could only—have that bird," he said. "I'd just, I'd just fuck her and fuck her and I'd never leave, I'd be with her every second, and if any other man tried to touch her I would—" He made a grand swipe with the edge of his hand to indicate: I would cut him to pieces.

"Aah, I thought you were sick," Spiegel said. "I was gonna call the hospital."

"*Sjukhuset*," said Luis, proudly.

"I was sick. I am sick. That you didn't introduce me to this bird."

"I didn't think—"

"You know America must be the greatest country in the whole fucking world," Jorge said. "You have birds like this, how do you say it, groping on trees?"

"Growing on trees," Spiegel said. "No, she's pretty special. But she's not just from America. She's from California."

"Oh," Luis said. "She's here on the California program. Now I understand."

"Understand what?" Spiegel said. "She's a junior at UCLA."

"Well, you know what I hear they call it: *UCIA*. They send people here for spies."

Spiegel heard one of the Estonians at a nearby table cough softly and set down his coffee cup. He knows more English than *he's* let on, Spiegel noted.

"To spy on what?"

"All you guys."

"Other Americans? No, I don't believe that," Spiegel said.

"What I hear," said Luis, "is some of the Californians are very, very good, you know, reporters. You should read the papers they send back home to their professors."

"Melissa doesn't know shit about the Americans here," Spiegel said. "I think I'm the only one she's met."

"They're not just interested in Americans," Luis said. "They're also interested in—people like me. Your Latin brothers. And others who could be planning to export the *revolucion*."

"How do you know this, Luis?"

But Luis didn't answer, just raised an eyebrow as if to say:
You'll see.

"I don't know, but if American birds are like that one I would
never leave that country."

"There is, you know, the matter of the war," Spiegel said.

"I'd fight it for sure. To be near her."

"But you see, she's here."

"Yes, that's true." Jorge finished his coffee. It was time to head
back to class.

The Polish agronomist was flirting with the Biafran nanny, no
language barrier there. The two Kurds were huddled by the radi-
ator, speaking in muffled tones, their eyes scanning the room as
if at any moment they expected an invasion of Turks. Karin was
fiddling with a film projector. Occasionally, the class branched
off into multimedia to learn such things as the rules of the road
or the Swedish currency system. She couldn't get the film to stay
in the sprockets, and the light from the projector accentuated the
harsh angles of her profile. Spiegel thought of the tricks he used
to play, as a kid in camp, with a flashlight, around the fire, casting his face as a Frankenstein mask. He doubted anyone in the
room could have had a similar experience. What kind of camp
would they have known? A military outpost, no doubt, a training
ground where they would have learned to march in formation,
to carry arms, to fight for—for what? National independence,
probably. Ethnic autonomy. Something no American has had to
think about, much less fight for, in two centuries. No wonder
they hate us so, he thought. No wonder we're always blundering
into wars on the wrong side.

At last, the film clicked into place and the sprockets whirred.
Karin stepped over and pressed the toggle to dim the lights. The
sound system clicked and sputtered, there was a tinny sound of
distant symphonic chords, and a voice began to speak in absurdly
clear Swedish, schoolroom enunciations, phrases such as, Spiegel
had come to realize, one never actually hears on the street.

Det här är svenska . . .

But on the screen was just a big square of light—no image.

Jorge tapped Spiegel on the shoulder and whispered, in the forbidden tongue: "A film for blinds."

They rode the bus home together after class. It was late afternoon, but already pitch-dark, even though the winter had passed its midpoint and the days were supposedly getting longer. The streets and sidewalks, Spiegel noticed, were kept clear of snow. Every shopkeeper and homeowner took on the responsibility of shoveling the snow away from his own doorway and whisking clean the nearby walkways and steps. But because the temperature rarely broke freezing all winter, the snow accumulated at the street corners in huge walls and drifts, which gave the city a mazelike quality. Often the only perspective was straight ahead, as if you were driving down a long icy chute, and Spiegel felt that the intersections would be really treacherous were it not for the extreme caution with which most Swedes seemed to navigate their way through the narrow passages of the Old City.

As the bus pulled out of town, crossed the river, nearly white with ice, and began the slow climb past the fallow fields out to the perimeter of settlement, Spiegel realized that the landscape, so strange and alien to him just a week before, had begun to take on a tinge of familiarity. He might have enjoyed the ride home except that Jorge had been bugging him, since class broke, for information about Melissa.

"Why are you so interested," Spiegel asked Jorge. "You've already got an old lady."

"A what?"

"It means . . . a girlfriend. But more than that. A serious girlfriend. A chick."

"You Americans," Jorge said, with mock exasperation. He looked out the window, examining his reflection in the glass. He gave his hair a slight pat of adjustment. "You don't understand."

"What's to understand? This great lady takes you, a penniless refugee, into her heart . . . "

"And into her flat."

"That, too. And you're looking to cheat on her. For what?"

"Every man, you see, needs two things. A wife and a mistress."

"You've got neither."

"Well, maybe it's different in your country."

"She is from my country, Jorge."

"But I'm not, and this isn't."

That was true enough. "Okay, you come by my room. We'll go up like I've got to lend you a language book or something, and she'll probably be there, in the kitchen, and I'll introduce you. Okay?"

"Super."

"And then we leave. We don't make a big thing of this tonight. See what you think after you meet her, and see what she thinks."

"Whoa, Lenny. What is this interest you show? Maybe I am invading on your territory."

"No, we're just friends. Not even friends, really."

"Then why do you protect her like a father? Is that an American thing, too? The big country protects the small country?"

"Aw, knock it off."

"What? I don't understand."

"You understand. You get my drift."

"Get my drift." Jorge spoke the words slowly, as if to test them out. "I like that."

Melissa was indeed in the kitchen, stirring some sort of rice curry in a big enameled iron pot. Jorge sat right down at the dining table. Spiegel, however, was distracted, for he had received a letter. And, to his surprise, it wasn't from America. It had a local postmark.

The letter was from Tracy, a simple, hand-scrawled note— *Sorry we haven't been to see you. Meeting tomorrow at 3. Be there?*—and the address of the American Resisters Movement— Sweden. Spiegel would have to leave class early, but he would risk missing the valuable lesson on supermarkets.

Jorge squirmed in his seat, kicking against the table leg, trying to get Spiegel's attention, until at last his impatience got the best of him. When Melissa turned from the stove, he spoke.

"My friend does not introduce us, but my name is Jorge Ramos."

"Gee, I'm sorry," Spiegel said. "This is Melissa."

"Thanks, I can do it myself," she said. "Melissa Layne. I've seen you at the school."

"Yes, I'm just starting. For the third time."

"What do you mean?"

"I mean I keep dropping out. I miss one lesson or two, and then when I get back to class, I've forgotten everything, and so I quit. And then start over again."

"You'll get screwed when you try to get credits," Melissa asked.

"I only take the class because of my residency permit. So long as I can be in class, I do not have to apply for a permit to work. And that is enough to make me want to stay in the class forever."

"Oh, I guess you're not here on an exchange," Melissa said.

"Sorry?"

"Exchange student. You know, from a college?"

"I never went to college. I was in business," Jorge said.

"That's *so* interesting."

"Yes, I will tell you sometime about my business."

"Jorge was the leading leather exporter in Europe," Spiegel said.

"Leather, ugh," Melissa said. "I like animals, so I use vinyl."

Except for the whips, Spiegel thought.

"Well, I wouldn't say leather," Jorge said. "I would say clothing. Flight jackets and so on."

"Oh, I hate that, too!"

"Well, what kind of clothes do you like?"

"You know, like this." She ran her hands along her soft, cotton khakis. "Natural stuff. Silk. Chinos."

"It was not the style where I came from, but maybe if it was big in California . . ."

"I don't know that it was big. What do kids wear back east these days, Lenny?"

"Don't look to me for fashion bulletins," Spiegel said. "I used to wear a bomber jacket, though. I thought of it as an ironic statement."

"I don't understand," Jorge said.

"Irony?"

"Yes."

"Why not?"

"It's not his native language, Melissa."

"No, really? I thought you were, like, English."

The guys laughed at that, and Melissa joined in, a little uncomfortably.

"I will take that as a great compliment. I love the English," Jorge said. "But my mother language is Portuguese. I am a native of Lisbon."

"Cool. You speak so well."

"You should hear me speak Portuguese."

"I wouldn't understand a word," she said.

"Then I would sing to you in Portuguese. Everyone understands the language of music. And of food. And of love . . . "

"Yikes, speaking of food!" From what they could discern, Melissa was not a kitchen whiz. Her method seemed to be boil water, add rice and curry powder, watch for smoke. The aroma of curry had filled the small kitchen, but it was beginning to be displaced by the acrid odor of scorched rice.

Melissa rushed to the stove and yanked the pot off the burner, singeing her palm. She began to shovel the rice out of the pot and into a soup bowl, scraping the burnt husks from the bottom.

"Shall I put that in cold water for you?" Jorge said.

"It'll clean," she said.

"No, I mean your hand."

"I'm okay. Are you guys hungry?"

"I have to be getting to my home," Jorge said. "But will you allow me to renew my offer?"

"Of cold water?"

"Dinner, *á la portuguese*."

"That's nice, but there's so many things I don't eat."

"There are so many things I don't cook."

"I'm a vegetarian," Melissa said.

"It seems to me damned hard to be a vegetarian in Sweden. No vegetables," Spiegel said.

"Sad but true," Melissa said. "But there's always rice. Sure you guys don't want some?"

"Rice, I can cook. But I will add something else, something you will like."

"Great, but maybe not right away. I've got rehearsals at night and all."

"Every night?"

"Every night this week."

"Next week, then," Jorge insisted. "Is that okay with you?" he asked Spiegel.

"Fine. Dinner's like a regular thing with me."

Jorge laughed. "If you like," he said, "invite a friend as well. We can be a quartet. Like the Beatles."

"Sure," Spiegel said. "I'll ask that *vackra svenska flicka* in our class."

Jorge looked at Spiegel, puzzled. "Karin?" he said.

"*Fröken Fält.*"

Spiegel saw Jorge to the door, and walked with him down the rough cement stairway—elevator still out of service—to the lobby. They stood for a moment in the courtyard by the front door. The ground was littered with the debris—planks, pieces of scaffolding, toppled buckets—tossed aside by the construction crew, which had left the job at sundown, that is, in the early afternoon. Jorge lit a Players and looked up at the windows in the adjacent building.

"I live up there," he said. "My old woman could be watching me, even now."

"Old lady."

"Yes. She trusts me. But you know, a man must have his, what do you say?—his foreign affairs?"

"Sure," Spiegel said. "It's a free world."

"It's good," Jorge said, "if she's looking, for her to see me here. With you." He took a long draw on the cigarette, then crushed it out in the rubble with the toe of his black boot. He blew out a last wisp of smoke, then he lifted his gloved hand, looked up, and waved at a row of dark windows. As he waved, a light flicked on.

4

A great paved wasteland split the city of Uppsala like an open wound. To the south was the old city and the pseudo-Gothic towers of the church, the castle, and the university. To the north lay the new city, office buildings of concrete and gleaming glass, the boxlike student tenements, and the long strips of residential housing that at last gave way to the farms and hills. The dividing line that separated the two worlds of Uppsala was the shopping mall, a long pedestrian walkway lined with window displays of teak furniture, stainless-steel kitchenware, cotton fabrics of bold geometric design, and ultralight winter clothing. Spiegel made his way among the drifts of crusty snow, stepping gingerly along the strips of cobbled pavement that had been cleared down to the bare ice. A wind cut to his bones, and he pulled the toggles to tighten the grip of his parka hood. This is not a day for people, he thought. It's a day for sled dogs.

When he reached the pottery warehouse at the far end of the mall, Spiegel stood in the doorway and slapped his mitts together to knock off the snow. It took him a minute to clear the steam from his glasses, another minute to kick the ice from the soles of his boots so that he could walk casually through the aisles, gazing up at the shelves stacked with teapots, canisters, Dutch ovens, and thousands of pieces of plastic dinnerware in a rainbow of colors. Suitable for play school or dollhouses, Spiegel thought. On display along the walls were radios and electronic appliances. Some men behind a counter in what seemed to be a repair shop were hunched over pieces of circuitry, probing about with stripped wire. A worker stood on a ladder, gently placing baskets on an upper shelf, while another ripped open packing crates stuffed with white straw. A bored cashier leaned against her register, flipping the pages of a fashion magazine. No customers, Spiegel noted. He made his way toward the back of the store, where he saw a man sitting on a stool by the doorway, idly polishing some wineglasses. The guy had dirty red hair pulled back into a ponytail and a scraggly beard, stained at the fringes by nicotine. He was wearing drab olive army fatigues, at least a size too large for his scrawny frame. He looked up from his work as Spiegel approached.

"*Vad kan jag stå till tjänst med?*" he said.

"I'm looking for—"

"You're Spiegel, right?"

"Yeah. Is this the place? I thought you guys would meet in a church or a union hall."

"Nope, you found us. I'm McCurdy."

He put down the stemware and held out his palm to Spiegel for a clenched-fist soul handshake.

"How long you been here, brother," McCurdy asked.

"Week or two," Spiegel said.

"It gets easier, man. The first weeks are the hardest."

"I'm not here to stay, though," Spiegel explained.

"You didn't come over the wall?"

"No, I'm just—"

"Another American looking for a home, right?"

"I'm here to help the movement is all."

"Come on," McCurdy said. "They're waiting for you."

McCurdy led Spiegel through a double door marked with a big red slash—no admittance—and they went down a stairway into the basement. They walked past several storage rooms packed floor to ceiling with shipping crates, and then to a doorway onto which someone had tacked a Vietcong flag and a photograph of Ho Chi Minh. McCurdy rapped on the door, and they entered.

Spiegel immediately felt as if he had stepped into another country. This was America, this was home. He could have been in the student union back on his own campus, or in the common room of any college dorm. The linoleum floor was cracked and stained with crushed cigarette butts. The corky walls were splotched with paint and papered with ragged posters promoting long-forgotten marches, rallies, and rock tours. Bulbs dangled from cords that drooped beneath broken ceiling tiles. An asbestos-draped heating pipe coughed and clanked and spit steam from its weak seams. A ratty sofa in a corner near the door was covered with drifts of mimeos and flyers. Tracy stood beside the sofa, folding papers and stuffing them into white envelopes. At the center of the room, Aaronson and two other men sat around a small card table, beneath a cloud of cigarette smoke.

"You found him," Tracy said, setting down a fistful of papers.

"Or he found me," McCurdy answered.

"How are you?" She rushed over to Spiegel and gave him a quick hug. "You settling in okay? "

"*Bara bra*," he said.

"I'm sorry we haven't been to see your new digs," Tracy said. "We've been so busy, trying to get this group off the ground."

"It looks as if you're underground."

"Exactly."

"So where's the meeting," Spiegel asked.

"This is it. It's like a board meeting, a steering committee," Tracy said. "Not the whole ARMS group."

Aaronson turned and waved to Spiegel. He gestured to an empty chair. "Good going, Worm," he said. "Sit down, take a load off."

"Worm?" Spiegel said.

Tracy tilted her head toward McCurdy.

"Yeah, they call me that," he said. "'Cause I unearth so much stuff."

"Like what?"

"Like you."

"Welcome to ARMS," Aaronson said as Spiegel joined the conclave. Aaronson set down his clipboard and his Styrofoam coffee cup to introduce Spiegel. "These are my main men," he said. Zeke, a black man wearing an Irish-knit sweater, had tied a red bandana around his forehead. He stood and reached his huge hand out to Spiegel. The other guy didn't budge from his chair. He was dressed in army khakis, cleaned and pressed, and his hair was clipped razor short, as if he had just come off the base. A Boy Scout, Spiegel thought, or else a new arrival. His name was Reston.

"You, too, Worm," Aaronson said. "Sit down." The Worm pulled up a chair, turned it around, and slouched over the backrest. He took a drag from a cigarette, one of three that had been left burning on the lip of a black plastic ashtray. When he set it back, its thin line of smoke floated up toward the gray cloud that had accumulated among the network of cables and heating pipes that crisscrossed the ceiling. It's like a little ritual offering, Spiegel thought—fumes of incense sent to the skies.

"We've been working," Aaronson said, "on drafting a statement—"

"And on some issues," Zeke said.

"Which I think is pretty much the same thing," Aaronson said. "We can't deal with the issues until we have a statement of purpose, a charter."

"And I'm saying you can't fight a battle on an empty stomach," Reston said.

"You're not starving, man," Aaronson said. "You're talking about maybe making your life here a little more comfortable. And I'm saying I don't think we should be comfortable. I think we should be goddamn uncomfortable so that we never lose sight of our focus."

"Which is what?" said the Worm.

"Which is going home. Which means making it possible for us to go home," Aaronson said.

Reston leaned back in his chair. He twisted his mouth into a crooked smile. "You can say that," he told Aaronson. "Easy for you to say we should live in misery. You come here right from college. You don't know misery. You've never seen a firefight, man, except in the movies. When you think of guns and napalm, you smell popcorn."

"Enough with that pulling-rank shit, man," Zeke said.

"Hey, if he wants to make it personal," Aaronson said, "let's do it. I'm as much at risk here as any of you guys, maybe more. Yeah, I appreciate it takes a lot of courage to leave the active service in time of war, facing the code of military justice and all that shit. But what about guys like me? Don't you think it's maybe even harder to give up your life when it wasn't in danger in the first place?"

"I think to the man there ain't a dime's worth of difference between you two. If either of you guys went home, you'd probably get a good white lawyer like Mr. Kunstler and you'd walk," Zeke said. "Me, I'd be doing time."

"But who's thinking of going home?" said the Worm.

Reston pointed at Aaronson. "He is."

"I'm thinking we should use our status here to try to end the war. We should make it known to our brothers in the armed forces that they could safely come to Sweden and be welcomed. And if enough come over the wall, it will put such pressure on the army that they will be unable to maintain the forces of occupation in Vietnam—"

"There's always more bodies back home in the ghetto," Zeke said. "They can replace every deserter ten times over."

"I'm talking moral pressure."

"But maybe Zeke has a point. Why not moral pressure on the Swedes as well?" It was Tracy. She had pulled up a chair and joined the meeting. "If there's one thing we know about them, it's that they're dripping with guilt. We could exploit that, make them see that they're not doing enough to integrate the Americans into Swedish life."

"What more do you want of them?" Aaronson said. "They give us residency permits, labor permits, housing allowances, free language classes, living stipends. What else could they do for us?"

"We need *more* money, man. It's not enough to live on," Zeke said. "And we need better social services."

"There's not enough language teachers," the Worm said.

"Or jobs. Or apartments. We need to be put at the top of the housing list. We're a priority case," Reston said.

"But there's a huge danger in that," Aaronson countered. "The more we publicize our difficult living conditions, the more we endanger ourselves politically."

"What do you mean?" Tracy asked him.

"I mean we can't expect a wave of recruits to drop their guns and cross the line if we go around whining about how hard life is in the socialist mecca," Aaronson said.

"Believe me, life is harder in 'Nam."

"You saying we should tell them life here is paradise?" Zeke asked.

"I'm saying we should focus on our long-term goals, and be willing to suffer to achieve them."

"Well, evidently you expect to go back to the States someday, but the rest of us do not," Reston said. "And our long-term goal is to make a tolerable life in this country."

"I think he's right," Tracy said. "I think we should draft a list of conditions and state our needs—"

"—our *demands*," Zeke said.

"—and present it to the newspaper—"

"—or the Uppsala city council."

"We could pass it along to the other groups of deserters around the country, get hundreds of signatures on a petition, and we could get the parliament to focus on our needs—demands—before the next national elections."

"I don't think it's an area we ought to get into," Aaronson said. "We have no role in Swedish politics, and if we try to step forward we'll get crushed like a bug."

"The Social Democrats have always supported us."

"And if we start speaking out and demanding more money, better living conditions, special treatment, we will be isolated. The Social Dems will back off fast, and the right-wing parties will step in to fill the vacuum. They'll stir up hatred against the American community so fast you'll wish you were back in the war."

"So you're saying—"

"Forget about Sweden. It doesn't really matter where we're living. We'll always be Americans, and that ought to be our focus, ending the war, bringing us home."

"I don't know, man," Zeke said. "No black man here would say that. We don't expect they'd ever want us back home, war or no war."

"You could choose to stay here. In seven years, you could become a citizen. But it would be your choice."

"I've made my choice," Zeke said. "I made it forever, the day I was born."

"Why don't we do one statement?" Tracy said. "A statement of purpose, calling on America to end the war of racism and oppression and calling on the Swedish government for continued and increased support of the American deserters and resisters."

"Our declaration of independence," Zeke said.

"More like *de*pendence."

"I'll do a draft," Tracy said.

"I can help," Spiegel put in, breaking his silence.

Reston turned sideways in his chair to look at Spiegel.

"Is that why you brought him in?" he said to Aaronson. "Is he a writer?"

"He's going to help us out," Aaronson said.

"What are you?" Reston said. He squinted, and scanned Spiegel top to bottom. "I can see from your hair, man, that you didn't come over the wall. You'd have been gone a long time to grow out that beard. Where you from? Another college student? Doing a term paper? Junior year abroad? You got your Eurail Pass? *Europe on Five Dollars a Day*? Instamatic camera?"

"I don't know why I'm here. Maybe I should go. I've heard enough."

"Maybe too much," Reston said.

"No, he's got to hear it all. He's got to be informed," Aaronson said.

"And why is that? He writing your biography, man?"

"He's sort of my representative."

"You a lawyer, man?" Zeke asked.

"No, I'm just his friend," Spiegel said.

"So this is a little reunion?" the Worm said.

"No. We never knew each other, back in the States," Aaronson said.

"Then how come he's here now?"

"I need him to help me while I'm traveling," Aaronson said.

"He's going with you?" Zeke said.

"An aide-de-camp," Reston said.

"No, he's staying here," Aaronson said.

"So how can he help you?" the Worm asked.

"We'll get to that."

"It depends how far he's going."

"This stays within the group," Aaronson said, "no matter what."

"Which group?" Zeke asked.

"This one."

"Not even Hyde—"

"Especially not Hyde. I don't want him to know where I'm going, or even that I'm gone."

"He's gonna find out, he's gonna want to talk to you—"

"Well, don't let him."

"Hyde?"

"He's been here longer than Aaronson, longer than any of us. Thinks he should run the show. You'll meet him—"

"—but try not to. At least not until I get back to Uppsala."

"Get back? Where are you going?"

"How much does he know?" Reston asked. "How much does he understand?"

"I don't understand a thing," Spiegel said. "Nobody explained."

"It's this," Aaronson said. "I've got to go check out some of our supplies."

"Supplies of what?"

"There's sort of a pipeline," Tracy said, "a network that helps guys get papers and cross borders, guides them into exile, settles them in. For security, no one knows more than one contact, one link on the chain. We're the end of the line, of course. The welcoming committee."

"And the filter at the end of the pipe," Aaronson said. "We keep out impure elements."

"He's got to go down to the border," the Worm said, "to make sure that we don't take in guys who would cut a deal with the man."

"Right," Aaronson said. "It would be extremely harmful if

we took in the wrong kind. We don't want anyone who would go back to the army and talk, in exchange for short time. So I have to screen anyone who's thinking about settling in Uppsala because there's always a danger that the army might have tapped into the pipe."

"What do you mean?" Spiegel asked.

"I mean they might send us a fake deserter. Send us a spy. Just to fuck us up."

"That's why everyone's so suspicious of newcomers," Tracy said.

"Nothing personal," Zeke added.

"I'm going to the border to deal with the latest deliveries. Check out the merchandise."

"Shipping and receiving," said the Worm.

"Quality control," Reston said.

"Well," Spiegel said. "I'll do what I can. That's why I came here."

"That's good," Tracy said. "That's why we're all here."

"So maybe we ought to adjourn this meeting," Zeke said, shifting his great bulk about on the spindly chair, "and reconvene in the *puben*."

"What the fuck is that supposed to mean?" Reston said.

"I mean let's go get a couple of beers."

"No. I mean the *puben*."

"*Puben* means pub, in Swedish," said the Worm.

"*Puben* means *the* Pub. The *en* ending means *the*, " Reston said.

"So what?"

"So you can't call it *the Puben*. That's like calling it *the the pub*."

"If you don't shut the the fuck up I'm going to hit you in the the nose."

"Okay, guys," Tracy said. "Take a stack of these flyers, each of you, on the way out, all right?"

The Worm, Reston, and Zeke fumbled with their caps and wool scarves.

"I don't know, man," Zeke said. "Last time I handed out flyers some pig comes up to me and says something I don't understand, and then he grabs me by the arm and shoves me right off that corner. I'm saying, hey, don't a guy have a right to hand these out? Ain't this a free country?"

"Well, it ain't a free country," Reston said.

"That's true," Aaronson said. "You need a permit for everything. Even for a demonstration."

"Can you imagine that, having to sign up for the right to protest?"

"But man," the Worm said, "it's the way they look at you. It's like they're looking right through you."

"Not me, man," Zeke said. "Most of them ain't never seen a black man up close before, except on TV. And they're like too polite to stare, except the children. They want to touch me, see if black skin feels the same. Like I'm in some kind of petting zoo."

"Kids always look at my long hair," the Worm said. "I guess they've never seen a guy with a ponytail."

"Yeah, well you could cut off your hair. Not much I can do about my color."

"Ain't no one saying you should, man."

"I'll catch up with you guys later," Tracy said, as Zeke, Reston, and the Worm shuffled out of the meeting room, trailing streams of cigarette smoke. They were off to spend their last few hoarded kroner on mugs of thin beer. Spiegel imagined them, shoulder to shoulder, gazing into the pools of amber, hoping to discern in the liquescence a muted image of a better life.

Aaronson led Spiegel into a little office he had fixed up in what had once been a storage closet. Stacked against the concrete wall were some packing crates of glassware and teapots. Next to the crates, Aaronson had set up a folding chair and a card table. He had draped an American flag over the table, which he was using as a desk.

"Nice lamp," Spiegel said.

Aaronson flicked on the handsome gooseneck that was clamped to one of the folds in the cloth. "There are advantages to renting space beneath an electronics store," he said. "All kinds of things pass through the warehouse, and sometimes they

get, uh, damaged during transport. Maybe I can manage to procure you something."

"I don't know that I really need a lamp."

"Well, anything."

"I was a little surprised that you guys meet in a warehouse. I'd
have thought you guys would want someplace more accessible."

"Why would we want that?"

"So people could be aware of the American community. They
could drop in, for information, for conversation."

"No, that's not really what we want. We'd rather go about our
business undisturbed."

"But here you have to pay rent."

"It's a very reasonable rate. The owners are sympathizers. And
we do some favors for them, too."

"Not in the janitorial area, however," Spiegel said. He looked
around, warily, at the accumulated debris and dust and crud.

"No, more in the area of shipping and receiving." Aaronson
laughed, and sat at the desk. "So, what do you think?" he
asked.

"It's okay for starters," Spiegel said. He sat down on one of the
crates. "Maybe someday you'll have a room with a view."

"I don't mean the office," Aaronson said. "I mean the guys,
the meeting."

"I think they want to learn Swedish," Spiegel said.

"You know what these guys really want?" Aaronson said.
"They don't want jobs, housing, welfare." He leaned across the
table and spoke quietly. "They want to get laid."

"Well, you've got an old lady, so I don't know that you're one
to judge—"

"I'm not judging. I'm just telling you all their complaints will
go away once they get their rocks off."

"So what are you wasting your time for? Why don't you just
start a dating service?"

Aaronson laughed. "You've got to realize, once these guys
start getting it, they're no good to the movement anymore.
They'll lose interest."

"You mean, they'll be happy."

"Contented cows," Aaronson said. "Ready to settle down beside a meadow and chew their cud."

"I think they deserve that, after all they've given up, and all they've risked. Look at the lives they've come from," Spiegel said. "There's nothing for them to go back to, even if there were a general amnesty. Here, they're free."

"Maybe," Aaronson said. "Until the government decides there's too many of us, that we're expensive and dangerous, that we corrupt the morals of Swedish youth. That we poison the air with our smoke and the gene pools with our dicks."

"What are you talking about?" Spiegel asked.

Aaronson explained that the Swedes had become wary of Americans and uneasy in their presence. The typical American on the street these days was no longer a college student with a backpack asking for directions to the *djurpark*. The Americans they saw these days were the high-school dropouts with tobacco-stained fingers and bloodshot eyes, trying to cadge a few kroner for a cup of coffee and a sweet roll. As a result, the sicknesses that had begun to infect Swedish society—guns, drugs, sexual disease—were associated in the public mind with the new immigrants, the refugees, and it would not be long before the fledgling right-wing parties began to exploit the nascent anti-American feelings to their political advantage.

"We're not citizens, you know," Aaronson said. "We live here on temporary residence permits. The official policy could change, and the permits could be pulled so fast—" He snapped his fingers. "Then where would we be?"

"Looking for a home?" Spiegel said. "On the road again?"

"But you know that's not going to happen." It was Tracy. She stood in the office doorway, clutching a batch of folded papers. From Spiegel's vantage, a large, shiny visage of Mao on a poster pinned to the far wall seemed to be watching them from over Tracy's shoulder. "There's no way they would pull our permits, unless we did something really fucked-up."

"Like what, Tracy?" Aaronson said. "Who's to define *fucked-up?* In this country, littering might be considered a capital offense. Maybe they could deport us for smoking in the wrong railway car."

"The pigs are the same all over the world," Tracy said, as she sat down on one of the crates. "I hope you weren't too put off by the guys," she said to Spiegel.

"They don't trust strangers. And rightfully," Aaronson said.

"It's okay," Spiegel said. "Neither would I, in their shoes. I mean, hell, I could be—"

"A spy. An infiltrator," Tracy said, ticking off the possibilities on her fingers. "Someone sent by the army, the criminal intelligence division, to file reports, to maybe try to talk a few of the deserters into renouncing the cause—"

"But at least you guys know that I'm clean."

"Sure," Tracy said. "That's why we wanted to introduce you to the steering committee. So that they would understand who you are, in case anything happens."

"You mean while I'm traveling," Spiegel said.

Tracy and Aaronson looked at each other, puzzled. "What makes you think you're going to be traveling?" Aaronson asked.

Spiegel leaned back against a heating pipe, and he smiled. "I figured it out. You're not going down to check out the new recruits," he said to Aaronson. "You can't risk crossing the border. That's why you wanted me to come to Uppsala. I look enough like you, so I can travel for you, I can travel *as* you, while you lay low back here, keeping an eye on things. That way, if I get picked up, everything's cool—at least for you."

"Hmm. Iris told us you were really smart, a quick study," Aaronson said. "And that's good. You figured out a really good plan, but you figured it wrong."

"I did?" Spiegel wasn't sure if he had been complimented or slyly insulted and put in his place.

"Or I guess I'd say you got it exactly right, but backwards. Like a mirror image," Tracy said.

"I'm the one who's going to travel," Aaronson said. "But I'm going to travel as you. There's a drop-off point in Denmark, and I have to go down there to meet some deserters who've just gone over the wall and get them safely into Sweden, without attracting the attention of the military police."

"I see," Spiegel said. "And you want to travel as me—"

"Because your papers are clean. And if I let my hair grow—"

"You'll look just like me."

"So if I'm stopped or checked," Aaronson said, "everything will wash."

"Will you give him your passport?" Tracy asked. She leaned toward Spiegel and placed her hand on his arm. "I know it could be risky for you, to be without papers."

"It's for the movement," Aaronson said. "We all have to take some risks. Think of the danger the deserters have braved. Anything we do to help them out is easy, by comparison."

"You've got to decide," Tracy said.

"I have decided," Spiegel said. "I decided before I left the States. I'd do whatever I could, whatever I had to do—"

"That's good," Tracy interjected. "That's great!" She stepped over to Spiegel and embraced him. On her neck he could smell a trace of mimeo ink—the perfume of the left. Spiegel felt a tenseness, an urgency in her embrace, however, as if she were eager to move him along before he changed his mind and pulled out of the deal. He let Tracy go and turned to face Aaronson. It seemed hard to believe that they had met only twice, for Spiegel felt that he had been living, for the past year, within Aaronson's gravitational field. Before, he had thought of himself as a meteor, adrift in space, which had been pulled into Aaronson's orbit. Now that they had met, he had begun to see that they had both been adrift, that maybe—from Aaronson's point of view—Spiegel had been the stronger force. Perhaps the truth was that they were more like double stars, spinning madly about an invisible axis, until either one of them would be cast off or they would converge at the center, obliterating each other in an all-consuming fire.

"I'll stop by tomorrow with the papers," Spiegel said.

"No," Aaronson said. "I need them as soon as possible. I have to leave right away, maybe tonight."

"Then I'll come down to your place tonight."

"I'd rather that we weren't seen together just now," Aaronson said slowly, measuring each word. "I don't want to attract too much attention to my movements. Why don't you just give the passport to Tracy? She can give you a ride home."

"Sure," Spiegel said. He set his hand on Aaronson's desk. His palm just about covered one of the fifty stars. "I understand where you're coming from," he said. "You're scared."

Aaronson looked up at Spiegel. "I'm scared of what?" Aaronson said.

"I mean, you're moving into the ring of fire. You could stay here, in complete safety, doing your work. And it's good work, important stuff, helping to establish the American community in Uppsala. Nobody would get on your case if you just hibernated in Sweden, building a new life for yourself, waiting out the war."

"No, I'm not scared," Aaronson said. He stood, and stepped out from behind his desk. "I mean, what's the worst that can happen? They arrest me, deport me, send me to prison? Sweden's a prison, too."

"Prison's the least of it," Spiegel said. "It's one thing to help the deserters once they're here. But bringing them in, underground-railroad stuff—that could be treason, in time of war. That's a capital crime, man."

"You have to wish me luck then." Aaronson grabbed Spiegel's palm, and they gripped hands in a strong, brotherly soul handshake, elbows crooked at right angles, joined fists upraised in the spirit of pride and defiance.

Spiegel thought, despite Aaronson's assurances, that he could see in his eyes and feel in the touch of his hand a slight trembling of fear, a nervous sidelong look of uncertainty. He was beginning to understand how strong Aaronson had to be to keep his doubts and fears hidden from view. As they said good-bye, Aaronson's features were set in a friendly smile, but Spiegel had the feeling that Aaronson's fixed expression was a facade, a mask covering his trepidation.

Tracy led Spiegel up the stairway and through the shop. A clerk was cashing out a register, and the workmen at the back were locking the repair desk behind a metal grate. It was dark outside, cold and still. The knife-edged wind had died. The pedestrian mall, lit by pools of amber light, was deserted. At the far end of the mall, a bus idled at an empty crosswalk.

"I think it's very brave of you," Tracy said, zipping tight her jacket.

"Why?" Spiegel said. "I basically don't have to do anything but wait."

"You could have said no. I thought maybe you would."

Tracy was silent for a moment. Spiegel watched her breath cloud the air, as if her unspoken thoughts had been made palpable, like a series of scalloped balloons in a comic strip.

"I mean, if anything happens to him while he's out of the country," Tracy said, "you're screwed, too."

Spiegel helped Tracy brush the light dusting of snow off the flat windshield and side mirror. Ice had clotted the trigger-grip handles, and he had to squeeze hard to pop open the passenger door. Tracy tossed her stack of flyers onto the cluttered backseat.

"You're right," Spiegel said, as he sat down in the car. His knees bumped the dash, and his breath frosted against the window.

"You're trying to keep clean, aren't you?" Tracy said. She turned to him, and reached out her gloved hand. "That's okay," she said. "You probably want to be able to go back home. We should respect that. We shouldn't fuck it up for you."

"I'll do what I have to do," Spiegel said. "Right now, I'm in your hands. Until Aaronson comes back, I'm going nowhere. I'll have no papers, my own or anybody else's. In the eyes of the law, I won't even exist."

"I'm Nobody. Who are you?" Tracy said.

"Are you—Nobody—Too?" Spiegel answered.

Tracy smiled. "You know that poem. Great." She turned the key. The engine cranked and sputtered and started up.

"Yeah, I was an English major, once upon a time," Spiegel said. He tried to remember the rest of the poem. "Then there's a pair of us?/Don't tell!" That was as far as he could get. As they rode in silence toward the lights of Flogsta, Spiegel thought that maybe if he held still for long enough he could disappear, like his frozen exhalations, vanishing into the clear, dark air.

MARCH

5

The sink was filled with snails soaking in water, and Jorge was involved with them up to his elbows. He swished them around in the grime, agitating the shells, cracking them against one another and against the stainless steel, and every couple of minutes he would pull up the drain and the sandy sludge would be sucked away with a huge slurp. Then he would refill the basin with a cascade of fresh, hot water that tumbled over the live snails and rattled them like chattering teeth. It was hard to talk above the noise.

"What makes you think she'll eat these?" Spiegel shouted.

"Well, why not? They are a food of love," said Jorge. He picked one up and held it in the light. "*Amore*," he said, and gave the snail a kiss.

"I think she's a vegetarian," Spiegel said. "It's part of being from California."

"Well, we can think of these as vegetables, can't we? They are more like a fruit than like an animal."

"A fruit? I don't think she'll buy that."

"I didn't buy them."

"Sorry?"

"I found them."

"No. *Buy that.* It means, I don't think she'll believe you."

"Okay." With a gulp and a belch, the gray water swirled down the drain.

"What do you mean, you found them?" Spiegel asked.

"Have you ever seen these for sale, in the greengrocer's?"

"The what? You sound like a Brontë novel."

"What is the word, then? Where one goes food shopping?"

"Supermarket. I guess the Swedish markets sell snails. They have everything, as long as it comes in a tube. Minute steak. Fried eggs. Malted milk. Codfish roe."

"But not snails. These I, how would you say it, gathered up?"

Jorge had put a big pot on to boil, adding oil and wine to the water. He had brought all the ingredients over to Spiegel's kitchen, carrying the bottles of oil, the wine, the spices, and the two plastic tubs of live snails, in big string shopping bags slung over his shoulder.

"You foraged. It means gathered your own food. Not a very common word."

"No, I wouldn't think so."

"And where does one forage for snails? In case I ever get a tremendous craving for snails in the middle of the night, when the kiosks are closed?"

"You wouldn't forage for snails in the middle of the night."

"Because they go to bed early?"

"No, because you find them in the graveyards. Is that the right word?"

"Oh my god." Spiegel felt a rising in his throat. He swallowed to repress the sensation, but he knew that he was turning white, or maybe green. Jorge had chopped some herbs, and he was tying the bundle inside a square of cheesecloth. "Graveyards?" Spiegel said, choking on the word.

"There's one down by the field at the end of the bus line." Jorge secured the knot on the cheesecloth and dropped the bundled herbs into the stockpot. "I go there when it's wet, and the snails climb out of the mud. They crawl on the gravestones. They must like the cold and damp. Maybe they munch on the minerals. Maybe the lime dissolves a little in the rain, and the snails like that. Maybe it helps them to build good, strong shells. I go with a little sack, and I pluck them off the graves. Sometimes, if I don't find enough on the stones, I dig a little in the mud with a stick. That stirs them up. It stirs up little bugs, too, but those I wash away, down the sink."

"Jorge, I think that's absolutely disgusting. How do you know we can't die from eating these?"

"Oh, at home I do it all the time."

"But these are Swedish snails. Maybe they're totally different, some deadly variety that just looks like Portuguese snails. This kind of thing happens all the time with mushrooms. Some poor guy goes into the woods and thinks he's found some delicious fungus, and he goes home and fries it up and it turns out to be the deadly nightshade. Just a whiff from the frying pan and his nerves are paralyzed and he can't breathe and he falls over dead."

"Yes, I have heard of such things. But those are mushrooms."

"Or blowfish. They have such lethal poisons that the chefs who prepare them have to be specially licensed by the Japanese government. A drop the size of a pinhead, if it gets onto a portion of fish that you're eating, it'll kill you. Your whole body goes numb, it's kind of pleasant they say, for a moment, and then you're totally paralyzed and then you die. It happens once in a while in restaurants, and it's part of the beauty of eating the fish: pleasure on the edge of danger."

"But those are eaten raw."

"But these come from graveyards, Jorge! Who knows where these snails have been? They may have been burrowing in the earth and eating the flesh of dead bodies, dead bodies of people. Who could have died from anything! These slimy things might be pockets of disease, little capsules of death!"

Jorge gave the snails a final rinse under cold water. "No, that is not how we think of them at home," he said. He sat down at the table with Spiegel and leaned forward so that he could speak quietly, almost in a whisper. "We think of them as wonderful food for lovemaking."

"An aphrodisiac?"

"Is that the word? Like an Afro hairdo?"

"No, different spelling."

"Okay. Snails give you great power, in love, you know. It is a secret of the French."

"Oh, come on, that's superstition, sympathetic magic, like the Chinese and powdered rhinoceros horn. It's just that snails

are soft creatures with hard shells, and their whole texture is
sexual—slimy and sticky—and the way they withdraw their heads
and then poke out their little horns, it's kind of vaginal—"

"Or like a prick, peeking out from its hood—"

"But it doesn't mean eating snails makes you more potent."

"It's not just for the man, though," Jorge said. The broth had
come to a boil, and it was steaming the kitchen with the fruity
smell of white wine and olive oil. Jorge lifted the colander from
the sink and carried the snails, dripping gray water onto the clean
floor, over to the stove and dumped them into the boiling broth.
As they hit the water, they made a slight hissing sound. Each snail
curled, like a little black thumb, then slowly sank beneath the
rolling surface to the depths of the roiling brew.

Melissa arrived late. She rushed home from voice auditions for
the peasant chorus. She had hoped to get the lead in *Miss Julie*,
but she couldn't master the Swedish. Oddly, the Australian
director knew no Swedish, either. He came to Uppsala with a
reputation as a wild man. He had done the famous Melbourne
No Exit *No Exit*, in which the emergency doors were actually
barred from the outside after intermission and the audience was
trapped in the theater for twenty minutes after the show. The
police closed down the production after three nights, but a crew
had filmed the panicked theatergoers smacking fists and purses
against the glass doors inside the lobby, stomping on one another
to get to the pay phones, and when the film was shown on TV,
the director—Mick Ryder—became red-hot. He topped *NENE*
with a nude *Godot* in Sydney that featured various lotions, lubricants, and live animals. The police closed that one down, too,
and it made tabloid headlines—Good Riddance! and Come no
More!—when Ryder left for a year's residency in Sweden.

His *Julie*, to everyone's surprise, and perhaps disappointment, was
so far looking rather traditional, perhaps because of Ryder's struggle
with the language. He was trying to cast the show by referring to his
English script while the actors read for the parts in Swedish, but he
seemed, according to Melissa, "lost in translation."

"I mean, he doesn't even look at us while we're onstage. His nose is in the book," she said. "I could be giving the performance of my life, and he wouldn't even know."

"Give him credit. He's trying to learn the language of the play," Spiegel said.

"I think tomorrow I'll do the peasant dance in the nude. I bet he notices that," Melissa said.

"Oh, from what I hear he's seen plenty of nudity. You'd probably make a bigger impression if you use some of your props."

"Props?" Jorge said.

"Things onstage during a play. Books, lamps, furniture, table settings." Melissa picked up some of the flatware. "Stuff like this."

"Guns," said Spiegel.

"There are no guns in *Miss Julie*. There's a razor, and a pair of boots, the count's boots, a very important prop. They sit onstage the whole time, and they symbolize the oppression felt by Jean, the valet."

"So come onstage wearing boots," said Spiegel. "A pair of big black American cowboy boots."

"And nothing else," said Jorge.

"He'd think I'm nuts."

"But, it would be a statement," said Spiegel. "A statement for women's rights. For sisterhood."

"Our bodies, ourselves," Melissa said.

"Well, look, if you want to stay in the chorus your whole life—"

"My friends, we must not argue," Jorge said. "This is a special night. I thank you for asking me over to your flat for dinner. And perhaps you can help prepare the dinner table by setting down the—props."

"Oh, Jorge, this isn't a play," Melissa said, as she began to help him set the table. Tracy was expected after dinner, but Spiegel set a place for her, just in case. She had called Spiegel in the morning and said she was coming to Flogsta. Spiegel hadn't seen her since Aaronson had left Uppsala, more than a week ago. It was obvious that she had been trying to keep her distance while Aaronson was gone. Maybe he's come back, Spiegel figured, and she's returning my passport.

The kitchen had become thick with the perfume of garlic and oil—just like home, Jorge said—and the Swedes who lived on the floor were gathering in the doorway, trying to make sense of this aromatic invasion. There were three of them—Lars, Brigit, and Sven—serious students who, Spiegel thought, had been through the wash cycle a few too many times. They were so fair-skinned and blond it looked as if the color had been rinsed out of them, along with most of the starch of personality.

"Have you guys eaten?" Spiegel called to them.

"Oh, yes," Sven said.

"Join us, join us."

"No, no."

Spiegel knew that they had eaten their dinner, white on white, some sort of flaky cod with potatoes and bread, as soon as they had come home from classes, and then they retreated to their rooms to study for the rest of the night. No one he knew in America worked so hard. The Swedes he had met were so different from what he had imagined. Back home, Sweden had a reputation as a country of license and liberty. Spiegel could see that the image was false. Swedes were free—free from government oppression, free from the need to atone for the sins of one's country—but they were not exactly liberated. They were shackled by an interior oppression, a product of their cultural and geographical isolation, and perhaps by a reaction formation, a self-imposed inhibition to compensate for the lack of legal restraints on their public and political behavior.

Spiegel thought that eating snails with garlic might do the Swedes some good.

But, having checked out the aromas, perhaps just making sure that the kitchen wasn't on fire, they returned to their own rooms, vanishing silently, like smoke in a breeze.

"What's for dinner?" Melissa asked.

"Jorge cooked up something really special."

"Will you try this food?" he asked. "It is from my country." He spooned a big helping onto her plate while Spiegel sliced up some sweet, yellow bread.

"Is this meat?" she asked. "I'm a vegetarian."

"You will like this," Jorge said. "It has shell."

"Like clams?"

"This is great," Spiegel said.

On the tongue, each morsel had a confusing resilience, as if it resisted giving up its flavor until fully masticated, at which point the flavor was released in a burst. The snails had absorbed the fruitiness of the wine, the grassiness of the herb bouquet, and a slight astringency from something more subtle—the garlic? a splash of vinegar?—that seemed to fill his whole palate with an explosion of sensation, complex yet harmonious. Yet beneath the exhilaration imparted by the garlic and the oils, he could detect—was it because he knew the source?—an undercurrent of earthiness, a darkness, a slightly burnt and muddy taste that made him think of death.

Melissa screwed up her face as she chewed. She had thought of herself as an adventuresome diner, but this was a long way from one of her curries. Bravely, she swallowed, then paused for a moment before speaking, to wait for her disordered senses to regain their equilibrium.

"Okay, I'll bite. Mushrooms?"

"No, escargots," said Spiegel.

"Snails. Oh, god," she said. She felt pinpricks of sweat break out on her face and neck. "I can't eat these."

"A snail is not much different from a vegetable," Jorge said.

"That's not why," said Melissa. "It's just too gross. It's like eating worms. Or rubber bands."

"I like it," Spiegel said. Just then, he heard someone at the doorway.

"Hey, like, what's cooking? And I mean that literally."

"Tracy!" She was carrying a big grocery bag, which she set down on the countertop.

"The elevator's broken so I walked up, and the door was open. Man, you can smell this all the way out on the highway. You can probably smell it in Norway. What is it?"

"I have prepared a special meal, in the Portuguese style."

"Tracy, this is my friend Jorge, and this is our friend Melissa."

"Yeah, I think I've seen you guys around town," Tracy said. "There aren't that many of us, you know."

"You're from California, too?"

"No, I meant foreigners. Outsiders."

"Do you really feel that?" Melissa asked. "Sometimes I think everyone here's an outsider. That's the beauty of a university town. Everyone's here kind of like on a visa. And they'll all be going home someday."

"We won't," said Jorge.

"That's true, but you won't stay *here*, will you? You'll probably settle somewhere else in Sweden. Everyone leaves Uppsala, eventually."

"You're saying Uppsala is a city whose whole purpose is to get people to want to leave it," Tracy said.

"Yeah," said Melissa. "Like a family."

"So, brothers, where can I dump this stuff? Don't you guys have coatracks?"

"My room's open," Spiegel said.

"You got a bathroom there, too?"

While Tracy was gone, Jorge bustled about, heaping her empty plate with a fresh serving of the snails. As he worked, he tried to grab Spiegel's attention. Standing behind Melissa, he gave a little cough and raised his eyebrows. When Spiegel looked, Jorge smiled and cupped his hands in front of his chest, as if to say—nice body, huh?

"I think Tracy has already eaten," Spiegel said.

"Oh, well, of course. But maybe we can entice her to a second portion. For the sake of—variety?"

"No, I don't think so."

"You'd be surprised, my friend, how many people like to dine on more than one dish. Am I right, Melissa?"

"I don't know what you're talking about."

"He's saying he thinks Tracy might be interested in me—"

"Now, now—" Jorge said. He seemed, to Spiegel's amusement, to be genuinely prudish when talking about sex in the presence of a woman. So he had been using circumlocutions. Perhaps he feared that speaking of sex, and of infidelity, would make his attempt to seduce Melissa more difficult. With Melissa, and no doubt with Lisbet and with any of the other girls in his past and his future, he would speak of sex, if he spoke at all, as if it were something holy and mysterious that had touched them, even for a single moment, with the blind force of its divinity.

"She's not interested in me," Spiegel said. "She's got an old man she lives with."

"She's the chick who lives with that deserter?"

"He's not a deserter. He's a resister." Tracy had come back to join them.

"What's the big diff?" Melissa asked.

"Deserters leave the army. Resisters take illegal actions against the war."

"Like burning draft cards and stuff?"

"More serious. That's like a speeding ticket. The resisters here are wanted on federal warrants. If Aaronson's caught anywhere outside Sweden, he'll do federal time."

Spiegel, stirred by Jorge's leering assessment, couldn't help but look at Tracy in a new way. Yes, she was cute, and now that she had shed her down jacket, he could appreciate that she had a nice, compact body and a liveliness about her step and her bearing that he found most attractive. Her expression was open and friendly. She had nice eyes and an appealing overbite. She would touch her teeth to her lower lip when thinking or when listening intently, and Spiegel liked that. It made Tracy look just a little bit aggressive, a little dangerous—as if no flesh would be entirely inviolate pressed close to hers.

"Well, I say thank god for Sweden," Jorge said, and he raised his glass. "If it weren't for Sweden, I might be lying dead on a beach in Africa."

"To Sweden," Spiegel echoed, and he raised his glass. "The last hope on earth for the oppressed—"

"Depressed—"

"Repressed—"

"Where Kurds and Turks, Egyptians and Jews, Ibo and Biafran can sit side by side—"

"—and learn to order cheese!"

They laughed and clinked glasses. Each of them took a long draught of the wine. Then they returned their attention to dinner, even Melissa, who decided, once she saw everyone else gorging on snails, that snails weren't really so bad. As members of the mollusk family, she reasoned, snails were perched low enough on the great chain of being that they didn't violate her vegetarian principles. She wondered if Tracy knew what she was eating, or if she cared. Something about those East Coast chicks—they were always hungry, always pushing ahead. She had known a few back in drama school at UCLA, the driven ones, the ones who wanted not so much the grades—who cared about that shit really?—as the contacts, a line to the producers, the directors, the casting agents. They drove her crazy, yet she had to acknowledge, as she watched Tracy sop up snail juice with a big slab of puffy bread, that she admired their drive and their spirit. She could learn a few things from Tracy.

"So look," Tracy was saying. "I've got some business to conduct here with Lenny, and you're welcome to watch—"

"Business? Whoa!" Jorge blurted. His face was a little flushed from the wine and the spicy food.

"I don't know what she's talking about!" Spiegel said, and his voice was louder than he thought it should be. He was feeling loose, too. It was more than the wine. The whole room, still pungent with cooking odors, seemed to be deeply intoxicant.

"Come on, I'll show you," Tracy said. She stood, and then they all did, a little shaky and uncertain. Melissa steadied herself by setting a hand on the table.

"What about all these dishes and stuff?"

"Later, later," Jorge said, grandly dismissive, a patron on his estate anticipating that the servants would see to the details, as Tracy led them into the hallway and to Spiegel's room.

"Great decor," Melissa said, as she stifled a giggle. Spiegel had added nothing to the room except his backpack, which sat in the corner, its flaps open, a change of clothes draped over the metal frame, a portable dressing bureau.

"I just had no idea how long I'd be here," he said. "Maybe I'll buy some posters for the walls."

"You need something," Melissa said.

"Why?" said Tracy. "I think he's got the right idea. Never accumulate more than you can carry on your back. Guerilla tourism."

"A lesson from the snails," Jorge said.

"Not for me," said Melissa. "Wherever I go, I like to make the place feel like home."

"So does your room look like Disneyland?" Jorge said.

"I'll show you. But first let's see Tracy's big surprise. Is it in those bags, Tracy? Did you bring dessert?"

"I don't know if I could handle dessert," Spiegel said. He felt a little weird, a bit feverish, and he wondered if it had been wise to eat those snails. Maybe Swedish snails carried a subtle, slow-acting toxin, whose poison even now was seeping through his veins.

"No, it's not dessert," Tracy said. "Come on, you guys can help. You got some newspapers?" She began to take things out of the bag: scissors, a battery-operated electric clipper, a hand mirror, a white sheet.

"What is this, a crafts project?" Spiegel said.

"Maybe you will bury someone and wrap the body in that sheet," said Jorge.

"I'm going to cut your hair," Tracy said to Spiegel. "Sit down."

"Why? I like his hair. It's cool," said Melissa.

Spiegel flushed. He thought of Iris running her fingers through his long hair, the last afternoon they had spent together. He had thought about getting his hair trimmed once he got to Europe—his wavy dark hair, nearly shoulder-length, made him stand out among the close-cropped, lank-haired Swedes—but every time he remembered how much Iris had liked the touch of his long hair against her face and neck he decided to let it stay.

"He looks like George Harrison," said Jorge. "It would be a terrible waste."

"All that work," said Melissa.

"Growing your hair long doesn't take any work," Tracy said. "It's about the only thing that you do by not doing something."

"Gee, what do you think, Lenny? It's *your* hair."

"Well, I guess I do feel attached to it," Spiegel said. "And for that very reason, it's probably time to cut." He wasn't sure if he really felt that, but he understood what Tracy had in mind. Spiegel remembered his first night in the country, how Tracy had made him stand beside Aaronson, how she had inspected the two of them while they examined each other, face-to-face, then side by side before the tall mirror. Neither of them could see the resemblance, but it had to be there, and Tracy had said that it was Spiegel's long hair that drew the line of demarcation between them. Tonight, Tracy would erase the line.

Melissa brought a stack of papers from her room and lay them on Spiegel's floor. Spiegel placed a chair at the center of the newspaper carpet, and Tracy draped the sheet around his neck, securing it with a safety pin.

"All set for the hanging," Spiegel said. "You guys going to watch, or do you get sick at the sight of blood?"

"It's just too sad," Melissa said.

"Don't worry, I know what I'm doing," said Tracy.

"Shouldn't we have some music?" Jorge said.

"We could sing a barbershop quartet number."

But in fact they were silent. Jorge and Melissa watched, mesmerized, as Tracy moved slowly, clockwise, around Spiegel, her scissors tapping out a steady, quiet rhythm of clicks and snaps. They moved about the room to see her work from various angles: over the shoulder, Spiegel in profile, Spiegel head-on, Spiegel from the back. Spiegel took a narcissistic delight in the attention. He was like a small sun with the planets of his solar system slowly revolving in their elliptical orbits, out there in dark space, beyond his line of vision. He felt calmed and cleansed, and he wondered if the toxins from the snails, or from who knows what Jorge might have slipped into the broth, had moved deeper into his muscles and nerves, gliding him past the point of flushed fever, then over the edge toward a pleasant narcosis, and maybe finally to the sweet sleep of death. He didn't care. He would sit and wait for time to pass, for Tracy, and for the snails, to do their work.

"There," Tracy said. She held up a pair of hand mirrors so that Spiegel could get a look at her accomplishment, front and back. "A new man."

"Did I sleep?" Spiegel asked. As he cast his mind backward, he thought that he could remember every moment of the haircut, Tracy's balletic movements, the light touch of the cloth of her loose shirt against his face and lips, her hands brushing against his neck, his throat. He could recall the banter of Jorge and Melissa, in the background, just out of sight. But at some point he must have dozed. Jorge and Melissa were gone—together?—and Tracy had finished her work. She was unpinning the sheet and shaking Spiegel's hair onto the newspaper mats. The floor was covered with knots and strands of his hair, dark and dull but punctuated with an occasional comma of gray.

"What do you think?" Tracy asked.

"I think no one would recognize me."

"You see now that you look just like him?"

"Is that what you want?"

"Yes," Tracy said. "I know Aaronson didn't explain much to you. He can't say much, to anyone. There's too much risk that the wrong people could learn what he's doing. But you're involved now, too, and I owe you an explanation."

"You don't owe me anything."

"Well, let's just say it would be better, safer, if you understood the situation. Not that I understand it all. Aaronson doesn't even tell me everything, and that's probably good."

Tracy had swept all the hair onto the newspapers and was rolling the papers into a neat cylinder. "Where can I toss these?" she asked.

"Why don't we save the evidence?"

"I'll send it home. Let your mom know you got a haircut."

"Send it hair mail."

Tracy laughed. "Where is your mom?" she asked. "Where did you grow up? You never told me."

"It's complicated," Spiegel said. "She's dead."

"I'm so sorry."

"It was a long time ago."

"And your father?"

"He's in the foreign service, diplomatic corps. He's stationed now in Africa."

"Cool! Would you go there to visit? There are cheap flights, I've heard. A lot of Swedes go to Tunisia on vacation, on charter packages."

"You know, I just don't see my dad that much. When he comes back to Washington, between postings, I get down there and we go out to dinner and stuff. But we're not really close."

"Maybe you should try? You probably have more in common, now that you're in college, traveling—"

"And getting a haircut?"

"Yeah," Tracy said.

"I think these days we'd have huge political differences, too. He's, like, the Ugly American and proud of it. I never understood that or thought about it till I met Iris, and you guys. Now, I don't know, the gap between me and my dad may be unbridgeable."

"I don't believe that," Tracy said. "I think people like you who have family in government ought to use that advantage to try to change the political structure. Imagine, if you could get your father to understand your point of view. Maybe he could open up some country in Africa as a refuge. That would be fabulous for the deserters, especially the black guys. They're just dying here, culturally."

"No, my dad would never do that. If he knew I was working with you guys he'd probably try to have me shot."

"Maybe not, though. Maybe the opposite. Maybe it would change his position."

"He's not really in that influential a position. I mean, he doesn't make policy. He does cultural stuff: runs the library, helps set up village schools."

"A grown-up Peace Corps."

"Yeah." But Spiegel wondered, even as he described his father's work in such benign terms, whether Tracy was asking him for information about his father or drawing him out, testing him to see just how much he would reveal. Tracy seemed to accept his ingenuous account of his father as a secular missionary. But he sensed that Tracy was not disclosing all that she knew.

Tracy brushed the last of Spiegel's hair off her blouse and into the wastebasket. She went over to the door and looked out in the hallway. No one was about. Melissa's door was closed, and the three Swedes were apparently deep into their studies.

"Let me tell you about Aaronson," she said.

"Has he come back?" Spiegel asked. "I thought he'd only be gone for a day or two."

"It was great of you to give him the passport. And you'll get it back. But things have become a little more complicated."

"You've heard from him?"

"Well, no," Tracy said. "And I don't expect to, not until he comes back to Sweden."

"How long can that be?" Spiegel said. "He's only gone to Denmark. He could swim home, if he has to."

"Actually, he's gone to Germany."

Spiegel swallowed. Why hadn't they told him the truth? "That's crazy," he said. "Germany's crawling with police. Half the country's in uniform."

"It's not the ones in uniform that worry me."

"True," Spiegel said. "What's he doing in Germany?"

"Aaronson has contact with a leftist student group in Heidelberg, the SDG, socialist *gesellschaft* or some damn thing. They've been working to set up connections to the army base."

"American army?"

"Of course. It used to be that posting in Germany was the best thing you could hope for. Mainly, that's where they sent the enlistees and the ROTC kids. It was a way to get people to sign up: If you enlist, you might go to Germany."

"No war in Europe that I know of."

"Right," Tracy said. "Great deal, for a while. But now they can't draft enough bodies to fight the war, so they're starting to send whole divisions over to Vietnam."

"Like from Germany?"

"Not yet, but there's talk, and plenty of guys are scared. And pissed. They thought they'd made kind of a deal—enlisting for three years instead of being drafted for, what is it, two? And now, it's no deal at all."

"Like junior year abroad turns out to be a year stranded in the jungle."

"I don't know if they thought of it as junior year abroad, but a lot of the guys stationed in Germany are college grads. A lot of them used a little pull to get assigned to a NATO base, where no one's shooting at you."

"So what's Aaronson doing? Enlisting?"

"Not hardly. He's helping the SDG with recruiting. The Germans hang around the off-base clubs, get to know some of the soldiers, talk to them, at first about, you know, movies, music, American TV. They get to know them a little bit, they dance and drink and smoke."

"The SDG has girls, too?"

"Of course. They flirt with the soldiers, maybe they even fuck. They make a date to meet the guys, somewhere off base, a German club, or someone's apartment. A group gathers there, a group of Germans, drinking and arguing, debating. The soldiers listen. They're smart, they're curious. They're hearing stuff they've maybe thought about but have never really dealt with before, arguments about racism, imperialism, American hegemony. Then the Germans start to ask the soldiers questions, about their background, their home, what brought them to the army, to Germany. They get them to think about the war, about how it's immoral, about how they're being used by the war machine. Coming from Germans, with their role in history, it's a really powerful argument."

"Enough to convince soldiers to desert?"

"These guys are really vulnerable. They're confused. And that's where Aaronson comes in. Eventually, when the SDG thinks they have a good group of candidates, they bring Aaronson into one of their sessions, a real American who has gone over the wall. He can talk to the soldiers in their own language, answer their questions about Sweden, show them it can be done, that they can live here in peace. He can lead the way."

"The Pied Piper."

"Moses. The Messiah."

"It's illegal?"

"Highly. By American laws, it's treasonous, I think—interfering with military operations during wartime. For that, they still have the death penalty, at least under the military code."

Son of a bitch, Spiegel thought. "And as he does this missionary work, what name is he using? Is he Aaronson? Is he me?"

Tracy paused. "Why would that matter?" she said.

"If he gets caught at the border, trying to cross using my passport, that's one thing. But what if he isn't caught? What if he's just observed? What if one of the SDG members is a spy or a mole, right? And he makes a report about this American who's trying to get soldiers to desert in time of war. But the only thing is, this American he's reporting on is me, right?"

"No!" Tracy said. She reached out and put her hand on Spiegel's arm. "That's not true at all. If anything happens, he would come clean and take the blame."

"Would he? He didn't the first time I was arrested, when he was in Canada."

"By the time he heard about that, you were free. And that's what gave him the idea that you could help him again."

"Great, but being arrested wasn't exactly the highlight of my life."

"No?"

And Spiegel realized that Tracy had a point. Perhaps being arrested in Aaronson's stead *was* the highlight. It was an epochal moment, a turning point that had given a new aspect to everything that followed. Since then, he thought of things as either "before I was arrested" or "after the arrest." And events on either side of the divide seemed so different that he felt at times almost as if he had led two lives, one that had ended that frozen night when he lost consciousness in the center of the swarm of cops, and a second, a much brighter life, full of possibilities and hope, that began when he opened his eyes in the hospital bed and saw Iris standing in the doorway.

"But nothing will happen," Tracy added. "He'll come home safe."

"Well, that's good. I've done my part."

"Not completely," Tracy said. "It's more than giving him the passport. We have to be careful until he does come back."

"I'm always careful."

"More than careful, then. I want you to be visible. Now that I've cut your hair so that you look like him again, I want you to be seen in public. I want people to think that Aaronson's still in Uppsala."

"Which people?"

"Anyone who's watching us," Tracy said. "I think you should move out of Flogsta. Temporarily, until he gets back. Move to our apartment. If we're being watched, it would be good if you were seen with me. You know, around town, shopping sometimes. It won't be so hard."

"I see," Spiegel said. "So if the SDG reports that I was in Germany, trying to pry deserters loose from the army base, Aaronson will have witnesses to testify that he was minding his own business back in Uppsala."

Tracy stood and walked to the window. She turned her back to Spiegel. "Oh, god," she said. "Will you stop being so fucking paranoid? If he gets arrested, that's it—they'll know who he is, and the whole pipeline will collapse. About ten soldiers will go to the brig, and Aaronson will be shipped home in irons and held in Leavenworth, and many people, good and sympathetic antiwar people, here and in Germany, people we don't even know about and never will, their lives will be ruined, too. Can't you see that we all have to take on some of this risk? That each of us has a really small part, but if we each do our part maybe we can all make a huge difference?"

Spiegel stood, too, and walked over to Tracy. He stood by her side, looking out over the dark fields. "I can do my part," he said. "But who knows that he's gone, other than us?"

"People are always watching ARMS, believe me: the Uppsala police, the CIA, the army's criminal-intelligence goons. Somebody may have noticed by now that Aaronson isn't around, and I want to divert them for a little while, so they won't start to look for him."

"The resisters know."

"Yes, they know he's gone. But only the three of them know

about you: Zeke, Reston, and the Worm. We'll have to keep the rest of the guys in the dark, at least until the end of the week."

"What happens then?"

"Aaronson was supposed to be on TV this week, on a panel discussion about Americans in Sweden. A couple of social workers, a minister, those types—and him."

"Can't he back out? Plead illness?"

"No, that would seem suspicious. What I think is, you're going to have to do it."

"Me? On TV? Oh, no."

"Why? It'll be easy. It's a big panel, you won't have to say much—we can teach you—and no one watches these damn shows anyway—"

"Except military intelligence?"

"So if they do, that's good, isn't it? Then they'll have evidence Aaronson's here."

"Unless they're watching him somewhere else at the same time. Then they'll have evidence they've been fucked."

"By that time, he'll be back in Uppsala. And you can vanish."

"If I want to."

"It might be better at that point if you did. If people do start spotting the two of you together, it could be awkward. I mean, you haven't done anything against the law. When he comes back, you could just go home."

"Or I could grow my hair back and stay here."

"Yes."

And Spiegel wondered if he could detect a hint of meaning, or of feeling, behind that "yes." Did Tracy want him in Uppsala? Did she need someone to talk to, another American, but one whose life was not so stretched out on the rack of politics and intrigue?

"It's late, Tracy," he said. "You could stay."

"No, really, thanks, I can't," she said. But had she understood him? Had he really understood himself? To start anything with Tracy could only lead to terrible complications and repercussions. Yet Iris was across the ocean and Aaronson, no matter where he was in Europe, seemed to be on the far side of some great emotional divide. Spiegel felt a sudden surge of passion for Tracy, a need to hold her, to touch her skin and her lips.

She was gathering her belongings, her scissors and clippers, and the thin sweater that she had tossed onto Spiegel's bed. She slipped it over her head and gave her hair a frisky shake.

"There," she said. "Will you come over tomorrow, though? I can take some of your things with me now, in the car."

"Okay," he said. "Tracy, I'm sorry. If I offended you. All I meant was, you could stay, and I'll sleep on the floor. It's snowing."

"I'm not offended. But that's not all you meant."

He walked her to the car. A light snow was falling and, as there was no wind, the flakes floated down like feathers. Spiegel watched the large, downy crystals as they came to rest on Tracy's hair and on her collar. Each flake shimmered for a moment and then, liquefied by the warmth from her body, became a little globe of water and then a teardrop. She brushed the thin, light snow from the windshield of her car while Spiegel cleared the windows.

He wanted just to rest, to let his thoughts and his feelings organize themselves, in sleep and in dreams.

6

Jorge stopped by to see Spiegel in the morning, having told Lisbet that he had left a scarf at Spiegel's flat after the poker game. His real motive was to see Melissa again, and perhaps climb into bed with her for a morning encore. But she had gotten up early and left for auditions. Spiegel, however, was awake, drinking coffee, and trying to sort through his feelings about Tracy. It stirred him that she wanted him to move to her apartment; he sensed that she had more in mind than simply ensuring Aaronson's safety. Again, he wondered if she felt a void in her life, a need for a friend or for a lover to keep her warm through the dark nights. His mind teetered, rocking back and forth between the alternatives and occasionally peeking over the edge at another, more disconcerting, possibility. Could it be that Tracy wanted Spiegel close by so that she could keep him under surveillance? He was troubled by her line of questioning about his father. She pretended to know nothing about his father, but perhaps that wasn't so. She might have known all along about the nature of his father's work for the government. And if she did, why would she trust him with sensitive information about Aaronson's travels?

It occurred to him—not for the first time—that he might be being used, that perhaps Tracy and others were feeding him a diet of misinformation in the hopes that he was passing false leads on to higher authorities. Or maybe, he thought, I am not being used. Maybe I am being held: a prisoner of war, who will be offered in exchange, if necessary, in case Aaronson is captured behind enemy lines.

Lost amid those thoughts, Spiegel hardly looked up when Jorge stepped into the kitchen.

"I can see that you had little sleep last night," Jorge said.

Spiegel put down his coffee cup. "I'm not myself," he said.

"Yes, I hardly was able to recognize you," Jorge said. "Sitting there in such silence, I took you at first for one of the Swedes!"

Spiegel had in fact adopted one of the Swedish practices. His breakfast consisted almost entirely of dairy products. He was spooning yogurt from a glass bowl, and he had before him a waxy brick of cheese that he had been scraping with a "cheese plane," an *ostraka*, then popping the little curlicues of cheese into his mouth like candy. He had made a small pot of filtered coffee, which he was drinking black. He told Jorge about his plan to move in temporarily with Tracy, skipping the details, of course, about Aaronson's being in Germany.

Jorge raised his eyebrows and broke into a laugh.

"Good for you, old chum," he said, and slapped Spiegel on the back. "I knew there was something cooking with that cute little dish."

"You've got it wrong, man," Spiegel said. But he knew that he couldn't explain, or explain away, too much. He was sworn to secrecy about the real reason for—for what? The haircut. The move to Tracy's. Perhaps even his presence in Uppsala. He knew that he would be better off, he would be safer, if he were to let Jorge go on with his ribbing. And perhaps Spiegel enjoyed hearing Jorge unleash the sexual drive that he had been holding in check, and he hoped or even believed that Jorge's innuendoes contained a hint of truth.

"Wrong? Come on, I know what went on last night with you two. I saw the sheets in the hallway, my friend."

"Those are just the sheets she used for the haircut. Nothing went on, Jorge. We're friends, that's all."

"And you're moving into her flat?"

"Just for a week. She needs help with a project."

"Whoo!"

"Come on, Jorge. Maybe it's different in Lisbon. But you don't understand American girls. Not everything's sex and love with

them, okay? They're more liberated. They can have a relationship with a guy that's just friendship, or maybe just political."

"Now listen to me," Jorge said. He had begun to help himself
to the food Spiegel had laid out on the table. He was spreading
thick lingonberry jam on a rye crisp and topping the jam with a
sprinkling of brown sugar. Jorge pointed the tip of the jam knife
at Spiegel as he spoke. "If I know one thing, it's birds, all right?
And it doesn't matter, Portuguese, Swedish, American, African.
The heart of a bird is the same all over the world."

"Well of course people are people, and there are certain things
we all have in common—"

"That's not what I mean. I mean that, when a girl comes over
to your flat for dinner and she goes into your room and you're all
alone and the door is closed, well, there's only one thing on her
mind, you see. And it's not, you know, politics."

"All she did was cut my hair."

"Then she must not have eaten the escargots."

"The snails? Why do you say that?"

"I told you. They are the food of love."

Yes, he had said so, and Spiegel had to admit that the snails
had carried some kind of potent message to his body. He had
felt weird all night, but not exactly sexually aroused, more as if
his emotions had been tuned to a different key so that whatever
notes of passion he had been hearing, love or sorrow or anger or
longing, had been played at a higher pitch, at greater intensity.

"I don't suppose *you* need snails, do you? You're always ready."

"*En garde!*" Jorge said, and began to flutter the jam knife
toward Spiegel's cheese slicer, a mock duel.

"Hey, cut it out," Spiegel said. His voice was sharp. He
was annoyed, at Jorge's behavior, and also at his insolence, his
assumptions. It annoyed Spiegel as well to think that there was
even a slight chance that Jorge was right, that he had missed—or
even actively resisted—an offered opportunity.

"No, you are correct," Jorge said, as he put down the knife,
gently, beside his breakfast plate. "The love food was not for me,
although I felt its powers, certainly. She has a lovely room, you
know. Most interesting. You have seen it?"

"I have. I like her wall hangings. Did she offer you a demonstration?"

"Yes. I asked to borrow her guitar," Jorge said.

"Did it work?"

"Of course. Why not?"

"It's just a stage prop. She brought it here in case she needed it for *Miss Julie*. I think one of the peasants plays a guitar during the interlude while Julie is offstage fucking her valet. But I guess the Australian director brought a guitar of his own."

"Well, it definitely was no Spanish guitar. You know, you have excellent guitars from America. The Gibson. The Fender. Oh, god, if I could have a Fender I would go for a year without fucking."

"By Christmas you'd regret it."

"Yes, by then I would be playing drums."

"So?"

"It needed tuning, and my ear is not really so good, but I tried. I was able to play her one or two George Harrison songs, and 'Norwegian Wood.' She sat on the floor as I played and crossed her legs. I think you call it the Indian style? Very American. No European girl would sit like that, so exposed in the, what do you call it?"

"The crotch."

"Okay. I will have to ask Karin what is the Swedish word."

"Fat chance."

"Sorry?"

"It means: You're out of luck. It will never happen. No way."

"Fat chance. So I am looking at her . . . crotch . . . and thinking I feel very hot, you know, and I just have to have this bird. But I feel also like I cannot move, it would take all my strength to stand up from the floor. The guitar, it was like it weighed a hundred stone. My fingers were like trees. Well, she must have felt this, too, because she asked if she could be excused for a moment and she went to the bath, the toilet. While she was there, I thought maybe I am making a big mistake."

"You felt guilty?"

"Oh no. I felt—have I turned her off? Perhaps my songs on

her cheap guitar were very boring to her. I thought, maybe I should play some Portuguese songs. We call them fado, have you heard them?"

Spiegel had not.

"Very passionate, romantic. Knights singing outside castle walls, lost loves, roses, eternal devotion, passion beyond the grave—that sort of thing."

"Not 'Norwegian Wood.'"

"No. So I thought I would ask her, when she came from the bath, if she would like to hear some of the music from my native land. I was tuning the guitar, my ear right to the strings while I turned a key, trying very hard to hear the note, because some music was playing in the next room, and then I look up and she is standing in front of me, in the middle of the room, naked."

"I guess you hadn't turned her off."

"She was," and Jorge leaned forward and whispered to Spiegel, "so beautiful! A natural blonde, you know. I laughed and then told her that I had been going to ask her would she mind if I took off my jacket. She said she would like to dance. So I did play her some of the fado. I would say, Lenny, that she knows very little about how to dance. She put her hands up over her head, like some casta-net dancer in a cabaret, and she wiggled around the room shaking her little muff. She was very awkward, and out of timing with the music. Of course my playing was a bit off, as well."

"Are you sure you need to tell me this?" Spiegel thought that he would be jealous hearing of Jorge's conquest, but he was not. He was, rather, a little embarrassed, and his own sense of prud-ery, or propriety, surprised him. He had never experienced that sensibility quite this way, a flush rising to his cheeks, a muscular contraction in his throat. Maybe he only wished to think of the sensation as embarrassment. Perhaps it was a mask for a deeper feeling, a jealousy that he did not care to recognize.

"Well, I will skip the intimate details, then," said Jorge. "Or save them for some other time. But now . . . I want to ask of you a favor."

"Come on, Jorge, how many girls here do you think I know?"

Jorge laughed. "No, not that of course," he said. "I need you to help me with Lisbet. She does not believe that I came here last night to play cards, with the boys."

Now it was Spiegel's turn to laugh. "Hey, look, Jorge. You can do what you want with Lisbet, Melissa, the man in the moon, I don't care, but don't ask me to cover for you. I won't tell Lisbet anything you don't want her to know, but I won't lie for you either." I'm doing enough of that already, he thought.

"No, I wouldn't ask you to do that," Jorge insisted. "But would you come to my flat and meet her? She would feel better about all this if she could meet you. She would like you."

Spiegel understood. Jorge had been given an order. He had come home, tail between his legs, stinking of perfume and cum, and tried to convince Lisbet that he had spent the night playing poker with the boys. So she had asked him to produce a witness, or some evidence: Go. Fetch. I'm a fool to be drawn into this, Spiegel thought, and Jorge is a fool to ask me.

"Come on," Jorge said. "Afterwards, we can borrow her car, and I can give you a lift to your new, what did you call it?"

"My new digs."

"Yes."

In Jorge's building, Spiegel got a sense of what the complex would look like if it were ever to be finished. The stairs were carpeted; the elevator hummed and dinged with efficiency. The hallways smelled of vinyl, of latex paint, and of the slightly acrid warmth given off by incandescent bulbs. Even the students looked more wholesome and complete; they moved about with a lively step, an alertness, so different from the ghostlike, almost lurking presence of the three Swedes on Spiegel's floor. Spiegel thought with regret about his own building, still slightly rancid with the smell of raw concrete, the interior lighting patchy and uneven, the drafts in the hallway, the midnight clanging of the warped glass door in the lobby, and the incessant knocking of the elevator cables. Spiegel had assumed that the other buildings he could see from the Flogsta courtyards were merely reflections of his own, but now he knew that rather than reflections the buildings were more like steps in an evolutionary series, of which his represented the protozoan stage.

Jorge's room was at the end of the hallway, a premier spot, as it afforded views in two directions. Usually, these rooms, the doubles, were let only to married students. Each double had a little sitting area nicely furnished with a table, desk, and chairs in addition to the small bedroom and closet-sized bath. It could hardly be called living in luxury, but by student standards the double was fairly spacious and therefore much desired. Either Lisbet had lied on her housing application, an almost unthinkable transgression among the law-abiding Scandinavians, or she was extraordinarily lucky when the lots were drawn.

She sat at the table drinking black coffee from a mug the size of a soup bowl. She was not like the other Swedish girls Spiegel had seen and not at all like what he had thought of as Jorge's type, the flashy and glamorous European or the sun-drenched, athletic Californian. Lisbet was small, and she had short brown hair straight as string. Her owlish glasses were set on the tip of her nose. She set down her mug and shut the glossy magazine she had been reading. On the cover was a lanky model in a dress that seemed to be made of aluminum foil. The Swedish *Cosmo*, Spiegel figured.

"You didn't tell me you were bringing company, love," she said.

Spiegel was astonished by her voice, or actually by her accent. Unlike the other Swedes, who spoke English in a soft, reserved Cantabridgian, Lisbet spoke with a thick Midlands accent. Perhaps that's what had attracted Jorge. Most of the Swedes speaking English sounded like Oxford dons, but Lisbet sounded like a British pop star, or a tart.

"I wanted you to meet my friend. Lenny, this is Lisbet Norstrom. Lisbet, Len Spiegel."

"Hi," he said, and reached out to her. He was surprised by the strength of her grip, hard and sinewy, as if, despite her tiny frame and the delicacy of her features, she had great reserves of power. Perhaps Jorge liked that as well, or perhaps not, perhaps her strength had intimidated him, had sent him out into the graveyards to harvest snails, had driven him to fabricate stories about midnight card games with the boys, all for what amounted to just a spasm of passion, expended on one of those aptly named "birds," sure to take flight. Why couldn't Lisbet entice Jorge to settle here by the hearth, Spiegel wondered, in this luxury suite, and cuddle up to enjoy domestic tranquility? Surely these Swedish magazines, like their American counterparts, have all sorts of tips for keeping your man content: advice on beauty, special recipes for chocolate delights, counseling on the techniques of sex.

"Welcome to our flat," Lisbet said. "Are you the one Jorge has told me about?"

"What has he told you?"

"There's only one American in his language class."

"*Det är jag*," Spiegel said.

Lisbet clapped her hands together, and smiled at Spiegel. "*Bra*," she said. "*Bara bra*. You are learning the language, which is more than I can say for some. See what you could do if you would mind the teacher?" she said to Jorge.

"I do mind her. I mind everything about her."

"See," Spiegel said to Lisbet. "Puns in English. He's good with languages. He'll learn Swedish in no time."

"He had better," she said. "I told him we could not announce our engagement until he can speak my language."

Perhaps, Spiegel thought, that accounts for Jorge's three languid tours through *svensk* for beginners.

"In America, all he would have to say is 'I do,' " Spiegel said.

Lisbet explained to Spiegel that Swedes take engagement seriously. To be engaged meant seeking the consent of both sets of parents, exchanging rings and gifts, setting a date, notifying the minister, filing documents with the parish, then hosting an intimate party for friends and family.

"And Jorge would be expected to give a speech," Lisbet said.

"I could do that now," Jorge said.

"Yes, but your speech would be about ordering a cheese sandwich."

Jorge and Lisbet laughed, but their laughter seemed to hold within it a whole conversation, a conversation that had been going on between them for months. Marriage was a subject that Jorge and Lisbet had worked over until it was raw, and just touching lightly on the topic had fired up their nerve ends. In Lisbet's laughter, Spiegel could hear a challenge, and in Jorge's something else, something like the last gasp for breath before submission to another's superior strength.

"In any case," Jorge said, "I found the scarf," and he held it up for Lisbet to see. It was white and finely woven, useless against the Arctic cold.

"That was my scarf, you know," she said to Spiegel. "He's so careless with my things. But let me just try to touch one of his precious items and—he explodes like a gong."

"Like a bomb?" Spiegel said, tentatively. He had learned that some Swedes did not take well to having their English corrected. Many had a false pride and liked to believe that their English was flawless, and it often nearly was, except for mastery of the idioms and pronunciation of the *w*'s.

"Yes, like a bomb. Thank you."

"You speak so well, though. Where did you learn?"

Lisbet laughed. "You mean my accent?"

"She grew up in Liverpool. She is John Lennon's half-sister!"

"Jorge!"

"It's true! If she could sing, she would be the fifth Beatle." He poured himself a cup of coffee and one for Spiegel.

"He's lying. I'm from the North."

"Of England?" Spiegel asked.

"No, of course not. Of Sweden. Norland, we call it. What do you Americans call it? Land of the midnight sun?"

" 'There is a house in New Orleans . . . ' " Jorge began to sing, as he strummed an imaginary guitar.

"So they speak English differently up there?"

"No, but we have trouble getting teachers, or keeping them. The only one that we could get for my school was from Liverpool. He taught us very well, but we all learned his accent, you see. It's rather funny. My whole little village, we all sound like the Beatles."

"All four of you."

"It's not that small," Lisbet said, laughing. "But it is terribly boring. I couldn't wait to get out. Right after high school, I went to Stockholm—"

"That's where we met. In a club—"

Lisbet took off her glasses, and set them down on the magazine. Spiegel noticed that she had left the pages folded open at a lingerie ad.

"You make it sound," she said, "like I was hanging around in a club, trying to catch a man!"

"Lisbet worked in the club," Jorge said. "She served drinks."

"I was trying to save money to travel, but look what it got me instead."

"A two-room suite," Spiegel said.

"I've told Lisbet that if she wants to travel, she has picked the wrong bloke."

"Now, Jorge, I've told you, we can get jobs on a cruise ship. I can be a chambermaid and you could—you know, work in the lounge and on the decks, keeping the ladies entertained."

"Oh, lovely," Jorge said. "You have a word for that in English?"

"Gigolo."

"While you entertain the lonely old men."

"The rich Americans."

"Left alone in their cabins while their wives—"

"—dance in the discos, with the handsome Portuguese prince—"

"—the count of Lisbon—"

"But you are forgetting about the problem with my passport, love," Jorge said.

"But once we're married you will be a citizen of the Kingdom of Sweden."

"I don't know that the dictatorship of Portugal would recognize my citizenship, if I should set foot on Portuguese soil."

"Well, in those ports you could stay aboard the ship, pretend that you're ill," Lisbet said.

"I would be ill. I hate ships. I think we should fly."

"Now who's unrealistic? Perhaps you picked the wrong chick!"

Spiegel felt totally weird. How had he stepped into the middle of this? Have they no shame? He got the sense, however, that Jorge and Lisbet needed an audience in order to act out their little dramas. They seemed to be playing to him, each angling for his support, hoping to draw him into the fray.

"I've seen you around the complex, haven't I?" Lisbet asked.

"Maybe you have, but I haven't been here all that long," he said.

"And already, he's moving out," Jorge added.

"What, you're going home so soon?"

"No, he's moving in with a . . . lady friend," Jorge said.

Spiegel raised his hand in protest. "Come on, Jorge, don't exaggerate."

"But I don't exaggerate! It is true. She is a lady and your friend. Is it not so?"

"Yes, but that's not the point," Spiegel said. "She's got an old man."

"Back in the States?"

"No," Spiegel said. "But he's traveling."

He regretted saying this, even as he spoke the words. He didn't like Jorge's insinuations—falsehoods actually—and wanted to set the record straight for Lisbet. Yet he didn't want to draw the conversation to Aaronson. The less anyone, Jorge especially, with his tendency to joke and to blab, knew about Aaronson and his travels, the better.

"Believe me," Jorge said, and he added a theatrical sneer. "I know plenty of birds who find someone to warm their nest while the old man is out hunting for the worms."

"Or playing cards," Lisbet said.

"Oh, when I play cards, I have no worries about you, love," Jorge said.

"I'm sure that you don't," Lisbet said. "What about you?" she said to Spiegel. "Do you like cards?"

"Not particularly," Spiegel said. Out of the corner of his eye, he could almost see the color drain from Jorge's face. "It's a chance to socialize is all," he added.

"You and the boys."

"Yes."

"You will have to invite the boys here for cards some night, love," she said to Jorge.

"I'm not sure," he said.

"You see," Lisbet said to Spiegel. "It's true what they say. Playing cards is just an excuse to get out of the house."

"But why would I need an excuse?" Jorge said, indignantly. "We are not yet married."

"Will things be so different when we are?" Lisbet asked.

"Of course," Jorge said. "Then I will stay home and you will go out with the girls and you can tell me that you are going shopping."

Lisbet had obviously divined the truth about Jorge's midnight rambles. But why had he raised the ante, with his insinuations about Lisbet's inconstancy? Was he sending a warning shot across the bow, or was he telling her that she need not worry, he was not the type to keep her tied to the mast?

"I think we all should go out some night, together," Lisbet said.

"The three of us?" Jorge said.

"Yes, like that French movie, about the girl with two guys—"

"That's *Jules and Jim*. I don't know as I want that movie to be the model for my life. Don't they all die in the end?"

"What, in a war, isn't it? It's terrible."

"No, that's some other movie. Maybe *Grand Illusion*."

"The French movies are all about sex," Jorge said. "The movies of Portugal, they are about—ideas."

"Which is why no one has ever seen one outside of Portugal," Lisbet said. "For ideas, how can you beat Ingmar Bergman?"

"Oh, who watches him?" Jorge said.

"He's very popular in America. Isn't it so, Lenny?"

"I'm not sure his movies are about ideas," Spiegel said. "They're about—conditions. Bleakness and depression. Back home, I thought it was all deeply symbolic and mystical stuff, but since coming here I've changed my mind. It's just social realism. Life here really is dark and gloomy, and everyone is full of angst."

"Well, you just have to wait until spring," Lisbet said. "Then, it's a new world."

"A whole new ballgame, we say in America."

"In the spring," she said, "Jorge will complete his studies, and we will announce our engagement. And you can help us to celebrate. Shall we make him the first to be invited to our engagement party?"

"Will I have to give a speech? In Swedish?"

"No, you will only have to make sure that Jorge does not disappear."

"And if I disappear, you will have to take my place," Jorge said. "Do you think you can?"

"I do," Spiegel said, and they all laughed.

There was a good three inches of fresh snow on the ground. Spiegel didn't mind at all. In fact, he liked breaking a path from the doorway to the parking lot. No one had come up to Flogsta to plow the roads or the walkways. The main streets in Uppsala were always scraped clean as bone, but on the perimeters of the city, particularly the student enclaves, plowing was much more haphazard. Spiegel noticed that Jorge had no idea what to wear in this weather. He had never seen snow until he fled to Sweden, except perhaps in spreads in fashion magazines. So he dressed as if the snow were a white background, a drop cloth, against which he could display his well-tailored jacket and pants. He was wearing a thin, dark-blue cloth greatcoat with brass buttons the size of saucers. His silky pants had cuffs as wide as those on pillowcases. His shoes were black leather. They had stacked heels and toes that came to needle-sharp points. The soles were soft, almost like velvet, and Jorge had mentioned that they helped him move like a butterfly when he stepped onto the floor at a "discobar." But in the fresh snow they made him slip and toddle like a drunken circus bear, and Spiegel expected that at any moment Jorge would tumble into a drift, scattering the stack of folded clothes and towels he was holding out before him. Jorge had the sense, at least, to wear gloves, for in that regard good fashion coincided for once with good practice, but Spiegel wondered whether the thin pigskin English driving gloves offered any protection against the biting cold.

"Where does all this stuff come from?" Jorge said. "You wouldn't think the sky could hold so much." He was trying to brush the snow from the windshield, using his elbow.

"Shit from the gods, a friend of mine once called it," Spiegel said. He set the bags he had been carrying on top of the Volvo and began to scrape the door handles clean. He, at least, had thought to wear good, thick mittens. "They say to die in snow isn't so bad. Jack London wrote a story about that."

"I don't worry about how it feels to die in snow. I worry about how it feels to live in snow." Jorge set the clothes down on top of a snowbank. He was blowing on his hands and smacking them together and stamping his feet in place, like a colt.

"You don't have to live in it, but you're going to have to learn to drive in it," Spiegel said.

"That, I like to do," Jorge said. "I'll show you."

Spiegel realized that he had been drawn into Jorge and Lisbet's relationship much deeper than he had wanted. He felt less like a Leporello and more like some gruff old father from a drawing-room farce or a comic opera, an old count booming: Make my daughter an honest woman! Marry her!

"Oh, but I will marry her," Jorge was saying as he revved the engine and flicked on the heater. Cold air blasted onto Spiegel's feet. He kicked his shoes against the mat to knock off the cakes of snow. "Perhaps when she finishes school."

"Then why do you need to be jumping into Melissa's pants?"

"I haven't married her *yet*," Jorge said.

"'You're gonna lose that girl . . . '" Spiegel sang.

"Oh, very good," Jorge said. "There is a song for everything, isn't there? It's just wonderful about the British pop."

"Don't change the subject," Spiegel said. "I mean the truth of it is—it's none of my business, and I don't really care what you do or what you two do or what the three of you do. Get together, all three of you, like in one of those French movies Lisbet was talking about. But don't drag me in to make it a jolly foursome."

"You could have told her, at least, that you like to play cards."

"I didn't want to lie. There's too much of that going around without my adding to it."

"Too much lying?"

"I'm thinking big picture," Spiegel said, changing the focus. "Johnson, Nixon, Kissinger, the Chicago police. Everyone knows they were under orders to bust skulls, to break up the peace demonstrations."

Jorge spun the car out of the parking lot and headed down the drive toward the highway into town. One lane had been plowed, and he slipped down the chute. If they had met a car coming up the hill, he would have had to turn hard and hope to slide off into one of the snowbanks to avoid a head-on collision. Spiegel got the sense that Jorge had never driven in snow. The rear wheels shushed and shimmied, and the car shook and spun as Jorge braked at the foot of the hill.

"In Portugal, when they want to clear up a demonstration, the tanks roll in. It rains bullets. And it is never reported in the newspaper."

"Then how do you know?" Spiegel said.

Jorge waved his hand, dismissively.

"We expect more from our government," Spiegel said.

"Maybe you expect too much." Jorge gunned the car out onto the highway. The road was clear, and they had it to themselves.

"We're idealists, I admit it. Most of us first got into politics when Kennedy was president. We expect our government to be more honest."

"More glamorous," Jorge said. Spiegel didn't answer. "So why is it," Jorge went on, "that you Americans don't like Sweden? It's the most honest government in the world, I think. And here we are, nobodies, you know? 'I'm a real nowhere man.' And they take us in and give us housing, schooling, freedom to do as we please. And all I hear from the Americans is they hate this country, it's mean, it's cold, unfriendly. What is it you want?"

"You haven't heard me complain, except this morning with Lisbet—"

"Yes, exactly! You are catching the infection, from your countrymen."

"Like who? I didn't think you knew other Americans here."

"Well, there was a group, in the language school. They left to form a class of their own, and the government even allowed this."

"Yes, the deserters and resisters. I know some of them."

"There you have it," Jorge said. "I would just say to you, stay away from them. Those fellows are trouble, and they'll, how do you say it, bring you down?"

Spiegel thanked Jorge for the warning. He thought that maybe it would be best if they just drove the rest of the way to Tracy's in silence. He wished there were some good rock'n'roll on the radio.

"Here we are," Jorge said, as he slowed the car. "Lisbet took me to this place."

"A shortcut?"

"No," Jorge said. "It is a place where we used to come to be free."

"That must have been before the winter. Now it looks like a place you would come to be stuck."

Jorge turned off the main road onto an unplowed lane that cut through one of the white fields whose ugly monotony had so disturbed Spiegel on his first bus ride out to Flogsta, weeks ago. The car cut its way through the fresh snow. The grip on the road seemed secure, and Spiegel realized that he felt safer off the road than on the highway. What could happen? There was nothing into which they could collide except a few snow-covered mounds. At worst, the Volvo would stall out, or Jorge would spin the wheels and lock the car in place, in a furrow of ice, and they would walk back to the road and he would catch the bus. Somehow, Spiegel knew, Jorge would extricate the car—or Lisbet would know how to do so. Maybe they would leave it in the field, a monument, awaiting the spring thaw.

But Jorge drove with care and precision. It was difficult discerning the course of the dirt roadway beneath the pure white field of snow. "Do you know what they are?" Jorge said. He gestured toward the mounds of snow.

Spiegel said that he did not. They looked like hayricks.

"Viking tombs, they say. No one knows how long they have been here."

"You'd think the government would dig them up. Or zap them with X-rays, to find out."

"Maybe the Swedes like the mystery. Sometimes it is better not to probe secrets, don't you think?"

"What do you mean by that?" Spiegel said.

"I mean sometimes if you start to dig too deeply, you may turn up ugly things that you would rather not have to see. It may be better, sometimes, to leave things as they are."

Jorge turned abruptly, and the Volvo slid down the lip that must have marked the side of the road. "Hold on," Jorge said, and he accelerated. The wheels spun in the snow for a second, then gripped dirt and the car kicked across the field toward one of the low hills. The ride was surprisingly smooth, Spiegel thought. The field must be unplowed. In spring, it would be a meadow. Jorge kept picking up speed as they approached the base of the hill. The nose of the car tilted upward at a slightly sickening angle. They had enough momentum that the car made it right to the top, where the hill seemed to flatten into a plateau. Just at the edge, Jorge pressed the pedal to the floor, and with a final surge and a pop they were on top of the hill. From there, Spiegel could see a new expanse of farmland. At the center of the landscape was a lake, its surface a white disk of snow and ice.

"Very pretty," Spiegel said. "A frozen pond."

"So smooth and clear. In Portugal, the only place we see such ice is in a glass of whiskey," Jorge said. "To see so much of it at once is like a miracle."

"Getting us out of here will be a miracle."

Jorge fixed his gaze on the pond. He stared ahead in silence, like a diver poised on the high board.

"Are you okay?" Spiegel said. He thought Jorge must have been recollecting a previous visit to this site. He could picture

Jorge and Lisbet, naked in the tall grass, making love in the shadow of the Viking tombs.

"Jesus walked on the water," Jorge said, after a while. "That, too, was a miracle."

"Yeah, and Moses parted the Red Sea. But the age of miracles is over."

"Let's find out," Jorge said.

Jorge let the Volvo begin its long roll down the far side of the hill, a much more steady and gradual descent than the steep slope that they had climbed. "Here we go," Jorge hollered, and he let the car pick up speed as it approached the pond, and then, on level ground again, he floored the accelerator and they shot across a band of snow and dropped onto the hard surface of the pond.

On the pond, the snow was only a dusting on top of the blue ice. The wind must have whipped the fresh snow over to the high banks, Spiegel thought. The next he knew, they were flying across the ice like a puck, and the tires whined and made a funny crackling sound, as if their passage were smashing the surface of the ice into millions of tiny crystals. Part of the world seemed to be slipping away from them, flattening itself out to a thin line, a nothingness obscured by the bluish ice and the gray-green sky. But another part of the world, or of their field of vision, the far side of the pond, by indiscernible increments assumed the recognizable shapes of a winter landscape: more white fields, thin pines, stubborn hills, and beyond the hills a mustard-yellow farmhouse with a red roof.

At the center of the pond, Jorge stomped as hard as he could on the brakes. The wheels seemed to lock, and the car went into a sudden spin. Spiegel was thrown against the door frame, then back into his seat. He braced his hands against the dashboard, to protect himself. The world whipped around him in a blur, a gray cyclone, and he was at its center, surprisingly silent, and thick with a cottony heat. He saw a tree trunk flash by his window, a branch seemed to scrape the windshield like a ghostly hand, and he felt a thud as the car bumped against a snowbank and then ricocheted out again toward the center of the pond. They seemed to be moving sideways, which Spiegel would have thought impossible, and then backwards, and he tried to regain his equilibrium by keeping his gaze focused on a bent pine in the middle of the white pasture. As they came at last to rest, Spiegel realized that he was drenched in sweat and shaking uncontrollably.

"A miracle," Jorge said, his voice shrill with excitement. "Another bloody fucking miracle!"

Spiegel thought that if he spoke he would break into tears and if he moved he would be unable to keep his hands from Jorge's throat.

7

"We have with us in our TVTwo-Uppsala studio tonight a founding member of a group called the American Resisters Movement—Sweden.

"Mr. Aaronson has deserted from the United States Army in protest against the war in Vietnam.

"Tonight, he will tell us about his views . . . "

It took a moment before Melissa realized that she was hearing English. She had grown accustomed to turning the TV on in order to tune it out. The noise secured her privacy when she was at Mick's. She was unaccountably shy about her visits with him. Maybe it was because of his flat, a garret above a row of shops and galleries in the minuscule artists' quarter—the artists' corner, Mick called it—on the banks of the river. The greedy landlord—a redundancy, Mick remarked—had split the loft into four units in order to circumvent Uppsala's laxly enforced rent-control laws. So Mick's flat was divided from his neighbors by a thin layer of peg-board overlaid, Mick thought, with nothing more sound-absorbent than a madras spread. Not only could they hear the comings and goings, and especially the comings, of the potter who lived in the flat to the right, a Don Juan in a clay-caked smock, but they got to enjoy the latest cuts from Pink Floyd and T-Rex and other hot sensations from the British scene, which were played ad nauseum by the would-be rock star who rented the flat to the left. All I contribute to this is the bubbling from my lava lamp, Mick said.

"Except when I'm around," Melissa answered.

Still, she liked to turn up the volume on his "telly" to mask the sounds of whatever it was they might get up to. She was a little shy, as well, because of the whole nature of their relationship. It was a bit of a cliché, wasn't it: the ingenue and the director, the American blonde earning the lead by auditioning on the casting couch? She shouldn't be with Mick, she knew it. Or she should wait until after the play, after the semester, to work out any relationship that might develop. But she wasn't that strong, and perhaps, yes, she was using him. But so what? It wouldn't be the first time.

"I think I know that guy," Melissa said.

"That's nice, love," Mick said. "You can tell me all about him later." They had just finished fucking, and Mick was curled up beside Melissa, his feet resting on the pillow beside her neck, his head resting on her thigh. He was licking her in a way that seemed to her almost feral, as if he were grooming her, combing her downy hair into place with his tongue. He was trying to arouse her again for, as he liked to put it, another shot in the dark, or as she said, the second coming.

"What is it with you Aussies?" she said. "You like it upside down."

"Down under, they call us," Mick said.

"I'm a California girl, remember."

"And how do California girls like it? Laid-back?"

"We like to call the plays," she said.

"Too bad. I'm the director."

"In the theater, yes." Melissa was uninterested in continuing the session, at least at Mick's level of intensity. Laid-back might be correct. She was trying to squirm her legs out from under his grip. But she didn't want to make it a real struggle, either. That might arouse him. She didn't want to get involved in another toss. "Come on, Mick," she said. "Easy."

"Yes, nice and easy, doll," he said, and gave the inside of her thigh a long, sensuous lick, ending with a little fillip right by her crack.

"I didn't mean *easy* that way," she said. "I meant, let's call it a night, okay?"

"A night? Why not stay over?"

As Mick sat up, Melissa got a better view of the TV, which was at the foot of the bed.

"I do know him," she said.

"Since when are you so interested in the telly?" Mick asked. "You can't even understand a bloody thing."

"Yes, look," Melissa said. "It's a show about Americans. I know that one." She touched the screen, as the view shifted to a close-up of Spiegel.

"He's speaking English, if you can call American English," Mick said.

"The American resisters," Spiegel was saying, "deserve the same rights and privileges enjoyed by all the citizens of Sweden: good housing, good schools, training for jobs . . . "

"I think it's a guy who lives on my floor, who showed up last month in the middle of the term."

"Probably some CIA spy."

"No, just your basic student."

"Another one of your—conquests?"

"No, he's got an old lady, in town. He's kind of moved in with her."

Aaronson's name was displayed across the bottom of the screen.

"But I guess I'm wrong. The guy I know is named Lenny Spiegel."

"All you Americans look alike, right?"

"Maybe from down under."

"No, from that perspective one can discern exquisite differences."

"Just how much experience have you enjoyed in that region, sir?"

"Not quite enough." And he slipped his face back down between Melissa's legs.

"Can I just, at least, watch the end of this show?" she said.

The camera panned to the right of the moderator.

* * *

"Also with me tonight," the moderator said, "are Miss Monika
Nuland, of the Uppsala chapter of the Swedish Student Solidarity
Committee, a group devoted to helping the American deserters
in Sweden, and Mr. Erik Edström, the founding member of the
Sweden First Party, whose slogan is *Sweden for the Swedes.* Mr.
Edström was an unsuccessful candidate for the city council, and
he has vowed—"

"This is a fucking setup!" said Tracy. Because there was no
extra seating in the broadcast studio, she was confined to the
station's lobby, where she was watching the show on a monitor.
She had been so concerned about preparing Spiegel for his role
that she had given little thought to who else might be on the panel.
She had heard about Monika Nuland and the SSS. The Uppsala
chapter had just been formed, and Tracy had intended to set up a
meeting with the new group. She was glad to see this Monika on
the panel. Edström, however, should not be there. All he would
do, Tracy thought, is stir public passions and align Swedes against
the Americans, subject us to a racist harangue—in short, provide
provocation. Aaronson could have handled him. He had run a lot
of meetings and faced down plenty of hecklers and right-wing
provocateurs, here and in the States. But she wondered about
Spiegel. He was so green, so naive.

". . . their drugs, their violence, their whole American
culture—these are things we don't need in Sweden," Edström
was saying. He spoke in Swedish, and an English text appeared
below him on the screen. "Now I for one have always been in
favor of providing sanctuary to true victims of political repres-
sion. But these Americans are not victims! They have left their
country in a time of war, in a time of great need. They have
turned their back on their motherland, and fled, leaving their
brothers in arms to fight their battles. Are we to consider them
heroes? Or are they traitors and bloodsuckers, looking now to
leech off the Swedish state?"

"Well, Mr. Aaronson, what is your answer?"

"Son of a bitch," Tracy said. She crossed the lobby and
punched the off button on the monitor. The tube uttered a little
click and a hiss and then went dark. The lobby guard, drowsy

beside his console, was stirred awake by the sudden absence of background noise. He scanned the room just in time to notice Tracy push her way through the door, to see her step into the hallway that led to the broadcast studio.

"My answer to that is simple," Spiegel said. He was sweating under the floodlights and squirming in his seat from tension and anxiety. He was trying to read Edström's words on the video monitor, which was small and set at an awkward angle. It was almost impossible for him to frame a thoughtful response and to talk slowly, as he had been counseled, so that the translator could type his words into Swedish subtitles. "You speak as someone who does not know the American resisters. If you were to know them, to know their stories . . . "

"Aw, what does he know," said one of the guys sitting around the small table in the warehouse basement. It was Hyde, dressed in his full combat regalia, with a black beret and a crimson sash slung over his shoulder and pulled tight against his pressed khaki shirt. He looked like a cross between Huey Newton and a French legionnaire.

Zeke had let the members of ARMS know that he would "borrow" a television and set it up in the meeting hall for anyone who wanted to watch "Aaronson" when he spoke on TV2. Four of the Americans were sitting at a folding table, where Zeke had propped the black-and-white portable that he had liberated from an untended storage room in the warehouse above the ARMS office.

"He was never in the fucking war," said another one of the guys, leaning forward to get a better view of the screen. The corner of the card table pressed into his gut, and when he leaned back to take a swallow of beer the table seemed to have left an indentation, like a finger poked into a puddle of bread dough. "They shoulda asked me up there."

"Yeah, but you can't read subtitles," Zeke said.

"Who says you have to read?" He took another big swallow from a tall can of Australian beer.

"How else would you know what the fascist is saying?"

"Which is the fascist?"

"See, that's my point. You don't even know what that guy

across from Aaronson was talking about, do you? 'Cause you didn't read the fucking subtitles."

"Aw, shit, I thought they were in Swedish, too."

"You really are stupid, man."

". . . much braver men to stand up against the military establishment and say, no, I will not kill, I will risk my life to end this killing. If more people throughout history had stood up to the forces of tyranny and dictatorship, well, we wouldn't have had concentration camps, we wouldn't have had, in my own country, a system of slavery . . . "

"I'm just saying," Hyde offered, "that I'm sick of this guy who never set foot in country telling us what to think and what to do, man. We've been here like two years, and the only person with a decent place to live and a car and you know—"

"—an old lady—"

"Right—is that motherfucker."

"That's right, Hyde," said a skinny guy, wiping suds from his Fu Manchu mustache. "You tell it."

"And what do we have?" Hyde said. "We've got like a handout from the government and enough Swedish to step up to a counter and order a hot dog. Now what kind of life is that? While he goes off traveling through Europe, staying at fancy hotels, flying in airplanes where they probably serve red wine and show movies, he's patting the asses of those stewardesses when they push the drink cart down the aisle, and—"

"Like where's he been, man?"

"It's not like he's gone off on a Mediterranean cruise, you know," Zeke said. "It's more like a guerrilla mission. He was down there looking for recruits, guys who wanna leave the show, and he's got to bring them up here safely. It's very risky stuff, man."

"He don't look like he's risking all that much right now."

"You think it's easy for him to be on the tube, speaking for us?" Zeke said.

"Don't look such a bad place to be," Hyde said. "Next to that old lady." The camera panned to show Monika Nuland, tossing her long hair back over her shoulder in a gesture of apparent contempt for Edström's harangue.

"Just look at these people," Edström said. "They live in the doorways, on the benches in parks and railroad stations. They drink too much, they smoke too much. They have money for these things and for who knows what else. But they do not work. Are we to support these so-called heroes? Why . . . "

"I have to admit there's some truth in what he says," Jorge said to Lisbet. "Most of the Americans are pretty grotty."

They were in the sitting room of Lisbet's suite. She was trying to study for an exam, but she was being distracted by the chatter from the television and by Jorge's hands, gently rubbing the back of her neck. Occasionally, a finger would stray and fondle the lobe of her ear, or his hand would slip inside the folds of her blouse to explore one of the hidden regions of her undiscovered continent. She alternated between putting him off—"Jorge, please!"—which would deter him for only a few moments, and leaning back toward him, involuntarily purring with pleasure.

"Oh, Jorge," she said, as she leaned away from him, trying to focus on her biology text. "That's so unsympathetic."

"You don't like what I'm doing?"

"With your hand? No, that's nice. I mean what you said. About the Americans."

"Ah, but it is true," Jorge said. "They're not, you know, the same as us. They seem to be from a different class of people. Much more—how do you say it?—cannibal."

"You mean primitive?"

"Yes, that, too, perhaps. They don't go to the school, they don't learn the language, they have no culture, no savoir flair . . . "

"It's *savoir faire*. And your friend has plenty of it."

"Of course, but he is very different, just look at him—"

"Where? That's not him on TV, is it?"

"No. No, I mean . . . just look at that American. He looks . . ."

"It does look like Lenny, my God."

"Well of course they don't have jobs!" Monika was on the edge

of her seat, really into it, giving it right back to Edström. "Who
would hire them unless they learn the language, the culture? And
isn't it the responsibility of the host government to bring them
into the culture, to treat them not as an invading army but to
welcome them with open arms . . . "

"Then why is it that you haven't learned the language, Mr.
Aaronson?" Edström said, turning to Spiegel. "I will tell you
why. I have evidence . . . "

"You see it is not Lenny. It is a man named Aaronson. Perhaps all
those Americans do look alike, after all," Jorge said.

"No, not all of them," Lisbet said. "He's cute, whatever his
name is. More than most."

"So you agree with me that most of them are of a lower
order."

"No, I didn't say that. Really, Jorge." She tried to get back to
her textbook.

"In Portugal, only the better sort of people refuse the military service. The working man, he would never dream of turning down the opportunity to fight for his king and his country.
It is his one chance in life to better himself and to see the
world."

As he spoke, his hand wandered farther to the south, his fingers gently exploring the many coves and inlets of the unsettled
coast, until eventually, a little Vasco da Gama, he rounded the
Cape of Good Hope where he caught sight of land, anchored,
and ventured forth into the dark continent.

". . . can you explain that?" Edström was asking. "The
entire American community in Uppsala dropped out of the
language classes. And you sit here and tell this audience that
it is the fault of the Swedish government that you have been
isolated and stigmatized."

"Is he correct, sir? " the moderator asked. "Did the Americans
quit the language school?"

"We thought we could get better instruction on our own,"
Spiegel said. "We hoped to find a teacher who would be free to

explain the lessons to us in English." But he really didn't know why Aaronson had drawn the men of ARMS out of the language school, other than to pull the group more tightly together and to fix a line between the Americans and the rest of the expatriates in Uppsala.

"But did you or did you not quit language school?" the moderator asked.

"Of course we fucking quit," the Worm sputtered. "Can't you tell him, fuckhead? Who would stay in that cesspool, with all those assholes from countries that aren't even on the map? You expect me to sit there and learn Swedish next to some farmer from Ethiopia? Or some so-called scholar from, what the fuck did he call his country? Bangledish? There's only one goddamn reason those greaseballs were in that class with us."

The Worm was getting used to talking to himself. In fact, he found himself to be rather good company when he was drunk, which was most of the time, now that he was living in Uppsala, free, alone, without a care in the world. He didn't need much to survive. His apartment, two rooms in a basement below a dry cleaner's, was almost bare: an iron bedstead and two straight-backed wooden chairs from a country church, bequeathed to the resisters by a sympathetic minister. A single pine table served as his countertop, dining area, and desk. The only window was set at street level, and it admitted no daylight. This was the best apartment the Worm had ever had.

"They were spies, trying to keep an eye on our community. Pretending they didn't speak English. Looking up every time one of us said anything about them. Then looking into their books and coughing. Ha! We could see right through them like they were made of glass. Dirty fuckers. Tell them that!"

"In my country," Spiegel was arguing, "we have this thing called the Statue of Liberty, and on its base there's written a motto, it's a sonnet actually, and it says—"

"I know what it says," Monika put in. "'Give us your tired, your poor'!"

"But we're not talking about his country," the moderator interrupted.

"If your country's so great, why are you here?" Edström asked. "We would be more than happy to see you and your compatriots to the border, and we would wave you good-bye. . . . "

But Spiegel was no longer concentrating on Edström's tirade. He had heard enough, and he was trying to figure out how to get off the set, out of the picture, out of this whole charade that had begun to consume his life, when he caught sight of Tracy. Because of the floodlights, he could barely see beyond the rim of the makeshift set—a small plywood platform designed to look vaguely like a living room. But he had heard some noise, the sound of a door slamming shut, and if he squinted he could make out, just over the shoulder of one of the cameramen, Tracy's form in the darkened studio. She was standing in the back of the room, behind a row of unoccupied chairs. It was hard for Spiegel to tell, but it seemed that she was edging her way forward, toward the pool of light, the heat of combat. He tipped his hand to let her know that he had noticed her.

"Wave us good-bye, I bet you would, you fat fuck," the Worm was saying. He was well into his second tall glass of—something. What was it he was drinking? It tasted, he thought, like perfume, or lighter fluid, or . . . who cares? It burned as it went down, and he felt as if he could breathe like a dragon and set fire to the world with his words, even with his thoughts. "Sweden for the Swedes. The master race. The blondes and the blues! *Sieg heil!*" He opened a drawer below the tabletop and pulled out a skin magazine. *Svenska militäriska flickerna*—the girls of the Swedish Army. They rode tanks, flew fighter jets, learned to shoot, fought with knives, marched through the mud. That's what he liked, the mud on their uniforms, how the wet khaki clung to their thighs and their breasts like a second, richer skin, deep and earthy and moist.

"You should be ashamed of yourself!" The voice came from nowhere, from the darkness, an epithet like a crack of thunder released by one of the gods.

The moderator flicked his head back and forth like a pigeon. *"Vem var det?"* he shouted. "Who's this? Where's this coming from"—and then a string of invective in Swedish, as Tracy went on shouting from the darkness.

"You don't represent the Swedish people. You have no right sitting on the stage with this man. Do you know anything about the war? Do you understand a thing about why he is here—"

The translator, thoroughly confused, was typing Tracy's words, in English, onto the screen. Edström couldn't read them. He stood as if to walk off, and the moderator put a hand on his shoulder, trying to calm him. But Edström took it the wrong way and shouted, first at the moderator, then at Tracy's disembodied voice.

"What the hell is going on?" Jorge could make no sense of it. Tracy was out of range of the boom mikes, so her voice was not picked up for broadcast. Jorge was watching Edström, red in the face, his voice rising to a shrill whine as he screamed at the moderator, but he was reading Tracy's words, picked up by the harried translator, scrolling across the bottom of the screen: *He came here because he loves peace! He came here because he couldn't take up arms against his brother!*

"It looks like a big fight, what's the word, a riot," Lisbet said, as she shifted her hips to pull her panties back up to her waist.

The moderator, a big fellow, was bullying Edström back down into his seat. Lisbet tried to translate for Jorge what Edström was actually saying, but it was getting harder to pick up his voice and in truth she was confused as well. English, Swedish, Portuguese, her biology text, his hands all over her—who could keep up?

"Jorge, love, maybe this isn't such a great idea," she said. "Can we stop?"

"But this is just now getting interesting."

"I don't mean the TV. I mean us," she said.

"Us? You mean, our relationship?"

"I mean, this sex, all this sex. I mean, can it wait? I have to study."

"Well, why can't that wait? Which is the more important?"

"To me? Right now? My biology."

Jorge stood, and began to pace the room. "Your biology? What about my biology?" He chopped the air with his hands as he spoke. "In my country, you know, this would never happen. No woman would deny her man his rights as a husband."

"But you are not my husband," Lisbet said. "And this is not your country."

"And it never will be. I will always be some sort of exotic to you—like a rare parrot, like an orchid."

"That's not true," she said. "That's not fair. I have been ready to announce our engagement. But what have you been doing? Sleeping late, skipping classes, staying out all night at cards—or so you say."

"What do you mean by that? Do you accuse me?"

"I accuse you of nothing but the truth. I hear what goes on, but I don't care. Go screw your American girlfriend. But you'll come back to me, I know. Because I've got something she can never give you."

"Do you think I would marry you just to become a citizen?" Jorge yelled.

"I think you would do anything."

"I have no girlfriend," he protested. "You know that I spend time with the Americans, yes. I know them from school. We play cards, talk, study our lessons. You can meet them. I will introduce you."

"Then we can all be friends together, you and I and your American whore."

Jorge stood before Lisbet and raised his hand high over his head.

For a second, Lisbet thought he was going to strike her. That would be the end, she thought. If he hits me, I will turn him out, I will never speak to him again. She closed her eyes, anticipating not so much the pain as the humiliation, the disappointment that would descend on her like a flood when she felt the force of the blow. She had fallen blindly into love with this man, and she would be knocked out of it, just as blindly, just as suddenly. But the blow never came. When she opened her eyes, she saw Jorge in the doorway, his jacket draped over his shoulders like a cape.

"You don't understand a thing," he said, as he pushed the door open. "I must go out, to walk and to think. I will leave you alone with your—biology."

Jorge shut the door behind him, and Lisbet set her book down on the coffee table. She pulled a tissue from a pack and wiped her face. She was surprised to find that she had been crying. The tears did not sting her eyes, but they flowed freely down her cheeks, as if some great pressure had been lifted from her soul, as if a band of tension had been snapped and her emotions, held within for so long, had been released. The hell with him, she thought. She held the tissue before her eyes, like a veil, and took in the scent of her own musky perfume. Lovely, she thought, as she gently touched the tissue to her neck and with her other hand grazed the satin fabric along the piping of her blouse. With her fingertips, she worked open a pearl button, and she could feel the nipples on her breasts rising like buds, like green shoots emerging from the dark soil. She arched her neck and spread her legs wide and lay there luxuriant, like an indolent goddess, basking in the flickering blue light cast by the television screen.

"Let's get out of here," Tracy yelled. She had stepped up onto the set, into camera range, as the moderator was trying to bring order back to the show. He stepped toward the camera for a close-up that would block the commotion from view. The television audience could see only his face as he ad-libbed an apology.

But the boom mikes were still above the panel, so while the moderator spoke, the viewers heard the words of Edström, speaking, for the first time, in English. "Typical Americans. When there's trouble, resort to violence. First chance you get, send in the troops, invade. Can't engage in civil discussion, have to shoot things out, like the Wild West."

"Don't let him bait you," Tracy shouted to Spiegel. "Come on."

"He's talking English?" One of the guys with Zeke, by now heavily into the Australian lager, was trying to make sense of the chaos on the set. "He's talking like a chick?"

"I think that's Tracy talking," Zeke said. He leaned closer to the portable set. "They pulled the mike off the guy on camera."

"What's Tracy doing there?" Hyde asked. "Why's she on this fuckin' show? She ain't never been near the army except in a parade."

"She ain't supposed to be there. She barged her way in."

"Well fuck me, why didn't I think of that?"

"Ain't we had enough TV? Let's go out and get drunk."

"We're already."

"More drunk."

"How you gonna manage that?"

"I got myself an unlimited capacity."

"But not unlimited funds, might I point out."

"I think," Zeke said, "it would be a right damn bad idea for four Americans to barrel stone drunk through the streets of Uppsala just now."

"What, are you afraid?"

"I ain't afraid of nothin'," Zeke said. "You wanna try me, boy?"

"Nah," the guy said. "I'se just asking."

"I'm just saying the worst thing we could do is go out there and tear up the town. It would be like proving that fucker's point, see."

"Well, this is the thing," Hyde said, as he crushed a beer can with his hand and tossed it across the room. "I think he's basically on the money."

Zeke and the other two men laughed, as the sound of a crash and breaking glass came over the air, and then nothing.

The screen went black, and then a test pattern appeared. What the guys had not seen, what no one in Sweden except for those in the studio saw, what even those in the studio could hardly believe because it happened so fast and the place was so hot and the lights were at once so bright and so blinding that everything at first looked too sharply defined and too real and then, when you turned away from the lights, everything was cloaked in pitch so that you were never sure whether to squint or to stare, to strain to see or to shield your eyes, was Tracy hauling back and slapping Edström across the face with the flat of her palm.

His head snapped back, and a spurt of blood appeared just at his lip. He touched his face, and when he saw the blood on his fingertips he muttered a curse in Swedish—*djävla!*—and then began to bark some kind of orders at the moderator. The producer had by this time run out from the control booth and was screaming at the two cameramen, one of whom, Spiegel noticed, had abandoned his post. The red light showed that his camera was still live, but it had swung around in its turret and the lens was aimed at the black studio wall.

"Let's go," Spiegel said, and he grabbed Tracy by the shoulder to lead her off the set.

Edström tried to protest, to block their way, but Spiegel pushed past him and guided Tracy toward the exit.

As he opened the door, he heard behind him someone call "Wait, please." It was Monika Nuland. She had run off the set to catch up with them. Spiegel stood in the doorway and got a look at her. Her deep-set eyes were bright with excitement. Her blond hair was pulled into a long French braid with a streak of black at the tip, as if she had dipped the ends of her silky hair in ink.

"*Hej*," she said to Spiegel. She was slightly out of breath. "I'm so glad you spoke up to him like that. You were wonderful!" She smiled, and took both his hands in hers. "If I had known they were asking that man onto the show, I would never have agreed to appear."

Spiegel nodded. Her hands were soft and warm, and her fingertips brushed his palms like feathers. He was afraid that his face was starting to flush. Somehow, he didn't want Tracy to see the pleasure he was getting.

"Yeah, I guess we were co-opted. I should have walked off the set right away," Spiegel said. "I should never have given him the chance to get into his rap."

"He got what he deserved," Monika said. She turned to Tracy and smiled warmly. "And thanks for hitting him like that. You American girls could teach us a lot about political action. With us in Sweden, it's always just words, words, words. I was even thinking that I should write a letter of protest to one of the left-wing newspapers. But then you hit him, and there was nothing more to say."

"I'm flattered. I'm overwhelmed."

"I hope the world saw what you did. I hope the newspapers report this tomorrow," Monika said.

"Peace protester packs punch, sets off studio scrap," Spiegel said.

"I've never hit anyone in my life," Tracy said. Spiegel could see that she was trembling, as if she was in shock. "I can't believe I did that!"

"I wish I had been brave enough," Monika said.

"Yeah, so do I," Spiegel said. He was feeling sheepish, a failure. He had neither played his role nor stepped out of it at the proper time. He had relied on Tracy to come to his rescue.

"How's your hand?" Monika asked.

"It's sore, but I feel great."

"This is Tracy, Tracy Green," Spiegel said. "She's with me. I mean, we're both with ARMS."

"I'm with SSS," Monika said.

"I've heard so much about your student group and the work you've done with the Americans in Stockholm," Tracy said to Monika. "We've been hoping to set up a meeting between ARMS and your Uppsala chapter."

"Well, the chapter right now is pretty much just me," Monika said softly. "But we should talk. We could go somewhere for coffee. I would like to show you that not all of the Swedish people are like those—pigs."

"Right now," Tracy said, "I think we should just get out of here, as fast as we can. But would you call me?"

Tracy gave Monika her number, and they agreed to get together. While Spiegel held the door for her, Tracy leaned over and gave Monika a quick kiss on the cheek, as if they had known each other for years, as if they were saying good-bye after a dinner party. That's just Tracy's way, Spiegel thought. She can bring people so graciously into her confidence, into her orbit. He envied her ability to touch people's hearts through the simplest of physical gestures, and he realized that he, too, might be falling under her sway.

"So are you satisfied?" Mick asked Melissa.

"Hmm, what do you mean?" she said. She had been lying back on the bed, and Mick had been gently stroking her as she shivered with delight.

"I mean with your bloody TV show. It just ended in a near fucking riot," he said.

"Yeah, me, too," she said. She turned away from him. It was actually a relief, she realized, to get away from his hand, so animated, like a little furry animal, a pet. "When did you turn it off?"

"The telly? I didn't. The screen went black. Weren't you watching? It was you who wanted it on, to see your American friend."

"Oh, I remember. But I don't know him. He just looked like someone."

"Well, he got into a rumble, and then a girl jumped up on the set and started hollering—"

"An American girl?"

"Yeah," Mick said. And he described Tracy.

"Maybe I do know them. They had dinner at my suite, and then—she cut his hair. Son of a bitch."

"She runs a salon?"

"Not quite," Melissa said. "I don't know what she's running. She cut his hair so he'd look like someone else. Probably whoever he was supposed to be tonight. He was playing a role. Like, acting."

"Well, if he was acting, he was good. I could cast him. An American Jean, to play against your American Julie. What do you think?"

"I think it's late."

Melissa began dressing. It would be a bad idea, she realized, to spend the night with Mick. There was enough talk among the cast about them already, too much talk. She should cool it with him, she knew, at least until after the show. Then—who knows?

"I do have an idea, though," he said. "A *Julie* in two languages."

"American and Australian?"

"Very funny. No, bilingual, with multiple screens and overhead projections. We'd use stereo sound. On one side of the stage, I'd set up a rock band, and on the other I could have a Swedish folk troupe. The clash of two cultures—"

"Good-bye, love," she said, and she kissed him on the ear. By the time she picked up her keys, Mick was in another world, scribbling on a notepad: *Setting: a disco club. Cast of characters: Julie, the cocktail girl. Jean, the barman. Time: the present . . .*

Tracy drove her red VW, Rosa, through the quiet streets. A soft rain was falling, the first of the season. The banks of snow that had accumulated through the winter were beginning to pock and heave apart, their slopes marked with jagged gullies through which the rainwater and snowmelt sluiced into the gutters, like rivulets off a mountainside, forming icy pools near the clogged storm drains and the high curbstones. The car sprayed a curtain of water as it rounded the corners to head up the hill toward the outskirts of town.

Spiegel had hoped that he might go back home tonight with Tracy, but he was reluctant to press his advantage. And perhaps he had no advantage. He had done what she had asked him. But had he done so to help the movement? Or to help her? He was a little bit ashamed of himself as well for the feelings he had begun to harbor, that she owed him something in return for his help. If he truly felt that, in what way had he sacrificed? To ask anything of Tracy would be to take advantage of her, as well—in her loneliness, in her anxiety about Aaronson, in her physical weariness and pain.

For Spiegel could see that she was favoring her hand when she shifted, and she was trying to steer with her left only. There was a welt across her cheek as well. Had Edström struck her? It had been impossible to see, at least from his angle and in the blinding light. Some hero he had been, in any case, letting her take a swing at his antagonist while all he could think to do was rush to the exit.

"Should you see a doctor, Tracy? Find the hospital or something?" he asked. "Your hand looks bad."

"I'm okay," she said.

"But you might want to file charges. It would help to document your injuries."

"You're forgetting that I hit him first."

"Not without provocation," Spiegel said.

She didn't answer. She braked for a light as the rain beat its steady tattoo on the roof.

"I shouldn't have agreed to sit in for Aaronson," Spiegel said. "I've just drawn more attention to him. After tonight, the whole fucking country's gonna want to speak to him, to interview him. And actually it would be great if he were here. It's the kind of opportunity he had always hoped would develop. But I can't go on with this any further. I'll just fuck things up even more, say things I shouldn't and get into more fights. . . ."

"You don't have to apologize," Tracy said. "I should have seen this coming. They were lying in wait for us. It was like an ambush. I'm the one who should apologize. I should never have let you get into that. I should have sent Zeke."

"But maybe you can't afford to risk Zeke. I'm more expendable."

"No, that's not true," Tracy said. "Not for me."

And those words were like a balm to Spiegel, soothing his wounds, wounds that were not visible like Tracy's but that hurt just as much, that stung him with the twined lashes of remorse and regret. In the end, he was glad that he had held back and did not ask if they should go back to her place for one more night. They had agreed beforehand that he would return to his student flat in Flogsta and resume his own life while they all waited for Aaronson's imminent return. Just as well, for Spiegel was beginning to see that the role of Aaronson was far too complex, and too dangerous, to play without a script.

APRIL

8

The rains continued for three days. Spiegel moved his belongings from Tracy's place back to his room at Flogsta. In a way, it was a relief to be alone. The steady vigilance required while pretending to be somebody else had worn him down. That, and the constant proximity to Tracy. More and more, Spiegel felt himself drawn to her, and he sensed that she liked him, too. But something within him, the remnant of a chivalric code of honor, probably as useless as a vestigial tail, had prevented him from taking advantage of his rival's absence. Or had it? Perhaps he was merely afraid of revealing his own ineptitude, or of facing Tracy's rejection and her contempt.

Spiegel began to think that maybe it was time to return to the States. He had skipped so many language classes while staying at Tracy's that he would have to start anew if he wanted to continue. Ugh! More instructions on how to buy a cheese sandwich! During his whole time in Uppsala, he had made no contacts at the university, so the dim hope of gaining academic credit for the semester had faded completely. Most of all, now that he had filled in for Aaronson on television and managed to screw that up so badly, Tracy would no longer need his help.

Yet Spiegel could not go home without his passport. Moreover, he hadn't heard a thing from Iris. Maybe her letters to him had been intercepted. Or maybe she had transferred her affections to somebody new. Could he really expect her to wait for him? Maybe he would return in the summer and resume the quiet life he used to lead before the police came crashing into his apartment and sent him flying out the casement window and into a new world.

He pulled a chair up to his desk, flicked on the lamp, and thought about beginning a letter to Iris. He scrawled the date at the top of a piece of writing paper, but that was all. His hand balked even at putting down the letters of her name. So he sat for some time, watching the rain blow through the courtyard and smash against the walls of the adjacent tower. The scraggly pines that had survived the onslaught of the cranes and bulldozers seemed to shiver in the hard wind, and the snow on the hilltops and the meadows was softening into a greasy-looking, grayish slush. Spiegel thought that he might leave Uppsala without ever seeing green stalks rise from the fields, without ever coming upon a quilt of wildflowers by the roadside, without experiencing the extraordinary stillness of the midnight sun. To be here through the darkest months would forever shroud his memories of Sweden in sorrow and gloom, in recollections of stormy days such as this, when he'd sat and watched the world at war with itself and wondered if he would ever find a peace that was not embedded in loneliness or a love that wouldn't tear him apart.

Lost in self-pity, he finally began to write, explaining to Iris, as clearly as he could, all the torments and dangers and disappointments that he had lived through since he'd come to Uppsala. He was surprised at how fluently his thoughts flowed from pen to paper, and he felt as if he could write all morning when he was surprised by a rapping on the door. Who knew that he had returned to Flogsta?

It was Jorge.

"I saw your light," he said. "Welcome home."

Spiegel noted that Jorge was clean and dry—blow-dried in fact—and without an overcoat. So he hadn't dashed across the rainswept courtyard from building one. Where had he been?

Jorge sat on the edge of Spiegel's bed and crossed his long legs. Spiegel noticed once again the fine cut of his clothes. He was wearing wide bell-bottoms with a sharp crease. They seemed to be of an excellent fabric, maybe linen, and the pleats made a soft swishing sound as he settled back. Beneath the cuffs, Spiegel

could see the tooled leather of Jorge's Western-style boots. It was
ridiculous, how clean he kept the soles, how he polished the sharp
points until the buttery grain seemed to shine with an interior
light. Spiegel imagined the boots after one day of work on a ranch,
caked with mud and shit, scuffed and wrecked and broken in.

"Are you back here for good?" Jorge asked.

"I never really left," Spiegel said.

Jorge shrugged. "It's too bad, then," he said. "She was a very
cute dish. I thought, once you got a taste of her, we would never
see you again at our table."

"But as you see, you were wrong," Spiegel said.

He cleared the papers from his desk. He didn't want Jorge to
see the letter he had been writing and to start asking questions
about Iris. Jorge's assumptions and insinuations about Tracy were
irritating enough already. Their friendship had been edgy ever
since that spin on the ice. Spiegel's initial fury had drained off,
but he had since then approached Jorge, the few times they had
run into each other in town, the way he would regard a snarling
dog. He knew that Jorge's polished surface masked a fierce and
reckless temperament, that Jorge was capable, when denied his
way, of doing nearly anything.

"Then welcome back to Flogsta," Jorge said. "And don't
worry about that one that got away. As your saying goes, there
are many fish swimming in the sea."

"What about you?" Spiegel asked. "How's school? How's
Lisbet?"

"Well, it's very awkward, you see. Do you mind if I smoke?"

Spiegel found a little tin can filled with paper clips. He
dumped them onto his desktop and gave the can to Jorge to use
as an ashtray. Jorge lit one of his pungent oval cigarettes and
inhaled greedily.

"I must confess that things are not so good. We had a little
fight, a disagreement, and, well, then I walked out."

"You what? Just like that?"

"When I came back to her, she had barred the door. I knocked,
but she would not let me in."

"When?"

"This morning. About two."

"I see. So where did you stay?"

"Well, you know, with a friend."

"Melissa?"

"Yes. I think Lisbet suspects that there is something between us. She no longer believes I go out at night to play cards with you."

Spiegel said that he was not surprised. "I wouldn't know seven-card stud from the *Seven Samurai*," he said.

Jorge nodded and took another hard pull on the cigarette. Spiegel guessed that maybe Jorge had been awake all night. The nicotine could keep him going, at least for a while.

"May I ask you a favor?"

"Do you need me to get your stuff from Lisbet's?"

"Oh no," Jorge said. "That won't be a problem." He reached out his hand and dangled a key chain from his index finger. The keys rang against one another like little chimes. "I can return to her flat, at my leisure." He pronounced the word in the English manner: *leh-zure.*

"Then what do you need?" Spiegel asked.

"It's just this. Lisbet and I had plans to go to a club, to hear music played by a friend of mine."

"Don't be ridiculous, Jorge. You think she's still gonna want to go?"

"Oh, yes. I think she was looking forward to a night, how do you say it, on the town?"

"So you want me to take her? I don't know as I could do that," Spiegel said.

"No, I will take her. I want you to take Melissa."

"You're nuts."

Jorge laughed as he crushed out the cigarette. "Nuts, tired, I don't know," he said. "She likes you. You—how does she say it?—speak her language."

"But why don't you just take Lisbet, if she'll go with you, and forget about Melissa, at least for tonight?" Spiegel said.

"Ahh, I wish it were so easy. I can't forget about her, though. She is in my bones and my blood. I have to be near her, you see, even if I'm not the one with her. Otherwise, the evening would be unbearable."

"Then why don't you just forget about Lisbet? Drop her."

Jorge screwed up his face for a second and looked at the ceiling. Spiegel couldn't tell if he was trying to summon up a phrase in English or if he was trying to figure out how to answer the question. Maybe the question had no answer, or no answer that an American could understand. Maybe this was just one of those peculiar European yearnings that one saw so much of in those ridiculous French and Italian films, the desire to create needlessly complex love relationships, the compulsion, no matter how seemingly successful the marriage, to carry an affair on the side. Spiegel had always thought the complex web of marital and extramarital relationships was a convention adapted for comic purposes in film and in fiction. But now he was beginning to believe that it was endemic to European culture.

"I can't, as you say, drop her," Jorge said. "We have plans to announce our engagement. Perhaps tonight. It is why I want you there, to be our witnesses."

Spiegel sat still, astonished. "Do you love her, Jorge?"

"I don't know. Perhaps a little."

"A little? That's not enough to be talking about marriage."

"You know, there are many reasons one might marry."

"What are you telling me, man? Are you saying she's pregnant?"

Jorge laughed, a bit contemptuously. "Certainly not. That would not be a reason to marry. It would be a reason to . . . see a doctor."

He stood and walked to the window. He scanned the rain-streaked view, then sat on the edge of the desk and leaned close to Spiegel, so that he could speak in a near whisper.

"My position here is not terribly secure," Jorge said.

"What do you mean," Spiegel said. "You're a political refugee, you're guaranteed sanctuary by the Swedish government. . . ."

"Not exactly so. You see, I was never actually drafted into the Portuguese army. Not yet. Perhaps I will be, perhaps I have been already. Until I am drafted, I am just here on a tourist visa, like you."

"I see. Well, what's the chance that you will be drafted?"

"Who knows? But you see my brother is a wounded war hero, so to speak. It would be a great shame to my family if I did not answer the call, when it comes."

"They wouldn't support you, if you decide to stay?"

"No. We see things very differently. They have abandoned me. What is the word? I am disinherited. My father has said that if I do not take up the arms in my brother's honor he will never see me again, not even in my grave."

"So if you are drafted, you would stay here."

"Of course I would stay. And then I would be safe. I would be a political refugee. Until then, I am without a clear status."

"Except if you marry Lisbet. She's your ticket to a permanent visa, right?"

"Yes, once we are married, then I will have a secure visa and I will be free to travel."

"I don't see that it's worth marrying someone you don't love."

"Maybe you marry for love in America and in storybooks. We Europeans marry for practical reasons. To build the family property. To create a . . ."

"Dynasty."

"Yes," Jorge said. He stood. The air between them seemed to have cleared. Jorge dropped the stage whisper and resumed his normal speaking voice. "Also, it will be much better for me," he said, "once Lisbet sees Melissa with you. It will put an end to her suspicions. I will go home and tell her, and she will feel better. We will kiss and make out."

Spiegel didn't bother with the correction.

"So you'll join us for a big celebration?" Jorge asked. "Tonight?"

"Sure," Spiegel said. "I'll be the beard."

"The what?"

Spiegel explained the term. "Like a mask. A disguise. When I'm with Melissa, it's like I'm covering for you."

"Right!" Jorge said. "Right on!"

* * *

By the time they left Flogsta that night, the rain had stopped, but the streets and sidewalks were wet and under the street lamps the city seemed to be bathed in a glassy sheen, a radiance that filled the air with shimmering light. Lisbet was driving. Spiegel sat in the backseat, next to Melissa. She seemed relaxed and light-hearted, amused by the whole setup. In fact, Spiegel wondered if this little drama had been her idea. Perhaps it was she who wanted to go to the club with Jorge and Lisbet, to see how Jorge interacted with her rival, to take her measure. But why? So as to know her enemy and to eliminate her, and to seize Jorge for herself? Or to get under Lisbet's skin and to make her life miserable, even if just for an evening? Or maybe Melissa just liked the innate drama of emotional disaster. Spiegel could picture her watching little creatures at play inside a terrarium. Every once in a while she would deign to reach out and rap against the glass and watch them scatter.

Jorge seemed happy and alive, as if he were excited by being in conjunction with not one but two women to whom he could lay some claim. He rode shotgun, and swiveled back and forth between Lisbet and Melissa, pointing out the sights of the city as they zipped past, waving and gesticulating, animated, even frenetic. He would describe some landmark to Melissa—"That's the old castle, where the botanist, what would be his name?, catalogued all of the flowers in the kingdom"—and then he would turn to Lisbet for some confirmation—"Isn't that so, darling?"—and pat her on the shoulder, and she would say, "Yes, dear, " and add some innocuous remark, like: "It was Linnaeus." And Jorge would turn back to Spiegel with a wink. Suggesting what? That everything was under control? Or that his relationship with Lisbet was meant to be taken ironically, as if between quotation marks?

Spiegel was surprised at how much he enjoyed being out, as Jorge had put it, on the town. He had not yet had the chance, or really the desire, to see "Uppsala by night," which was a bit of a local joke. Swedish students tended to be so serious and focused except on the weekends when most were either back home in the provinces or blind drunk that the most happening places, someone had remarked, were the university library and the infirmary.

Going out for the evening to a club—even one chosen by Jorge on who knows what basis and with a date arranged by Jorge for his own mysterious purposes—Spiegel felt relaxed for the first time in days, even weeks. Tonight, once again, he could be himself. Until he had given up the role of Aaronson, Spiegel hadn't realized what a burden he had been bearing.

Because nature had made him and Aaronson into virtual twins and fate had placed them together at the same university, it was assumed that they would be alike in certain interior ways and that Spiegel could slip into Aaronson's persona as easily as if he were borrowing one of his sweaters. But Spiegel had found that it wasn't so. Becoming Aaronson was not so much a matter of pretending as of learning, absorbing a whole history and way of being, and then suppressing his own personality. It was not that he treasured his personality so much. For years, he had been trying to discover who he was and to solve the puzzle of his own existence. It was only through his freak encounters with Aaronson back in the States that he had begun to approach a solution. Since then, he had begun to see himself as he was seen by others. Without any clear convictions of his own, he had let Iris and her allies in the student-worker movement determine what role he should play in their struggle to end the war. Yet by acceding to their wishes, he had set the foundations of his personality on a bed of shifting sands. For what would happen if while he was away from Iris his image were to fade from her memory? What would happen if he were to become so enmeshed in the tangles of Aaronson's life that people forgot about Spiegel altogether and he began to vanish from their minds like smoke in light air, like a dream on waking? What would happen if his heart were drawn to the emotional vacuum left by Aaronson's absence and he were to find himself, even just a little bit, in love with Tracy?

It was better to be away from Tracy for the night, to be next to this crazy Melissa and to smell her musky perfume and to relax as her long blond hair brushed against his cheek when she turned to look at a sight Jorge pointed out as they whisked down the street. Spiegel cranked open the window, and gusts of humid air swirled against his face and neck.

By the river, the streets narrowed. The pavement was made of cobblestones. Lisbet slowed the car, and as it bumped along the uneven roadway Spiegel and Melissa were jostled against each other in a pleasant manner. Spiegel felt as if he were a child, being bounced on someone's knee.

The buildings in this part of the city were made of a rough, sandy stone, set against one another at odd angles, which made this section, the Old City, or the Gamla Stan, as it was called, a little warren of confusing corners and intersections punctuated by slits and alleyways not much wider than a man's shoulders. The buildings presented a drab facade at street level. The doorways were of heavy oak, and the windows were tiny squares of rippled glass crossed by wrought-iron grates. The roofline of Gothic spires and arches was like a spidery script written across the night sky, breaking the moonlight into strips and fragments so that no place on the street was either fully lighted or completely in shadow. To Spiegel, the Gamla Stan, a quaint and well-preserved relic hidden behind the modern apartments and office buildings of the city center, seemed like a village out of Grimm transposed into the modern world. He felt a spasm of disgust and disorientation, as if he had come across a dark mushroom among the offerings in a bowl of fruit.

Jorge had assured Spiegel that he could get them into his friend's club, no problem. Spiegel had assumed that meant he could cut the line, but what he meant apparently was that they would have no trouble getting in because the club was nearly deserted, although Jorge insisted that the club was merely "undiscovered" and that once Swedes learned about the place they would jam the streets with their Saabs and Volvos and line up at the doorway for the chance to descend to the stone-walled basement, sit on pine benches, drink overpriced Mateus or black instant coffee, and listen to a would-be Left Bank chanteuse strum a badly tuned guitar and sing in an execrable accent barely recognizable versions of tired antiwar ballads and early Dylan.

One of Jorge's countrymen owned the club. There was a small community of Portuguese refugees in Uppsala who had met through the language school and who stayed in touch during the warm weather through a football league and during the winter months through occasional gatherings for boiled squid and fado music. Jorge had mentioned that the club owner, Mario, had worked his way up, starting with a little grilled-sausage stand that he expanded to a food shop and then into a snack bar that did a sideline in postcards and souvenirs, which he sold to the occasional busload of blue-haired American ladies who came up from Stockholm to tour the botanical gardens and to marvel at the Domkyrkan—that is, the church—and the great castle, the Slott, that sat at the center of the old city like a black heart.

Mario had opened the Penny Lane—Jorge had proposed the name—during one of the great storms of the hard winter. He had thought that the long winter nights would be good for the café business, that Swedes would want to dissolve the hours of darkness in heroic bouts of song and drink. But if that was so, they apparently didn't want to pass the night hours in a club that was carved out of the rock beneath the city, for business had been terrible, so far. Mario's hopes now were for the summer tourist trade, and he had plans to put a few tables with umbrellas out on the tiny sidewalk in front of his establishment, although Spiegel couldn't imagine how he could do so without forcing the foot traffic over the curb and into the roadway. Cars already had to navigate through the many oddly placed granite hitching posts and iron pikes, relics of the agrarian age that today had become annoyances, even hazards, for driver and pedestrian alike.

"Welcome, welcome to my club," Mario called when he spotted Jorge at the doorway. Mario embraced his countryman and greeted the two women, European style, with a kiss on both cheeks. They all followed him down the winding staircase into the maw of the club.

"This place should be called Le Cave," Spiegel whispered to Melissa.

"Or Dante's Hell," she said.

Spiegel imagined that a century ago the space had been a wine cellar. The ceiling was low and uneven, and the few lights hung, like stalactites, from spars that seemed to have been jammed into fissures in the sedimentary rock. The walls had a disconcerting jaggedness to them, as if the space had been created by blasting or some other process of destruction rather than by design.

Mario led the foursome to a table near the small stage. Two guys near the back were in the far stages of inebriation, and smoke from their French cigarettes swirled toward the ceiling, where it massed like a storm cloud.

Two ice buckets immediately appeared beside Jorge. One held a bottle of Swedish aquavit and the other a cheap Spanish champagne. Jorge began pouring liberally, and Lisbet drank hers down even before Jorge finished the round. Spiegel thought that she must be determined to get very drunk or very sick. Her voice, her laughter, had been rising in pitch through the evening, and he had begun to realize that she wasn't laughing out of gaiety but out of hysteria, that her laughter was a release of tension, even a sneer, an attack.

Melissa, meanwhile, was becoming more cool and glassy. She drew on a long cigarette as if she could suck nourishment from the smoke, from the tip of the flame, and Spiegel wondered if such aggressive smoking was in fact an act of erasure, an attempt to fold the outer world into oneself and to conceal it, a way of withdrawing from the world by breathing it in.

Jorge tapped the edge of his knife against one of the ice buckets and raised his glass of champagne. "I would like to make, here in the presence of my dear friends, a little pronunciation," he said. "Lisbet and I have decided that on midsummer eve, which we will celebrate with her family, we will announce our engagement. And we wanted you, our American friends, to share with us the pleasure of this announcement."

As he spoke, his hand tipped and he spilled champagne onto the tabletop, where it pooled into a little lake of foam. Spiegel noticed how the texture of Jorge's English, usually so smooth and supple, like the fabric of his clothing, seemed to fray under the influence of—what? Alcohol? No, he had been with Jorge before during some long evenings over wine. Jorge's English unraveled when subjected to the stress of hypocrisy. For Spiegel knew Jorge's position, his bad faith, and he was convinced that Lisbet knew as well. She had to know. But why did she put up with this treatment, with this charade? Maybe the script was hers, her way of forcing Jorge into a public renunciation of his transgressions. If so, she had evidently given up on her demand that Jorge learn Swedish before they announce their engagement. She must be determined to take Jorge on in whatever language she could get him to say "I do."

"Well congratulations, love, that's wonderful news," said Melissa. She leaned across the table to give Lisbet a kiss, and the silky fringe of her shawl brushed dangerously close to the candle. Spiegel had to steady her with his hand as she sank back to her seat. She, too, was pushing herself to the limit, licking drops of aquavit off the rim of her shot glass.

"Thank you, darling," said Lisbet. She leaned toward Jorge and gave him a kiss on the cheek. "I can't wait, really. I wish we were announcing our engagement tonight, instead of in June."

"Well, you sort of have announced it," Spiegel said.

"No, we've only said that we're going to announce it."

"But isn't that announcing it?" Spiegel said. In fact, the distinctions between engagement and announcement were all beginning to blur in his mind. Maybe it was a matter of semantics. Maybe the very words *engage* and *announce* meant something different in Swedish, in Portuguese, in English, and while they all thought that they were talking about the same thing, each meant something different. Or maybe it was the bad air and the wine.

Lisbet held her glass right in front of her face and tipped it at a precarious angle. Spiegel couldn't determine if she meant to finish the champagne at a gulp or to hurl the glass across the room. Was she thinking about a Swedish toast or an English one? She stared at Spiegel, across the rim. He could see a smear of lipstick on the glass, which reflected the candlelight. If he lowered his head, Spiegel could examine Lisbet's features through the refractions of the wine. The bubbles rising in the pale liquid looked like tears coursing across her lips, her fine cheekbones, the soft ovals of her eyes.

"Lenny? Lenny?" It was Melissa. Had his head dropped right to the table? Had he nodded for a moment? Or was he just locked away in private contemplation of the image of Lisbet, preserved in amber? Melissa raised her glass slightly and looked at him with raised eyebrow. He realized that he was expected to propose a toast to Lisbet and Jorge.

"Yes, I'm sorry," Spiegel said. He tried to stand, but his knees felt gelatinous. He wasn't sure they would hold him. It took all his concentration to raise his glass, and his voice.

"I, too, would like to make an announcement," Spiegel said.

"Here, here!" Someone from a table at the back of the room spoke up. The two drunk guys were sitting on a bench backed up against the wall of rock. In the weak light, Spiegel couldn't see them well. The one who spoke wore a cable-knit sweater. He had hair cut so short that his scalp bristled like sandpaper. The other had a thick, walrus-like mustache. There was a bottle of whiskey on their table, and tall glasses.

"Thank you," said Spiegel. "May I continue?"

"*Skål!* To your health," the brush-cut one said, raising his glass.

"I would like to express my hardest—I mean my heartiest—congratulations. You know they say that opposites attract, and, I'm not saying Lisbet and Jorge are opposites but, well, like north and south, like the Baltic and the Mediterranean, like Sweden and Portugal—"

"Like Ringo and George!" said Melissa.

"Yes, they're different but perfect together."

"Bravo!"

"Will you tell that guy to shut up?" Lisbet said.

"Together, may they form their own Atlantic alliance," Spiegel continued.

"A NATO pact," shouted Melissa.

"Oh, well, nothing military," said Jorge.

Lisbet poured some aquavit straight into her champagne glass.

"A Common Market, then," said Spiegel. "And may they produce a fine crop of olives and . . . hey, what the hell do you grow in Sweden, Lisbet?"

"Old," she said.

"I know who you are," said the brush cut. "You're a star."

"No I'm not," said Spiegel. "You don't know me."

"Down the hatchet," said the mustache. He gulped down a slug of whiskey.

"Sit down," Jorge said. He was tugging at Spiegel's sleeve. "Let it be."

"No, no, I want to finish," Spiegel said.

"Let the American finish," said the crew cut. "He's a star. He's a hero."

"Now cut it out—" said Spiegel, and he turned toward the Swedes. But Jorge grabbed him by the wrist and nearly toppled him back into his seat.

"It's time for some music," Jorge said. "Listen. A surprise."

And when Spiegel turned he saw on the makeshift stage Luis, his Mexican pal from language class. Luis had on a bandanna around his forehead and a suede vest with long fringe and colorful beadwork, and he carried an acoustic guitar richly inlaid with mother-of-pearl. He was adjusting a thick cloth fret band and trying to get the instrument in tune. He leaned close to the strings, but it was almost impossible to pick up the tones because of the echoes off the rock ceiling and the screeching feedback from the standing mike.

Luis's difficulties with the guitar at least had the virtue of diverting the drunks. They began to applaud as he worked the tuning pegs, tightened the mike stand, adjusted his finger picks. Spiegel hoped that they would shut up once Luis began to play. He thought that if they ragged Luis, he might find himself in the midst of his second fight in two days. And he wasn't yet drunk enough to think that he and Jorge—two reeds, two gnats—could prevail if they tried to sting the two drunken bears.

At last Luis launched into a long flamenco ballad, followed by some traditional Mexican folk tunes, and then he slipped north of the border for a country number. Jorge's friend Mario, wearing an apron wet with dish suds, stepped out from behind the Japanese screen that demarcated the kitchen and grinned his approval, applauding each number with his soapy hands. Jorge offered words of encouragement in his pidgin Spanish: *Esta es, bueno, muy bueno*. And the drunks applauded so loudly between the numbers that Spiegel thought he could detect a strand of mockery. Why are they here? he wondered. Why don't they just leave?

After his set, Luis squeezed a fifth chair to the table and sat down. He untied his bandanna and dabbed his forehead. He had worked up a little sweat. Mario appeared with a mug of lager, and Luis tilted his head back and finished it in a long gulp.

"You were thirsty, man," Spiegel said.

"In my country we say: Your tongue is like a tie," Luis said. "There's a joke, you know. An old man is going to visit a young lady who lives on the top floor, and he says to his friend: I'll take the stairs.

"His friend says: But your tongue will be like a tie!

"The old man says: Yes. That is what I want."

"I don't get it," said Lisbet.

"Then you should talk to Jorge, sweetie," Melissa said.

Oh, boy, Spiegel thought. This could get ugly.

Mario came back with another bottle of champagne, Möet. "This comes from the two gentlemen in the back," he said, as he settled the bottle in the bath of ice. "It is for the star."

Luis turned to the two men and waved his thanks.

"Not for you, amigo," the brush cut said. "For the gringo. The television star!"

"He means you," Jorge said to Spiegel. "He thinks you were on television. A show I saw the other night had an American deserter, and he looked like you. We even thought—Did you see it?"

"Umm, yes," Melissa said. "It was on. But I wasn't focused."

"Look, fellas," Spiegel said, turning around. "Thanks for the wine. But I wasn't on television. It wasn't me. Wrong guy."

"No, we saw you, for sure," said the brush cut.

"Maybe we should send this wine back," Spiegel said to Jorge. "I just don't like the vibes here. These guys are getting to me. I mean, this is not a friendly gesture. This is . . . "

"Enemy action," said Melissa.

"Yeah, this is not normal, man. I mean, I don't want to be paranoid, but just who are those guys? Why are they here? Are they, like, great lovers of flamenco guitar? Big fans of Mario's cuisine?

Your basic Uppsala pub crawlers? No. You know what they look like to me?" He leaned forward so that he could whisper. He spoke so softly that his words barely swayed the candle flame. "Cops."

"Like what?" said Jorge.

"Police. Fuzz. Pigs. Gendarmes. *Polizei*. Whatever word you have for it in Portuguese."

"Oh, you are being paranoid," said Lisbet. "I mean, they're not even Swedes. I don't know what they're talking. Finnish, I think."

"I think they're following me," Spiegel said.

"From where, though? All the way from Flogsta? I would have seen them in the mirror, you know. But the roads were empty, after the rain."

It was true. No one had been near them when they drove into Gamla Stan, and no one knew they were coming to this club. Maybe Lisbet was right and Spiegel was being paranoid, a remnant from his early student days when he imagined that behind every cloud of marijuana smoke lurked a narcotics detective and a federal drug agent. It took him years to settle down and realize that no one cared what kind of chemicals he was mixing into his bloodstream. It was just as well, to the feds, if every student in America majored in pharmaceutical applications. Keep them high, keep them happy, and let us wage our war. Opiates are the opiate of the people.

But once Spiegel abandoned drugs for politics, he found himself in faster, more dangerous company. No cops ever bothered the potheads, but the activists, as he had learned, were likely to find themselves at the receiving end of a billy club. Though Spiegel felt safer, and more free from police harassment, in Sweden, he knew that he would be wise to keep in mind one of the tenets that he had often heard preached from the pulpits of the movement: The pigs are the same all over.

"I don't know. I just don't like their attitude is all," Spiegel said. "Maybe we should call it a wrap."

"Sorry?"

"Call it quits. Splitsville. I mean, let's go."

"But Lenny," Jorge said. "You can't mean that. It's—how do you say it? The night is young?"

"Well, maybe I oughta go alone, and if either of those guys makes to follow me . . . "

"We call the cops, right?" said Melissa.

"I guess not. I guess you and Luis come after me, carrying wine bottles. Unless you've got a knife, Luis."

"Sure, I'm a real bandito," he said. He smiled and pulled a Swiss Army knife out of his jeans pocket. "It's got a corkscrew."

"That's ridiculous. You guys can't go chasing those two thugs out to the alleyway. They'll carve you up. They'll kill you."

"Thanks for the vote of confidence," Spiegel said.

Melissa screwed her face up into a childish pout. "So let's just stay here and wait them out. They won't do anything to you as long as we're in the club."

"They won't do anything at all," said Lisbet. "You Americans are so crazy. Too many Westerns. Shoot-out at the old salon."

"Saloon," Spiegel said.

"America is a violent country, honey," Melissa added.

"Now let's not talk about these things," Jorge said. "What I wanted to do here, if I might, was sing a song for my dear friends, and I was hoping that I might borrow Luis's guitar."

"You're going to sing?" said Lisbet.

"Of course. Why not?"

"In Mexico we have a saying," Luis said. "Not my gun, not my horse, not my woman, not my guitar. But I will make an exception for you, Jorge."

"And lend him your horse?"

Everyone laughed, and Jorge took Luis's guitar and stepped up onto the stage. He sat on the three-legged stool, hit one loud chord, and began to sing, early Beatles.

"Jorge has no trouble tuning," Spiegel said to Luis.

"Because I had tuned it for him," Luis said.

"Or because his ear is not so good as Luis's," said Melissa.

"Or because it's better," said Lisbet.

Here we go, thought Spiegel.

"Do you two play together," Melissa said. "Duets?"

"Oh no," Lisbet said. "I just listen. He's the caballero."

"The wandering troubadour, huh?"

"He doesn't wander so much. Not so much as you think," Lisbet said to Melissa. "When he does, he always comes back home, you see."

"Oh? I thought he spent many nights out with the boys. Playing cards."

Lisbet turned away to look at Jorge. But Jorge's eyes were locked on Melissa as he sang.

"Bravo, bravo," Melissa shouted, applauding over the music.

"Cool it, Melissa," Spiegel said. "Let him sing."

Spiegel felt a hand on his shoulder. The drunk with the brush cut was standing beside him. His face was flushed, and his stance was unsteady. He stared down at Spiegel with pig-red eyes.

"You are the guy. The American who was on television," he said. He pronounced it: *tele-wision*.

"Not me," Spiegel said. He was looking directly into the man's round gut. He was getting annoyed. "Now just leave us alone."

"But you are a hero," the man said. "I hate America. I hate your fucking war. I hate Wiet-nam. You are a good man. Let me buy you another bottle of wine."

"It's not my fucking war, and I don't want your wine," Spiegel said.

"We can drink to the death of America!"

Spiegel turned to check out brush cut's partner. He was gone. To wait for them in the alleyway? To slash the tires of Lisbet's Volvo?

"That's fine, you hate America," Spiegel said. "I don't. I'm going back there. I live there. Now get your paws off me."

Spiegel looked around furtively to see if anyone could help extricate him from this guy's grip. No one was paying any attention to him. Mario was clearing the back table. He was agitated, worried that the drunks were trying to slip out without paying the bar bill. Lisbet and Melissa were staring at each other. Jorge had eyes only for Melissa, and Luis had his gaze fixed on the precious guitar.

"Fuck President Nixon. Fuck Henry Kissinger. Fuck the war!" the guy shouted.

Jorge was leaning into the mike, trying to boost the volume.

"I am not so blind. I know what goes on," Lisbet was saying to

Melissa. "I am only saying: It is over. I am warning you. We have made our announcement. He is mine now. You touch him, you die."

"What makes you think I have any interest in Jorge?" said Melissa. She leaned across the table and kissed Spiegel hard on the lips. The music stopped.

"Hey, what are you doing?" Jorge shouted to Melissa.

"He's my date," she said, stroking Spiegel's face and neck. "I dig him."

Lisbet stood and turned to Jorge. "Why do you care who she's fucking?" she cried.

"I don't care. I'm just . . . interested," he said. The mike began to screech with feedback.

"Then take her!" Lisbet yelled. "The two of you! She's nothing but a whore. And you—"

"Fucking Americans," said the brush cut.

"Who's fucking Americans?" Luis said.

"He is, she is, they all are," Lisbet shouted, gesticulating wildly.

"I don't care what you say about him," Melissa said. "But watch what you're saying about *me*, bitch."

"You watch this," Lisbet said. She reached back and then her arm uncoiled and her fist shot out as if it were on a spring and she landed a shot right to Melissa's jaw. Melissa went down.

"Why did you do that?" Spiegel called. He tried to step between them, in case Lisbet planned to continue her assault.

"Baby," Jorge yelled, but not to Lisbet. He jumped off the stage to help Melissa, and as he did so he dropped the guitar. It hit the floor with a deadening *thwunk*, followed by the asynchronic reverberations of a popping fret board.

Luis screamed. *"Madre de dios,"* he yelled. "You bastard!"

Luis jumped toward Jorge, with his hands stretched out as if to throttle him, but Spiegel held him back. "Calm down, calm down," he hollered, in anything but a calm tone.

"You get away from her, Jorge," Lisbet shouted. "She's a *putain*! American whore!"

Melissa sat up and wiped a smear of blood from her mouth as Jorge leaned above her, solicitous and terrified. With a silk handkerchief, he dabbed the blood from Melissa's lips.

"Take her then, you twig, you coward," Lisbet went on. Her face was red with tears and excitement. "I could rip each of you apart with my hands. You deserve each other, you puff of smoke, you blade of grass, you nothing!"

Luis was gently fingering his damaged guitar, like an archaeologist studying a shard of rare pottery. He was muttering in Spanish, bringing down the curses of the ancient Mayan gods on Jorge and all his descendants for three generations.

"Come on, let's go," Spiegel said to Lisbet. He steered her away from the wreck she had made, hoping to extricate her before she could bring about any more carnage.

"Oh sir, sir," Mario called as Spiegel walked to the steps. "Your bill, sir. You have not paid, not to mention these damages—"

"I thought this was on Jorge," Spiegel said.

"He said the Americans would pay, sir," Mario said. "The Americans."

"What's he talking about?" Spiegel asked Lisbet.

"Then get it from *her*," Lisbet said, pointing to Melissa. Melissa was standing, wobbly, leaning her hand on the table, as Jorge fluttered around her like a hummingbird. "She's an American."

"But you must see what you have done to my club," Mario cried. He looked ashen in the smoke-strained light.

"Let's go," Lisbet said. She grabbed Spiegel's hand and pulled him to the stairway.

"You will hear about this," Mario called after them. "I know people at the embassy!"

At the doorway, Spiegel, like Lot's wife, took one look backward to assay the scene of destruction. The guy with the walrus mustache had vanished. The brush-cut drunk had collapsed beside a pine bench in the corner, his feet propped against an upturned table, his thick hands resting on his gut. He looked as if he were dead to the world, but his eyes, two red-rimmed slits of ice, were fixed on Spiegel, as they had been all night.

"Fucking Americans," he said. "Make trouble wherever you go."

9

Spiegel's mouth felt like sandpaper and his head like a Japanese lantern, a thin membrane filled with hot tongues of light. Every movement churned his stomach, and waves of dizziness flowed through his body as he tried to stand. His legs trembled and his knees fluttered. He sat on the edge of the bed to steady himself. He breathed deeply. His stomach calmed a little. The pain in his head narrowed to a spot of fire that burned behind his eyes. Slowly, sensation returned to his limbs, and eventually he felt that if he were to stand and walk to the bathroom his body might be willing to comply.

How did he let himself come to this? He hadn't been so drunk, nor so hungover, since . . . when? Since he had discovered, in a sense, who he was. And perhaps that was why he had let himself go last night. He felt that he was losing that self-awareness. Since returning to Flogsta, it was no longer clear to him that he was on a mission, that his presence in Uppsala was part of some grander purpose. He had come all this way, and at such great expense, jeopardizing his academic standing and, as a result, his draft deferment, to what end? What was he doing here? Whom had he become? He had never enrolled in the university, he had pretty much dropped out of the language class, he would probably earn no academic credits, the friends he had made as Spiegel he had spurned when he posed as Aaronson, the celebrity he had gained as Aaronson he had renounced when he returned to his life as Spiegel. His abnegations and sacrifices had, so far, led only to confrontations and confusions. The movement in Uppsala, without Aaronson's leadership, was drifting aimlessly, no more able to stop the war than a skiff can stop the tide. Across the world, the firefights raged in the tropic air, the bombs dropped on the rice paddies, the body counts tolled on the news night after night—and the Americans in Sweden were up in arms about housing vouchers and vocational training. If they knew how ineffective we are up here, how mired in trivialities and in petty bureaucratic disputes, they would put all the would-be deserters and resisters on the Baltic Express, Spiegel thought. The war machine runs more efficiently without us.

Perhaps they want us here.

But no, that couldn't be. For life in Uppsala, in Sweden, despite the cavils and complaints by the Zekes, the Worms, the Aaronsons of the world, was, all in all, pretty soft. The housing was good, the government took care of your most basic needs, the wages were decent, the working conditions were excellent, there was always an open door to further education, and, let's face it, the girls were stunning. And if most of them turned out to be as cold and unfathomable as glacial ice, there were some whose hearts would melt at the approach of an American war resister, a streak of light across the dark skies of their isolated and seemingly predestined lives. If the American soldiers, the kids being drafted out of the deadliest urban ghettos or the remote Midwestern prairies knew that, with little risk, with near impunity, they could lay down their arms and establish a new life in a secure and prosperous nation, how many more would desert? How many would shed their citizenship like a second skin and slip into the silky borrowed robes of expatriate sanctuary? The movement would be like a river flowing north, spreading like a flood across the plains, obliterating the landscape, soaking the dry earth with a great tide of peace.

And if that were so, if the army's criminal-intelligence division had any concerns at all that the trickle toward the north could become a stream and then a torrent, the smartest thing that they could do would be to let the resisters alone to squabble among themselves, to pick one another apart, to complain like spoiled children about their mistreatment by the Swedes, to gripe about their rights and to file grievances about perceived wrongs, in short to present a tear-streaked, pouting face to the world and to make the movement seem to be petty, impulsive, and doomed.

I must have been a fool, Spiegel thought, to agree to stay in Uppsala until Aaronson comes home. How long might that be? Tracy had heard nothing from Aaronson for weeks. Maybe Aaronson would remain out of touch for several more weeks, maybe for months. Maybe he had left forever. If that were so, Spiegel had no more reason to stay in Uppsala. He could go to the American embassy, tell them he had lost his passport, and apply for a replacement. And if his doing so threw a spotlight onto Aaronson, so what? Spiegel had already given him enough time to get himself home free and out of danger.

Yet how could he explain that he had lost his passport? The American officials would believe that he had given, or sold, his documents to the antiwar movement. They would hold him, interrogate him, threaten him with fines and with prison. They would open his case again, back in the States, figuring that he had been part of Aaronson's conspiracy from the beginning, that he had not been just an innocent dupe busted because of police incompetence. They would suppose that he had been a straw man, set on fire to distract the pigs, a blaze that burned bright but quick to give Aaronson enough time to escape.

Maybe if he did walk into the embassy, they would spring the trap. They would sit down across from him with steely eyes. They would hold the pen out toward his shaky hands, and when he signed his name to the long confession that they had typed, they would pat him on the shoulder, hand him a new passport, and look at him as if to say, "What took you so long?"

Grappling with these thoughts cleared Spiegel's head. He swung his feet out of bed and took a few long gulps from the glass of water that he had with foresight set on the floor. His tongue felt like a cardboard blotter, and it swelled as his body absorbed the liquid, seemingly directly into his cells. Sunlight was streaking through the slats in his window blinds, and from the courtyard below he heard the sounds of the students rushing out to catch the early bus into town. He heard the rise and fall of Swedish, the vowels skipping over the hard consonants like rocks bounced off the surface of a lake. He could decipher a phrase now and again, but he could not fit the elements together into a coherent structure. He had been exposed to the language long enough so that he could see some phrases as distinct units in his mind. But when he heard the language spoken, the sounds all jumbled together.

Spiegel stood and stepped gingerly toward the desk. He picked up the letter to Iris that he had begun the day before. He folded it and slipped it in among his books. Maybe writing to her, at least while Aaronson was still out of the country, was not such a hot idea. Who knows who might see the letter? Spiegel fingered through his language book, *Svensk för er*—Swedish for you. Or, Swedish for the ear, as he called it. Maybe he should get back to the classroom. It was a new week, and he could make a fresh start, pick up where he had left off, consummate that sundered relationship with Fröken Fält. If he took a quick shower, he might catch the late bus and get to class before the first break. As he set the book back on his desk, he heard a rapping at his door.

"Lenny, Lenny, are you awake?" It was Jorge.

He had been with Melissa, evidently. It looked as if they had spent the night in a state of war. Jorge's eyes were dark, his skin scored with scratch marks. His hair, usually sculpted with architectural precision, was a matted tangle of black wire. He was wearing a silk robe without a belt. He clutched the folds closed with his fist.

"It was your little dish Tracy on the telephone," Jorge said. Spiegel had given her Melissa's number—Melissa was the only one he knew in the complex with a phone in her room—in case she had to reach him in an emergency. "I think she must be interested in you, still."

Spiegel was in no mood to snap at the bait. If Tracy had called him, at this hour, something had gone wrong. "Tell her to hang on," Spiegel said, slipping into a pair of jeans. "I'll be right over."

"No, don't go anywhere," Jorge said. "That was her message."

"You mean she hung up? Didn't she want to talk to me?"

"She said she would be coming to Flogsta. She wanted me to make sure you stay here. She is on her way."

"Okay," Spiegel said. "I'll shower and get dressed."

"Then come to our suite. She will meet you there."

"Lisbet's?"

Jorge looked at Spiegel and laughed. "Of course not. Melissa's."

Spiegel had not been in Melissa's room for several weeks. The place was much more cluttered than it had been when he first visited her. The walls were still hung with her neatly arranged displays of black-and-white photography and psychedelic poster art. But the floor was almost unnavigable. Heaps of clothing, men's and women's, had been tossed into the corners. The bedding was scattered across the floor. The rya rug was strewn with matchsticks and ashes. Candles and wads of incense were massed on the desktop and the bureau. Many of the candles had been toppled, and they sat in pools of hardened wax. The room had the air of a votive shrine that had been sacked by Vandals.

Melissa stood at the mirror, brushing her hair.

"How are you feeling, after last night?" she asked.

"What's the Swedish word for Alka-Seltzer?" Spiegel said.

"I don't know. Maybe, *skål*?" She turned to look at him. There was a slight cut above her lip.

"Your mouth okay?" he asked.

"Bitch wears a ring."

"Her engagement ring, perhaps."

"Look, it's broken," Melissa said. She leaned close to Spiegel, and touched the top of her finger to her mouth.

"Her ring?"

"My tooth."

"You could get it capped."

"I think it will make my smile more sexual. It will give me the damaged look."

"Yes, you'll look feral," he said. She looked at him, puzzled. Let her guess, he thought.

Spiegel could hear the shower running. Tails of steam puffed from beneath the jamb of the bathroom door. He imagined that Jorge would be in there a long time, tending to his grooming.

"I'm sorry Tracy woke you up," Spiegel said.

"I'm late for rehearsal, anyway," Melissa said. "Can you hand me that?" She pointed to a small steel box, jammed between her mattress and the wall. Spiegel had to sit on her bed and lean over the feather pillows to reach the box. A spicy scent rose to him in a little cloud as he sat back on her crumpled coverlet. He felt a slight stirring of sexual arousal until he realized that the perfumes he had detected were not from Melissa's hair and skin. The scent was Jorge's.

"Thanks," Melissa said, and popped open the case with a small key. She removed a stack of papers and shuffled through them.

"What are you doing?" Spiegel asked.

"It's my script." She was mouthing lines to herself as she tucked her blouse into her black jeans.

"I thought you were in the chorus."

"No," she said. "I've been discovered. I might get to play Kristin, if I can learn to cook. She spends most of the first act fucking around in the kitchen."

"I don't think you want to do that," Spiegel said, remembering her curry.

"Yeah, I really want to be Julie."

Spiegel leaned back against the wall and asked Melissa about Tracy's call.

Melissa turned to him and spoke quietly, her voice almost drowned by the steady cascade of Jorge's marathon shower. "She was worried," Melissa said. "She thought you had gone."

"Gone where?"

"Jorge told her he thought you had gone home with Lisbet."

"He what? Why would he think that?"

"It would have made things more interesting."

"You mean, more convenient. For him."

"What about for you?" Melissa said.

"Maybe I still have a little sense of loyalty to Jorge. I think you'll be through with him soon enough, and he'll go back to her like a dog with his tail between his legs."

"And until then? What's wrong with Lisbet?"

"I'm not sure I'm a match for her."

"No? That's too bad," Melissa said. "Then I guess I'll have to beat the shit out of her myself."

She might be serious, Spiegel thought, and he was about to answer when there was a knock on the door. "It's me," a voice called from the hallway. "Tracy."

Melissa let her in.

"Thank God," she said, and she dashed across the room. She clutched Spiegel tight to her, startling him with the strength of her embrace. "I'm so glad I caught you here. You haven't gone out this morning yet, have you? You haven't been out at all?"

"I was thinking about going back to class," Spiegel said. "But I was afraid I missed too much and they'd make me sit in the corner."

"Well, you're not going back, so don't worry."

"I wasn't worried," Spiegel said. But he was starting to resent her presumptions, the way she had begun to appropriate his life as if he were no more than a tool in her hands, a little chisel with which she could chip away at a block of wood or, if necessary, pry open a door.

"I see we have a visitor," Jorge said. He emerged from the shower followed by a cloud of steam and cologne. His silk robe swished as he stepped into the room, and Jorge's thin frame and hollow chest seemed lost amid the voluptuous folds of the fabric. He set down his chestnut-wood hairbrush and took Tracy's hand to his lips. "Welcome to our house," he said.

"Look," Tracy said. "I think the shower was a good idea."

Jorge let her hand drop and looked at her in amazement. "You would like to shower?" he asked, puzzled.

"No, the water. Keep it running. In case anyone is trying to tape us."

"Tape-record?" Jorge said. "But why? I do not sing in the shower."

"Anything could be going on here. This place could be bugged. With the water going . . . "

"You've read too many spy novels," Melissa said.

"Or not enough."

"Okay, forget it. I'm probably being paranoid," Tracy said. "I can trust you guys, though, right? I have to."

"What's the problem, Tracy?" Spiegel asked. Despite his smoldering annoyance at her untimely visit and at her proprietary tone, he realized that she would not have driven out to Flogsta on a whim. Something must have troubled her, frightened her. He had no idea how he could help, or even if he should.

"You don't read the newspapers, do you?" Tracy said. She looked around at all three of them.

Jorge shrugged. "Just the photographs," he said.

"Just the reviews," Melissa said.

"Just the obituaries," Spiegel said. "Just kidding," he added.

"Then you haven't seen the story," Tracy said. "There's a warrant out for your arrest."

"Arrest?" Jorge said. "For last night? Surely it was not his fault, about the fight. And as for the bill, I will speak to Mario—"

"They should arrest that bitch," Melissa said.

Tracy ignored her. "Someone's been seen trying to cross the border illegally," she said to Spiegel, "and the police have put out the word that it's you. Here, look at this." Tracy pulled from her purse a rolled-up copy of the morning paper from Stockholm.

Spiegel scanned the story. The only words he recognized were those of his own name. His hands began to shake. "Holy shit," he said. "How did you find this?"

"Monika. She called me yesterday."

"The girl who was on the TV with me?"

"Then it was *you* that we saw on that show!" Jorge said.

"Those goons in the club last night were right," Melissa said. "You're a TV star."

"You better explain everything to them," Spiegel said.

"Yes," Tracy said. "You have to know." She explained that she had come out to Flogsta that night to cut Spiegel's hair so that he could pass for Aaronson. She told them about the television show, and how it had ended in chaos.

"And after that," Spiegel said, "I thought I was done. I could come back to Flogsta and enroll in school again and maybe earn some credits and go home at the end of the semester, having done my bit, played my part, carried my share of the weight."

"Man, you have carried more than your share," Jorge said.

"So what happened at the border?" Melissa asked. "Can anyone read that newspaper?"

It was just a short item near the bottom of an inside page. In the margin, Monika had scribbled a rough translation:

The Swedish border police have issued an arrest warrant for a man, believed to be an American student, who was seen attempting to enter the country via the Hälsingborg ferry while carrying a handgun.

The man was identified as Leonard Spiegel, who has been active with the antiwar student movement at his university in the United States.

Spiegel had been arrested in America and charged with damaging government property, a military draft office, but the charges against him were dropped.

It is unknown why he was carrying a handgun or where he had obtained the gun.

It is believed that Spiegel was enrolled as an exchange student at Uppsala University. It is unknown how long he had been abroad or where he had traveled. The border police have stated that they intend to turn Spiegel over to American authorities, who will hold him for questioning and for possible deportation or trial.

"Aaronson," Spiegel said. "He's screwed."

"Yes. Somebody must have been watching him. The police caught up with him, they wanted him for questioning, but he eluded them once again. They think he's you."

"Just what you wanted."

"Hey, easy," Tracy said. "At least he's not under arrest."

"But why did Monika call you?" Spiegel asked. "How did she know anything about me?"

"She didn't, at first," Tracy said. "We got together for coffee yesterday, and we had a long meeting. She asked me for help.

Her student group monitors all the papers. The Stockholm headquarters had just sent her this news clipping. They asked her to find out about 'Leonard Spiegel,' and if he was really an American student in Uppsala."

"I see," Spiegel said, although he was not sure that he did. "So how much did you tell her?"

"I told her everything," Tracy said. "How you have always been mistaken for Aaronson, how you took on his role, his life, that you even took his place on the TV broadcast."

"Why did you tell her?" Spiegel asked. "The fewer people who know that Aaronson's gone, the safer he is. Why not let her just go on thinking I'm Aaronson until we figure out exactly what happened at the border?"

"She can help us figure that out," Tracy said. "We need help."

"I do, too," Melissa said. "I'm confused." She turned to Spiegel. "So this guy Aaronson was the one they saw at the border? And the police think he's you?"

"Right," Tracy said. "He'd been using Lenny's passport. So now we have to lie low and give Aaronson a chance to get back across the border."

"He can't cross into Sweden with my papers, now that I'm a wanted man."

"He'll find another way," Tracy said.

"I ought to try to get out the word, at least to the people who care about me, that I'm here, that I'm safe."

"I don't think so," Tracy said. "We have to wait them out. Either they'll drop the charges against you or they'll take some steps to find out more about you. But until we know that Aaronson is safe, you have to come home with me. You have to go back to being Aaronson, to give him some cover. Can you do it?"

"Of course," Spiegel said. "But so many people know who I am. They've seen me, since the TV show. It will be hard to convince them, to make them believe that I'm not here, that I haven't been here . . . "

"We'll have to work up a story that you left the country for

Denmark a few days ago," Tracy said. "When was the last time you went to language class?"

"Not for nearly a week. But other people have seen me."

"Like who?"

"We won't say a word," Jorge said.

"I know you won't, but there's Luis, and Lisbet."

"I will talk to them," Jorge said.

"And those drunks in the club last night."

"Yes. At least *they* thought you were Aaronson," Melissa said.

"But I told them I wasn't. I told them I'd never been on TV."

"Fuck, we can't waste any more time," Tracy said. "We have to get you out of here. Let's just pack up your stuff so it looks like you went away for a weekend or something and get you back to my place."

"Come on, Jorge," Spiegel said. "You can help me pack. And when I'm gone, if you want it, you can have my room."

"Thank you," said Jorge. "I will treat it like one of my own."

"Yes," Spiegel said. "I'm afraid you will."

Not until that evening, when Spiegel had unpacked his duffel once again and settled back into the by now familiar environment of Tracy's apartment, did Tracy tell him all that she knew about Aaronson.

They were sitting at her kitchen table, drinking tea. For two days, the phone had been ringing. People wanted to talk to Aaronson about his fight with Edström. The *Herald Tribune* was asking for an interview. The Social Democrats offered support and asked if Aaronson could speak at one of their May Day rallies. The American Deserters Committee in Stockholm issued a call for a nationwide mobilization to combat racism and violence, and they were pressing Aaronson to release a statement and provide testimony. Tracy had been fending off the requests, telling everyone that Aaronson had to "get his head back together." She had also been trying to work things out with ARMS. She'd called an emergency session of the steering committee and told Zeke, Reston, and the Worm what little she knew about Aaronson. She told them of her plan to have Spiegel continue living with her until Aaronson's safe return to Uppsala. The guys were willing to go along with her scheme and to shield Spiegel, even from the membership of ARMS, at least for a short time, but not forever. Their loyalty to Aaronson, or their dependence on his skill at organization and finance, was waning during his long and troublesome absence. "He's supposed to be our leader, and he ain't leading us nowhere," Zeke said.

But Tracy argued that if Aaronson took a hit it could be fatal to the whole ARMS movement, that they could not abandon him in his time of crisis, and her arguments prevailed. "We'll give him a week to show his face or to get us some word of his plans," Reston said.

Give him to May Day, Tracy pleaded. Till then but no longer, they said.

"If he ain't back by then," Zeke said, "I'm taking over the leadership, and Reston will handle the finances."

Tracy agreed. What did it matter to her? If Aaronson was still gone by May Day, there would no longer be any reason for her to stay in Uppsala. Trying to hold together the ARMS movement, trying to keep Zeke and Reston in line, she felt like a thin tether between two wild dogs tied to a rotting post. At some point, the tether would snap.

She explained the deal to Spiegel: He would have to keep a low, almost a flat-line, profile. She would tell the ARMS rank and file that Aaronson was exhausted after his trip to Germany, that he was leaving the daily operations up to the steering committee. Spiegel would have to stay in the apartment, and if he did leave he would have to avoid going to places where people might recognize him as Spiegel.

"I guess I am under arrest," Spiegel said.

"Does it feel that way?" Tracy asked.

"No. Prison would be different. There are parts of this I like."

"The food? The view?"

"The company."

"Yes, I think we can make the most of this."

Spiegel wondered then, for a moment, exactly what she

meant, if her insistence that he move back to her apartment could in any way be taken as an overture. He liked being near her. He regretted not pushing his advantage right after the TV show. He should have gone back home with her that night. His long night of drinking in the Penny Lane, he realized, was a kind of penance for his foolishness. But fate had done for him what he could not do for himself, restoring him to Tracy's proximity. This time, he would not give way to a ghost.

Tracy broke the silence that had set in between them. "I have a confession to make," she said.

"Bless me, Father, for I have sinned."

"Not that sort of confession." Tracy smiled. "I just want to clear the air a little bit here. I want to straighten some things out because we may be together for a while."

"Sure," Spiegel said. "Go ahead." He could feel his heart race. He was drawn to Tracy, and his longing for her was something light and delicate that could be lifted into the air by the slightest wisp of feeling. But it could easily, if it were caught in adverse currents, crash to the ground and be crushed beneath the weight of words.

"It's about that guy who gave you that pamphlet, the guy you fought with on the train."

Spiegel let out a little hiss of air. "I thought you were going to say something about you, about us."

"It is about us. It affects both of us, and Aaronson as well. You have to know."

Spiegel looked out the window to shield from Tracy's view his reaction, his disappointment.

"We know that guy. Or maybe not him exactly, but we know his group, his church. Aaronson had some contact with them when he first arrived in Europe."

"He converted?" Spiegel turned back to Tracy, eager to catch all the nuances of what she was about to say.

"Hardly that. They're insane right-wing fanatics, vowing poverty and eternal devotion to some divine priest who's supposed to live on an unmoored boat that drifts around the Baltic. That's not really Aaronson's style of worship. But he was forced into some business dealings with the church, in order to arrange his safe passage through Europe. I don't know all the details. But I know there was some unfinished business, too. He was going to handle another shipment to the church. I don't know what and I don't know when."

"So you're saying it wasn't just chance that one of the believers sat with me on the train and tried to beat me into submission."

Tracy nodded.

"They thought I was Aaronson."

"Yes," she said. "They were trying to convey a message to him."

"But how did they know he would be on that train?"

"That's one thing I don't understand," Tracy said. "Someone must have tipped them off, told them to keep a watch on the Gare du Nord. It had to be someone who knew when you were traveling and who wanted either to screw Aaronson, or to screw you."

Who could that have been, Spiegel wondered. Iris? Brewer? Tracy? Aaronson himself? Nobody else knew the details of his route or his destination.

"They've been watching you closely ever since you were arrested in the States," Tracy said, "and since you took up with Iris and Brewer and their crowd on campus."

"Who's *they*?" Spiegel asked.

"The CIA, the FBI, the military police, everybody. They knew you were coming here. They're still watching you. It's just that . . . they're not sure who you are."

Spiegel was silent for a moment.

"If they do get Aaronson at the border—or anywhere in Europe—his best hope is to keep your identity and face whatever charges they're going to lay on him as you," Tracy said. "You have a clean record. The worst they'd do to you is pull your passport and ship you home. Aaronson could handle that. He could figure out a way to get himself back here to Sweden, so long as you let him hang onto your name. That's another reason why you have to get used to being Aaronson."

"I have gotten used to it. I am used to it," Spiegel said, and he reached across the table to take Tracy's hand, to draw her toward him slowly, to test her resistance. The room was silent, and the air between them was still. Spiegel parted his lips, just slightly, not to speak but to signify, through a gesture, his vulnerability and his readiness to unfold, like a tender plant exposed to the first sunlight of spring, beneath her radiance and her warmth. Tracy gripped his hand, and her fingers were pliant, alive, like small wild creatures. He could feel her breath on his face, and as her soft lips touched his he set his hand on the hollow of her back. She was standing above him, and the tendrils of her hair brushed against his face, like rain. He reached up to hold her, to touch her shoulders, to bring her down to him. But his hands could not find her, and suddenly she was not there. She'd broken the embrace, the contact, and stepped away from him. Her hip bumped the table, and the dishes rattled.

"I'm sorry," Tracy said. "I can't. Not now."

"It's okay," Spiegel said, although he didn't mean that. He was shaken, and a bit angry, as if he had been led on, perhaps by Tracy, perhaps through a willful misinterpretation of her feelings, fed by his own stunted desires. "When he comes back, I would let you go."

"It's not just Aaronson," Tracy said. "It's Iris."

"Iris? But we agreed, before I left, that we would both be free—"

"How would you feel if you learned she was with somebody else?"

"I'd feel all right," Spiegel said, without much conviction. "I haven't heard from her once. I don't even know where her head's at right now."

"But she's my best friend," Tracy said.

"And she sent me to you."

"It would be too confusing for me," Tracy said. "You're too much like him. I don't know." She shook her head, and turned away from Spiegel. "I have to think about it," she added.

"Yes, there's a lot to think about," Spiegel said. "It's been a hell of a long day."

What he thought about, that night, as he lay across the thin mattress on Tracy's living-room floor, looking up through the tall windows at the circles of lamplight and the bare branches that tipped in the night breeze and scraped against the casements and the glass like bony fingers, was the image of Tracy, hovering above him like a cloud, permeating the room, the air, his flesh, as if she were a thick fog that surrounded him, smothered him, and he was lost inside her, groping to find his way out into the clear.

In the next room, Tracy lay quietly, straining to hear the sounds of Spiegel's fitful sleep. She could hear him rustling against the sheets, shifting and tossing like a ship held at anchor on stormy waters. She flicked on her light and shook loose her long hair. She walked softly into the living room and stood by the window. The night had grown wild and stormy. The street lamp cast Tracy's long shadow across the floor, to the edge of the mattress where Spiegel sprawled, a castaway washed up on an island, wrestling with his dreams. Tracy stepped closer to the window, and she leaned back against the cold glass so that her shadow moved and her image spread itself toward Spiegel like an inky tide. She waved her hands and let the shadows dance over the walls and the floor, enjoying the sensation of being a solitary form at play over a sleeping figure, shielding him from the storm, keeping him in the dark.

10

"Hej," said the man at Tracy's doorway. He had walked right up to the second-floor landing. She had been careless and left the foyer door unlocked. It had been a crazy night.

"*Kan ni prata svenska?*"

"Only a little," she said. "English would be better."

"English it is," he said, with a goofy enthusiasm, as if Tracy had just guessed the answer to a profound and complex riddle. "I like to speak English, every chance I get. Especially with Americans. The English of the English, that's almost a dead language, don't you think so? Like Latin."

"I really don't know."

"But you Americans speak the living tongue. Westward the course of empire, and so on."

The man was tall, even for a Swede, but gangly, Ichabod Crane–like, and he seemed to stoop even in Tracy's high-ceilinged Victorian entryway. He had thick brown hair that stuck straight up like the bristles on a shoe brush, and he wore heavy eyeglasses set in square steel frames, like girders that seemed to brace his eyebrows together, giving his face the look of a project under construction.

"Who are you?" Tracy asked. "What do you want?"

"To talk, of course," the man said. "You're Tracy Green, aren't you? I have been following your career for some time. So I consider us to be practically old friends, you know."

"But I don't know you," Tracy said.

"A technicality!"

She grabbed the handle, ready to shut the door on him.

"Don't do that," he said. "You know that they're all going to want to talk to you, once they find out where you live. But I think you should talk only to me."

"Because we're old friends?"

"Because I was the first to find you."

"Great, you win the scavenger hunt."

"Sorry?"

"It's sort of a game that kids play, that—why am I talking to you? I don't know you."

"But you do know something about my character. Here," he said, and handed her a business card.

Gunnar Mendelsohn. *Uppsala Tidskrift. Editor och ecrivit.*

"You're a reporter," she said.

"And editor. It's good that way. So when I fall asleep on the job or take the day off to go fishing, my editor, I mean me, does not get too mad. Unfortunately, I also have to fill in for myself when I take a holiday because someone has to be there to do the work."

"How many people work there?"

"It's very small."

"I don't really want to talk to the press," Tracy said.

"Have you read the *UT,* though?" Mendelsohn said. "Probably not, because it's printed in Swedish, of course. I mean that's the language that we speak here, in Sweden, and—"

"I try to read the paper," Tracy said, "as a way to keep up on the news, and the language, but I read the—"

"*Svenska Dagbladet.* But that is the paper of—how do you say it? The Establishment. Or maybe you have not noticed?"

"Well, I don't read the editorials," Tracy said. "My Swedish is not that good."

"You can tell things without reading the editorial page, though. For example, the kind of stories they write, or do not write. Have they, for example, written at all about the Americans in Uppsala?"

"A little."

"And when they write about Americans, do they come here, to see you?"

Despite herself, she was beginning to like this guy. Maybe she should invite him in for coffee. She wouldn't have to give him an interview. But it might be a good idea to have a friend in the press, someone to turn to if the hounds got too close to her heels.

"So if they're the Establishment press, what are you?"

"We? We are the journal of ideas. People read the other newspapers in Sweden if they want just the facts. They read the *UT* if they want to think. Our readers expect us to question authority. So we never accept the official version of the news events. We follow our leads as far as they will take us, until we find the truth, the real story."

"You're saying you print stuff that no other paper prints? Like *Ice Age Creature Devours Helsinki? Girl Gives Birth to her own Grandmother?*"

"No, no, no, not like that. We are interested in political stories, issues, investigations. We have sources in many agencies that speak only to us, especially when they want to expose their views to the Swedish people. So when people read an article in the *UT*, even if no other paper has the story, they know there is some truth, or somebody's true beliefs, behind what we write. You have to read the *UT* to get the whole picture."

"Even if I don't read Swedish?"

"May I come in?"

Tracy apologized about the condition of her place. Spiegel's belongings spilled from his upturned duffel, and his clothes from the night before lay scattered about the living-room floor. Somehow, Spiegel had rolled up the mattress and pushed it into a corner beside the couch. The sheets and thin blanket had been tossed over an armchair, like a shroud. She could hear Spiegel fumbling with the faucets in the bathroom.

"I'm sorry," Mendelsohn said. "You have company."

"No. He lives here," Tracy said. "You'll meet him in a minute. He slept in."

"I see," he said. And Tracy was afraid that he did see, that as he scanned the scene, like a classicist among the ruins of ancient Troy, he would detect that he was walking on the grounds of a battlefield, not poking about among the pottery and utensils that would mark the site as a family domicile.

She was pouring coffee through the drip filter as Spiegel stepped into the kitchen, toweling dry his hair. She introduced him as Aaronson, "my old man."

"Yes, yes, great to meet you," Mendelsohn said, holding his bony hand out to Spiegel. "Your group, wonderful, the things you've done for the Americans in Uppsala, I couldn't agree more."

"Thanks," Spiegel said, and he gave Tracy a look, as if to say: Who is this nut?

"Gunnar Mendelsohn is with the press," she said.

"I thought—"

"Now I'm not doing a story on the Americans, per se," Mendelsohn said. "Though I think it's a great topic, and I would like to, someday—"

"Then why is he here?" Spiegel asked Tracy. "He's a reporter, and I thought we were going to stay clear of all that—"

"Yes, I don't blame you, not a bit," Mendelsohn said. "Saw you on that panel. It was horrible, what they did to you. But as I was explaining to Tracy, here—"

"He's on our side," she said. "The left-wing press. And in fact—"

"In fact I was telling Tracy that I'm here to try to find out about somebody else, you see, another American, a friend of yours I suppose."

Spiegel joined them at the table. "Do you mean Lenny Spiegel?" he said.

"That's the one."

"Yes, we read about him," Tracy said. "He tried to carry a gun onto the ferry."

"Oh? You did know him then?"

"Of course. There are so few Americans in Uppsala. We pretty much all know one another."

"And he was from your college, back in the States."

"Yes," Spiegel said. "But we didn't know him there."

"Just a coincidence he came here?"

"Not exactly," Spiegel said. "He did look us up once he got to Uppsala. We have friends in common at home. So maybe he decided to stay here because of us, because he met us."

"But then, he didn't stay, did he?"

"What paper did you say you're from?" Spiegel asked. This guy's goofy looks were deceiving. With a strange acuity, he could spot the chinks in a story.

"The *UT*. We're more like—how do you say it?—a weekly: commentary and analysis, the odd feature story, that sort of thing. You should give us a look."

"My experiences with the press have not been all that good."

"Wrong press then, I think. Have they been bothering you, trying to find out everything you know about this Spiegel fellow?"

"No," Tracy said. "You're the first to bother us."

"I'm sorry."

"It's just that, you know, we didn't know him all that well."

"Are you sure?" Mendelsohn said. He took a long, greedy sip of the coffee. "Fellow American, same college, he looks you up once he gets to Uppsala, surely he must have told you something about his travel plans."

Maybe Mendelsohn knows that we're putting him on, Tracy thought. Maybe he has been watching us from a distance for weeks, months. Maybe he's leading us along, playing a game with us before he pounces.

"We don't really know him or his plans," said Tracy. "Could be it was Lenny Spiegel they're looking for at the border. Or it could have been that they want someone else. It might be a case of mistaken identity."

"Such things do happen," Mendelsohn said. "But usually not as a mistake. Perhaps they are seeking someone who was using Leonard Spiegel's passport. Or someone who has stolen it."

"Why do you think that?" Spiegel said. "Do you have any information about Spiegel?"

"Do you?" Mendelsohn asked. "If you do, perhaps I can, as the saying goes, put two and two together and make—five."

Spiegel and Tracy looked at each other. This guy had to know something. He was plugged into the circuit, and the circuit was alive. How else would he have known that Aaronson, Tracy, and Spiegel were connected? How else would he have followed the loose wire back this far, right to their lair? They didn't speak, but somehow the understanding passed between them: They should open the door a little to Mendelsohn, let him learn a little bit about what they knew, and see if he could somehow lead them to Aaronson.

"Lenny Spiegel is not in Denmark," Tracy said. "We believe that someone else was using his passport."

"As I thought," said Mendelsohn.

Spiegel swallowed and tried to catch Tracy's eye again. How far would she go? He thought she had gone far enough already, maybe too far.

"It just made no sense to me that someone carrying a gun into Sweden, if in fact he was doing so, would carry his own passport," Mendelsohn said. "But then, why would this Spiegel give up his passport? Was it politics? Money?"

"What makes you think he gave it up?" Spiegel said.

"Well, how else would the gentleman have come upon it? A passport isn't something that one finds lying about in a hedge-row, is it? I think someone must have approached your friend with an offer. Just wanted to borrow his passport, for a week, you see."

"And who would have done this?"

"Whoever wanted the services of a man with a gun. Perhaps the Sweden First Party. They're the ones you had your little tiff with, on the air. They don't like immigrants, as you know."

"I don't think Spiegel would have had anything to do with those creeps," Tracy said.

"But he wouldn't have known who they were. They might have told him they were part of the resistance, your antiwar movement. Maybe he loaned someone his passport in the mistaken belief that it was for the cause. Was he foolish enough to do that?"

"Lenny is sort of naive. I mean, he had very little to do with the antiwar movement back in the States, or here for that matter. But he's no fool."

Spiegel was relieved to hear Tracy say that. The words sounded good to him, even though he knew that she was just blowing smoke.

"Or maybe he knew he was helping that fascist group," Mendelsohn said. "Maybe he only pretended to be sympathetic to your antiwar movement. Maybe his real mission in Sweden was to help crush the movement. Maybe he was an enemy agent, placed in your midst. Did you do a background check on him, ever?"

"No," Tracy said.

"That's too bad. No telling what might turn up. They say that his father works for the American government, you know."

"America's a big country. Lots of people work for the government," Spiegel said. "But that's beside the point."

"I think the real point," Mendelsohn said, "is to find him."

"That won't be easy," Spiegel said. He was anxious. Mendelsohn was the first person he had come across in Uppsala who seemed to know about his father's work. How could that be? Spiegel wondered. Had Mendelsohn been sent to convey a message, to him, or to Tracy?

"It shouldn't be so hard to find him," Mendelsohn said. "If he gave up his passport, how far can he have gone? He must be somewhere in Sweden, of course."

"I don't think so," Tracy said. "We were told he went off on a trip, to Denmark."

"Yes, he could have sold his passport there," Mendelsohn said. "Then he would report the papers missing, stolen, whatever."

"No, you've got him all wrong," Tracy said. "He wasn't hard up for cash. And he wouldn't have sold his passport for a kick."

"But you said that he was . . . naive. And I had heard that, too. That he was a bit of a simpleton, a fool. Came here looking to get involved, not sure why, one of those aimless, wandering Americans that one sees in all of the train stations of Europe, asleep on the benches, their blue jeans ripped at the knees, resting their heads against aluminum-framed backpacks that cost as much as a small Italian car."

"Spiegel wasn't like that," Spiegel said, a bit defensively. Who was it, he wondered, who called him a simpleton? Or was he being baited?

"He was maybe naive," Tracy added. "But he learned from experience. Maybe he did come here to find himself. But he came here with a purpose as well. . . . "

"Which was?"

"Let's just say, to help the movement."

"Then why would he leave?"

"Maybe he'd served his purpose."

Mendelsohn shook his head no. "You have told me some things, and now I will tell you some things, in the hope that we can work together. I will help you find your friend. And you will help me to get my story. Because when we find him, I want to talk to him. I want to be the only one."

"An exclusive, we call that in America. A scoop."

"What is it you can tell us?" Spiegel said. "Because I don't think there's that much we can do until Spiegel surfaces, you know, comes up for air. As you say, he's not going to get far without his passport."

"Well, that's just it," Mendelsohn said. "He hasn't gone very far. In fact, I think that he is still in Uppsala."

"Why do you think that?" Tracy said, and Spiegel thought that he could detect a slight weakening, a hesitation in her voice. Did Mendelsohn know much more than he had let on? Maybe they had been far too trusting in talking to him.

"I talked to someone who saw him," Mendelsohn said.

"You did? Where?"

"I was at Flogsta, where Spiegel lives, or lived. His room there, pretty much cleared out, yes. But he didn't take care of the details one looks to before leaving the country: the postal delivery, some food in his cupboard."

"Of course, he planned to come back. He was just traveling."

"And while I was there I talked to a fellow who had been placed on Spiegel's floor, across the hallway. He has watched Spiegel's behavior for some time now."

"That guy Lars, the engineering student?" Spiegel asked.

"You know him? Curious little fellow," Mendelsohn said.

Curious little rat, Spiegel thought. Who had been paying Lars to spy on the foreign students? And how did Mendelsohn know to seek him out?

"What was he, a friend of Lenny's?" Tracy asked. "He'd never said—"

"I don't know about a friend," Mendelsohn said. "But he told me he saw Spiegel there this weekend, and Monday morning as well."

"Doesn't this guy have anything better to do than stare out his window?"

"Who said anything about a window?"

"Didn't you say—"

"He never told me how he saw Spiegel. Maybe in the corridor. Or maybe he observed him from afar."

"Okay," Spiegel said, and he resolved to keep the rest of his thoughts to himself. If Mendelsohn was going to track the scent, let him do so without any further help from the quarry.

"He said something else odd," Mendelsohn added. "He said that he thought he saw you there as well on Monday morning, Tracy."

"Yes, of course I was there," she said. "By that time I was worried about Lenny. We both were. I drove up to Flogsta to see if maybe anyone, any of his friends, had heard from him."

"But I guess you're not a very good reporter," Mendelsohn said. "You learned less than I did. Or perhaps you talked to the wrong friends." And he laughed, showing his yellowed teeth.

Mendelsohn thanked them for the coffee, and told them to stop by his office any time. But he had to get back, to work on some real stories, stories that had, as he put it, "legs to stand on." The search for Lenny Spiegel, while a fascinating pastime, might turn out to be absolutely worthless, from the news point of view. Spiegel could already be on his way to Kennedy Airport, or maybe he was "shacking up" somewhere in Uppsala with some *vakra svenska flicka* he had met at a dance or a club and he would turn up in a day or two at their doorstep and say: Why all this fuss?

"Maybe," Tracy said. "But somehow I doubt it."

"A nice place you have here," Mendelsohn said on his way out. "I like these old-fashioned buildings, high ceilings and all that. Old Vics, we call them. Don't see many in Uppsala, after all, do you?"

"No. Most people like the newer buildings."

"But you prefer an older building. Or was it all you could get, on the housing list?"

"There was plenty available," Tracy said.

"You could apply for a bigger flat, you know. An extra bedroom. Then maybe, well . . ." Mendelsohn shrugged, spread his palms. "A little extra space. It never hurts. There may be guests, people dropping in. You could put them up more easily, you see. I get the housing list in advance. We publish the list in the *UT*, along with the government notices. But I could let you see the list, before we publish it. That way . . . well, that is, if you think you might need better housing."

Tracy's hands were shaking as she told Monika Nuland, later that day, about the strange encounter with Gunnar Mendelsohn. Tracy called Monika after Mendelsohn had gone, leaving behind a business card on which he had scrawled his home phone number, and Monika invited Tracy over for tea. She told her to bring Spiegel along so that they could all try to figure out the significance of the recent news reports. They would try to make sense out of Mendelsohn's visit, as well.

Tracy and Spiegel agreed that there was something underhanded about Mendelsohn. Tracy argued that if he had been driving all around the city, dropping in at odd hours on strangers, without calling ahead, he was in search of more than a news story. She thought he had been sent to track down Spiegel, that he was some kind of police agent, either from the Swedish government or in the pay of the army's criminal-intelligence division.

"Why? What makes you think that?" Monika asked.

"The things he said about me," Spiegel said. "He knew too much."

"He said he had heard about his father," Tracy said.

"What about his father?" Monika asked.

"We try to keep this quiet because it would just make it impossible for him to operate within the movement," Tracy said. She explained about Spiegel's father and his work for the government.

"Are you in touch with him?" Monika asked. "Does he know you are in Sweden?"

"No, we hardly speak. He heard the news when I got into trouble last year, in the States. He offered to bail me out, pull some strings in the judicial branch. But I got out on my own—"

"—time off for good behavior," Tracy said.

"And since then I just drop him a card now and then. I wrote some out before I left the States. A friend back there mails them, once a month. He thinks I'm still at the university, I guess."

"Then it's no problem," Monika said.

"But how did Mendelsohn know about him?" Spiegel said. "I don't believe that he just wandered up to Flogsta and by chance found someone who knew me, who had seen me there on Monday. I think he has been in touch with someone up there who has been watching me the whole time, ever since I came to Uppsala."

"That engineer on your floor? Lars what's-his-name?"

"Apparently, but probably there's someone who knew me better. Someone who was able to lead him to you, Tracy."

"Oh, it's not so surprising he came to call on Tracy," Monika said. "Everyone in Uppsala who knows anything about the political scene knows Tracy. You're a celebrity," she said, raising her teacup and clinking a toast.

"*Skål*," Tracy said.

The teacups were filled with straight vodka. As Spiegel could see from looking around Monika's place, a small cottage on the grounds of the botanical gardens, Monika was a woman of contradictions, but she'd drawn the contradictory elements of her interests and her personality into a pleasant and comforting harmony. Through her mullioned windows Spiegel gazed on neat rows of tufted thistles and pale flowers, their soft petals undulating in the gentle spring breeze. Inside, however, the timbered walls of the cottage were papered with screeds against injustice and oppression, huge posters demanding that the masses take arms against the imperialist dogs and the capitalist swine. The message, trumpeted from the doorposts and the walls, could not rouse Spiegel from the drowsy comfort he felt in Monika's presence. He should probably be holding high a banner and marching in the streets, but he would much rather sink down among the soft cushions of Monika's overstuffed chairs and watch the sun set as he drank her vodka chased by herbal tea.

From the moment he had seen her in the TV studio, Spiegel had been curious about Monika, attracted both by her serene beauty and her ardent political convictions. He was taken, from the first, by her soft and lovely features, her heart-shaped face and her mouth like a teardrop, her breathy and almost girlish voice, her English laced with the fetching hint of a British accent. When she spoke, she stated her views with clarity and confidence; she had stood unafraid before the hectoring of the opportunistic politician and the cynical goading of the spineless moderator. He was sorry, at the time, that he had to deceive her, to make her believe that he was Aaronson. He thought he would like to meet her and to set things right, although he feared that she had hardly noticed him, that in her mind he was just a faded image, obscured by the brighter presences all around him. Monika would never be able to make him out among the long, dark shadows cast by Aaronson and Tracy.

On the way over to Monika's cottage earlier that afternoon, Spiegel had learned from Tracy some of the details of Monika's life. She had grown up in a small village in the far north, and directly after high school had moved to the city, to Stockholm, to work in a counseling center for refugees. Most of her time had been spent trying to get housing vouchers for Turkish construction workers and talking to homesick teenage Finnish maids who wanted to break their contracts and take the ferry home to Helsinki. But she did meet a few of the first wave of American deserters, and she listened to their tales of the horror and the stupidity of the war. Moved by a heartfelt sympathy for the displaced Americans and by a messianic outrage about the war

itself, Monika set up a social-service team that would be devoted
to the needs of the small American community in Stockholm.
They helped many of the deserters to find their first jobs and
apartments. After two years of working in Stockholm, Monika
enrolled in the university in Uppsala to take a joint course of
study in counseling and international politics and to establish a
new branch of the student antiwar society, the SSS. But Spiegel
suspected that there must have been more to her decision to
leave Stockholm. Perhaps her involvement with the Americans
had gone beyond the level of professional services. Perhaps she
had been wounded in love and she had come north to take refuge
from the field of battle, an exile in her own right.

Monika refilled the cups and lit a set of tapered white beeswax
candles that warmed the room with a liquescent, shimmering
light. "I don't think he's a spy," she said. Spiegel, lost in ruminations, had almost forgot that they had come to Monika's to get
the lowdown on Mendelsohn. "He is a real editor. His newspaper
is quite good, actually."

"Maybe he's a spy on the side," Tracy said. "Sort of like a
hobby."

"Hmm. I don't think so. He's not even Swedish, you know."

"No? What is he?"

"A Dane. That's why everyone in Sweden reads his paper so
carefully. He's an outsider. He brings a fresh point of view."

"Which is what?" Spiegel asked.

"Not so much right or left, but inside, under the surface. He
seems to hear about things before anybody else, and when he
prints a story, even if it seems outrageous, everybody knows that
there must be truth in it. He has excellent . . . what's your word
for it?"

"Contacts? Sources?"

"Yes. As you have learned."

"I'm not sure I should stay in touch with him," Spiegel said.

"Oh, don't worry about that. He'll stay in touch with you,"
Monika said.

"Then maybe I should just stay out of his way," Spiegel said.
"I don't think it's such a good idea right now for me to be inter-

viewed by the press. The TV show was one thing, but I don't think I could pretend to be Aaronson through a whole interview. Eventually, I'd slip up, and Mendelsohn would know for sure who I am and that Aaronson's in Europe."

"So if he calls back, I'll just tell him we're lying low," Tracy said. "No press. I'll keep him away from you."

"You could move in here," Monika said, "until you hear from Aaronson again. Until he returns."

"No," Tracy said abruptly. "I want him to stay with me. People may be watching my flat. We have to do whatever we can to make it look like Aaronson is still in Uppsala."

"Do you know where he has gone? If he's okay?"

"I hope he's already made it into Sweden. If not, he'll have trouble at the border with Lenny's passport."

"It's a big country. It's not exactly surrounded by an iron curtain," Monika said.

"More like a Marimekko curtain."

"He'll find a way back," Monika said. "Or he will get word to you."

Monika took a long sip of her tea. Spiegel let his gaze wander from Monika to Tracy and back. Somehow, by her suggestion that Spiegel could move in with her, Monika had raised the temperature of the room. More was at stake than Aaronson's safety, Spiegel realized. For reasons of her own, Tracy wanted him near her. He was flattered and moved by her sudden and unexpectedly firm refusal. But he was stirred, as well, by Monika's solicitude. He smiled at her, although she didn't notice.

Monika put down her teacup. "My group in Stockholm has contacts with the student movement all through Europe," she said. "Perhaps we could get him a message, send him some new documents to help bring him back home. If he is in danger, we could arrange for his security. We have houses, places of hiding, all through Europe. We have used them to shelter others who were running from danger or waiting for new papers."

"Yes, he may need protection," Tracy said. "There's no telling what kind of trouble could be chasing him."

"What do you mean?" Spiegel asked.

"Depending on what Aaronson has done and where he's been, the American government may want to bring criminal charges against him. They may try to convince the Swedish authorities that he's not an ordinary war resister and that his residence permit should be pulled."

"You mean," Spiegel said, "even if he gets back safely to Sweden, he could be held, and deported for trial."

Tracy nodded. She turned to Monika. "If he's in trouble, could your group hide Aaronson for a while?"

"For as long as you need."

"That's good," Tracy said. "We'll talk about that. But first we have to try to find him."

"And then we have to find a way," Monika said, turning to Spiegel, "to make you disappear."

"I'm good at that," Spiegel said. In truth, he felt a strange excitement at the prospect of becoming someone else, a deep sexual shudder that reminded him of the sensation he would sometimes experience as a child, when he thought about diving into the water with his clothes on, as if what he was about to engage in was a both a playful indiscretion and a more serious violation of taboo.

"You don't have to be good at disappearing. All you have to do is be Aaronson," Tracy said. "And we have to make it seem as if Lenny Spiegel has vanished. We don't want people trying to find him in Sweden."

"You're thinking about Mendelsohn."

"Yes. Right now, he believes that Lenny's passport was stolen. Eventually, he will ask the next question. Where has Spiegel gone?"

"Do you have a plan?" Spiegel asked.

Monika stood, and stepped over to the window. She brushed in passing against a small pot of geraniums, and a faint scent of powder drifted through the air, mixing with the vapors rising from the teacups. Monika turned to look outside, at the darkening sky and at her flickering reflection in the window glass. The twin candles cast a double image of her silhouette onto the slope of the low ceiling.

"I don't know," she said. "Do you want to take a walk? I'll show you guys the gardens. They are beautiful at night."

"I think we should probably get home," Tracy said. "You could walk us part of the way."

"That would be nice," Monika said. "But if you both are going home, I think I'll stay here. What is your expression? I have to get my head together."

"Yes," Tracy said, "we all do."

Spiegel stood. His legs were wobbly, and he felt tipsy from the vodka and the sweet tea. He put his hand on the table to brace himself. He turned to say good-bye to Monika, to thank her, but she had stepped aside, and he found himself about to speak to a face on a tattered poster that had been tacked to a kitchen cupboard. He was staring into the shaded eyes of the Black Panther leader Huey Newton, a sash across his chest and a carbine slung over his shoulder, his clenched fist raised in a salute. *You are either part of the problem or part of the solution*, the block letters above him screamed. *You must choose, brother, you must choose!*

Absurdly, Spiegel mumbled something to the poster.

"I'm sorry," Monika said. "Were you speaking?"

"Right on," Spiegel said. "I just said, right on."

"You were talking to the wall? You Americans really are crazy." Monika laughed.

"I like your taste in art."

"You do?" Monika said. "I'm surprised. I think most of these posters are ugly, but I like what they say. I look to them for inspiration. Would you like one?"

"No, I think it would depress me," Spiegel said. "It would feel like someone's in the room yelling at me all the time. But thanks."

"It's nothing. And if you change your mind, well, I have some art posters, too. In my room."

"Yes, and thanks for your offer," Tracy said. She was standing at the doorway, impatient to be going. Monika folded her arms and made no move toward the door. "To get word to Aaronson, I mean," Tracy added.

"Sure," Monika said. "You just let me know what you need, once you decide."

"I will," Tracy said.

Somehow, Spiegel felt that all evening the exchanges between Tracy and Monika had been floating way above his head, like clouds, but that suddenly their words had sharpened and the syllables were zipping past his ears like bullets. Their voices burned through the fog of his vodka-clouded thoughts like two search beacons, revolving in the night, bright enough to alert him to a proximate danger but not sufficient to reveal its magnitude or its source.

11

The office of the *Uppsala Tidskrift* was in the older section of the city, not the quaint Old City where tourists walked the narrow, cobbled streets that zigzagged up the gentle slope from the church to the castle but the working-class quarters, a patch of barracks-like apartments and commercial buildings set on the flatlands beside the railroad tracks and the factories. The broad main street had buckled from hard use and long neglect, the concrete sidewalks had been broken apart by frost and weeds, and every exterior surface felt slightly gritty. A residue of ash that had been spit from the kilns of the nearby brickyard and the smokestacks of the power plant accumulated on the rooftops and window ledges. The newspaper was housed in a low, cinder-block building whose facade was drab and unadorned save for two rectangles of glass brick on either side of the steel door. The windows stared out at the dull street like two dead eyes.

Inside the office, Gunnar Mendelsohn sat at his rickety wooden desk, leaned back in his swivel chair, and propped his feet on a stack of papers and magazines. His worn-down right heel rested on a glossy image of a woman's bare breasts. He was reading over some notes he had typed after his interview with the two Americans. He was trying to decide if he should pull these scraps of information together into a story. An American student living in Uppsala goes on the run. So what? Would the readers care? What they really want from a newspaper, Mendelsohn knew, was the minutiae that affects their lives: schools, crime, culture, and taxes, taxes, taxes.

He employed no staff to speak of, just an occasional intern from the university to help with the layout and skilled workers from the trade school to handle production and distribution. So he couldn't really compete with the daily paper and didn't try to. If readers had to know about the water board, the health commission, or land transfers, they would have to read the daily, and most of them did. But Mendelsohn had attracted a loyal readership by paddling away from the mainstream and following the stories that he alone wanted to explore. If the readers stayed with him, Mendelsohn thought, he could offer them a journalistic product unique in the land, eccentric, unpredictable, quirky, passionate, all in all a newspaper created pretty much in the image of its editor.

And the story he was after this week was about to fall apart just as he should have been going to press. He had to tell the production crew to put everything on hold. The workers were huddled in the back of the plant by the idle presses, grousing, but they had been through this kind of crisis together before, plenty of times. The men would work through the night, like an army besieged, and they would get the job done—at time and a half.

But first, Mendelsohn had to make sense of his story. What he knew was that his instincts had been right. No American exchange student would try to enter the country carrying a gun. But if Spiegel was not really the one that the Americans wanted, Mendelsohn was left with two questions: Who had been seen at the border? And where was Spiegel? And that's where his investigation was falling apart. His Danish contacts, usually extremely forthcoming, referred all inquiries to the Americans. The only response from the Americans was that the matter was under investigation. *Tack så mycket*, Mendelsohn thought. Thanks a lot, for nothing.

But at least he knew that someone had tried to cross the border using Spiegel's passport, and then eluded the authorities. So where was Spiegel? Eventually, he would have to surface to reclaim his papers. If he didn't, the Americans—the State Department, the CIA, Congress, somebody—would begin to look for him. They would demand an investigation. They would

want to know how someone else came to be in possession of
Spiegel's passport. Had he lent it or sold it? Had it been stolen?
Why hadn't Spiegel reported the theft? Had he been silenced,
killed, dumped in the Copenhagen harbor? Wouldn't his fam-
ily want to know where he had gone, where he might turn up?
Wouldn't his friends want to know? Wouldn't everyone?

Yes, they would, but Mendelsohn guessed that the Americans
in Uppsala knew more than they were letting on. Tracy and
Aaronson seemed surprisingly cool about the whole issue, acting
as if they barely knew Spiegel at all. Well, that wasn't so. They
had been seen together throughout the past two months. And,
friendship aside, the disappearance of an American student and
his possible link to a concealed gun could be a huge problem for
the other Americans in Uppsala, further evidence that Americans
were a violent and unstable people and that the resisters were the
worst of a bad bunch. They would never integrate into Swedish
culture. They would bring with them their drugs, their diseases,
their ways of death, all views that were prevalent throughout the
city but were anathema to Mendelsohn himself, who recalled
with a shudder of horror his own shattered childhood, his flight
across the frontier just ahead of the Nazis, family members and
friends left behind to live under the boot heel of the occupation,
forced to wear the yellow star, while the Mendelsohns wandered
like spirits, forever unsettled, moving incrementally, village by
village, up the coast, his father finding piecework as an itinerant
tailor, the shadow of death falling all across Europe but not on
the Mendelsohns, survivors of the wreck, flotsam on the surface
of the neutral land.

Mendelsohn would always be grateful to Sweden for taking
him in, grateful yet slightly resentful of the nation that continued
to treat him like an outsider. He had spent his childhood trying
to find his foothold and his adolescence trying to fit in, and his
life had been torn between proving to others that he was excep-
tional and proving to himself that he was ordinary, just another
Swede. So he understood the forces that were tearing at the
Americans, the strange, combustible mixture of pride and shame
that battled within the soul of all political refugees, shame for

the degradation that had fallen on their native land and a right-
ful pride in their own moral superiority for having turned away
from their country's dishonor. Mendelsohn was determined to
use his resources to help the Americans, his brothers in exile. He
would learn what he could about their missing compatriot, that
Spiegel, and he would tell the Americans what he had learned,
even before he went to the back shop and gave the order to set
the story into type.

"So," Tracy said to Spiegel, later that morning, as they lay on
their backs and watched the sunlight streak through the blinds,
"how does it feel, to have vanished?"

"Hmm," Spiegel said. He turned to nestle against Tracy's
warm body. "Like the old joke about the guy who jumps out the
window. Halfway down, he says: 'So far, not bad at all.' "

"You're an optimist." Tracy sat up, shook her hair loose, and
pulled on a T-shirt that she had tossed to the floor sometime
during the night.

"I tend to look on the bright side," Spiegel said. He was still
curled up in the blankets. He was determined to model his life
on Aaronson's as closely as possible, right down to the bad hab-
its. Sloth, he found, came to him rather easily. "If this is what it
means to disappear, I can take it."

"It's not all that it means. You know that. You're not done
disappearing."

"You mean when he comes back," Spiegel said.

"Then you will really have to vanish."

"But, Tracy—" Spiegel said. He suspected that her attraction
to him had been impulsive and would soon be laced with guilt
and regret. But he was hurt that she voiced her reservations so
readily, practically on waking.

"It's not a question of which one of you I'd like to be with,"
she said. "It's where you can be most useful. We need people back
home who can keep us on the political agenda. I mean, Kissinger
keeps talking about a negotiated withdrawal, and I think for most
of the Americans, that's really all they want: Get us the hell out

of Asia. We don't care if you end the killing. Just save our asses.
Let the gooks kill one another. And I think when he pulls it off,
or pulls us out, which I think he's got to do so they can win the
next election, these guys here will just be forgotten. No one will
remember that they were the first to say no."

"Okay," Spiegel said. He was annoyed by her sudden harangue,
her shift from tenderness to rhetoric. "If you still feel that way,
when Aaronson comes back, then I'll go." But he wondered if by
then it would be so easy for him, or for Tracy.

The night before, she had fought for him and won him like a
prize, a trophy. He'd been full of joyous resolve when they left
Monika's. The night was cool, the sky was starry. They walked
home, along the borders of the botanical gardens, through the
quiet shopping district. The crystal vases and shiny chrome
appliances behind the plate-glass windows looked like jewels and
artifacts on display in a museum. Tracy remarked that she would
never need such material possessions, never want them. To own
a piece of crystal is to make your life as fragile and delicate as
crystal, she said. A sudden move, a loud noise, and everything
would shatter. Tracy wanted a life of—what? Plywood, cardboard, rolled-up mattresses, a cheap car and cheap gasoline, said
Spiegel. How nice it would be, she said, to go places, see wonderful sights, eat strange vegetarian dishes on cliffs overlooking the
wild ocean, if someday we can be free again.

I can travel, Spiegel told her. I'm still free. He was a little
drunk on Monika's vodka and on his own soaring spirits. Would
she travel with me? Spiegel wondered. Can I become a part of
her life? He took her hand, and he felt shy and tentative, like a
schoolboy. She did not resist. She let her hand rest in his.

He accepted that as a signal. It was what he had wanted since
the first night, at the train station, months ago, when he saw her
delicate face in a cloud of frost. He knew even then, it seemed,
that there had been a terrible mistake, that fate had sent him
on the wrong journey. His path had somehow been crossed
with Aaronson's; he was the one who was meant to live here in

Uppsala, in Tracy's arms, in her life. He had the odd sense that, ever since his arrival, the gods had been struggling to right their mistake, to place him on the right course. Aaronson, he was convinced, could sense this, which was why he had been gone so long. It was why he had made no serious attempt to communicate. Only Tracy failed to comprehend the rightness of Spiegel's presence in her life. But perhaps this would be the night. She would grasp his hand and they would leap together, off the precipice, into their fate.

He approached her as she stood before the kitchen sink, gazing out the window at her own reflection, slightly distorted by the mottled glass. He rested his hands on her shoulders and drew her to him with a slight but steady pressure. It's for the movement, he tried to joke, for verisimilitude. In case someone's watching us. No, she said, we can't do this. Is it because of Aaronson? Spiegel asked. You love him that much? I'm not sure who I love, she said. I'm not sure that I love. You could love me, he said. Who knows where he is? Maybe he's left you. Don't worry about him, don't think about him. He tried to kiss her, he leaned his face down to meet her lips, and she was there for him, warm and inviting. His tongue explored the contours of her mouth, the texture of her face, her neck. His fingers played across the light bones of her shoulders and her back, the little bones of her neck, like small shells, the fine and almost musical curve of her ribs, the strong musculature of her legs, her thighs, her ass warm to his touch. Her clothes fell to the floor beneath them. It was as if the fabrics melted away and she stood naked, in a pool of light. She led him back to her room, and he followed her as if he were floating down a river, moving with no effort, drawn by the silent flow of the deep water.

I don't know, she said afterward, as she held him close to her. I just don't know. Her body was slick with sweat, glowing with a feverish heat. Her legs were wrapped around him, locked behind his back, so that he pressed against her, salty and rough.

He spent the night tossed about among weird and violent dreams: He was in a zoo, behind the bars, while a parade of people, grotesque and gargantuan, went strolling by, pointing and laughing, throwing peanuts. He was in an airport, trying to buy a ticket, and the woman at the counter would not speak to him, even though he shouted: Don't you know who I am? Don't you know who I am? And toward morning he dreamed that he was back home, at his doorway, but the door was made of glass and inside he could see Iris. She waved to him, walked to the refrigerator, and stepped inside. May I help you? a voice said. Yes, let me in, Spiegel answered. I'm sorry, said the voice. There's no one here by that name.

"But Tracy," Spiegel said, as he, too, got out of bed, "do you really think that Aaronson is coming back?"

She sighed, turned away. "Yes," she said. "And maybe you think, after last night and all, that I don't care, that I don't want him back. But I do."

"And what if I were to you tell that, after last night and all, I don't?"

"It wouldn't surprise me. That's why I think we made a huge mistake. As soon as sex enters the picture . . ."

"It was always in the picture."

"But now our relationship is sexual instead of political. And now you'll probably . . . oh, forget I said that."

"In other words, you can't trust me anymore? You think I'll do something to jeopardize Aaronson, like spill my guts to Mendelsohn, just so I can have you to myself?"

Tracy didn't answer. Spiegel knew that was exactly what she was thinking. It had crossed his mind as well. He could go to Mendelsohn, explain how he had been brought to Uppsala as Aaronson's double, and Mendelsohn would write a big story.

"I won't do that," Spiegel assured her. "But we have to get the word to Aaronson, maybe through Monika, that if he doesn't come back soon there will be nobody here waiting for him."

"Nobody? Are you so sure?"

Somehow, he was. He knew that Tracy, whether she left with him or not, could not wait forever, Penelope-like, for the return of her wandering hero. "You won't stay in Uppsala, Tracy," he said.

"You've fallen into a bad dream that you'll wake up from, someday, and then you'll head back home, back to a normal life."

"Just click my heels, right?" Tracy took a brush from the dresser top and began combing out her tangled hair.

"You're not facing any charges. You could fly home today, if you could afford the ticket."

"I may not be facing charges right now. But a lot depends on what happens with Aaronson. Haven't you ever heard of a thing called aiding and abetting? Didn't Iris explain that to you? She must have learned about that in Criminal Law one-oh-one."

"You mean, everyone's fate is tied to Aaronson's. If they catch him, we're all in the noose."

"Exactly."

"All the more reason that you should go back to the States while you can. If he gets back here safely, you can always return."

"No, I have to stay," Tracy said. "And we have to do every-thing we can, while he's gone, to give him cover, to make it look as though he's never left Uppsala. We have to think of ourselves as actors, and we have to play our roles every hour, every day."

"Yes, I can do that," Spiegel said. He felt as if their relationship, already framed, so to speak, by his usurpation of Aaronson's identi-ty, was about to be placed at an even further remove, like an object left between facing mirrors, its doubled image arcing and fading away toward an unseen vanishing point. It seemed that Tracy was telling him that they could continue to be intimate only as long as he pretended to be Aaronson and she pretended to believe it.

"And we have to begin right away," Tracy said.

"What more can we do?"

"I mean we have to clean up the evidence, wipe you from the slate. Don't forget, if the police find you, Aaronson is exposed, too. Mendelsohn was just the first one. Pretty soon, the cops will be combing through your place, trying to come up with clues."

"Well," Spiegel said, "it will just look like I've gone away, for a weekend trip or something. They'll find some groceries, my clothes, my books." Spiegel tried to picture his room, to recall what else he might have left behind, and he felt a sudden hollow-ness in his stomach. As his mind's eye scanned the shelf above his desk, he could see a white corner of folded paper, rising above the spines of the books like the flat palm of a drowning man.

"What is it?" Tracy said, alarmed.

"I started a letter to Iris. It may have written down some things . . ."

"And you left it in your room?"

Spiegel nodded. "I folded it and stuck it between some of my books. It must still be there, unless Jorge cleared it out."

"Why would he do that?" Tracy asked.

"To make room for his hairspray?" Spiegel offered.

"I ought to go up there and look," Tracy said.

Spiegel asked if he should come along, but Tracy told him that he had to stay away from Flogsta. Why give Lars another chance to file a report on a suspected Spiegel sighting? The place would be under thorough surveillance soon, Tracy said, with Mendelsohn poking around and the police sure to follow. Unless, Spiegel thought to himself, Mendelsohn and the police are one and the same.

But Tracy need not have worried about surveillance. At midday, when she pulled into the muddy lot, Flogsta was deserted. All the students had gone into town for classes. The six looming towers were empty and still, like shrines. Tracy entered Spiegel's old building. The door at the entryway, improperly fitted, swung loose on a bent hinge. She took the stairs to Spiegel's floor. Her footsteps scratched against the sandy cement. The hallway to Spiegel's room looked like a passage through an Egyptian tomb, a mausoleum. A rhomboid of gray light from the emergency door at the far end of the corridor lay across the salmon-colored carpet, like a floating patch of skin. From behind Spiegel's doorway, Tracy could hear the dull rush of an electric blower. Jorge was at work fixing his hair.

Jorge had settled into Spiegel's room, camping around the few items of furniture that Spiegel had left behind. The Levi's and flannels had been cleared from Spiegel's tiny closet and replaced by silk shirts, flared pants, and black boots of tooled leather. On the countertop, Jorge had set out an opulent display of lotions, ointments, combs and brushes, and exotic colognes in tiny glass ampoules. On the bed, cradled in a nest of woolen blankets, lay Jorge's guitar.

"He wouldn't mind, would he?" Jorge said, as he led Tracy into the room. "I thought, as long as he wasn't going to be needing the room for a while, I would just clash."

"Crash, you mean."

"Yes, make myself a home."

"Sure, it's okay," Tracy said. "When Aaronson comes back, I'll send Lenny to move in with Lisbet. He'll disguise himself as you."

Jorge laughed. "Oh, yes. We wear exactly the same sizes, although we do not share the same taste in clothes. Fortunately, from our wardrobe you can tell us apart."

"I never noticed," Tracy said.

"Lenny and I could pass for brothers, you know. Under the right conditions, even Lisbet might mistake him for me, if he could play the guitar," Jorge said.

"I know you love that instrument," Tracy said, pointing to his guitar nestled on the coverlet. "But do you sleep with it?"

"Oh, I never sleep here."

Yes, she could see that. The room, in spite of all of Jorge's accouterments, did not have the feeling of a space that had been inhabited. Everything seemed arranged, as if for display, for safekeeping. Jorge had been living with Melissa, and he used this room, it seemed, only as a storehouse for his material possessions. Jorge liked to maintain his sense of identity by direct physical contact with his belongings. His passions were strong, deep, turbulent, and quickly spent. But his material possessions endured and gave him comfort.

She recalled Spiegel's story about how Jorge had fallen for Melissa when he first set eyes on her back in the language school, how he had vowed that if he could "only have that bird" he would do anything for her, he would devote his life to her, he would become her slave. Spiegel said he had never believed Jorge for a second, but it turned out that Jorge had been telling the truth. He had given up everything: his peaceful and rather domestic relation with Lisbet, his claim to a student visa, the likelihood of permanent-resident status. But Melissa would grow bored with Jorge, sooner or later, Tracy thought. He would no longer seem to her so exotic, so sensual, and his attentions would eventually feel demeaning and obsequious. His needy, clinging devotion would lower him in her estimate, and she would discard him and move on to a new phase in what Spiegel called her "life experience."

"How is Melissa?" Tracy asked Jorge.

"Always at rehearsals, it seems."

Tracy was surveying the room. Jorge had neatly stacked a few record jackets on a corner of the writing desk, but Tracy saw no sign of Spiegel's books. Perhaps Jorge had removed them because they did not fit with his idea of decor. "When's the show?" she asked.

"Sometime next month. Do you want to see it?"

"It depends," Tracy said.

"On what . . . happens? I mean with Aaronson."

"Yes. Jorge, you and Melissa, you've kept your word, haven't you? Nobody knows?"

"Who would we tell?" he said.

"No one has been around, asking for Lenny? Asking about him?"

"Not that I know," Jorge said.

"Because," Tracy said, "a guy came by to talk to us. He said he was a writer, a reporter. He was going to do an article about Lenny."

"And what did you tell him?" Jorge asked.

"Well, we didn't tell him that Aaronson was out of the country, of course. But he seemed to know a lot already. For one thing, he seemed to know that Lenny was still in Uppsala. He said he had been up here, talking to students. And one of them had seen Lenny."

"I did not squeak," Jorge said.

"No," she said. "We think he might have talked to Lars, at the end of the hall. He said he saw me up here, too."

"He saw you?"

"All of which means," Tracy said, "I can't hang around here

long. If people see me, it could raise questions. I just came here to get some of Lenny's stuff that he needs and to bring it back to my place."

"I thought he took his stuff," Jorge said.

"He left behind some books."

"Take whatever you want," Jorge said.

"His books are gone," she said. "You seem to have rearranged everything." On the bookshelf, Jorge had set his combs and brushes in a neat row, like soldiers.

"I moved some of his things across the hallway," Jorge said. "Maybe they got mixed in with Melissa's books. We could check."

It was always a little creepy stepping into Melissa's room, which had been transformed into a strange hybrid of California surf palace and Ripley's museum. She had tacked corny posters of Pacific sunsets and Hawaiian volcanic beaches alongside her framed art photographs and her private museum of whips, scabbards, and swords—the props. Her collection of shades, sweatbands, bikini halters, and other paraphernalia of sun worship had come out of trunk storage, and the colorful items were strewn across the dresser top, among the stray pantyhose, tank tops, shorts, sweats, and faded jeans. Melissa's better clothes—some short skirts, cotton pullovers, a cashmere sweater—were piled on the floor at the foot of the bed.

"She was putting away her winter wardrobe," Jorge said apologetically. "We don't usually live this way. She would be angry if she knew—"

"Where would she even find room for books?" Tracy said.

"There are some books beside the night lamp." Jorge gestured to a narrow shelf resting on wall brackets above Melissa's bed. "Have a look."

Tracy put her knee on the bed and reached across to the shelf. A scent of roses and funk wafted up from the spongy mattress. The bed was soft, creamy. Melissa's white coverlet was puffy yet evanescent to the touch, like a cloud. Suddenly, Tracy felt a hand on her shoulder. The mattress pitched, and Tracy almost tumbled forward into the cottony pillows, huge and thick, like laundry bags.

"Get off of me, you pig," she yelled.

"Melissa won't mind," Jorge said. His teeth were clenched, his eyes filled with tears, from the effort to subdue Tracy. She was much stronger than he had thought and much more resistant to his charms.

"Fuck you, Jorge, I mind," she said. She twisted hard, pulling free from Jorge's grip and knocking him off balance. He fell face-first onto the bedding, and Tracy pinned him. He was like a trussed chicken. His arms, pulled behind his back like wings, were thin as sticks. His waist was like a reed, his legs like pencils or straws. There's nothing to him but hair and clothes, she thought, as she gritted her teeth, planted her feet on the floor, and leaned backward to drag him off the bed.

He struggled and rolled to the side, knocking over Melissa's Tensor lamp. It fell off the shelf. The bulb popped, sending sprinkles of glass among the condom wrappers and the opened tubes of lubricants on the floor between bed and wall.

"I give up, I give up," Jorge said. "I was wrong."

Tracy released her grip, and Jorge stood. He was out of breath. His cheek and forehead bore a faint red abrasion, an imprint of the pattern from the quilted coverlet. "How will we explain this?" he said. He wet his thumb to lift a crystal of the shattered bulb from the pillow.

"That's your problem, isn't it?" Tracy said.

"It might look to anyone who came in here as if we had enjoyed ourselves," Jorge said. "Look what we have done." He leaned across the bed and picked from the floor a crumpled foil packet. He dangled it over an exposed corner of the mattress. A few drops of liquid slipped from a jagged corner and fell like tears to the ticking. The thick fabric sucked in the oils.

"You're trying to threaten me with Melissa?" Tracy said. "What a joke."

"She can be dangerous," Jorge said. He gestured toward the wall, where her armaments were on display.

"Yeah, and I hear she's a hell of a bar fighter, too," Tracy said.

"She was taken by surprise," Jorge protested.

Tracy turned to the mirror to straighten her blouse and to

shake free her hair. "They tell me Melissa got a big part in *Miss Julie*," she said.

"What do you mean?" Jorge asked.

"I just wonder if she has a special friendship with the director, is all. "

"She has been at rehearsal every day," Jorge said, suddenly indignant. "Every night, she studies her script . . ."

"You know where Spiegel's books are, don't you?" Tracy said.

"You're fucking him. Aren't you?"

Tracy was silent for a moment. "Let's agree, then, that we all have our secrets."

"You believe Melissa has been spying on the American community, and I am lying to protect her?" Jorge said. "You are wrong. But I will try to find his books. And I will try to find out if what you say about Melissa is so. If I learn that she has been fucking somebody else, I will—"

"You will what? Move back to Lisbet's? Do you think she would have you, after all this?"

"I will look through Melissa's papers," Jorge said, "and see what I can discover."

And Tracy realized that she might have made a mistake. She should never have revealed to Jorge how badly she needed to find Spiegel's books. He had figured out that she was searching for more than idle reading matter, that among the books must be something on which she would place a great value. Tracy had placed too big a marker within Jorge's grasp, and she had no idea what price he might exact for its return.

It was evening when Tracy pulled into the courtyard in front of her apartment. Gunnar Mendelsohn was sitting on the front steps. He stood to greet her, or to block her way to the door. By the clumsiness with which he moved, she guessed that he had been sitting for several hours.

"You could have rung the bell," Tracy said. "Aaronson would have let you in."

"I didn't want to see him," Mendelsohn said. "I wanted to talk to you." He seemed to be a patient man. A professional asset, no doubt, she thought. Like a duck hunter or an ice fisherman, the reporter must wait stock-still until the quarry arrives in his sites.

"Do you want to go for coffee or something? I haven't eaten," Tracy said.

"I would rather talk here," Mendelsohn said. "I will have to rush back to my office as soon as we finish. We are past my deadline. I am keeping the pressmen on overtime because of this story."

"Which story? You've found Spiegel?"

"I've been doing some research," he said. "I looked into the background of your friend Leonard Spiegel. Are you familiar with it?"

"A little," Tracy said. "We had friends who knew him back in the States."

"Friends, yes, but it is impossible to talk to any member of his family. His mother is deceased. His father worked for intelligence and now is apparently with the Foreign Service, at a posting somewhere in Africa. I cannot find anyone who knew Spiegel until he entered—what was the name of your school?"

Tracy told him.

"Exactly. Before that time, he is hard to locate. No good records, transcripts, that sort of thing until he transfers to your school. He becomes there a student in, I think you call it pre-law. Or so I am told. The school has no record of him, you see."

"No?" Tracy said, a bit surprised. "Maybe the police seized all his records when they arrested him that time, by mistake."

"No, not because of that. The school administration told me it was because he never received any credits. He may have enrolled in courses, they said, but he never completed any. So they have no official record. He did, apparently, live in the city, near the school. He was arrested, as you know, not on the campus but at his home."

"Yes, he was mistaken for Aaronson. The cops let him go, but by then we were safely out of the country. It worked out well for us," Tracy said.

"Exactly. How convenient for you," Mendelsohn said. "As it

happens, the police in your city will release no records of the arrest because, as they told me, all charges have been dropped. So I cannot confirm anything from that source. All I have to go on, to learn about Spiegel's arrest, is news reports. And your word."

"We weren't there, of course. But from what we know the school tried to turn in Aaronson, but gave out the wrong ID card because Spiegel and Aaronson are practically twins. Spiegel had never been involved in the movement."

"Until then," Mendelsohn said. "Then, he became involved. He leaves the States, comes to Sweden, doesn't exactly enroll in the university but takes a room at Flogsta. He signs up for the Swedish classes at the institute. And then, he follows his pattern."

"Which is what?" Tracy asked.

"He disappears. Two months after he gets to Uppsala, he vanishes. He doesn't finish the language class. They say at the institute, yes, a student named Leonard Spiegel did register and attend classes for several weeks. But he never finished even the first unit of study. At Flogsta, the records show that indeed a Leonard Spiegel rented a student flat. But now, he has disappeared, and it seems that another foreign student has occupied his dwelling. And except for one student who says that he saw your friend this week, no one that I talked to in Flogsta seems to remember when it was that they saw him last. All of which I find very odd indeed."

"He . . . kept to himself a lot," Tracy offered, lamely.

"No," Mendelsohn said. "You can't lead me on any more. I understand your game now." He leaned close to Tracy and spoke quietly. "What I want from you is confirmation, before I write the story."

"I suppose," Tracy said, "if you know, you know. What is it you're going to write?"

"The truth, of course," Mendelsohn said. "That Leonard Spiegel does not exist."

Tracy froze. She was startled by a jingling sound. She had forgot that she was clutching her key ring. She looked, and saw that her hand was shaking.

"Ha. You didn't think I could figure that out," Mendelsohn said.

"No. How did you?"

"Simple. It all added up. There never was a Leonard Spiegel. His name appears here and there, in the news, on certain lists, transcripts. But he has passed through life like wind through a forest, moving the branches around for a minute but changing nothing, leaving no mark. He is, how to say it? Your invention. He allowed you to escape from America, and perhaps, for a time, he even allowed your friend Aaronson to travel around the continent, until the military police got wise to your game and decided that if you were going to pretend that there was such a person as Leonard Spiegel, they could pretend to put out a warrant for his arrest. That would make it impossible for you to use him any longer for your purposes."

"But why don't they just arrest Aaronson?" Tracy said.

"Here in Sweden? Don't be ridiculous. But you got the message, didn't you? I think it's clear. They will no longer live by the rules of your fiction. If your friend Aaronson tries to leave Sweden again, he will be subjected to Spiegel's fate. He, too, will disappear. I would like to write this in my story. That Leonard Spiegel does not exist and never has. But I wanted to check with you first. A word from you can stop me. Have I come upon the truth?"

Tracy nodded in confirmation. "Yes," she said to Mendelsohn. "There's truth in what you've told me. I won't admit everything you've said is true, but I won't call the other papers to deny it, either. I won't stand in your way. Go ahead," she said, as she turned from Mendelsohn to slip her key into the door lock. "Write that story."

MAY

12

It had been daylight for so long that it felt like high noon by the time the march began. But it was only ten o'clock. The crack of dawn, Spiegel would have called it, back in the States. Now, as the days grew and stretched and threatened to consume the darkness altogether, like some monster from a Grade-D horror movie, the creature that devoured the night, Spiegel found himself awake at unthinkable hours. Three a.m. Four-thirty. He had never before seen those moments—at least not from the waking end—in his life.

Each morning, Spiegel would find himself awake, listening for the sounds of birds, of traffic. He would lie in bed, his hand resting on Tracy's back, thinking that he should get up, do some work, get on with his life. Here he was, after more than three months in a foreign country, and what had he to show for it? He knew hardly any Swedes, for one thing. Other than Monika and Lisbet, his only friends were Americans and a few other foreign students like Jorge. For another, he hadn't left Uppsala since he'd arrived at the railroad station. Shouldn't he at least try to see part of the countryside, and maybe even Stockholm, before he went back to the States? And the language. Ever since he had begun to represent himself as Aaronson, he had stopped going to language classes. He knew hardly a word of Swedish, couldn't carry on a conversation, could barely even order a cheese sandwich at a kiosk, lesson number-one in language school for immigrants. Well, he could read the banners unfurled in the great courtyard in front of the old castle. *Arbetares frihet för arbetare.* Freedom for the workers, he figured. Or maybe it was the name of an Uppsala rock group. *Låt oss bli fria!* The last shall be the first? Lassie, come home? *Ut ur Vietnam, USA imperialister!* That one he could understand. He had learned that, just as there is a universal language of love, and of sex as well, there is also a universal language of hate, and of violence. So he didn't need to speak Swedish to make his feelings known. All that he had to do was join the May Day crowd, marching as one from the park behind the castle—he knew the word for that, *slottsbacken*—through the center of town to the factory yards by the river. He would be one with the masses. He was glad about that. He did not want to take a place at the podium. Monika had urged him to speak to the crowd, said it would be great to have a voice from the Americans as part of the citywide, nationwide, worldwide—so far as they knew—demonstrations. But Spiegel said he couldn't do it, and Tracy backed him. They both knew why he had declined. He would rather preserve his obscurity than bask in a false glory behind the guise of another's name.

The events of the past month had been wearing Spiegel down. He hadn't slept much, and it wasn't just the dawn awakenings. It was also the sheer physicality of a new sexual relationship. Loving Tracy was not something he was able to step into easily, gracefully. He was always stumbling over something, something that wasn't even there. Even when he and Tracy were in their deepest moments of passion, moments that made Spiegel feel as if his body had been transformed into light, into pulsating waves of energy, she would sometimes turn her head in such a way, pulling back from him slightly with a faint look of puzzlement, and she would utter a soft sigh not so much of pleasure as of regret, and Spiegel would know that her body was with him but that part of her being, part of her consciousness, still rested with Aaronson. What he couldn't determine, and what Tracy could not or would not tell him, was whether her love for Aaronson was fading and growing dimmer or whether it still burned strong. And if it did, maybe Spiegel's passion was inadvertently keeping the fading ember alive. Maybe he wasn't the fire but the air that the fire consumes. If so, he was doing Tracy no favors. His presence in her life might be giving her a false hope, making it harder for her to relinquish her memories of Aaronson, keeping her in a constant state of anticipation, of readiness for his return. Yet if there was anything Spiegel had come to believe in the past month it was that Aaronson was not coming back to Uppsala.

If he were, he would have been there for May Day. He would have wanted to lead the Americans as they marched, chanting and waving banners, through the city. The deserters looked great, Spiegel thought, like an invading army come out of the bush after a month's maneuvers. Most of the guys wore their khakis or camouflage. Some, despite the bright sun and the surprising heat, wore beat-up leather flight jackets. One guy wore a grimy gray sweatshirt, the sleeves cut off, a deep blue tattoo of a devil's face on his bulging biceps. Another guy sported a beret, and another had slung a heavy rucksack over his shoulders. They all had full beards or stubble, stringy hair shoulder-length or longer, droopy mustaches. The Swedes, in contrast, even the leftists who had organized the march and the old socialists who came out to wave the banners and sing the "Internationale" every year, looked diminutive, well-groomed, and disciplined.

Spiegel saw the Worm at the edge of the crowd, pacing nervously, scrutinizing a flyer someone had handed him. Spiegel waved, but the Worm didn't look up from his reading. Spiegel couldn't spot Reston in the crowd. Zeke, he knew, would be at the speaker's podium at the head of the march, with Tracy. It had been the plan to have Tracy read a letter from ARMS at the May Day rally and then present the ARMS petition on jobs and housing to the delegates from the Uppsala City Council. At the last minute, Zeke had raised a fuss and insisted that as leader pro tem of ARMS he should be the one to present the petition. Tracy objected at first, arguing that Zeke's presence on the podium would raise questions in the press about Aaronson's absence, but eventually she yielded for fear of alienating Zeke or pushing him to the point where he might betray her trust. She offered to hand Zeke a final draft of the petition and join the men in the line of march. But Zeke insisted that he needed her on the podium for moral support. He wanted Tracy to stand beside him.

A guy with a megaphone handed Spiegel a mimeographed sheet: a list of the phrases they would chant as they marched into the city. Each was numbered, one through five. Spiegel wasn't sure he understood all of them. One was clear enough: U.S. out of Vietnam. Another seemed to call on Nixon and Kissinger to end the bombing, end the war. One called for NLF victory; another sang the praises of the wise man Ho Chi Minh. The fifth troubled Spiegel: *Vietnam, Palestina, samma kamp*. Vietnam and Palestine, same struggle. Were they really? He didn't care to mix up his wars. I'll keep my mouth shut when the march leader calls out number five, he decided.

By the time the head of the march had begun to move down the hill, the Worm had worked his way in next to Spiegel. Although it was early, the sun was well above the horizon. The day had become hot. Spiegel wished that he had brought a hat. There was shade beside the castle and in the narrow streets of the Old City, but as the line passed through the shopping district they would be marching in direct sunlight.

"Do you fucking believe this?" the Worm was saying to Spiegel.

"This?" Spiegel wasn't sure what the Worm meant, and he didn't want to talk to him for a whole hour as they marched. He pretended to be studying his mimeo.

"This whole scene," the Worm said. "It's more like a July Fourth parade. I mean, when I go to a demonstration, I wanna see someone kick ass, you know what I mean?"

"Maybe you will," Spiegel said. "The day is young."

"I don't even understand this stuff." The Worm slapped his hand against his flyer. "What's this stuff about *Norska fiskare?*"

Spiegel looked at the Worm's handout. He couldn't make sense of it either.

"I think you got the wrong one. This one's something about fishing in Norway. Maybe it's the group against North Sea oil?"

"What'd you get?" the Worm asked.

Spiegel showed him his sheet.

"Yeah, Nixon, Kissinger. That's where I wanna be. I'm gonna get rid of this *fisk* shit and find the right guy." Spiegel was about to offer the Worm his hymnal, but before he could offer it the Worm had sunk back into the throng. Spiegel turned, and he could see the Worm making his way, against the flow of the crowd, toward the stragglers and the latecomers at the rear.

By that time, most of the marchers had already set off from the castle grounds. Spiegel was relieved to see that the neat lines of march were breaking apart and the order imposed by the organizers was beginning to disintegrate. Some people who had been consigned to the back had sprinted on ahead of their groups. The chanting of slogans from the many teams and contingents was overlapping, forming a multilingual cacophony that echoed off the stone walls of the castle. Organizers down the hill piped on whistles in vain attempts to bring the marchers back into line and the teams into synchronicity. But the shrill whistles and the booming megaphones just added to the tonal disorder and tended to pull the rest of the marchers into further disarray.

Spiegel found his place behind the Vietnam War banner. Other Americans in the contingent recognized Spiegel, or thought they did. "Where you been, man?" said one lanky guy in combat fatigues and black boots. "Welcome back, brother," said another, gripping his hand in the soul handshake.

"How you doin', Hyde," Spiegel said. Hyde and his partner fell into step, one on each side of Spiegel.

Hyde edged uncomfortably close to Spiegel's shoulder while his partner marched in lockstep, a pace ahead of Spiegel, boxing him in. "We got to have a talk," Hyde said.

"Yeah, maybe after the rally," Spiegel said. "Tracy said something about a meeting." He looked to his sheet. He wished someone would call out a number. He wanted to shout slogans. It would be better than talking to Hyde.

"We ain't met for how long now? Three weeks? You know, pretty much since you've come back."

Nixon! Kissinger! Vietnam! As the march passed below the castle into the narrow cobbled streets of the Old City, the sounds crossed and reverberated. It was hard to distinguish one chant from another. Spiegel was feeling closed in as the lines of the march compressed. His two comrades, bumping and jostling him, were swelling with a bad attitude.

"I'm thinking maybe you ain't so interested in the group anymore," said Hyde. He wore a sash across his khaki shirt and a ranger hat, which made him look like a combination of a Boy Scout and Black Panther.

"No," Spiegel said. "There's just been tons of pressure. Since the TV thing. Threats and stuff, and I've laid low."

"But what about us, man?" said the lanky guy. He had a sick-looking blond beard, and he was missing an upper tooth. "I'm talking about our reserve fundings. Like, it's time for you to kick in."

"Well, things are just, like, out of joint this month." Funds? Tracy had mentioned to him the so-called emergency fund that Aaronson had established, and Spiegel knew that several of the deserters had come to Aaronson from time to time to tap into that source. Had it gone dry? And how could the well be replenished? He would have to ask Zeke, discreetly.

"We're glad you done come back," Hyde said. "We thought maybe you'd been dipping into our funds for, like, an airline ticket."

"Now what the hell good would an airline ticket be to me?" Spiegel said. "I'm grounded here. Besides, I get scared shitless flying."

"Ha, ha," said Gap-tooth. "Maybe we could have a meeting, and talk about that. Maybe we could see what kind of souvenirs you brought back from your last trip."

"Okay," Spiegel said. "Maybe." And then he focused on the mimeo he had been carrying. He had crushed it in his sweaty hand so that the only line he could read was number five: *Vietnam, Palestina, samma kamp.* When the squad leader called for it, he joined in, as loudly as he could.

Hyde and his comrade dropped back into the wall of olive-green fatigues, the scruffy and bedraggled deserters who had dusted off their salvaged uniforms and wore them proudly, like Legionnaires on Memorial Day back in the States.

From the windows above the shops, restaurants, and galleries of the Old City, young people—the artists and students who had been drawn to the quaint district, Uppsala's Left Bank, as they called it—opened their wooden shutters wide and leaned out, over iron parapets and window boxes filled with red flowers. They waved small flags and shouted to the stream of people passing raucously below: *Hej, amerikanare!* And the deserters waved back, fluttered their flags, pumped their fists, one or two even saluted. Today, they were the heroes.

These heroes were resentful of Aaronson for his absence, for his abdication. And they were separated from him, as well, by a matter of class and social status. Most of the deserters were poor and poorly educated, but here, they had come to realize, they outranked Aaronson. They respected his brains and his daring, but they looked askance at him as well because he had never been in the army, never seen Vietnam except on the news. Whatever danger Aaronson had faced, whatever taboo had been violated to bring him to Uppsala and to keep him in exile, it could not be so great as the horrors they had seen and the risks they had run to save their souls. They couldn't help but think that he, a college boy, could always fly home and buy his way out of trouble. But they were here forever, consigned to purgatory, an alternative they had chosen at great price after looking into the pits of hell.

The roadway widened as the march passed through the gates of the Old City and onto the shopping concourse that sloped down toward the river. Spiegel remembered how inhospitable the downtown streets had looked in winter. Seeing this part of the city for the first time since winter, Spiegel noticed that the streets looked so much more airy and open than he had recalled. The sunlight was shining off the great plate-glass windows with their tasteful displays of crystal and luggage, the trees modulated the intense light with their feathery green leaves, flags at the street corners snapped in the breeze. The bystanders, few but enthusiastic, cheered the marchers as they passed along. One young girl ran out to the Americans and handed them small white flowers.

Spiegel slowed his pace so that he could drop back in the line of march. He wanted to talk to the Worm. Maybe the Worm could shed some light on Hyde's insinuations. But the Worm, it seemed, had fallen well behind the ARMS contingent. Trailing the Americans was a group calling for Macedonian independence, then a small but energetic squad of Basque separatists. Spiegel stood to the side and let them pass. If he didn't find the Worm, he would either jog ahead to the deserters or keep pace with one of the "Greens," the Whole Earth enthusiasts who were the wagging tail at the shaggy end of the parade. That's where he saw the Worm, marching beneath a street-wide banner that depicted a breeching whale.

The Worm waved to Spiegel. "Why'd you end up here?" Spiegel asked him.

"I believe in ecology," the Worm said. "It's everywhere."

"No, man, you fell back when those two dudes squeezed in next to me."

The Worm looked straight ahead. Around them, tall blond people, healthy-looking even for Swedes, chanted *Norge, Nej!* It had something to do with the Norwegian whaling fleet, Spiegel assumed. Someone a few steps ahead of them wore a tall hat shaped like a smokestack. Every twenty steps or so, a puff of gray smoke belched from his chimney, and the spectators cheered and applauded.

"Answer me," Spiegel said.

"I just thought they wanted to talk to you alone is all," the Worm answered.

"Do you know Hyde?"

"Sure. Been in ARMS since before I got here. He's from Oakland. Claims he grew up with Bobby Seale, but who knows."

"So why did you disappear when he showed up? Did somebody warn you or something?"

"Warn me? What about?"

"I think they meant to give me some shit is all. Not me, exactly, but that fucking Aaronson. They want to know why he hasn't been running meetings, where he's been since he came back from Germany, other stuff, too, that I didn't understand. I think you do. I think you know that someone's going to try to clip Aaronson, and since they think I'm him they're gonna end up clipping me."

"I only know some of the guys wanna have a meeting. They think you, I mean Aaronson, ought to resign. They want someone with credentials, I mean a real deserter, to run the group. Not everyone agrees."

"Do you agree?"

"I don't care, except the group's about broke, you know. They're gonna kick us out of the warehouse, and we'll have to move into like a church basement, or a fucking rectory."

"What's so bad about that?" Spiegel asked.

"No smoking, man."

"I'm thinking," Spiegel said, "that I can only hold out so long, waiting for Aaronson. I can give it maybe another week. Then, I'll have to level with the guys, tell them what I've been doing to run interference for him while he ran his mission. But right now, I don't know where the fuck he is. Maybe he's being held somewhere, or maybe his travels took him farther than he let on to us."

"Do you know," the Worm said, "exactly what his mission is all about? 'Cause I suspect it involves more than bringing deserters back to Uppsala."

He looked around to make sure that no one could hear what he was saying to Spiegel. No one could. The march, at least at its tail end, had broken down into disorder. People from the sidewalk crowds had joined the flow, and the once-disciplined ranks had degenerated. The squads by now were so intermingled that when a leader called a number through a megaphone some people would be chanting about Vietnam, some about apartheid, and others about British coal miners. Spiegel noticed that the pace had slowed and the crowd thickened as the procession approached the narrow pedestrian bridge that crossed the river.

"I can tell you that there's other stuff involved," the Worm said. "I don't know what. Maybe drugs, maybe guns. I don't know how he's moving them. But I think he's paid well for his troubles, and that the money finds its way to our treasury. Some of it finds its way out, too. Maybe that's what they were asking you?"

"Maybe," Spiegel said. He was thinking that, if the Worm was right, it could explain why nobody had heard from Aaronson.

Tracy had said something about Aaronson's handling a shipment of material to the church. Maybe he had been captured while he was smuggling arms or drugs, and the police really thought he was Spiegel. Maybe they were keeping it quiet, waiting for Aaronson to start talking, to reveal the network of his contacts on both sides of the border. Spiegel suspected that Aaronson would crack. Spiegel bit down on his lip, shook his head in worry. I'm dead if he starts talking, he thought. But how lucky for Aaronson, if luck it was, to be out of the crosshairs when the shooting was about to start. Once again, Spiegel would find himself pinned to the target while his doppelgänger danced away, floating off the range and out of view.

Spiegel stepped ahead of the Worm onto the footbridge. He was nervous about crossing the water. He wondered if the crowd might be testing the old bridge to its capacity, or beyond. The copper railings, green with age, looked flimsy and malleable. The pavement itself seemed to buckle and to undulate as the marchers stomped across, in rhythm to the pounding of a bass drum that could be heard coming from the park on the far bank. Spiegel looked over the railing to the swirling river below. The snowmelt and the late-spring rains had raised the water level high up the embankments, so the surface of the river nearly kissed the girders beneath the bridge.

Just as Spiegel reached the apex of the bridge, the procession halted. The crowd had filled the near end of the square where the rally was to be held, and the police had started to direct the last of the marchers down a side street, toward a less populated section of the plaza, distant from the grandstands. Spiegel felt the footbridge sway as the advancing crowd pressed ahead. The marshals, whistling and shouting, telling the squads at the rear to halt, to back up, could not prevail. The procession continued to roll forward like a tide. Spiegel was locked into place, between opposing forces. He knew that he would have to begin to move, in one direction or the other. To stay put would be to risk being crushed, like a rock beneath a glacier. He looked back to see if he could find the Worm, but the crowd had swallowed him.

The shrill whistles from the leaders of the squadrons piped

from both sides of the river. The sounds seemed to bounce off
the factory walls, to echo one another, to reverberate with a con-
tinuous increase of intensity. Far away, Spiegel could hear the
electronic screaming of the loudspeakers that had been set up
to broadcast the speeches at the rally. If he went back to the
embankment, he might be able to walk through the city to
the auto bridge and cross the river in time to hear Zeke. But
the crowd behind him seemed to have become thicker. There
was a real chance that the throng would burst the railings and
people would tumble into the rushing water. Spiegel decided
that his best chance was to find within the crowd a rivulet that
was flowing forward, to join in, and to press ahead toward the
site of the rally. He craned his neck to get a better view, then
leaned out dangerously over the railing to see if he could detect
any movement. His heart stopped. There, at the far end of the
bridge, scanning the crowd, stood a tall man with a jagged red
scar across his jaw.

He had been looking across the water, trying to scan the
marchers who were retreating from the footbridge. He was
bouncing on the balls of his feet, edgy, even frantic, like a caged
animal. As soon as he recognized him, Spiegel turned and burrowed into the crowd. He shouldered and shoved against the
wall of marchers, working his way inch by inch off the bridge.
He could feel the crowd parting behind him, making way for
someone in pursuit. Ahead of him a young woman held a peace
sign aloft on a bamboo pole. Spiegel grabbed the pole from her.
Djävla! (hell!) she screamed as he called to her, *Förlat* (sorry).
Now people got out of his way as he pushed through, swinging
the pole. He bullied his way in retreat, and he could hear behind
him a steady rumble, the sound of his pursuer working his way
up the ramp of the footbridge, fighting against the tide.

Spiegel fought, too. He had no time to assess the damage he
might be inflicting, no time to think about that. He swung the
pole, and the crowd parted. He had to work like an automaton,
a threshing machine. If he was in pain or injured, he hadn't yet
noticed. If he injured others, he would suffer the consequences
later. Whistles blew, and horns and sirens, but he didn't hear.

People shouted at him, but he couldn't understand. He thought he heard a scream behind him, a crash of metal, a shattering of glass, but he did not pause to look. He told himself that he must keep swinging the pole until he reached the embankment. Then, he would drop the peace banner on the grass and run, lose himself among the alleyways of the Old City.

The last of the marchers, sensing that something had gone terribly wrong up ahead, halted at the foot of the bridge. Through the crowd, Spiegel could see a patch of green, a corner of the sloping parkway alongside the river. He dropped his pole and sliced his way into the clear. He felt a shock of dizziness and relief, like a diver who has been submerged too long breaking out to the surface and gasping for air, as he sprinted down a cinder pathway toward the city streets. And then he saw why the crowd had stopped moving. The police had arrived, on both banks of the river. Their sirens howled and screamed across the water, calling to each other. A police wagon—Spiegel was surprised at how much it resembled an American ice-cream truck—had pulled onto the paved turnaround at the far end of the footbridge. Its horn blasted as the heavy notes of the national anthem, broadcast from the loudspeakers at the rally site, rolled over the water and echoed off the stanchions of the bridge and against the glass walls of the city's office buildings and the stone face of the castle, high above them on the hill.

Ahead of Spiegel, at the end of the cinder pathway, a black Volvo jumped the curb and slammed to a stop, cutting slashes in the grass. Two policemen leaped out and stood shoulder to shoulder on the sidewalk, blocking Spiegel's way. He thought of trying to barrel through them, but he knew that he no longer had the strength, or the momentum. The policemen were huge, and planted as firmly as trees. He would bounce off them like a football scrub crashing into the tackle dummy. So at the last second Spiegel pulled up short. His lungs were burning, and he felt a pain in his side as if someone had stabbed him with a sword. He leaned forward, as if to vomit, and he thought he might drop to the ground, but a big hand gripped his shoulder and held him aright.

"Hello, Aaronson," a voice said.

Had the Uppsala police been following him all through the march? Or for much longer? Spiegel tried to steady his breathing enough so that he could speak. "I didn't do anything," he protested. "You can't put me under arrest."

"You're not under arrest," the policeman said.

"Come, let's go," said the bigger of the two. Spiegel had no choice. Nor did he desire to resist. To go with them could be no worse than waiting on the bridge to confront his fate, his accuser, his demon.

The Volvo whipped through the city, the wail of its siren streaming behind them like a long ribbon of sound, a pennant trailing in a breeze. Spiegel leaned back in the hard leather seat. He caught his breath. He felt comfortable, and surprisingly relaxed. It was as if he had been placed inside a capsule and lifted above the noisy discord and partisan bickering of the day's events. He knew that he had narrowly escaped what might have been a mortal threat, but he felt strangely removed from the experience, as if he could set his chin on his palm, gaze out the tinted window, and watch the narrative of his life unfold, like an astronaut staring bemusedly at the watery globe from the weightless silence of space.

Crowds parted before them as they rolled along the main thoroughfare, like a pinball shot from a chute. As they approached each intersection, uniformed police officers held back traffic and waved the unmarked Volvo on its way.

Spiegel's head was spinning with questions: Why had the Uppsala police suddenly materialized and pulled him to safety? Were they planning to arrest him? And if so, what for? He had done nothing wrong. He was being chased, and he'd run. If he had created a disturbance, if anyone had been injured, that was not his fault.

But Spiegel knew that if the Uppsala police learned his true identity, they would turn him over to the American authorities in Stockholm. Then, anything might happen. If the Americans learned that he had given up his passport so that Aaronson could travel illegally to Germany, Spiegel could be deported and held on federal charges. He could even be linked to Aaronson's attack on the draft board, and charged with conspiracy. It would hardly matter that he hadn't known Aaronson at the time of the sabotage. Conspiracy charges, especially in federal courts, were tremendously elastic and could stretch to include the most disparate and nebulous of actions, as anyone who had followed the Chicago Seven trial knew all too well.

The radio crackled, and one of the Uppsala cops barked something back into the speaker, orders, a location check, Spiegel couldn't tell. The words were coming at him in short, static-filled blasts, apparently reports on the march and demonstrations from around the city. Spiegel wondered if the rally would come off and if Zeke would get to give his speech. He wondered about Tracy, how she would learn that he had been taken by the police. No doubt the Worm would tell her. He must have seen everything from his vantage on the bridge. Would she bail him out? It might be better, though, if Tracy didn't show up at police headquarters too soon. Spiegel didn't want her saying anything before they had a clear picture of the battlefield, or at least of the face of their antagonist.

Lost in his ruminations, Spiegel barely noticed as the Volvo pulled into the basement garage beneath police headquarters. "Here we are," said the driver. "Special delivery." The other cop grabbed Spiegel roughly by the arm, and led him into the building. Spiegel was not afraid, but he was tired. Perhaps he had been half-asleep in the car. The whole day seemed to him like a dream. It was only early afternoon, but he felt as if he had been awake for many hours. That incessant sunlight had been eating through his sleep.

An automatic glass door slid open at their approach, and standing in the doorway was a small man in a tan summer suit. He had jet-black hair that fell across his forehead, nearly draping his deep-set eyes. It looked as if he had been wearing a wig that had slipped forward after a sudden stop. The man held his hand out to Spiegel and introduced himself as Inspector Svenson, detective division. His hand, in Spiegel's tentative grip, felt like a toy. Svenson said something to the uniformed cop, thanking him, apparently, for the good work, and the cop released his grip on Spiegel's arm. Svenson led Spiegel into the station.

Inside the doorway, on benches along the wall, sat three men wearing torn white shirts stained with sweat and dried blood. One was shaking with a death-rattle cold, his teeth chattering like hail on glass. Another, clutching a leaflet that he must have carried from the May Day march, was staring blankly into space, as though he were trying to discern, at some faraway vanishing point, the faint inscription of his fate. The third, his eyes sealed closed, folded his arms and rocked from side to side, as if in prayer.

"Sorry to lead you this way," Svenson said. "We had to clear certain elements from the line of march. To keep it clean, you know. We let them cool down, then release them. Or take them to hospital." Svenson guided Spiegel down a long hallway to a bank of elevators.

The elevator, shiny steel polished to a mirror finish, smelled of fresh oil. The smell of guns, Spiegel imagined. Yet the building looked much more like a corporate office than a police station. Spiegel had seen police stations back in the States, and had hoped never to see one again, at least from the prisoner's perspective. He still had fixed in his memory a vision of shattered ceiling tiles, asbestos hanging from the heating pipes, cinder-block walls painted a dead-moss green, windows thick with protective wire, the glass brown from years of cigarette smoke, the floor an unfinished concrete, cold and rough, with a dark sewer drain set in the corner like an open wound.

But the room Spiegel found himself in now was entirely different from the holding cells where he had cowered in pain and terror until Iris managed to get the charges against him dropped. This room was like an office, perhaps a consulting room for a successful but nonostentatious therapist, furnished with a comfortable couch whose bolsters were covered in canvas ticking in bold floral patterns. Across from the couch were two chairs of Danish teak. Slouched in one of the chairs was the guy with the walrus mustache, whom Spiegel had last seen at the Penny Lane.

"They got you, too," Spiegel said.

Svenson laughed, and said something in Swedish. Spiegel could see the man's eyes crease and the fringes of his mustache lift slightly, like a stage curtain budged by a distant tug on the pulley cords.

"Oh, you're a cop, right?" Spiegel said. "You've been fucking following me." The man didn't answer. Perhaps he didn't understand English.

"Where's his partner?" Spiegel asked Svenson.

"Pardon me?"

"Partner. The guy he was with, hair shaved down to spikes, tried to buy me a bottle of champagne. Bleated about how much he hated 'Wiet-nam,' until he passed out underneath a bar stool."

"*Kan ni förstå?*" Svenson asked. Can you understand? The man shook his head.

"He works alone," Svenson said to Spiegel. "You must have seen him on a case. Someone he was following when your paths crossed. Allow me to introduce you to Walter Brunius, special officer, Uppsala police." Brunius held out his thick, paw-like hand. Brunius, how apt, Spiegel thought. A bear, with the face of a walrus.

"And you, of course, are Leonard Spiegel," Svenson said. "The vanishing American."

Spiegel said nothing. How long had they known? How long had they been on his tail? Well, there was nothing more to hide. The tail had caught the dog.

"*Var så god och sitt,*" Svenson said, the universal Swedish greeting. Please have a seat.

Spiegel sat on the sofa, sinking down into the pillows. A square of sunlight fell on the thick rya rug. Svenson went to the window and turned the cord that twisted shut the interior blinds. The room dimmed, and it seemed suddenly cooler, as if someone had snapped a switch. Svenson closed the wooden door, and it locked behind him with a satisfying click.

"I haven't done anything wrong," Spiegel said, rather pathetically.

To speak to the men, he had to look up slightly, which made him uneasy. Spiegel realized that they knew this, intended it.

They wanted him to be so comfortable that he became ill at ease and was at a disadvantage, like a guy in a polo shirt trying to get a car loan from a banker in gray flannels.

"Oh, we are not accusing you of anything," Svenson said. "We would just like to have a . . . conversation. Would that be okay to ask?"

Spiegel didn't answer. If he were at home, he would know his rights. He had learned them from Iris. Don't say anything without the presence of your counsel. Here, who knew? Sweden was of course a liberal democracy, but Spiegel understood nothing about its system of justice. The Swedes might have all sorts of anachronistic practices. They had a king, after all. Maybe they still practice flogging, or beheading. The right thing to do, in most circumstances, would be to ask to see the American consul. Yet in Spiegel's situation that might be the most dangerous thing he could do, for him, for Tracy, and of course for Aaronson.

"At least you should be grateful to us," Svenson said. "We saved you from that mob, didn't we? If we had not brought you here, well, I don't know where you would be. Somewhere worse, no doubt."

"Maybe, maybe not. At least I'd be free."

"Oh, you are still free. We would not want to place you under arrest, and create—how do you say it?—an international incident. But we could make things difficult for you, if we wished. For example, we could ask you to produce your passport. That could be a problem for you, couldn't it, Lenny? I would hate to have to ask, and to be forced to turn you over to the American authorities."

"My passport was stolen," Spiegel said.

"Was it? Has this been reported?"

Spiegel didn't respond.

"Perhaps your American friend still has your passport?"

Spiegel held his peace.

"You don't think so?"

"Why are you doing all the talking?" Spiegel asked Svenson. "Doesn't Brunius speak English?"

"Only when drunk," Svenson said. Brunius smiled. "But he does understand us rather well," Svenson added.

"Yes, a little," Brunius said. His voice was surprisingly high-pitched.

"Do you have my passport?" Spiegel asked.

"Of course not. We assume your friend still has it."

"Aaronson?"

"Of course. Doesn't he?"

"I don't know," Spiegel said. "I don't even know where he's gone."

"Liar," Brunius put in, and Spiegel knew why Brunius was there. The conversation with the elfin Svenson had been, or had seemed to be, civil, cordial, even amicable. But Brunius was all business. It would be difficult to put him off, impossible to lie to him. His eyes were tiny, like pebbles, beneath the eaves of his thick brow. His mouth was hidden behind the fringes of his drooping mustache. His face, as a result, was nearly devoid of expression, and the word had the sharp ring of a command.

"Is he drunk now?" Spiegel asked.

Svenson laughed, but Brunius just stared at Spiegel. Maybe he didn't understand the quip.

"We all want to know where Aaronson is," Spiegel said. "We haven't heard from him since . . . several weeks."

"Since he went to Germany."

"I don't know where he went."

"Come on, Lenny, don't give us the bullshit. You know he went to Germany. That's why he brought you to Uppsala. To help with the exchange. Everybody knows this now. But the question is: Did he come back? Where is he? We know you are just trying to protect him, but as you can see, you are doing him no good, and you are putting yourself at great risk."

"I'm not sure—"

"You don't really know where he gets his money, do you?"

"He gets donations." He and Iris had even sent a few bucks over, stuffed into a letter, shortly before he'd agreed to come to Uppsala.

Svenson barked out a little laugh. "Oh, yes. Donations. Your friend Aaronson has done a good job, since he arrived from— where was it? Canada?—attracting small funds to support your little group. American leftist sympathizers, French Communists, Italian anarchists—"

"A redundancy," Spiegel put in.

"But would you say that was enough to support his way of life?"

"Sure. Why not?" Spiegel said. "He's not into material things."

"But did he seem to have a regular income, would you not say? A nicer flat than most of the other Americans? Money for a car? Enough to support a lady friend? A few extra kroner to spread out among the boys when they were, how do you say it, short?"

"None of the deserters is rich."

"But he had enough to set him apart."

"So what are you saying?" Spiegel asked.

"Has it ever occurred to you," Svenson said, "that Aaronson is in the business of selling information?"

"You're asking me if Aaronson is a spy? That's ridiculous."

"Believe me, it is not so ridiculous. We have seen it before. A nice fellow like Aaronson, a college student, in a moment of excitement does something stupid like he did to that draft office, and he finds himself on the run and far away from everything and everyone he ever knew, alone in a foreign land. He needs money. He has no idea where to turn when somebody approaches him— in a club, let's say—and buys him a drink and tells him how much he hates the Vietnam War, how much he respects the American deserters. Do you follow me?"

"Yes, I think so," Spiegel said cautiously.

"Good. Eventually, this man, let's call him—"

"Igor," Brunius put in.

"Igor convinces Aaronson that they can help each other. In return for regular contributions toward the welfare of the American community, Aaronson will make available to Igor certain facts. Not the kind of facts that could hurt anyone. Just the names of the other Americans, where they live, what they are planning, what they are doing, hoping, basic dossier material—"

"The Russians," Brunius said. "It was Russian money."

Spiegel looked at Brunius and read nothing in his eyes, his expression. He turned to Svenson for help in decoding this cryptic message.

"So what?" Spiegel said. "Why should you care where the money comes from? ARMS is a private organization."

"Private, but with Soviet backing," Svenson said.

"How do you know all this?"

"It's his job," Svenson said, nodding toward Brunius. And Spiegel understood that the man he had seen with Brunius was not a drunk, belligerent Finn but some sort of Soviet agent.

"Okay," Spiegel said. "Say I believe you." Brunius snorted, and Svenson smiled benignly, his eyes bright beneath the fringe of hair, like diamonds hidden in dark straw. What an unlikely policeman, Spiegel thought. What an unlikely Swede.

"Why not just let the ARMS movement take its course and get its money from whatever country offers to help?" Spiegel said. "God knows Sweden hasn't offered much."

"Because we are not the only ones who have been tracking the Soviet money," Svenson said. "We have reason to believe that the American military police, the criminal-intelligence division, as they call it, has been watching the banking transactions of your group. We understand that they intend to encourage Aaronson to expose the ARMS group as a Soviet cell. They will use him like a lever to pop the lid off the whole antiwar movement. And beneath the lid, what will they see? A swarm of maggots. Everything will be revealed—how deserters are recruited, how they are smuggled north, who pays for their life support—with the obvious political consequences."

That's possible, Spiegel thought. He had heard that the military police had been trying to infiltrate the deserter groups in Stockholm, to get some of the brothers to denounce others, to stir up a climate of hate and distrust, to make the deserters look self-ish and cowardly in the eyes of the world. If they could depict the Uppsala group as a tool of the Soviets, it would discredit the anti-war movement in America and become a powerful political symbol for the hawks on the right, at home and in Sweden as well.

"You mean the deserters would not be welcomed home if the American public knew they had been nourished on a diet of rubles," Spiegel said.

Svenson waved his hand dismissively. "The politics of America is of no consequence to me. My concern is for the political stability of Sweden. If the ARMS group is tied to the Soviets, the SFP would surely use that issue as—how do you say it?—a platform. Certainly they would try to turn the country against foreigners, against Americans."

"The Sweden First Party?"

"Yes, the ones who appeared with you on that television show. They have been watching you very carefully."

"But, I mean, they're so out on the fringe they're barely in the picture," Spiegel said. "I can't believe you take a threat from them seriously."

"They are small, but deadly serious. And with a break like this, they could grow, win some seats in the parliament, maybe even claim a cabinet post. All they need is for Aaronson to talk."

"Aaronson will never talk."

"You may be right. But they would like to hand someone over to the American authorities."

"You're suggesting . . ."

"You. If they can't find Aaronson, they will deliver you. That's why we were hoping that you could lead us to your friend. Unless you want him to take his chances on his own."

"I've told you the truth, though," Spiegel said. "I don't know where Aaronson is."

"That is a shame," said Svenson. "We were going to offer to help, if you could lead us to him."

"Help with what? I don't need help."

"Maybe Aaronson does. We could offer him some protection."

"From who? From what?"

"From the charges he would face: espionage, treason. Those are serious matters, when your country is at war."

Spiegel looked from Svenson to Brunius and back, the one so volatile and intense, the other so phlegmatic and still, his heavy features set as if his face were carved in stone. How could he trust them? Were they truly hoping to protect Aaronson, or were they plotting to do away with him and then to smash ARMS apart. Perhaps, Spiegel thought, they are just angling to get into position for the perfect shot: Spiegel would betray Aaronson, reveal his own true identity, and then he and Aaronson, Tracy and all, would be knocked off the table and dropped out of sight.

"It is only a matter of time before Aaronson renews contact with you," Svenson said. "Keep in mind that when you hear from him, we will be ready to help. We would like to help him to disappear. We would agree to do that. But we need help from you, too."

"Okay," Spiegel said. "I'll think about it." But he knew what kind of help they would want: reports on membership, on new recruits, on contacts with the States and with foreign governments, all the things that he had done his best, so far, to know nothing about. "But what if I do help you?" Spiegel added. "Then what? After Aaronson is gone, and military intelligence, so-called, goes off following another scent, what happens to me?"

"That depends on what kind of help you would like," Svenson said.

"I need papers," Spiegel said. "I need a residence permit."

"Is that so?" Svenson said. "I would have thought, once Aaronson has gone, there would no longer be a reason for you to stay in Sweden. I would have thought you could be more useful elsewhere."

"So are you offering to help me disappear, too?"

"You?" Svenson said. He leaned toward Spiegel, and his dark hair flopped down, nearly concealing his bright eyes. "But have you forgotten? You have already disappeared."

"The vanishing American," Brunius said.

"Nobody in authority knows that you are still in Uppsala, except for us. And we can be very—what is your word?—discreet."

"You mean even this meeting," Spiegel said. "We're off the books? Nobody else in the department knows who I am or why you brought me here?"

"At this point, that is correct. As far as our official reports are concerned, you are merely a voluntary participant in one of our ongoing investigations, nothing more."

"Then I'm free to go," Spiegel said.

"Of course," Svenson said. "Anytime." He stood and turned

the knob to unlock the door, a subtle reminder, Spiegel felt, that despite the protestations he had been held captive. "Let us just consider this a friendly conversation. How do you say it? A pre-liminary exchange of ideas."

"Yes, like the Paris peace talks," Spiegel said. "Preliminary to the bombing."

Svenson let out a sharp laugh, and Brunius joined in, his laugh so high-pitched it was almost a giggle, though Spiegel doubted if Special Officer Brunius understood the reference.

Spiegel stepped into the corridor. Svenson and Brunius stood behind him, in the doorway. "It's too bad about your friend, though," Svenson said. "I mean the little fellow that was with you on the bridge. What is it you call him?"

"You mean the Worm?"

"Yes, that one. I don't think he looked so good."

"What are you talking about?"

"The river. He fell over the bridge. When you were running, swinging that stick and all. You caused quite a bit of trouble. Maybe even injured your friend. There could be issues we might have to raise, charges. For now, though, let us say your friend was injured in an accident. But we could change our minds after we investigate. Yes, we could change our minds. Good day, Lenny."

"Good day," Brunius said, and raised his flat, paw-like hand. For the first time, Spiegel could see an expression on his face: a big, self-satisfied grin.

13

After Spiegel left the police headquarters, went home, and
filled Tracy in about the interrogation, they agreed that the
Swedes didn't want the U.S. military using Uppsala as a
proving ground for its cold-war battles. Any attack on the
credibility of ARMS would only strengthen the platform of
the right-wing, isolationist fanatics, like Edström and his
Sweden First Party. So the police had been ordered to clear
Aaronson out of their jurisdiction before he could cause any
more problems.

"Then I've got nothing to worry about," Spiegel said.

"Unless they can't find Aaronson, and they decide to throw
someone else to the wolves," Tracy said. "A sacrificial lamb."

They would have to keep tabs on the Worm, to make sure
he didn't turn. They didn't want him talking to the police about
Aaronson's journeys, and they didn't want him agreeing to testify
against Spiegel—swearing that Spiegel tried to knock him off
the bridge, or whatever—in return for a guarantee of citizenship,
of housing vouchers, or other tempting benefits laid out on the
welfare-state *smörgåsbord*.

The next day, they visited the Worm in the hospital, a
sprawling, two-story, crescent-shaped building set in parklike
grounds in the fields behind the botanical gardens. The place
looked more like a country lodge than a health clinic. Dappled
sunlight filtered through the abundant, leafy trees and sparkled
in the hallways. Nurses in crisp uniforms walked silently down
the wide corridors, pushing big steel trays filled with cups and

vials. The only sounds were the occasional beep and ping from monitors concealed behind closed doors.

The Worm was sitting up in bed, propped on bolsters. He was sipping orange juice that had been brought to him on a cafeteria tray.

"Splendid digs," Spiegel said. "When can I move in?"

"All you gotta do is get sick," the Worm said.

"Welcome to socialized medicine," Tracy said. "I could get to like this." She fingered the fabrics on the armchairs. The wall hangings were plush and luxurious. In place of a dresser there was a large oak armoire that held a color TV and a small but excellent stereo.

"Yes, a room to die for," the Worm said.

"I wouldn't go that far," Spiegel said.

"How are you?" Tracy put in. "So tell us what happened."

"They're saying you did it," the Worm said. "At least, asking me if you did. Which tells me they want to put the finger on you, but—"

"Hold on," Spiegel said. "Who's saying? I did what?"

"Cops. They were all over me, as soon as I got shifted to this, what do they call it, *sjukhuset*?"

Hospital—literally, the sick house—was one of the hardest words for an American to pronounce. The only one harder was *sjuksköterska*, nurse, or sick sister, which was supposed to sound like "shook-shooterska," with the *sh* containing the hint of a whistle. The Worm pronounced all of his Swedish the same way: badly.

"Transferred you from where?"

"I couldn't really tell. A horrible clinic, dirty and smelling of bleach. When they pulled me from the river, I was barely alive, coughing blood and brine. Each cough I think I'm spitting up pieces of my lungs. I'm screaming for air. By the time I know what happened, I'm on a cot, next to a junkie with the shakes, sweat and vomit all over his face. I'm waiting for a doctor. A cop shows up, says in pretty good English that they can get me out of there, into a real hospital, if I can help with their investigation. I don't argue. I can still hardly speak. I can't even see. My eyes are stinging from the river water, I guess.

"They put me in a wheelchair. On the way out I saw the rest of the clinic, men like scarecrows with hollow eyes, shivering in their thin green hospital gowns. Awful. They wanted me to see—that's where I'll be if I don't cooperate. Then they took me here."

"And they want you to tell them that I pushed you into the river?"

"They want me to say that Aaronson did."

"The Uppsala police know who I am. Do they know you know?"

"I don't know."

"So what did you tell them?" Tracy asked.

"That I wanted a lawyer."

"Ha," Spiegel said. "You know, here, you've got no Miranda rights."

"No what?"

Didn't everyone know the term?

"Anyway," Spiegel said, "they haven't accused you of anything. You're the victim."

"But I bought time," the Worm said. "I ain't gonna lie. There was a real stampede when you were running the wrong way off the bridge, swinging that pole. I was trying to keep an eye on you, to see where you were going, when I felt a smack against the side of my head." The Worm touched his cheek to point out the purple stain of a bruise.

"It could have been an accident, someone else with a banner, turning around too fast, catching me on the blind side with the butt end of a pole.

"I went down against the railing. Then two hands came toward me, I thought to help me up. I reached for them, and, bang, it was like a ramrod hit me in the chest, and I was falling backward toward the water. As I dropped, all's I could see was Reston leaning over the railing, a big smile on his face."

"You saying he pushed you in?"

"I'm not saying. I can't say. I don't think he was sorry to see it happen, though."

* * *

"I'm calling this meeting to order." Hyde was speaking. Today, he wasn't wearing his beret. He wore khakis and camouflage, like the rest of the deserters. He slammed his hand against the desktop, trying to get the meeting under control.

"Who drafted you?" one of the guys shouted from the back of the room.

"Yo' mama," someone called from another corner.

"She got better taste than that," someone else yelled. There were sparks of laughter as Hyde kept whacking his hand against the wood. With each slap, the desk lamp beside him leaped and worked its way closer to the edge. Either he gets this meeting going or the lamp hits the floor, Spiegel thought.

Spiegel sat in a straight-backed chair next to the makeshift dais. He felt like a prisoner in the dock, which in a sense he was. Hyde had called for the meeting—the first ARMS gathering in a month—to discuss the organization's finances (shaky), its leadership (lacking), and its political influence, which had diminished to the point of near invisibility following the May Day fiasco. Because of the stampede and the riot, which forced the organizing committee to cancel the afternoon rally, the deserters had become pariahs among their former allies in the student left and the labor unions, and the city council, fearful of associating itself with a violent international movement or perhaps just taking the opportunity to play out for political advantage some long-held but seldom expressed racial and ethnic prejudices, had refused to receive the ARMS petition. Spiegel understood. Aaronson was to blame for the decline and fall of ARMS. He had abandoned the men in their time of need, and now the Vandals were storming the gates, with blood in their eyes and smoke on their tongues. Spiegel knew that to save himself he might have to proclaim the truth. He could protect Aaronson only for so long. It was hard work, playing a role, and it had got him nowhere, nothing—except that it had brought him to Tracy. And he had been wondering: When the moment came, as he believed that it had, when he would have to give himself up—or more accurately—relinquish a false identity and reclaim his own, would he have to give up Tracy as well?

Gradually, the noise abated and the men settled into position, some in chairs, some standing. They began to focus on Hyde at the front of the room, still slapping his hand on the table for order. A gray cloud of smoke hovered near the ceiling, fracturing the light into discernible shafts. It had been some time, Spiegel thought, since he had been in a room that was thick with the bitter scent of tobacco. Swedes, he had noticed, tended to restrict their cigarettes to the outdoors, as if smoking were a sport. The Americans tended to smoke indoors, and for them smoking was an act of assertion, even aggression, a way by which the men stained the air and marked off a bit of territory as their own. Spiegel saw Zeke sitting near the rear of the room, sucking powerfully on the last nub of his cigarette so that the glowing ash tip was pulled almost to his lips, a kiss of fire. Sated with the fumes, Zeke dropped the butt onto the floor and squashed it with his heel, as if it were a bug.

"Now, no one of us ever was elected officer or president or anything like that," Hyde was saying, "but somehow Aaronson got himself appointed leader of this here group. Maybe he appointed himself. I don't know. But long as I've been here in Uppsala, we all have gone along with that, and it's been okay. Our housing ain't so bad, we all have pretty secure resident status, we got enough scratch to get by, all that shit. But the past two months, some of us have noticed, things ain't been right. Aaronson goes off to . . . somewhere, supposed to be to recruit new members, but he comes back with nothing. No one's joined us here since the winter. And he goes on TV, a disaster far as I can tell, and then he ain't heard of no more. He gets like real tight with his old lady, and he ain't got no more time for this group. He won't call a meeting, he won't write the May Day speech, he won't even stand up at the rally and present the petition to the city council. So we're wondering: What's going on? Is he trying to back away from this ARMS group because he knows something's coming down and he wants to be out of the free-fire zone when the shit hits? So we start looking into Aaronson and what he's been up to, and we find out about these other problems."

"That's right, you tell it, brother," one of the guys called out from the floor. Spiegel thought it was Hyde's gap-toothed partner from the May Day march.

"It's the money, man," Hyde went on. "Now most of you all know that Aaronson, when he came to Sweden, brought with him a fair bit of cash, and he used it to set up a bank account for the movement. And that money grew, man, though none of us really knows how. We make it our business not to know, okay? Maybe he's dealing in something, maybe he's got a rich grandmama who believes in our cause. I don't know, don't wanna know, right? But there's a purse full of money, and Aaronson's holding the strings. He'll loosen up and let a piece out now and then, and each of us has probably gone to him for a little float to tide us over some rough passages. Each of us knows about the money and we're, how do you say it, beholden to him. Nobody wants to talk about this situation, even to the other brothers, 'cause we're afraid Aaronson will turn off the tap. And we long for that money, even a drop of it. It's like a drop of water for a parched man. So the money's Aaronson's little secret source of power, held over our heads, and just out of reach. Am I right?"

A few of the men nodded in agreement; others bleated out the responsory, "That's right," as if Hyde were running a revival meeting. Spiegel knew what he was talking about, too. The cops had been watching the bank account. Apparently Hyde had been watching it as well.

"So Reston has begun to look into Aaronson's transactions, and I turn the floor over to him to tell you what we've learned."

Reston stood and took Hyde's place at the front of the room. He kept his back to Spiegel, unwilling to meet his contemptuous gaze. Reston pulled some papers from one of the flapped pockets on his flak jacket. "Now, I'm not so good with numbers and all, so you guys will have to bear with me, but what I've got here is a copy of the bank statement of the account that Aaronson set up for ARMS. For us. Now, it says here that it's in his name, I can make that out, and then some words that I'm told mean it's an account held for all of us, like a group, but with him as the, like, the trustee or treasurer. It means anyone can put in money. But he's the only guy who can take it out, right? Him and the person who co-signed the account, his old lady."

"Sounds like a pretty good deal, for him," one of the guys said, and pointed at Spiegel. There was some laughter, scattered and sharp, like buckshot against tin. Spiegel looked straight ahead. He would hold his peace until Reston and Hyde finished their assault.

"What we see here," Reston continued, "is, from the time Aaronson arrived in Uppsala and set up this account, it kept growing every month, till there was, it shows, about twenty-thousand kroner in there, and that's more than five thousand bucks. Then, he takes out about a thousand kroner in March, and that's to pay for his trip to Germany, yes? All through April the account keeps growing and then, bang! Look what happened last week. The account is just about cleared out, wiped off the slate. Somebody goes in, pulls eighteen-thousand kroner, and that leaves us just about at empty. You can see this for yourself." And Hyde handed the crumpled copy of the bank statement to one of the men, who studied the columns of numbers and then passed it on so that it would circulate around the room. It would come to Spiegel last, if at all.

"Thanks, brother," Hyde said, taking the floor back from Reston. "So the question is, and we will ask our comrade to explain it to us, what the hell happened to all this money? It was not flowing into Uppsala for the personal and political benefit of Aaronson. It was meant for ARMS, for the movement. So where did it come from, where is it going, and what are you going to do to replace it?"

"Could I speak to that? Could I speak now?" Spiegel asked. But he wondered, if they gave him permission to respond to the accusations, what he could say. He knew the source of the money, or thought he did, but so did Reston. The money had come from foreign governments, most recently from the Soviet Union, but laundered and filtered through some obscure, gauzy network of charities and trusts and relief agencies so that no one, not even the cops or the spies, could say for sure which blocks of cash came from what source. But where had the money gone? Had Aaronson somehow managed to tap into the account from abroad? Had Tracy acted for him?

"A moment, in a moment," Hyde said. "We will want to hear

from you. But first I want the brothers to hear all the charges I am bringing against you."

"Charges? Am I on trial?" Spiegel said. " 'Cause if I am, I'd as soon resign and be done with it."

"Resign from what?" Hyde said. "We ain't got no officers, no constitution. That would be hierarchical bullshit, as you've taught us. It would be a replication of the authoritarian military culture, if I am quoting you correctly. As a result, we don't have officers. As a result, there is no office from which you can resign. Am I correct?"

Spiegel nodded. There was no way he could stop Hyde, who was like a train rolling downhill, picking up speed. All Spiegel could do was wait and maybe hope to jump when the runaway freight slowed at the next crest.

"At the same time that you have taken money from our treasury, without explanation, a number of strange and inexplicable events have transpired here in Uppsala," Hyde continued. By this point, Hyde had changed his focus and was speaking directly to Spiegel, to the accused.

"Tell it," someone shouted.

"You have been seen," Hyde said, "in the company of the notorious journalist Gunnar Mendelsohn, long suspected of being a collaborator with the U.S. military police."

"He was doing an article, and—"

Hyde cut him off. "That is true! And his article would give one the impression that you fooled the authorities into thinking there was another American, who bore the name of Leonard Spiegel, who was brought to Uppsala to act as your cover, to enable you to sneak off on your travels. His article contained the revelation that Leonard Spiegel does not exist, and that the American spotted at the Swedish border and wanted by the military police was somebody else, a courier for one of your foreign enterprises. But we happen to know that Gunnar Mendelsohn's story was a lie, planted in the press by the CIA. Because Leonard Spiegel does exist. We have found him out. And he is a spy, a snake, that you have brought into our midst." The men burst into hissing noises, and some stamped their feet.

"Do it," someone shouted.

"Tell it," said another.

"Now that's ridiculous," Spiegel muttered.

"Is it? Well, we have had documents supplied to us that show that Leonard Spiegel's father is an operative for the U.S. Foreign Service, based in the Lagos embassy in Nigeria. Which is to say, he is in the direct employ of the CIA, and his son, who was sent here no doubt on government orders, was no more than his father's agent." Hyde held aloft a bound pamphlet. Spiegel could see that it was papers, transcripts, supplied by his college. How did Hyde get those? He felt ambushed, crushed.

"His father works in Africa, yes," he managed.

"And if we find this Spiegel," Hyde shouted, "if he ventures among us, we will pounce on him, and we will smite his head with our heel!"

"You won't see him," Spiegel said. "He's long gone."

"Moreover," Hyde continued, "at the height of the May Day riot, just before the police descended and broke up our rally, before Zeke or any of the expatriates had a chance to address the crowd, you were observed leaving the scene of the march, being whisked away to safety, by a squadron of the Uppsala police."

"Not to safety, man," Spiegel protested, although his spirits were waning, and he knew that there was nothing more he could say to avert the course of the proceedings. His fate had been determined. "I was under arrest!"

"Silence!" Reston shouted.

"Finally," Hyde went on, "we believe that you were a knowing collaborator with the turncoat Timothy McCurdy, formerly known as the Worm, who, in his earth-dwelling, lowly, foul, and rank ways, has wriggled himself into a path underneath our feet and burrowed his way to freedom by rooting below the very soles of our shoes. He shall henceforth be known as the Pig!"

The men burst into hoots, howls, oinks, and snorts.

Zeke had not said a word. It was obvious to Spiegel that they had turned on Zeke as well. Zeke's known ties to Aaronson and to the Worm were being held against him.

And now, Reston and Hyde stood before the membership of

ARMS, accusing the Worm of being a turncoat and a liar. When had they learned the truth about the Worm? Before they had tried to drown him, or afterward? For though Spiegel knew, or at least believed, that the Worm was an innocent, he realized also that there was something about the Worm's obsequious personality that made it seem as if he deserved his fate.

The Worm was gone. The Worm had grown wings and, through a gestational miracle, he had turned into a bird. He had stopped by to see Spiegel and Tracy, when he was released from the clinic, and he had tearfully confessed. He was holding an open return ticket to the States and a valid passport. He had never deserted, never been in the service, except for a stint in the Maryland National Guard. True, during his time in Uppsala he had missed his monthly Guard meetings. But he wouldn't have faced a legal crisis until the summer, when he was due to report for his two weeks of active-duty maneuvers. He told Spiegel and Tracy that he would try to rejoin his unit. It would be better than allowing himself to fight in the war. He wished that he could stay and make Sweden his home, but he had learned the truth about himself. He was not strong enough to desert.

But in his downfall, there was salvation. By leaving, the Worm had managed to avoid the obligation to offer his testimony, to identify Spiegel, and to explain what he knew about Aaronson's travels. Spiegel was left alone to confront his accusers.

Spiegel understood what he would have to do as well. He would have to be strong, like the Worm, by being weak. He would have to practice what the Taoists called moral jujitsu, the power of nonviolence. He would have to overcome the aggressor by giving in to his superior force. Before the meeting, he had stepped into Aaronson's place. Just in time, he understood that doing so would be to step into the trap that Reston had set. Reston knew Spiegel's true identity, but he had convinced the others that Spiegel was a fifth columnist who had conspired with Aaronson to loot the ARMS treasury, or maybe worse. The men were angry at Aaronson, but they were also gunning for the mysterious, elusive Leonard Spiegel. Maybe the Worm had understood that as well. Certainly, Zeke understood.

That's why Spiegel couldn't catch Zeke's eye. This meeting was a crisis for him, too. If Spiegel called upon Zeke to confirm his identity, which he had planned to do, Zeke would be ostracized. Well, if I have to go down, Spiegel thought, I won't take Zeke with me. They will never know that he knew. He wished that there were a way that he could signal Zeke, to let him know that he was going to hold fast to his false identity. He would be Aaronson, to the end, even if in being true to Aaronson he had to be false to himself. All he was able to say, before slinking out of the meeting and leaving Hyde in charge, was that he regretted his failures and that if anyone were to blame—for the disappearance of the funds and for the inroads of the CIA—it was Leonard Spiegel. He swore to the men that he would not return to them unless he could bring Spiegel to face their retribution. He reached for Hyde's hand, but Hyde refused the gesture. The men were silent. Spiegel had come as close as he dared to an admission, in Aaronson's name, of guilt. But the men held for their founding leader an almost nostalgic affection. He was the one who had brought them together and who had guided their way as they took their first steps into a new life. They were uneasy, for they sensed that in the past months, for reasons that they could not understand, Aaronson had abandoned them. Watching Hyde's vengeful attempts to assume his authority allowed the men to see something horrible, if only for a moment. Hyde would be a wrathful god. He was one of the thousands of casualties uncounted on the nightly news. The war had injured him, as it had injured even those whose skin had never been singed by its flames. His would be a reign of terror.

Spiegel walked home from the meeting. He was alone, and he felt lonelier than he had ever felt before, though he was no longer truly alone. He had Tracy, and waiting for him in the States he had Iris. But here he had to live with his sense of failure and betrayal. He had come to Uppsala to help the movement, and all he had done was damage, particularly to Aaronson. If Aaronson ever came back, what would he find? That Tracy had been unfaithful, his comrades had turned against him, he was wanted by the Uppsala police, and he was being stalked by a religious zealot.

It was evening, but the air was still and the sky was bright. Along the sidewalks, tulips and violets grew in large wooden planters. Couples walked the pathways beside the riverbank, holding hands and talking. Groups of young people lingered by the tiny kiosks and sausage stands, laughing and sipping tall drinks. Old men sat on wood-slat benches reading newspapers and magazines, nodding to one another in mutual commiseration about the peculiar state of the world. It was as if the fine weather had melted the icy reserve that, through the long winter, had kept the people of Sweden apart from one another. During the months of darkness and cold, everyone rushed to get indoors, to the shelter of their narrow, isolated lives. Now, people seemed to thrive in the warmth and the light and in one another's company. It was as if they had been released from bondage into freedom, which in a sense they had. But it was a freedom that, to Spiegel, seemed false because it was a freedom that he could not enjoy.

For he knew that he would have to leave Uppsala. He could offer nothing to the movement except more trouble. If he stayed, the police would question him. They would want a dossier on Hyde, on Reston, maybe on Zeke. And would they believe him if he told them the truth, that he had been exiled? No, they would see his action as subterfuge, refusal to cooperate, and they would serve him up to the dogs, like meat. His best chance—not simply for freedom but for his actual survival—might be to head for a city, for Stockholm, alone. There, he might be able to blend into the background, living at a hostel or a cheap rooming house for a few days, until he could make the right contacts, maybe with a foreign embassy. Perhaps he could get a visa for Russia or for Cuba and he could live there safely and Tracy could join him and they would work side by side in a factory or on a farm, in total obscurity, out of the glare of history, until the war ended and a new generation of Americans opened their arms in forgiveness to those who first followed the paths of peace.

* * *

At home, the blinds were closed, casting the rooms in the pearly gray shadows of winter. Tracy must have gone out. Spiegel went to the kitchen to put some water on to boil. He tilted the blinds at the kitchen window to let in some of the evening light, and he froze in place. Aaronson stood there, on the landing, looking in at him. He was hovering, above the ground, ghostly and pale, his eyes wide and his mouth open in a frozen expression of disbelief. And then Spiegel realized that, of course, he was looking at his own image, there in the glass. He stood, regaining his composure, for more than a minute, gazing through his reflection, to the clear air a few feet beyond the windowpane. Spiegel stared through the cloudy image of his face to the empty courtyard, the tobacco shop, the city streets, and he suddenly understood why our deepest thoughts are sometimes called "reflections." We come to know ourselves, and to grow, through doubling, or more precisely through splitting. Every new phase in his life, every step he had taken, he had prepared for by imagining a new self and project-ing his double into a region, of space or of time or both, that he had yet to inhabit. Our lives, he thought, are a process of creating these self-reflections and then transposing ourselves into these projected images, until we can look back at the life we had left behind and see that it has become much like an image, a reflec-tion, as well. We are constantly turning our present life into a reflection to be seen in the future—into memory.

Spiegel was wakened from these dreamlike thoughts by the double chimes of the telephone, much softer and less insistent than the shattering, interruptive ring of an American phone. Still, Spiegel jumped. He and Tracy rarely used the telephone because they were incapable of speaking in Swedish and unwill-ing to say much in English, for fear of surveillance. He stepped away from the window and tentatively picked up the receiver on the fourth ring. It had to be Tracy. She must have heard about the meeting, Spiegel assumed. But why had she gone out rather than wait home for him, and why would she risk discuss-ing the day's events with him on the telephone?

"Hello, Tracy?" Spiegel said. "You know I've been waiting—"

"No, this isn't Tracy," Spiegel heard.

"Monika," he said. "I'm sorry I sounded so paranoid. Things are a little intense right now."

"I know. That's why I've been trying to reach you." Her voice, with the slight musical lift she gave to the vowels and her soft, almost powdery enunciations, stirred him, for a moment, with curiosity and desire. "You've been out for quite a while."

"So Tracy hasn't been here, either," Spiegel said.

"No. Nobody answered."

"I guess she had to keep her distance from me," Spiegel said. "I'm persona non grata."

"You're what?"

"Like the poem says: 'I'm Nobody! Who are you?' Do you know it?"

"I don't know it. Are you okay, though?"

"Where are you calling from?" Spiegel asked. He leaned against the countertop and with his free hand lowered the flame beneath the coffeepot. "Are you nearby?"

"I'm at home."

Spiegel tried to picture her, sitting by the window, her crisp white shirt tucked into her black jeans, her fine hair like filaments of gold, glowing in the evening light.

"Would you like me to come over there?"

"I . . . don't know," Spiegel said. "I'm waiting for Tracy . . ."

"Then you haven't heard the news," Monika said.

"No," Spiegel said. "What news?"

"Nixon. He's bombing Cambodia."

Spiegel gasped. "I don't fucking believe that," he said.

Nixon and Kissinger had been talking about a peace plan. Apparently, this was it—expand the war to all of Southeast Asia. Spiegel felt, for the second time that evening, as if he had been kicked in the chest.

"It seems like this war will never end," Monika said. "We try to stop it, but it just grows and spreads, gets bigger and bigger."

"Like a monster," Spiegel said. "Like a disease."

For a moment, they let a heavy silence hang on the wire between them while each was absorbed in thought.

"I . . . I called to tell you that I have to leave Uppsala for a few days," Monika said. "The SSS has called an emergency session at headquarters, in Stockholm. We will be planning a national student strike. I have to go down there, tonight."

"How long will you be gone?"

Monika said she didn't know for sure.

"Maybe I should go down there, too?"

"Hmm. But what about Tracy?"

"I could leave her a note."

Monika laughed. "I think you should wait there for Tracy," she said. "Maybe she went to the Uppsala student union. They could be working on some plans or some ideas."

"Yes," Spiegel said, cautiously. He was unsure how much to reveal over the telephone. "I've heard a few things, today, about Tracy." He paused, but Monika was silent, waiting for him to proceed. "There's a bank account, which had been set up for ARMS. I think it's possible that she might have been ripping off that account."

"Why would she need to do that?"

"I can't really say," Spiegel said. "Maybe she was planning to travel."

"I don't think so," Monika said. "She wouldn't do anything like that without talking to you."

"Maybe things came up all of a sudden. Maybe there are things she doesn't want me to know."

"Everybody has secrets," Monika said.

"She may have her reasons for hitting on the ARMS treasury, but I'm the one taking the heat. So I think she ought to clue me in on what's been going down."

"Maybe sometimes it's safer to be, how do you say it, in the dark?"

"Ignorance is bliss?"

"Yes, something like that."

"We also have another saying: Knowledge is power. Is that what's going on here? Are you holding out on me?"

Monika paused and sucked in a little puff of air. "*Nej*. I don't know anything about a bank account or about what Tracy has done or even where she is tonight."

"I think what I'm saying is, I have to leave Uppsala. Too many people are closing in too tight," Spiegel said. "I don't think I can hang on here much longer."

"You mean, you're thinking you have to leave the country?" Monika sounded incredulous. "You can't do that."

"I know," Spiegel said. "There's nowhere I could land safely. I'd need to apply for a new passport, for an entry visa. And I can't risk stepping right into the hands of the American authorities: Here I am, the guy you've been looking for. Give me a new passport and I'll quietly go away. I think they'd have their own ideas about how to help me leave—in chains."

"We can't let that happen," Monika said. "I could find a place for you. My family has a small house in the north where you could stay until the danger has passed."

"It may never pass."

"You should stay with us until Tracy can get you the documents and visas that you will need to travel. She could send them to you or meet you at a site that would be secure. We have done things like this before, for other political refugees. It's no problem."

"That might be what we have to do," Spiegel agreed.

Monika had been planning to drive north to visit her family at the end of the spring term. She could bring Spiegel with her, and he could wait while Tracy, back in Uppsala, worked out the final arrangements for him to stay at a new refuge in Sweden, or else for his flight.

"If you're still in danger, I will talk to Tracy when I get back," Monika said. "I'm sure she'll be cool with the plan."

Despite the horrible events of the day and the demoralizing developments in the faraway war, Spiegel felt as if he had settled into a strange, Zen-like state of composure, a willingness to accept his fate. Talking with Monika seemed to have that effect on him, soothing his nerves and helping him to understand that political engagement can grow out of something greater than self-interest and self-preservation. It was easy to see why people like Zeke, Hyde, Aaronson, even he himself had joined the antiwar movement at home or the resistance movement abroad. The specter of war had set its bony hands upon their throats, and they were struggling to get free. But Monika had become involved in the movement out of her sense of missionary zeal, her saintly devotion to what increasingly seemed like a hopeless, quixotic cause. Until he had met Monika, Spiegel had felt a spiteful contempt for the Swedes and other foreigners who picketed the embassies and denounced American imperialism. They should mind their own business, he thought. Let them get their own houses in order. But he had changed. He could not help but recognize and admire the pure and altruistic nature of Monika's commitment, the authenticity of her spirit, in the way that even an untutored novice can distinguish a fine varietal wine from a harsh blend or a genuine Ming vase from a cheap, factory-made export.

Following the skein of these thoughts, trying to sort through the many images he had of Monika—fired up in righteous anger that night in the television studio, sitting cross-legged in her cottage sipping vodka and herbal tea, standing in her doorway with her lovely face back-lit by candles as he and Tracy walked through the botanical garden to find their way home—Spiegel's mind became snarled. He kept stumbling across the tangle of his relationship with Tracy. What had she done? Despite all that he had heard at the meeting and all that had been implied by Monika's evasive answers to his inquiries, he refused to believe that Tracy had betrayed him. How could he believe that she had turned against him without a word, without a touch of guilt or remorse? But how could he explain the bank account? Could she have withdrawn funds to divert to some private purpose of her own? What expenses did she have? The rent? The upkeep on the VW? She seemed, to Spiegel, totally unaffected by material needs and by the drive to accumulate capital, a living refutation of all the theories of Marx and Engels.

During the fateful ARMS meeting, Spiegel had assumed that Reston had been lying about the bank account in order to tighten the knot around "Spiegel's" neck. As he sat at the kitchen table, sipping the dregs of his coffee, enjoying some momentary solitude during the few hours of darkness, anticipating the sound of Tracy's key turning the door lock, Spiegel began to realize that Reston might have been telling the truth. Beneath the surface of his public attack, Reston might have been trying to slip Spiegel a private message. He might have been trying to let Spiegel know that Aaronson had returned to Uppsala. But if that were so, where was Aaronson hiding? How much had he observed? How much had Tracy revealed?

What will I say to him, Spiegel asked himself, when he learns that I have broken my word? What will he say when he finds out that he has been driven out of ARMS in disgrace, that the whole movement has been blown apart, scorched to the earth, like a jungle village strafed by firebombs? How can I account for all the rubble and the ruin, all the damage I have done?

14

"I found you!" Melissa was standing in the vestibule, at Tracy's doorway. She looked white as paper, but with a ghostly glow, like a TV screen with the brightness turned up too high. Her eyes had a wet and glassy look, as if she had been awake for many hours through pharmaceutical aid. "I've been looking for you, for, shit, I don't know. I've been in rehearsals all week, and we opened last night. I think it was last night. Did you read about it?"

"I heard it was a smash," Spiegel said.

"Oh, yeah, the play. What a scream. You should've come to the opening, joined us at the cast party." The memory of the cast party seemed to make her shudder a little, like the thought of a stiff drink after a night of far too many. She put her hand to her forehead, as if to wipe off a thin residue of perspiration.

"Are you okay?" Spiegel asked. "Do you want to come in?"

Melissa wanted a cigarette. It would calm her, she said. She had, in fact, been up pretty much straight through for two days, since the show, the all-night party, the anticipatory hours before the first reviews, the full day of meeting the press. Mick's take on Strindberg, now called *Ms. Julie*, had become his latest *succès de scandale*. He costumed Julie—Melissa—in a low-cut black cocktail dress, and Jean, the valet, had become a Black Power revolutionary, with a bandana wrapped around his head and an ammunition belt strapped across his chest. The men in the cast, Strindberg's peasants, wore U.S. Army fatigues, and the women were dressed as Vietnamese bar girls. A crowd of pickets, claiming that Julie represented "American imperialist hegemony," had marched in front of the theater and stormed the stage during the "peasant chorus" at the end of act one, throwing the theater into turmoil until the Uppsala police arrived to restore order and to establish a "military occupation" to keep the peace during act two. It was later revealed that the pickets had been aspiring actors and the police had been hired for the occasion, uncredited extras working on a per diem.

After the reviews came out, Melissa, still in costume, accompanied Mick on his rounds. She was supposed to give the photographers something to focus on other than Mick's sunken eyes and waxy skin, maybe to get a chance to answer some questions about the show and get her own name in the papers. But any chance she'd had, she totally fucked, she said. She sat beside Mick in a TV studio, trembling from the aftershock of a long night of Finnish vodka laced with meth. Maybe the reporters had asked her stuff, but she had no idea what she'd said although she was sure that none of it was quotable. So much for advancing her acting career.

Mick, she reported, was on a high, totally psyched about the *Ms. Julie* reception, talking about putting the show on the road, taking it to Paris, London, New York. Melissa wasn't so sure. Once the audience learned that the demonstrations were part of the production, the element of surprise would be eliminated. Mick, though, said he could make it work. "We can pack this show in a box and sell it like waffle mix," he said.

"Come on in. Sit down," Spiegel said. He led Melissa in from the doorway where she would stand and talk forever, if he let her.

Tracy was sitting on the floor, legs folded, working on some meditations. She raised her hand, Buddha-like, a silent gesture of welcome.

"I didn't mean to bust in or anything," Melissa said, "but I had to find you guys to talk, and, the phone . . ."

"You're right about that. I wouldn't trust it."

"Can we go somewhere where we won't bother her?" Melissa said, nodding toward Tracy.

"We won't bother her. She has maximum powers of concentration." Spiegel led Melissa into the kitchen. Coffee would be a really bad idea, he thought, looking at her shaking hands. He offered to cook up some eggs, and she said okay. He wondered how long it had been since Melissa had eaten.

"It wasn't easy to find you guys," Melissa said. "I went to the ARMS office and asked where to find Aaronson. And some dude said he had no fucking idea, that Aaronson was no longer a part of the American movement, that he had been exposed as an agent of the forces of imperial aggression and he had probably gone home to wallow in the muck of his pigsty."

"So they gave you the impression they're no longer fond of him," Spiegel said. "They think he betrayed the movement, stole money from the treasury." He had a feeling that Melissa knew this already and had known for some time.

"So I asked," Melissa went on, hardly noticing anything Spiegel said to her, "about Tracy. Where I could find her digs. Nobody knew a thing about Tracy, either. So they said. But I knew that was bull. The whole friggin' bunch of them's been to Tracy's at one time or another. Hell, every American in Sweden came here for the party she threw after the, what was it, Byrds concert?"

"Traffic."

"Yeah. But they wouldn't say where she lived. Then I remember Jorge telling me something about a . . . what do you call it?" Her speech processes seemed to be deteriorating, as if her mind were a machine on tightly wound coil springs that had begun slowing toward a dead stop.

"I don't know."

Melissa pointed out the window, then gestured with her hand, waving her cigarette.

"*Tobak.*"

"Yeah, tobacco shop. So I knew pretty much the neighborhood, and when I got here I asked around about cigarettes and shit, where I could get them. And then I saw Tracy's Volkswagen and everything. And I'm here."

"Yes." Spiegel put the plate of fried eggs in front of her, along with some bread and butter on a small wooden board.

"Go ahead, eat it, Melissa. You'll feel better." Tracy was standing in the doorway. She had finished her meditations and was wiping her face with a kitchen towel. She looked at Melissa with contempt. Even Tracy, Spiegel thought, whose mission in life seemed to be to rescue strays, would not reach out to Melissa. There was something about Melissa that put off other women. She was a threat to them and a challenge, and they didn't mind seeing her suffer.

"I don't know," Melissa said, shaking her head. "I'm not all that hungry." She poked the eggs around on the plate with the tines of her fork.

"Suit yourself." Tracy went to the stove to fix coffee.

"So," Melissa said. "I can see, by looking around here. That . . ." Her face seemed to crumple like paper as she broke into tears. She opened her palms and lay her head in her hands and cried. Her blond hair fell forward to the tabletop, surrounding her sobbing figure like a curtain and giving her the illusion of privacy.

Spiegel and Tracy looked at each other. It was obvious that the girl was having a breakdown. Whatever drugs she had been riding had just given out.

"Do you want to go to sleep?" Spiegel asked. "Do you need a place to crash?"

"It's not me," she said. "It's him. I was hoping I'd find him here. But no. You haven't seen him, then, have you?"

"You mean Mick?"

She shook her head "No," she said. "I'm worried about Jorge."

Melissa had stayed as long as she could at the cast party. Mick had rented a hip boutique for the bash, and the party was just screaming far-out, she said. All the extras showed up, the guys in their fatigues and the chicks still in their kabuki makeup. The cops that Mick hired to stage the bust showed up, too, but they hung at the edges, drinking cheap Australian wine. Everyone else tried to stay out of their line of sight by hiding, like, behind the mannequins and stuff to pop their pills or sniff their—whatever. Then they'd step out from the clothes racks and make like they were just having a cool time, drinking wine and eating little smoked-fish sandwiches on rye crisps. The models who worked at the store walked around with trays, wearing skirts about as short as a snakeskin belt. Way past midnight one of the cops got real drunk and made a move on an Asian chick, and she whacked him with her tray. There were bits of canapé everywhere, even on some of the clothes racks. Guys started stuffing their appetizers into the pockets of the jackets on the mannequins in the windows and even inside of the cuffs of the pants draped on the racks. The same cop, by dawn, was so out of it, he made a pass at a mannequin, Melissa said.

It was already morning when they left the party, but she was still so high on the show that she forgot she had been kicking it all night. Mick ran out and got a couple of morning papers and one of the kabuki ladies translated all the reviews for him and he thought that they were pretty cool. So he said, come on, let's go celebrate. Melissa said, Let's crash. But Mick said, No, he's got to do a TV show and some other interviews and he wants to go home and get changed, so Melissa thought, Okay, how often am I going to get a chance to be on TV, even if it is TV2 that nobody ever watches? At least it's a credit.

They walked back to the theater, where Melissa left her car. Melissa was hoping he'd drive, but not sure she should let him. He had no license and drove by Australian rules, he said, which had something to do with rugby or water polo. Goal, goal, he'd shout. He went to the driver's side and opened the door and who popped out?

"Jorge," Spiegel said.

Absolutely, Melissa said. He had found her car behind the theater and hid there all night, waiting. At first, maybe he'd just been looking for a place to rest, or maybe he wanted a ride back home and some sort of reconciliation. But as the night went on he'd gotten angrier, obsessed, blaming all his troubles on Melissa. When she showed up, hungover, maybe still a little drunk, alongside Mick, who was so high he could suck lightbulbs from a street lamp, Jorge went nuts. He took Mick by surprise and smacked him hard, knocking him to the ground, but Mick, his courage stoked by the chemicals racing through his veins, popped back like a toy on a spring and started beating the shit out of Jorge.

"How's Jorge now?" Spiegel said.

Well, that's the point, Melissa continued. She'd gotten between Jorge and Mick, taken a few body blows doing it, but got Mick to back off, draw a breath, dust off his jeans, while Jorge slumped to the ground. There was blood coming from a gash above his eye. "We've got to get him to a hospital," she had said, but Mick said, "Like hell."

Melissa went on. "And I said, like, we're gonna just leave him here? He could have a concussion. He could be dying! And Mick goes, well, that's the fucking point, that's why we're leaving, and I said we can't do that, and he says—so why don't I just go to the bobbies and sign a bloody confession, why don't I? He starts talking about how the publicity would be sure to bolster his career: 'Director booked on murder rap; It's curtains.' So I tell him I'm taking care of Jorge no matter what you say, and Mick storms off down the street."

Melissa leaned over Jorge, who was slumped against the side of the car, sitting in a puddle of water. She could see a large bump rising on the side of his head and a crease or indentation across his cheek where Mick had smashed his face against one of the ridges of the door frame. She touched his forehead, wiping a dollop of blood away from his left eyebrow. Jorge opened his eyes and looked at her. His eyelids fluttered. He had a glassy, faraway look. It seemed to take him a few seconds to recognize Melissa, to focus on her face, and when he did it was as if his eyes sharpened like pencil points and he screwed up his mouth into a tight little knot of contempt and said to her, "Whore."

"I couldn't believe it," Melissa said. "Here I am, literally lifting him out of the gutter, and he's accusing me of all sorts of crazy shit."

"You mean he got up and started talking?" Tracy asked.

"Oh, definitely. You can beat the crap out of his little popsicle stick of a body, but you can't shut up his mouth unless you've got a fistful of epoxy. He can barely stand up, he's wobbly like a drunk or a two-year-old, and he's shoving some papers at me, talking about love notes, says he's been on to me all along, that I've been fucking all night with that kangaroo, that he's through with me, I'm dead, worse than dead."

"So at least he's okay, right?" Tracy said, her interest in Melissa's story now kindled by her sympathy for Jorge. "Mick didn't kill him."

"No, but this is the thing," Melissa said. "I made a huge mistake."

Melissa had told Jorge, right there on the street, that he was right, she had been seeing Mick, that things got out of hand a little, stuff like that happens in the theater all the time, the lines between the stage and reality tend to blur and you confuse your life with your character's life and before you know it you're fucking someone your character's in love with for no reason other than that it's in the script.

"But the show is over and it's over between me and Mick and I never should have done it and let's just go home and patch you up and patch us up," Melissa had concluded.

Jorge slowly stood. He was silent during the ride back to Flogsta, and Melissa was concerned. Maybe he was just spent, or maybe he was gathering his thoughts, because God knows his thoughts—if you could call them that—were by now scattered all over the city. Or maybe he had really been injured by the beating and Melissa wondered if she should take him to the *sjukhus* instead of back to Flogsta. And looking back, she said, that's what she ought to have done. But she'd thought it would be better to get Jorge home and let him rest. And also, she admitted, she'd been thinking of Mick, because if she showed up at a clinic with Jorge bashed about, bruised and pulpy like a piece of old fruit, someone was sure to ask her, "What happened to your friend?" And Jorge would tell them, "A guy beat the hell out of me." And the cops would come for Mick, probably right in the middle of the TV2 interview. They would yank him out of the studio, cameras rolling.

"So I thought I'd take a chance and see if I could get him back to his room and let him sleep it off, you know, keeping his head cool and level, watching his pupils, that kind of stuff."

Spiegel looked at Tracy. She shook her head as if to say, This lady's crazy.

"Mel, are you a nurse or something?" Spiegel said. "Because a head injury is like something not to fool around with."

"No, but I've watched that stuff a lot on TV."

"So now he's back at your room—"

"He's in your old room, actually. Or he was this morning, when I went to the studio, with Mick. When I got back home, though, the door was locked, and he wouldn't answer."

"So he could be in there, in a coma or something—"

Melissa nodded. "I thought you might still have a key," she said.

"No, he has the only one," Spiegel said.

"We should get him to a hospital," Tracy said. "I can tell them we just found him in his room like that. . . ."

Melissa was sobbing. Her story, or her portion of Jorge's story, was finished. She had plunged in much deeper than she had ever meant to go. She had turned to Spiegel and to Tracy in desperation.

"I'm talking to you, Melissa," Tracy said, and Melissa nodded, but it was unclear how much of what Tracy was explaining to her she could comprehend. Maybe some of it registered and was filed away, and when the spasms of emotion and guilt eased she would be able to recall Tracy's words and make some sense of them.

"Lenny and I have to get the hell over to Flogsta as fast as we can and get some help for Jorge. The less we know about him right now, the better. As far as we're concerned, you told us nothing, we never saw you. We were just worried about Jorge because we haven't seen him since he split from the show, you dig?"

Melissa looked up at Tracy with wet eyes. She had nothing more to say.

"As for you," Tracy went on, "you've got to get out of here. Go to Mick, but don't tell him anything. I don't want the whole world to know we're covering your ass, and his. I don't want to see this in his next fucking play: Hamlet beating Polonius's head against the hood ornament of a Karmann Ghia. Do you understand me, Melissa?"

"Yes," she said.

"Then go. Now."

Melissa said okay, and stood. "I don't know how, you guys, I mean . . . " And she fell into Tracy's arms. Tracy held her in a motherly embrace, and Spiegel could see the gentling effect she had on Melissa. It was as if some of Tracy's power and determination was being passed on directly to Melissa, by contact, calming her nerves and her heart.

"I'm ready now," she said. "I'm okay."

Melissa left, heading for Mick's. Tracy and Spiegel hopped into the VW and took off for Flogsta. Spiegel's knees shook from fear and anxiety.

"How bad do you think it'll be?" he asked Tracy.

"Head injuries—I don't know. They can become real serious really fast. Swelling of the brain and stuff."

"She should never have left him alone," Spiegel said.

"No shit. If anything happens, she's as much to blame as Mick."

"Maybe she didn't know."

"Hell, of course she knew," Tracy said. "Didn't anything strike you as really strange about her story?"

"Like the whole fucking thing," Spiegel said.

"Yes, but strangest of all. She was so particular about tucking Jorge into bed all snuggly and warm. Now how often do you think he's been sleeping in your old room?"

Spiegel understood. Never. But Melissa wanted to make sure that if anything went desperately wrong it wouldn't happen in her room and that whatever happened, whenever it happened, she would be far from the scene.

"You mean she was just putting on an act for us. She knew exactly what to do about Jorge, but she was playing the role of the helpless ingenue, the space ranger, strung out on vapors and meth."

"We ride off to the rescue," Tracy said, "while she and Mick wash each other's hands."

They drove the rest of the way in silence, each lost in thought.

* * *

It had been more than a month since Spiegel had been back
to Flogsta. He was amazed to see the changes. The earth was
no longer gashed with tractor treads nor scarred by tailings of
cement. Grass flourished, and conical plantings cast shade across
the fresh, undulant lawns. The bulldozers, earthmovers, and
cranes, which had huddled in the snowdrifts like great yellow
reptiles, had been replaced by a fleet of Saabs and Volvos, parked
at identical angles, in neat rows, on the newly paved lot that had
been carved into the hillside. The six towers, which in the winter
had been framed by scaffolding, draped in bright blue tarpaulins,
and limned with orange power cords that traversed the temporary facings like veins, had been unshrouded. The buildings
stood on the hilltop, six gleaming obelisks of glass and steel, each
one cold and isolate, like modules for a lunar colony.

Spiegel was disoriented by the evening light. The sky was so
bright, the light so clear, that Spiegel had to remind himself that
it was nearly six o'clock. A small group of students, their day's
work done, stood in the long shadows of the Flogsta towers.
Spiegel thought that the architects might have placed the students on the lawn as an element of the design, to mark the blank
tablet of the otherwise deserted campus with the ornaments of
habitation and community as a landscape artist might sketch a
row of sheep grazing on a hillside to imply a human presence
that lies just outside the frame. Spiegel thought of all the signs of
student life, as he had known it, which were missing in Uppsala:
no Frisbees, no tattered backpacks, no golden Labs on frayed
leashes, no thumping rock bass from a portable hi-fi, no stink
of incense and marijuana, no bleach-scarred jeans and tie-dyed
T's, no unruly hair and bloodshot eyes and mouths concealed by
the scruff of a black beard, no bandannas, no woven magic-eye
necklaces, no bracelets of Navajo beads, in short, none of the
symbolic assertions that had set the current generation, Spiegel's
own, apart from the rest of American society.

The lobby of Spiegel's building, which he remembered as a
tomb framed in rough cement, had been transformed. The floor
was covered by a sisal carpet, the walls lighted by recessed bulbs
placed discreetly above the doorway. The elevator seemed to

float between floors, and its arrival was announced with a soft but satisfying *ping*.

It was all Tracy and Spiegel could do to keep from shouldering open the elevator doors and sprinting to Jorge's room. But they had agreed that they would approach the scene as if nothing were wrong. And their caution was rewarded when they saw, by the kitchen, one of the Swedish students who lived down the hallway. Spiegel remembered his name.

"*Hej*, Lars," he said.

"*Hej*. You're back." Lars set a saucepan on the stove and stepped over to greet Spiegel. "Welcome."

Spiegel wondered how much Lars had read, or been questioned, about his disappearance. "I'm just here for a moment. I'm just visiting."

"We're here to see Jorge," Tracy said, cutting Spiegel off. "Is he home? Have you seen him?"

"You, too," Lars said. "Everybody's after that guy, this evening."

Tracy and Spiegel looked at each other.

"Who else?" Tracy asked.

"First Melissa asked me if I had seen him. Then some girl from building one."

That must have been Lisbet, Spiegel realized. Was Jorge still seeing her, too? Perhaps, while Melissa was pursuing her extra-curricular interests, he had been involved in a bit of recidivism.

"Is he around?" Spiegel asked. "Did they find him?"

"The girl had been knocking on his door, but he didn't answer," Lars said. "She was all dressed to go out—makeup, stockings. I could smell her perfume from here, like a cloud of violets."

"It's not like Jorge to miss a chance to be with one of his birds."

"Maybe he's just asleep," Lars said. "Like the last time you were here."

"Last time?" Spiegel said.

"You know, last week. When you came back, from—wherever—and you found him in your room."

A chill shook Spiegel's body. He suddenly understood what

was happening. Aaronson had been here, trying to make contact. Perhaps he didn't want anyone in ARMS to know that he was back in Uppsala. But why had Aaronson come to Flogsta and not to Tracy's?

"Have people been looking for me, as well?" Spiegel asked.

"No one this week. After you moved out, there was that newspaper fellow. And some calls from the States, I think."

"What did you tell them?"

"Nothing. I didn't know where you had gone. I said to talk to Jorge, that he might know."

"Yes," Tracy said. "We've got to talk to Jorge, too."

Lars shrugged, as if to say, suit yourself. For a guy who has done a lot of observing, Spiegel thought, Lars comes across with very little information. Maybe you have to pay him for his information. Maybe somebody has. There was always something creepy and conspiratorial about Lars, and Spiegel sensed that Lars was part of the network or circle that had been surrounding him, just beyond the margins of his vision. Now, he could see signs of its presence everywhere he turned.

He and Tracy walked quickly down the hallway to Jorge's room. The door was locked. Tracy whacked her palm against it and called Jorge's name.

"But maybe he's not there," Spiegel said. "He could have gotten up, felt better."

"And then?"

"He would have looked for Melissa. Most of his stuff is in her room, anyway."

Melissa's door had been left ajar. The stench of cigarettes and incense seeped from her room into the hallway. Inside, it looked as if the room had been ransacked. Clothing, books, and papers were strewn all over the floor. Record albums were fanned out on the desktop. Some had been stripped from their paper sleeves. One black disk with a bright green island at its center, exposed to the direct sunlight, had begun to warp. The room was uncomfortably hot. A plate of cheese and sliced salami had melted into little pools of oil that reeked of garlic and smoke. Several tall glasses left beside the window were streaked with a dark but translucent film. The rya rug had been kicked aside, its long fibers greasy with wine stains and the grainy residue of ashes and cake crumbs. The coverlet, sheets, and bedding had been stripped and left in a pile by the closet door. The bare white mattress looked odd amid the chaos, like a well-trimmed boat passing through a sea churning with wreckage and debris.

"Someone tore this place up," Tracy said. "No one could live like this."

"I'm not sure," Spiegel said. He had seen plenty of other rooms in such disarray, had even awakened in some of them. "Maybe she just left in a hurry."

"No," Tracy said. "Someone's been through here, either looking for something or trying to send Melissa a message."

"You think it was Jorge?"

"Maybe he woke up this morning, before Melissa left for the TV interviews, and they had a fight. . . ."

Spiegel looked around the room. "Jorge doesn't fight that well," he said. "You'd have to be really strong to fight long enough to do all this damage."

"But it must have made a lot of noise," Tracy said. "Wouldn't someone have heard and come in to see what was happening?"

"People here tend to mind their own business," Spiegel said.

He stepped cautiously through the rubble, turning this way and that, trying to reconstruct from memory the room as it was when he had first met Melissa. He picked up some cosmetics that had been knocked to the floor, straightened a mirror on the dresser top. It was a fine mirror, with beveled glass and a frame of darkened ivory, nearly the color of tortoiseshell. African, possibly, Spiegel thought. He wondered whether it was Jorge's or Melissa's. He couldn't manage to make it stand properly on the dresser because of a slight irregularity at the base, as if the dimensions of the frame had been subtly adapted to natural contours of the bone. Spiegel noticed a clasp on the back, however, and realized that the mirror must have once hung from a small hook that he saw protruding from the wall. Before he could replace the mirror, he caught sight of his own image in the glass. It still surprised him to see himself with such short hair. In the months that he had been in Sweden, or perhaps just in the time that he had been living with Tracy, his face had filled out and his eyes had become more alert, his lips more prominent. The set of his face conveyed a new serenity and self-confidence. Spiegel wondered if somehow he looked even more like Aaronson than when they had agreed to exchange identities and to step into each other's lives.

Just then, an odd thing happened. As Spiegel looked at his reflection, his own face seemed to speak to him, to form some words, inaudible and barely intelligible at first, but words that seemed to present to him a riddle that he could not solve. "Which one am I?" the face in the mirror seemed to be whispering from somewhere deep within the glass. What's going on here? Spiegel wondered. He tried to look away from the mirror, but his own image held him fast. Was he actually saying these words, or was it just a nervous tic that had always lain dormant or, more likely, that he had never before had the capacity to observe, some spasm that forced his mouth into a set of shapes that looked like words? Or perhaps the words, which he could not at first comprehend, had risen from a deeper region of his mind where they had been hidden, coagulating for years, like a bubble of petroleum lying unseen beneath desert sand.

"Are you okay?" Tracy asked. For a full minute, she had been watching Spiegel, transfixed by his own image. "Why are you staring like that?"

The words seemed to pass from Spiegel's image directly to his lips, and as he said them—"Which one am I?"—the words tasted peculiar on his tongue. It was as if someone else had spoken through Spiegel's body, as if he were just a medium.

"What are you talking about?" Tracy said.

Spiegel set the mirror back on the dresser. He felt cleansed and lightened, as if a weight had been lifted and he was free to move again, to speak in his own voice. His muscles felt loose and flexible, the air itself seemed thin, pure, and he thought that if he relaxed he could lose his grip and float to the ceiling, as if the oxygen in his blood had been transformed through some intercession, some sudden and obscure chemical phenomenon, into helium. He knew that these thoughts were absurd, yet the perception itself was persistent, overpowering. Have I fallen into the clutches of some exotic West Coast hallucinogen that Melissa had sprinkled on the carpet like talc so that the merest human stirrings would cloud the air with the infectious powder? Or am I in the aura that passes through the mind like a wave of light before an epileptic seizure?

With a click, like a case snapping closed, Spiegel remembered where he had come upon the words uttered by the face in the mirror. He scanned the framed posters and the photographs on the walls. The thumbtacks had been removed from the lower corners of a poster of a surf bum, and the picture had begun to curl toward the ceiling, like a tailing ocean wave. Two months' worth of grime and smoke stains had clouded the plastic laminate that protected Melissa's art photographs. The images, which once had given the room the look of a gallery, had become blurred and obscure. With the side of his hand, Spiegel wiped away an oily palm print and leaned close to peer at the double-exposed image of the Venus flytrap and the Botticelli Venus. He could read the legend beneath the images: *Which one am I?* Next to the photograph, a display case was hanging limply from a single hinge.

"Tracy, look," Spiegel said, in a voice that startled him because it was once again his own. "Someone pulled it from the wall."

The case used to rest on a set of brackets, directly over Melissa's bed. One of the brackets had been wrenched half-loose from the plasterboard. The other had been twisted, as if a hand had tried but failed to tug it free.

"Yes, so what?" Tracy said. "The way this place looks right now, wall decor is not an issue."

"It's what used to be there," Spiegel said. "Her gun. That's where Melissa kept her pistol. Someone took it."

"Are you sure it's not buried in this clutter?"

They looked, but found no sign of the gun. A whip and a long sword and a scabbard that Melissa had also placed on display had been tossed into a corner among the bedding. The gun was gone.

"My God," Tracy said. "What do you think—"

"We've got to see if he's in his room," Spiegel said.

They rushed back across the hall, and Tracy began bashing her palm against Jorge's door. "Jorge, if you're in there, open up," she called above the tattoo of her slapping hand. "Unlock the door, Jorge." But there was no answer. Spiegel could see tears on her face, tears that seemed to have been wrung out of her by sheer exertion. She leaned her forehead against the door frame, panting for breath.

Lars had stepped out of the kitchen. He was watching Tracy, placidly, from his station in the hallway. Spiegel turned to look at him. He felt like telling Lars to screw.

"I thought I could help," Lars said.

"We have to get into this room," Tracy said. "Jorge may be hurt."

"Does the housing office have a master key?" Spiegel asked.

"But it's closed," Lars said. "Closes at six." He tilted his wrist to show Spiegel the face of his watch. "Maybe you could call the police. Just press emergency." Spiegel knew what he meant: the red button with the Munch scream that had startled him the night he arrived at the Uppsala station. The last thing Spiegel wanted would be to bring the police onto the scene.

Spiegel thought for a moment. "The girl from building one who came here," he asked. "Did she say anything to you? About Jorge?"

"I can tell you exactly what she said. She said she would like to kill him. She said he'd stolen her fucking car."

"Her car?" Spiegel looked at Tracy.

"I think we have to talk to Lisbet," Tracy said.

Spiegel and Tracy found her standing at the edge of the parking lot, her hands squarely on her hips. She was wearing a tight mini and black fishnet stockings. Her short hair had been tousled by the gentle evening breeze.

"Lisbet!" Spiegel called.

She turned to him, and squinted. She was no longer wearing her owlish eyeglasses. Her face was done up with black eyeliner and purple mascara that made her milky skin look so white it gleamed like fresh paint. "I knew you hadn't gone away," she said.

"No, I never left Uppsala. I just moved into the city. I moved in with Tracy."

Tracy introduced herself to Lisbet. Lisbet took her hand. "Forgive me," Lisbet said. "It has been a strange day."

An hour back, Lisbet explained, she had been on her way out to meet some other "birds" at a club in town, but when she got to the lot she couldn't find her car. Now it's true she'd had nights where she came in so late and tired—smashed, in other words, Spiegel interpreted—that the next day she couldn't remember where she had parked, and other nights she'd lent her car to a friend who had to leave after the last bus—in other words, Spiegel thought, to some guy she'd picked up who had to get out of her life by dawn—but this was different, she was sure. She had come in at a reasonable hour the night before, gotten some sleep, awakened in the morning in time for her classes. She rode the bus into the city and spent the afternoon in the library, thinking about studying for her exams. She caught the bus back to Flogsta at four o'clock and fixed herself an early dinner, or some semblance thereof, most likely—from what Spiegel remembered Jorge's saying about the diet he would have been subjected to had he let Lisbet cook—jam smeared on a roll and potato soup sipped cold from the can. She changed, did her hair, stepped out for the night with a lucid mind, and her car was gone, vanished.

Her first suspicions lit on a guy she had been seeing since Jorge left, one of the workmen who had been stringing electrical cable in building five. An expert on wiring, he told her that if she refused to come home with him to the Bosporus, he would give her car a "hot start" and drive it all the way by himself. The Volvo would give him something to remember her by. So she suspected Arne, but she couldn't very well wander into the workers' quarters to find him, not dressed like this. The men were breaking down the encampment, packing up for home, blasting away their final payments with a night of beer and herring and bonfires and who knew what else? Who could go there for her? She didn't want to involve the police, if she could help it. She thought of Jorge. He was crazy enough that this kind of mission would appeal to his Mediterranean sense of chivalry. There was still a force between them, Lisbet felt, a connection that united them despite Jorge's peregrinations and her own, like a thin span crossing a gorge high above the waters of a swift and sinuous stream. She went to his room to call on him for help, and only as she was rapping on his door, under the sidelong observations of the seemingly indifferent but curiously ever-present Lars, did the truth strike her. Jorge had kept her spare set of keys. Jorge had taken the car.

"So you haven't called the police," Spiegel said.

"No. They wouldn't believe me. They would think I have lousy screws."

Spiegel didn't correct her idiom. He rather liked it, the hidden truth her malapropism revealed, for the police would be sure to think that Lisbet got just what she deserved. They would look at her, hear her story, and determine that she was a slut who liked foreign boys, hippies, longhairs, drug addicts, perverts, and naturally those guys would rip her off, rob her blind, and if one of them even took off with her car, well, what else would you expect?

"I'm glad you kept the police out of this," Tracy said. She didn't want to tell Lisbet about the gun. There was no point in further upsetting her. "I think Jorge might be in trouble. It will be better if we find him ourselves."

"Not better for him," Lisbet added. "I am not as tolerant as the police."

Spiegel drove Lisbet and Tracy directly to Mick's flat in the commercial district. He sensed that Jorge would have gone there first. They circled the block, trying to spot Lisbet's Volvo. If it were parked nearby, they would see it, for the shops were closed and the lots nearly empty.

"Jorge's not here," Tracy said.

Lisbet cared less about seeing Jorge than about recovering her car. If they saw her Volvo parked on the street, she was prepared to hop in and drive it home and have the ignition pulled the next morning. She would rather do that than make Jorge hand back her spare key.

"What if we see him driving it?" Spiegel asked. He thought

that maybe Jorge was cruising the city, trying to find his way to Mick's apartment.

"Can you follow him and wait till he gets out?"

"Not without him seeing us. He knows this VW. He'll know we're tailing him."

"Then knock him off the road."

She's seen too many American movies, Spiegel thought. He had no intention of using a car, particularly a VW, as an attack weapon, and he knew that a chase through the city streets would probably get all of them arrested, or even killed. Plus, there was the matter of the gun Jorge might be carrying. A gun would tip the balance, in any confrontation, in ways that Lisbet, who was unaware, had not considered.

They turned a corner onto the street directly behind Mick's building. "Shit, look at that," Spiegel said.

"What? I can't see," said Lisbet. She was crowded into the backseat, her legs folded up almost to her chin.

Spiegel tapped Tracy on the knee and pointed. Tracy saw it, too. Spiegel looked at her, wondering what to do. He had forgotten that they had told Melissa to go to Mick's, never thinking that they would show up an hour later with her old sparring partner. Maybe they should just drive on and pretend they hadn't seen anything. But what would they say to Lisbet? And where would they go?

"What's the matter?" Lisbet asked.

"It's just that I think Mick might have company," Tracy said.

"Cool, a party," Lisbet said. "Let's crush it."

Spiegel pulled Tracy's VW in next to Melissa's car. It doesn't matter if Melissa is entangled with Mick, he thought. Let Lisbet draw what conclusions she will. Maybe she will be happy to see Melissa flinging herself at someone else. In any case, they had to find out about Jorge.

Mick's flat was on the fourth floor, in a garret below the eaves. Even from the ground floor, they could hear the sound of human voices raised in anger, and as they climbed the stairs the random sounds became more distinct. Gradually, like a picture slowly coming into focus, the declamations sorted themselves into words until at last, by the time the three of them had reached the fourth-floor landing and stood breathless before Mick's doorway, they felt as if they had already been part of the argument that was raging between Mick and Melissa.

Spiegel knocked, and Melissa pulled the door open without even a pause in her tirade.

"Well, you're goddamn lucky it isn't the fuzz, and if I had anything to say about this it would be, 'cause you keep this up and—"

"Me keep this up? What about you!" Mick was collapsed on a beanbag chair, drinking whiskey straight from a bottle. "How could you let him in like that? And now you just open the door to whoever—"

"It's not whoever," Melissa said.

"It's us. I'm sorry, we didn't mean to intrude," Spiegel said, "We just—"

And at that moment, Lisbet pushed her way through the doorway. She was so quick Spiegel didn't even feel her rush by. She was like the wind, passing through him as if he were just a spindly branched tree. One moment she was behind him in the hallway and the next she was nose to nose with Melissa, swinging her short arms in a blur, like a window fan, trying to get at Melissa's face, to grab her by the collar. But Melissa, quick and strong, her strength fueled now by pure fear, batted Lisbet's peppery punches away while she crouched slightly, spread her feet apart for balance, refused to give ground.

"It's you again, you bitch," Lisbet screamed, her voice ratcheted instantly up to the high decibel level that Melissa and Mick had already reached. "Where is he? What did you do with my bloody car!"

"Get her the fuck off me," Melissa called. But Mick didn't move and Spiegel hardly dared. He had seen these two go at it before and he didn't want to mix. Only Tracy, out of bravery or ignorance, stepped forward.

"Back off," she said to Lisbet as she struggled to grab her from behind in a bear hug, immobilizing her arms. "She didn't do anything. It's not her fault."

"Fucking-A right it's not her fault," said Mick, nearly supine. "It's that wag of hers, the greaseball teddy, he's totally bonkers, off his nut, he is, tried to fucking kill me—"

"You? He tried to kill you?" Spiegel said.

"Stop her, stop her and I'll explain," Melissa said. She had her arms raised to eye level now, like a karate boxer, ready to snap to the defense.

"*Låt mej gå*," Lisbet yelled in Swedish, but Tracy was not about to let her go until she calmed.

"I won't hit you," Melissa said to Lisbet. "Just back off, and I'll explain—"

"Fuck-all explain," Mick said. He was really drunk. He took a final swig from the bottle, finishing it off, and tossed it into a cardboard box near the kitchenette. "There's nothing to explain except this guy comes in, she lets him in—"

"—I thought he was hurt," Melissa said. "I thought you'd beat him to death. I was worried sick—"

"—Well I guess I bloody well didn't beat him hard enough, because he shows up here and she opens the fucking door for him and tries to give him a big kiss on the lips—"

"—I only asked him was he okay," Melissa said.

"—When he shoves her aside and comes at me, firing, like this is a fucking Western saloon."

"He what?" Lisbet said. "A fire?"

"A gun," Mick said. "He had a gun. He shot me. Look!"

"Oh goddammit," Tracy muttered through her clenched teeth. She relaxed her grip on Lisbet.

"He didn't shoot you," Melissa said. "That's what I'm trying to say!"

"Then what's this?" Mick pulled up his shirt and showed an ugly red gash along the side of his chest. "Bastard just missed my heart, he did."

"He didn't shoot you," Melissa said. "That's a burn, a powder burn. There was no bullet."

"I think your heart's on your left side," Spiegel said. "Unless it's different down under."

Mick looked at Spiegel as if he were made of dirt.

"It's just a damn starter pistol. It fires blanks. It's a prop for a play. Hedda Gabler shoots herself with it—although she better not hold it to her ear or she'll be deaf for a week."

"It's not a gun. It's not a gun," Tracy said, repeating the phrase like a mantra.

"Nobody told me," Mick said. "It sure as hell felt like a gun."

"How would you know?" Melissa said.

Mick backed off to the corner to soothe his wounds and to get out of the next round of fire.

"And the Oscar goes to . . . Mick Ryder," Melissa said.

"Oscar?" Lisbet said. She was lost.

So was Spiegel. "What happened?" he asked.

"He sure acted like it was a gun," Melissa said. "Would've convinced me."

She explained. She had just got to Mick's place, ready to give him hell for what he'd done to Jorge, when they heard a screech of tires out on the street. They looked out the window. A red Volvo had pulled halfway up the curb and was tilted precariously onto the street.

"My car," Lisbet said, mournfully.

Jorge nearly toppled out the door, then called something, incoherently, from the sidewalk.

"Like in *Streetcar*," Melissa said.

She realized later that Jorge had no clear idea where Mick lived. She should have kept quiet. Jorge might have gone away. But she was so startled to see him, and relieved to see him, in a way, that she leaned out the window and called to him.

"Like Juliet," Lisbet put in. Melissa looked at her as if to say: Idiot. She went on with the story.

Jorge didn't answer her call. He just darted into the building's foyer, and they could hear him pound his way up the steps, across the landings. When he got to the fourth floor, he called her name. Then she made her second mistake. She opened the door. He pushed his way past her into Mick's flat. She tried to hold him, to soothe him, to make sure that he was okay. He didn't want to see her or to touch her. "Where is he?" Jorge called. That's when Melissa noticed that Jorge was carrying a gun. She recognized it right away.

"Me, you looking for me?" Mick had said, as he stepped in from the kitchen. "Didn't you get enough last night?" He moved toward Jorge, fists held high, not really wanting to go at it, but trying to scare him off, when he saw a flash of silver. Goddamn, he yelled as he tried to dive for cover, but in the tight space there was no room to maneuver. Mick backed into the couch as Jorge stepped toward him, pushed the gun into his chest, and fired. There was a flash, a pop, a wisp of smoke, and Mick fell over the back of the couch and onto the floor, landing squarely on his shoulder. No, Melissa screamed, no—meaning he's not hurt, there's no bullet, but Jorge, in the face of what he had done or thought he had done, turned and ran. Melissa vaulted over the couch to see what had happened to Mick. She could hear Jorge wailing as he scrambled down the four flights of stairs.

"I thought he fucking shot me," Mick said. "I really did."

"You did not," Melissa said. "You took a dive to scare him off, you bastard."

"So you're saying," Spiegel put in, "that Jorge left here thinking he'd shot Mick? Maybe killed him?"

"And just as well," Mick said. "He tried to. Let him think he did. Let him sweat."

"But where did he go? Where is he?"

"And my bloody car, he took my bloody car," Lisbet whined.

"Should we call the cops?" Melissa asked.

"Let's keep them out of it," Tracy said.

"What about my car?"

"If he's driving the way he was when he took off out of here, they'll be after him."

"If they catch him," Spiegel said, "who knows what he might do? He might hold the gun on them—"

"Are they armed, Swedish cops?" Tracy asked.

"I bloody well hope so," said Mick.

"I think we ought to find him," Spiegel said. "Maybe Tracy and I can go. If we tell him everything's cool, Mick's okay, he should just kind of settle down—"

"And bring me back my car," Lisbet said.

Spiegel didn't say anything about it until he was alone in the VW with Tracy, but he was pretty sure he knew where they could find Jorge, if he could remember how to get there. He knew it was a long country road heading north from Flogsta, out into the untended fields, past the town limits, out beyond the farthest hills, the burial mounds that according to legend housed the remains of the Viking warriors. He hadn't been among those hills for months. In his memory, they were a kind of icy blue, and the fields were a sheet of white snow. But at this time of year the hills were mottled, brown and green, clusters of pine interlaced with windings of rich mud. The road forked in several places and they seemed to proceed for long stretches in a great arc, so after a time Spiegel was no longer sure if he was heading back toward the city or deeper into the heart of the country. He would not have found his bearings at all except that almost by chance, at a junction in the highway, he saw off to the side down a long embankment to his left a farmhouse painted the color of mustard, and he remembered that place, although the last time he had been here he had seen it not from the roadside but from across the vast expanse of snow-crusted fields.

He pulled to a stop. Behind the farmhouse he could see a large pond, almost a lake, blue-green in the late sunlight. Along the margins, in the shadows of a row of spruce, the waters looked dark, black as pitch.

"Jorge used to come here," Spiegel said. "He took me here once."

He turned the car down a long dirt driveway that led past the farmhouse, bumped a rocky course alongside a barnyard and some outbuildings used for silage and milking. Several cows stood by as the car crawled along the edge of their pasture. The road diminished into a grassy landing near the weedy shore of the lake. Spiegel pulled the car up beside a tree stump. Someone had recently cut a clearing, perhaps for firewood or for lumber. The smell of pitch hung in the still air.

"Here?" Tracy said. "Jorge took you here? What on earth for?"

"We came that way," Spiegel said. "Over the hills once, in the snow. He did it for kicks. For a thrill."

"Did what?"

"Drove onto the lake. Onto the ice."

"Oh God," Tracy said. She pointed off by the row of spruce. In the waning light, they could just make out a metallic dome breaking the surface of the water like a smooth rock. Beside it, like a single reed, a steel antenna pointed toward the sky.

JUNE

15

Spiegel felt a hand on his shoulder, shaking him awake. He didn't know if it was day or night. Even a quick peek at the alarm clock—a little past two—was no help. Day and night, by now, looked exactly the same to him. Out of habit, he had been keeping the blinds closed at night, to help him sleep. Out of inertia or indifference or perhaps a secret wish for more security, he had taken to leaving the blinds shut in the day as well, so when he was indoors, which was much of the time, he went about in a gloomy half-light that reminded him of dusk.

"Come on, Lenny, wake up." It was Tracy's voice. "You have to get moving."

Two o'clock. Spiegel began to realize that it was two in the morning. There was no noise whatever from the streets and shops outside. Tracy herself spoke in a whisper, as if she were afraid of disturbing the stillness of the night.

What had he been dreaming? For the past few days, his dreams had been filled with images of the dead: a body floating facedown in the muddy waters of a harbor, a blackened human figure dangling from a steel pipe that protruded from a wall of concrete. The figure reached out to him with a spectral hand. Spiegel tried to bat it away, but the hand kept coming toward him, pointing at his eyes and then closing into a clenched fist that grabbed at his clothing, his skin, his flesh. He tried to shake the bony hand away, but he couldn't do it. And that's when he slipped out of his dream and saw Tracy.

He closed his eyes and nested his face within the folds of

the coverlet. He would rather sink into the deepest torment of his dreams than emerge from sleep and have to confront his thoughts and feelings and memories. The last days were a blur, or more precisely they were a wreck, a scene of turmoil, an explosion. It was as if his mind had been blown apart and all the pieces shattered, and on waking he would have to resume the task of reassembling the fragments into some semblance of a whole.

All he could remember, as he cast his mind backward, was kneeling on the pebbled shore, oblivious to the sharp, gray rocks pressing into his shins and his knees. He'd lifted his hands up toward the pewter-colored sky and cried out, a pure and unanticipated howl of lamentation, a scream that came not from his throat or his lungs but from somewhere deeper inside, from a region that no terror or sadness he had felt before, not even the death of his mother or the pain when he was beaten by the city police, had ever touched. He tried to raise himself, to run to the shoreline, and he would have plunged forward into the cold, black water, but a hand gripped his shoulder, squeezed the cloth of his shirt, and held him in place.

"That's Jorge! He's down there," Spiegel called, and a voice behind him said, through clenched teeth: "I know, I know. You have to let him go. We have to leave."

Leaving Jorge's body, untended and unmarked, entombed in the sunken Volvo, mired in the watery grave, felt to Spiegel like a sacrilege, like a sin against the laws of a God in whom he no longer thought he believed.

Tracy let him stay by the lakeside, crying himself out, for what seemed like hours but what really might have been no longer than a moment, yet it was a moment wrested out of temporal context by its intensity, like a picture snapped in darkness by the light of a flash. Tracy sat beside Spiegel, wrapped her arms around him, and stilled his sobs and eased the spasmodic shivering of his shoulders and his limbs. She knew that it was okay, even desirable, for Spiegel to drain himself of anger and remorse. She wanted him to be able to think clearly before they returned to town. He had to see that it would be reckless to report Jorge's death to the police. She dreaded being caught in the web of an investigation. Jorge's death, she understood immediately, could wrap itself around them like the snarled filament of a fishing line, and the more that they fought against it, the more they tried to clear themselves away from its tangles, the harder it would tug on them until they were immobilized and dragged to the bottom.

She urged Spiegel to leave Uppsala before the police came upon Jorge's body. Though Spiegel thought about breaking away from Tracy and cutting his own deal, offering to tell Inspector Svenson what he knew about Jorge Ramos in return for, say, a U.S. passport or even a valid Swedish residency permit, in the end Spiegel decided to play the game by Tracy's rules—for in truth he was scared. The warning Svenson had offered to him after the May Day rally had turned out to be on the mark. Once again, someone wanted Aaronson, and Spiegel had drifted into his sights. It had become obvious that whenever Tracy went into town she was being trailed. A uniformed member of the Uppsala police department had stopped by one day, with a well-dressed American along to help interpret, and tried to ask Tracy some questions. They told her that they knew she had been living with Leonard Spiegel and that they had reason to believe that Aaronson was back in the country. They asked if she would inform them as soon as she had contact from Aaronson—for his own safety. She demurred, but she and Spiegel both got the message. The noose was tightening. Whoever wanted Aaronson—the American military police, the enforcers hired by the church, some rogue operation within the Swedish government, the CIA, the KGB—had been informed, through a network of contacts, that Spiegel was the wrong guy. But Spiegel also knew that if the American authorities wanted to make an arrest for purely political purposes, to discredit the deserters or to advance a rightist agenda in the Swedish elections, it didn't matter which of the Americans they nabbed. His own head would be perfectly acceptable, if served on a platter.

And in fact, Spiegel began to suspect that he might have become the real quarry. What good would it do for the military police to arrest Aaronson and ship him home so that he could stand before a court of law and become a martyr? But if the military police were to arrest Spiegel instead and send him home in shackles, that could be devastating to the movement. If the police could frame him by revealing his patrilineal ties to what till now Spiegel had referred to euphemistically as the "foreign service," he would be exposed as an infiltrator, a fifth columnist. The movement would be wrenched by spasms of rancor, accusations, incriminations; it might never recover. Yes, the authorities might want to grab Spiegel, but when, where, how? They could take him at any time, he knew. The Uppsala police had demonstrated that once by plucking him to safety during the May Day uprising on the bridge. They just had to wait for the opportune moment, when his arrest would do the greatest possible damage to the cause.

So Spiegel agreed to leave Uppsala right away. Once the police discovered Jorge's body, they would be sure seek out Spiegel for questioning, for there was really no one else left in Uppsala who knew anything about Jorge's life. Lisbet had gone home for the summer, believing that eventually Jorge would drive her Volvo into a lamppost or park it illegally outside some Stockholm disco where the police would find him drinking champagne from a shoe. Melissa, far less sanguine, believed that she was under a constant threat while Jorge was at large. She knew that he was crazy, volatile, and obsessed, and that if he learned that Mick had survived the shooting he would return to her, an abject slave. Unable to face him, unwilling to turn him in, she and Mick packed what they could fit into Melissa's Saab and set off for Paris, where they hoped to revive *Ms. Julie* with an *en plein air* performance at Place Bastille.

"Let's go," Tracy said, nudging Spiegel once more. "Monika will be here soon."

"I'm awake," he said. "I was dreaming."

"It's good you slept. I've been up." Tracy, even more than Spiegel, had trouble with the constant daylight. She said it was her concern for Spiegel's safety and her thinly veiled paranoia that kept her from sleep. "Who knows what might happen once I shut my eyes?" she said. But Spiegel thought that he might be to blame for Tracy's condition. She had been avoiding the small brushes of intimacy, a foot tap under the table, a hand resting lightly across the other's wrist, that had graced the early days of their relationship. Sex with her had become not perfunctory but strangely aggressive, as if they brought their bodies together to fulfill an appetite rather than to express intimate feelings. He had begun to think that perhaps she wanted him to leave not for his well-being but for other reasons. Maybe she was worried about her own safety and she wanted to be out of the range of the moving target. Or maybe she had simply grown tired of living with him, as she had, earlier, to Spiegel's advantage, become impatient waiting for Aaronson.

Spiegel slipped into jeans and a sweatshirt. He had packed in the evening. Nearly all his gear fit snugly into a backpack and small duffel. He had come to Uppsala with very little, and it seemed that he had been shedding belongings ever since he arrived, leaving bits and pieces of his life, scat and detritus, at every turn. I'll be lucky if I can leave this country with even a change of clothes, he thought.

While Tracy made coffee, Spiegel sat by the window. He was watching for Monika's car. They had agreed that the quicker the turnaround, the better. They had no idea who might be eyeing Tracy's flat or from what vantage. But they were willing to risk that there would be no surveillance at this hour. If they were wrong and someone saw Monika stop by and pick Spiegel up, it would be easy to spot a tail on the highway. If anybody was after them, they would abort the journey and come back to Uppsala. Spiegel, still shaking the dreams from his skull, thought that their plan was crazy. Maybe he should have gone off alone and met Monika somewhere outside of the city. Or they should have set up some sort of decoy, a late-night party or cell meeting, to distract the attention of any external observers, allowing Spiegel and Monika to slip away unnoticed. But his qualms had come too late, he realized. They had plunged ahead in their usual reckless fashion, and now they were committed to the journey. To delay would lead to further anxiety and risk. If anyone really wants to follow us, Spiegel thought, let them. They'll have little to see.

* * *

The night was so silent, he could hear Monika's car approach long before he saw it nose around the tobacco shop and pull into the courtyard. Monika parked by the doorway. Spiegel knew that she wouldn't touch the horn. He tilted the blinds twice to let her know that he had seen her approach. "Trace," he called softly.

"Yes," she said. "Here, take this." She handed him a china mug, filled with black coffee.

"No, we'll stop," he said.

"No." It was one of those ridiculous conversations about practical matters that one clings to in times of stress, a floating log in a sea of trouble. There were a thousand things they should have said to each other, but neither wanted to acknowledge the gravity of the moment. They hoped that by treating the departure lightly, casually, they might alleviate the intensity of their emotions. But they were wrong. We always remember endings and departures, so much so that they sometimes eclipse the entire antecedent experience, crushing all the subtleties and nuances into a single sensation.

Tracy followed Spiegel out the doorway and watched as he dropped his bags into the trunk. There was nothing more to say. They held each other, and he took in the scent of her hair, a grassy perfume, rising above a slightly astringent aroma of soap. I'll be okay, he assured her. She told him she would be okay, too, and that she would send word to Spiegel as soon as she had worked out his passage to safety. Yes, he said, I'll see you soon, but the words felt dead even as he spoke them.

Tracy turned to Monika. Take care, she said. Monika nodded and pulled Tracy to her for a quick embrace. Spiegel got quickly into Monika's car, according to plan. He was pretty sure that nobody had been posted in the tobacco shop or in one of the adjacent apartments to observe them go through the gestures of departure, but still—it was no time to take chances. It was time to go.

The highway out of the city was a good, four-lane road that traversed the west shore of the Baltic all the way to the far north, Norland, where they would veer away from the coast and head into the spruce-covered mountains near the Arctic Circle. They were bound for Monika's village. Her family lived on a small lake beside a little fishing resort. Behind her house was a summer cottage that she and her sister had once used as a playhouse. They had long outgrown the cottage, but it was still furnished and it even had a working sink. Monika had suggested that Spiegel could stay there until the situation cleared back in Uppsala. In the north, no one cared about anyone else's background or political views. It was a land of tremendous conformity, but also of tolerance. Her family, her village, would accept Spiegel's presence among them, Monika said, and they wouldn't question him too closely. They understood full well why people moved to the north, and they knew that a man will share his history with strangers only if and when he pleases. Usually, never.

Monika said little, conserving her energy for the long drive. The radio played softly, some old jazz numbers, Lionel Hampton or someone from that era on the xylophone. Spiegel thought about trying to drop back into sleep, but his mind was too stirred by thoughts about what he had left behind and worries about what lay ahead. He turned and looked out the window, where he sometimes caught a glimpse of the Baltic when there was a break between the monotonous, seemingly endless forest.

"It's not really very pretty," Spiegel said, breaking the silence.

"The Swedish countryside? Please don't judge it all by this," Monika answered. "There are parts you haven't seen, beautiful places. Maybe you'll get to see them, if you stay."

"We have a saying in English, though. Beauty is in the eye of the beholder. Do you understand it?"

"Hmm. Yes," she said softly, considering the words. "When you feel beautiful, things look beautiful to you. I think it's true. I hear people complain a lot, for half the year about the darkness and then the rest of the year about the constant light that keeps them awake. I think these people are just saying that they're unhappy."

"Foreigners, mostly?"

"Swedes, too. But I think foreigners have the hardest time. I used to think that you Americans could never get used to our land. But now, you've made me think, maybe it's because so many of you have come here under such unhappy conditions. You're just . . ."

"Projecting. Putting our own personal feelings outside of us, onto the landscape. They're easier to deal with that way."

"Yes." She drove in silence for a while longer. Their plan was working, Spiegel was relieved to see. No cars were following them. They had hardly seen another on the road. Once in a while, a huge logging truck, a thick mountain of spruce strapped to its long flatbed, would whisk by them heading south. Otherwise, the road was theirs alone and the pathway north was unobstructed.

"And you, Lenny," Monika asked. "Why are you so unhappy?"

"I'm in mourning for my life," he said. She turned to look at him, puzzled. "It's a line from Chekhov," he explained.

"Your life," she said. "It's just begun. How old are you?"

He told her.

"Would you go to Vietnam, if they draft you?"

He told her that he would not be drafted.

"Then you are lucky. But you are also brave. Most Americans, if they could get out of the war, would just stay home and do whatever Americans do. Make money, I guess."

"I didn't come to Sweden for any great moral reason," Spiegel confessed. "I came because I wanted to prove something."

"To yourself?"

"No, I was in love. I wanted to prove it to her."

"To Tracy."

"No, not Tracy. I didn't know Tracy in the States. I met her in Uppsala."

"And now, she's the one you love. And you have to prove yourself to her."

"I think by now," Spiegel said, "I don't have to prove anything to Tracy. Now, I'm proving something to myself."

"No," Monika said, after a moment. "I don't believe that. I think now you have to do what's right. Even if that means—"

"Abandoning Tracy?"

"Or giving her up. That's why you're unhappy. Am I right?"

Perhaps, Spiegel thought. He didn't feel as if he were giving up Tracy, for he had never been sure that she was his alone. As he rode farther away from Uppsala, the whole city, the whole episode of his life that had passed there, seemed somehow dreamlike and unreal. Yet it didn't feel as if he had begun a new journey. Spiegel felt as if he were continuing along a passage that reached far back into his past and also far into the future. In short, it felt good to be on the move again, even though he was leaving the unsettled and heading for the unknown.

It may have been his imagination working, but it seemed to Spiegel as if the air, the sky, the quality of light itself became more weak and diffuse as they drove north. The Baltic Sea looked gray and cold, like metal. The fields along the roadside were barren and rocky. The low hills were patched with thin stands of spruce that disfigured the topography. Occasionally, they passed a farming village where the houses seemed to huddle together as if for protection from the great, harsh emptiness that pervaded the landscape. It's like a desert with trees, Spiegel thought, severe, extreme, inhospitable to life. He could sense that they were approaching the top of the earth. He imagined what he would see if they continued north. The vegetation would give out by nearly indiscernible gradations until the forest had imperceptibly dwindled into tundra, and then the tundra would succumb to the vast reaches of polar ice.

Monika's village sat in a quiet valley less than an hour from the north coast of the Baltic and within a day's hike of the Arctic Circle. She had told her family that she was bringing home a friend from school, an American, who wanted to backpack along the Kungsled, the national trail that passes through the mountains near the Norwegian border. Monika thought that hiking the trail would be a great experience for Spiegel; it would give him "a taste of the real Sweden." But he wasn't so sure. The real Sweden, to him, still tasted like cheese in a tube, which he could buy at the Uppsala train station. Since his days on the Ohio beet farm, Spiegel felt a mild revulsion toward all recreation associated with the great outdoors. A sleeping bag rolled out on a parquet living-room floor was about as close to nature as he cared to get. He would prefer to camp out in Monika's guest

cottage until Tracy sent word. She had promised to dispatch
Spiegel's papers, along with a plan to get him safely out of the
country, to a postal box at the railroad junction near the frontier,
a two-day hike from Monika's village. In return, Spiegel pledged
he would keep the plan secret, even from Monika.

It was about two in the afternoon, some twelve hours after
Spiegel had been shaken out of his dreams, when they turned
onto the gravel road that led to Monika's family home. Her
parents lived five miles from the nearest town, and they were
five difficult miles, even in summer. In the winter, the road was
nearly impassable. Monika slowed to a crawl, as the road surface
was gashed with ruts carved by the spring rains and the steady
runoff of snowmelt. Sometimes a fresh stream spilled across the
roadway, like a ribbon of silver. For a long stretch, the gravel had
been entirely washed away, and they rattled along on an under-
bed of raw rock. The car was jostled from side to side, and stones
cracked against the fenders like gunshot. At last, they came to a
wooden signpost where Monika turned to the right onto a dirt
lane that hugged the weedy shore of a lake. Gradually, the lane
dwindled into two broad wheel ruts pressed into the soft earth,
and then it vanished altogether and the car nosed its way through
high meadowgrass and came to rest at the edge of an unmowed
field. "This is ours," Monika said. "We're home."

Her parents and her kid brother lived in a sprawling house set
on a grassy hill just above the shoreline. There was something
immediately pleasing to the eye about the house: the gingerbread
carvings above the porch railings, the excellent carpentry of
the doorways, the windowsills, the moldings and cabinetry, all,
Spiegel learned, the handiwork of Monika's father. The comfort
was not only in the details but in the satisfying proportions of the
dwelling. The interior was cozy, even quaint, with its low ceilings
and many small windows made up of multiple panes of thick glass
that had begun to ripple and bubble with age, but the house was
also spacious and generous in the way it opened to the out of
doors and allowed for a comfortable flow of traffic from room to

room. In all, it reminded Spiegel very much of Monika's cottage nestled in Uppsala's botanical gardens.

"Welcome to my house," her father said, extending his hand to Spiegel. It was the traditional Swedish greeting, and in this case fully appropriate, Spiegel thought. The man and his house are as one. All the family members, including some aunts and cousins who had come by for the occasion, embraced Monika one at a time, and then in clusters of three or four. They couldn't get enough of her. She had been home earlier in the spring term, Spiegel knew, but they acted as if they hadn't seen her in years. Perhaps it was a function of the loneliness and isolation of the setting. The appearance of a stranger or the return—even after a brief absence—of a loved one, had an intensified effect.

While the kid brother ran around in the fields chasing butterflies with a long stick, Monika's father ushered Spiegel and the assembled company into the dining room. A table of sandwiches, cheeses, and sausages had been laid out, and Monika's dad immediately set to pouring tall glasses of foamy dark beer from a big pitcher. There were "*skåls*" all around and the clinking of glasses, the *ting* of silverware against china. Spiegel found himself with a full plate of sliced ham in one hand and a glass of beer in the other. He drained off the beer. "My dad makes it himself," Monika said. Spiegel nodded: very good.

As he went for a refill, he began to realize, however, that he was the center of attention. Everyone was too polite, or too reserved, to stare at him. And his Swedish was so awkward that none but Monika could carry a conversation with him beyond the plane of platitudes. But Spiegel could discern, from the way people approached Monika, tilted their heads toward him as they spoke, caught his eye and met his gaze with a knowing smile, that they were asking her about him and sizing him up. He wished his Swedish were better. He felt as he had when he had first arrived in Uppsala, his voice and even his thoughts nearly drowned by the unknown language that washed over him as he struggled to stay afloat in the choppy waters. At Monika's, though, the still indiscernible words sounded to him much sweeter. The lilt of the Swedish language, with its sudden and surprising interspersals of the elongated *sh* sounds between the hard K's and V's and the loopy vowels and swooping, softened consonants, seemed to him like a flock of birds dipping and diving through wild air. Perhaps he was drunk.

Monika was laughing as she spoke, gaily shaking her head, no no no, and holding her hand aloft in protest. The guests were teasing her about something, making her blush. More people had joined the party, and the crowd had begun to spill outward, drinks in hand, to the porch and front lawn. The whole village must be here, Spiegel thought, the whole county.

By what according to Spiegel's best guess must have been early evening, some of the men went outside and built a small fire of birch logs in a stone-lined pit. From a kitchen shed, Monika's mother wheeled out a table on which sat rows of long metal frames. On each frame she set a whole fish, a silvery salmon, scaled and boned. She snapped the frames shut so that each salmon looked as if it were clinched in a tiny cage. These racks were to be smoked over the hot stones around the fire pit.

Neighbors had brought other delicacies, pickles and jellies and cream pastries and long links of blood sausage, which someone had pierced with sticks and shoved one by one into the dancing fire. Spiegel found himself biting into a sausage, smoky and hot, and the juices burned his tongue. He cooled his throat with more of Monika's dad's dark and bitter beer. The fire crackled, and the smoke drifted off above the spruce, a thin trail rising into the weak light of the evening sky.

After dessert, which Monika's mother ladled from a copper tub of vanilla cream dotted with fresh, dark berries, Spiegel felt like toppling over into the tall grass. His head was light, his stomach was full, and his arms and legs were cramped with exhaustion. But he could not get away graciously. The family, the villagers, crowded around him, asking him questions in broken English or in Swedish, which they spoke slowly and loudly, as if that would make up for his linguistic deficiencies. Sometimes, their conversations degenerated into little games of charades. He would hold his hands together and pretend to scrutinize his open palms as if he were reading a sacred text, and someone would laugh and say, Ah, student! An old man with a grizzly beard pointed his left arm at Spiegel, sighted down his shoulder as if he were looking through a scope, and clicked his fingers like a trigger. Vietnam, bad, bad, he said. Spiegel nodded warily, and smiled.

At last Monika came to his rescue. She was clutching a stalk of dried flowers. Spiegel plucked one, and placed it in her hair. Two of the neighbors, watching, clapped in approval, and Monika's brother yelped out something, which brought on more laughter. Spiegel took another flower and put it in his own hair. "San Francisco," someone called, and everybody laughed again.

"Come on, let me show you around the place," Monika said. She took Spiegel's arm and led him toward the lake. From the shore, they could see the few other houses of the village, neatly spaced at even intervals along the waterfront. Near them was a weathered dock. An old rowboat was tied to a piling, and a green canoe rested on the beach, like a mossy log.

"Can we swim here?" Spiegel asked.

"Yes, but it's filled with weeds," Monika answered. She walked ahead of Spiegel toward the dock. He looked for stones that he might skip. Perhaps he could show her something new. Maybe skipping stones was unknown to Sweden, like baseball. But all the stones were rounded. He tossed a few into the lake and watched the circles form, expand, and pass through one another in intricate patterns.

"Do you know why they're laughing?" she said, as she sat down on the canoe.

"They're drunk." They could hear the sounds of the festivities, magnified, it seemed, by the properties of water and by the reflective surfaces of the surrounding hills. Insects droned all around them as well, a steady background noise that patched out the occasional intervals of silence.

"No, they're not drunk. You have to understand life in the north. The winters are so long and dark, and the distances so great, so in the summer we take advantage of all this light and we see one another every chance we get."

"You mean you guys party all the time up here?"

"No, but every party tends to . . . stretch out. Sometimes people stay all night because . . . "

"Because how can they tell. It could be midnight now. It could be the next day. I have no idea. It's funny," Spiegel added. "I can't even tell if I'm exhausted or not. I think I am."

"If you want, I'll show you where you'll sleep. You could, what's your word?"

"Crash?"

"Yes, like a car."

She led him to the little summer cottage behind her parents' house. It reminded Spiegel of the sort of clubhouse he'd played in when he was a boy. The walls were bare wood, a knotty pine that gave off a faint, resinous odor. A plain mattress on bare planks served as a bed. There were simple crates and boxes for furnishings. An oil lamp sat on a dresser beneath the small window. Monika drew the curtains, thick muslin drapings that hung from a bare steel rod.

"This is dark enough for sleeping now," she said. "That's why we have these little houses, for the long summer nights. My dad built it this way, with only the one window. I call it a box of darkness."

She struck a match and touched it to the lamp wick. "There," she said.

"I liked the darkness," Spiegel said. "I miss the darkness."

Monika extinguished the match, with a little puff of breath. "You were wrong, before," she said, turning to Spiegel. The shimmering light from the lamp illuminated her hair with a beautiful backlight so that the loosened strands seemed to glow like incandescent filaments.

"Wrong? About what?" Spiegel asked.

"They're not drunk. The people here, they could drink through the night and not show it. Then go to their work. It's the way of life."

"I wasn't accusing anyone. . . . "

"No, I don't mean that," Monika said. "I mean, that was not why they were laughing. They were laughing because . . . they are remembering the last time."

"The last time? What do you mean?"

Monika sat beside Spiegel on the bed. "My sister came home one summer with a friend, an English boy. He was going to visit for a day or two and then take the train to Norway. But he stayed on for several days, then weeks. She married him, you know."

"Are they here, tonight? Have I met them?"

"We never see my sister," Monika said. She turned her face away from Spiegel. He felt an urge to touch her, to set his hand on her arm or her shoulder.

"They were married that summer, at the church in town. The whole village came to the wedding. We danced all night and in the morning rowed across the lake. It was a wonderful time, but we all knew why she married Paul. That was his name. He promised to take her away. Once she went south to university, it was impossible for her ever again to live in the far north. She wanted to live in the bigger world, the world of day and night we sometimes call it. I don't know if she loved Paul. I don't think she did. But I think she was not brave enough to leave Norland on her own."

"He was her ticket out," Spiegel said. "A one-way ticket."

Monika nodded. "Of course my parents knew, all the time," she said. "They knew once my sister left for school that they had lost her forever. The north is dying. In time, there will be no one left here. You must have noticed, at the party. There were no young people, no children."

"And you, Monika," Spiegel said. "What do they think about you?"

"Can't you tell? They expect me to do the same. That's why we are celebrating. That's why they have left me alone, with you."

It was probably no longer a time to talk, but a time to take Monika in his arms, press his lips to hers, so that the two of them, for the moment, could huddle in their world of dark shadows and flickering light, could obliterate all thoughts and memories of lovers left behind, of the betrayals of friends and of parents, of the war on the other side of the world. But Spiegel felt smothered by Monika's expectations. What kind of customs do they have here? he wondered. He remembered the peasant dance in *Miss Julie*. Maybe they still do such things. Had he inadvertently become the prize in some sort of mating ritual, complete with toasts and libations and, now, the retreat to the bridal chamber? He felt like a missionary who had wandered into an aboriginal enclave and been forced to wed the chieftain's daughter in a ceremony witnessed by the whole village. He imagined that Monika's family even now was strewing flowers on the pathways, dancing a fertility rite as they circled the little cottage, staring through the muslin drapes at his silhouette projected on the back wall, waiting for his shade to disappear beneath the much larger shadow cast by Monika.

She was beside him now, and he could feel the warmth from her skin, a comfort in the chilly air. She brushed some strands of hair from her eyebrows. Her cheeks were flushed, her lips trembled. She waited for him to come to her, and when he did not, her eyes moistened.

"How much do they know about me?" Spiegel asked. "What did you tell them?"

Monika smiled. "They know everything they need to know, about you and about me," she said. "They know why you're here, why I brought you to the north."

What Spiegel sensed, though, was that Monika deliberately kept her parents in the dark about his activities and about her own, and that they preferred it so. It was part of the Norland code of living. Don't ask anyone, even your children, about their lives. Keep silent, and keep your distance. Each man is an island.

Monika lifted her hands to Spiegel, touched his shoulders. They could hear laughter from the lawn. Someone was playing a guitar, and there were sporadic attempts at singing. Spiegel was dizzy, not quite drunk but light-headed from the air, the light, the noise, the smoke, the lack of sleep. Did it matter whether Monika loved him forever or just for a moment or not at all? Perhaps she was using him. She could be like some petulant Nordic god, holding Spiegel in thrall to retaliate against the alien spirit that had imprisoned the soul of her sister. Or perhaps Monika was a secret agent, trained in the ways of dissembling, enchanting Spiegel with her siren song in order to lure him into a trap, into the hands of his enemies. Or was she a warrior, flaunting her captive like a hunter's prize, posturing and gaining status before the elders of her clan? It didn't matter. Her words could mean everything, or nothing, for words, gestures, love itself took on strange new configurations in the far north, and whatever passed between them would have to sort itself out once again when they returned to the land of day and night.

Spiegel took Monika to him, and her lips opened and her tongue, quick and alive, found his. She felt light as summer air against his skin, and she was as soft and tactile as wet silk. She slipped out of her jeans, and in a moment she was beneath him, open, undulant, gentle as the calm waters of the sea. Oh, she moaned softly, and her voice rose and joined with the birds of morning that were whistling in the mountain spruce and with the floating chords from the guitar someone was playing while the villagers sang round the fire and paddled in little boats along the lakeshore. For a long time, Spiegel held her, drifting in and out of sleep, while she brushed her lips against his face and his hair and watched their shadows dance in the flickering light.

16

From across the water, the distant shoreline looked flattened, two-dimensional, so it seemed that the farther Spiegel rowed the more the village he was leaving behind him was transformed until eventually it looked like a photograph, a picture postcard. From this distant perspective, Spiegel could no longer discern the intricacies of the shoreline, the coves and inlets and the little finger-like fishing docks that probed the margins of the lake. But for the first time he noticed the hills and meadows that rose from the shore, and among the hills he saw the houses that punctuated the whole vista like end points after the long stretches of unbroken spruce. Only from here could he appreciate the village in relation to its landscape. How small it looked when seen as part of the vast expanse of water and sky, forest and field, bright air and dark earth! Each house on the shore was like a single note of music, lost within the rising swells of a grand orchestral chord. He was sorry to be leaving.

They had set out in the morning, after breakfast, from Monika's dock. Monika sat in the stern, a picnic lunch in a basket at her feet. A straw hat shielded her eyes from the sun. Wisps of her hair fluttered in the soft breeze. She put her hand to the brim of her hat and leaned back occasionally, arching over the transom so that the stray tips of her hair brushed the surface of the water and scrolled a trail that drifted along behind them between the brackets of their wake. Spiegel stared at the soft skin of her white neck. She slipped her feet out of her sandals and rested her bare soles against his ankles.

In the bow sat her brother. His name was Per. He held in his lap a bag of nuts and raisins, which he was supposed to conserve for a snack on the return trip. But he had begun to munch shortly after they left the dock and soon, bored and impatient and incapable of setting anything aside against future want, he began tossing the bits of food onto the water in hopes of attracting fish. *Titta, titta*, he kept shouting, look, look. A gray bird circled overhead. Per pointed and sang a few phrases. Monika laughed, and told him to hush, but Per persisted and then broke off his song, seemingly in mid-verse, to set forth on a soliloquy that Monika assured Spiegel did not warrant translation. In short, he was a pest. Or in other words, he was a typical eight-year-old kid brother who was alternately confused and fascinated by this older visitor who did not speak his language and who, in some way that he could not fathom, had aroused his parents' solicitude and awakened his sister's sexuality. Spiegel had initiated, in three days, a seismic shift in the family's dynamics, and Per was determined, through his probing and nudging, to work out the mystery.

Per rested his heels on Spiegel's backpack and bedroll. For balance, it would have been better to place the heavy pack in the stern, but how could they trust Per to keep his kicky feet away from the picnic basket? So, with too much weight in the bow, rowing was hard work. The boat lurched drunkenly forward with each stroke.

They would arrive at the far shore by mid-morning, before the sun was at its height, so that they could have lunch in a grove that Monika knew of from previous outings. Maybe Per would go for a swim or take a walk along the pebbled beach, and Spiegel and Monika could find a few minutes to be alone. Spiegel felt torn inside. What had happened in the past three days between him and Monika had made him reassess everything he had come to feel, and to believe, about Tracy and therefore about himself. He was convinced that, for several months, he had been in love with Tracy. But he was sure, now, that his feelings for Monika were so much more powerful, more elemental, than anything he had felt for Tracy, or for Iris beforehand, that he wondered if he had ever known love. If what he felt for Monika was love, the answer was no, for he had never felt this way before. But was he in love? Or had he turned to Monika out of fear, loneliness, confusion, conditions that might pass if he ever returned to Uppsala? Perhaps what he felt for Monika was merely a matter of opportunity. Perhaps he was so weak that he had no will of his own but was simply dominated by the strongest proximate personality, as an iron filament is drawn to the nearest magnetic field. He would have to step with caution as he set out to navigate the treacherous passage between Monika's will and Tracy's.

Spiegel had told Monika nothing about Tracy's scheme. He had no idea what papers Tracy had dispatched to the railroad junction, whether she had managed to procure a passport that would allow him to leave the country or a residency permit that would allow him to stay or no documents at all. When he left Uppsala, he had felt that he was placing his life in Tracy's hands, that his fate, and hers, depended on whatever official papers she could buy, steal, or fabricate for him, for them. But in the past few days, the earth had shifted, the stars had been realigned, the rivers had reversed their flow and once again his life, which had seemed so torpid and sedentary, had branched, flooded, and altered its course. He would have to summon all the strength he had left to fight against the swift current, for, whatever plan Tracy had devised, now Spiegel could neither leave Sweden nor resettle elsewhere in the country except with Monika.

During the next few days, Monika planned to visit her aunts and uncles and cousins who lived in the surrounding villages, each a good hard hour's drive from her parents' place. No one would speak English at these gatherings, so there would be nothing for Spiegel to do except eat and grin and feel like a specimen on display, genus *Americanus*. Spiegel told Monika he would use the time to hike into the back country for his taste of the real Sweden. The thought of that seemed to amuse Monika. She laughed as she tried to picture Spiegel, the American pioneer, hacking his way through the wilderness, like Daniel Boone. Think of me more like Thoreau, Spiegel said. How did Thoreau put it? I would rather sit on a pumpkin and have it all to myself than be crowded on a velvet cushion.

Yes, she said, he could roll out his bag and rest his head against a cushion of moss. He could dream of her, as she would dream of him, his bright eyes and his friendly laugh, his long fingers and his cock that grew hard so quick it almost jumped when she touched it, as if her hand carried a spark. And what would he dream about? she asked.

He didn't want to dream of her, he said. He wanted to be with her, to watch her in the morning as she ran a silver brush a hundred times through her fine blond hair, as she walked in her long skirt through an unmowed field, the grasses and flowers parting before her as if in homage, to hear her voice calling him from a distance and to feel her silky skin warm and alive against him in the night. Although he wouldn't say so, he was afraid to leave her, for his feelings for her had emerged with such sudden and unexpected force and intensity that he worried about what would happen when he left the source. Would she fade from his mind, like a dream on waking? Was his passion just a passing thing, some atmospheric turbulence that ripped through the sky and shook the trees, filled the air with wind and rain, and then dissipated, like a summer storm, leaving the ground fresh and light but, in essence, unchanged? Would she waken and realize that her passion for him was a delusion, a midsummer night's dream?

Late in the morning they reached the far shore. Per leaped off the gunwale into the shallow water, soaking his sneakers and cuffs. He grabbed the painter and lugged the rowboat onto the rocky beach. Spiegel helped Monika to disembark, and they carefully transferred the picnic basket and his backpack onto dry land, then dragged the empty boat above the waterline. The boat listed on the beach, a clumsy thing when out of its natural element.

"What do you think?" Monika asked. They had put in at a small inlet notched into the thick grove of spruce that limned the shore like a green wall. Hills rose behind them, the foothills to the great snowy mountains of the north. A stream tumbled down from a ledge into an icy pool of black water. Per had yanked off his sneakers and was trolling a stick along the water's edge.

"It's beautiful," Spiegel said. "Great."

"*Great.* Such an American word," Monika said. "As if beauty has to be a matter of size."

"Okay. It's *bara bra.*"

She took his hand. She had just been joking, teasing him. He understood. Spiegel looked back across the lake, trying to find the village. It had disappeared around the promontory at the head of their cove. From his current vantage, all he could see was the unbroken forest, a monotony of shape and hue. He imagined that the land stretched on that way for hundreds of miles, all the way to the Baltic, to Finland, to the Russian steppes and beyond. He was glad that soon he would be climbing above the treeline, where he could look down from a lofty perspective. From on high, he thought, from a tower or an airplane, a city always looks slightly toylike, with antlike people and cars like drops of mercury slipping silently along the slender, glassy tubes of the roadways. He wondered if the forest would look different from above or if it would look just the same, grand and immense and timeless, seemingly unmarred by human presence, concealing all within its cloak of green.

He and Monika walked along the inlet to the trailhead. She suggested that they have lunch soon and then say good-bye. She didn't want to row into an afternoon headwind on her way home across the lake. And Spiegel would have a substantial hike to reach the first of the mountain huts.

They called to Per. He slung the basket over his shoulder and ran to them, hopping along the boulders. Spiegel could imagine, with a single missed footing, Per tumbling into the water along with their provisions. But, with a final leap of joy, Per landed unsullied at the picnic grounds. Monika spread a cloth and laid out a plate of open-faced sandwiches. Per smeared red jelly onto torn yellow hunks of soft, sweet bread.

After lunch, Monika told Per to run along to the boat and wait for her. She said she had to help Spiegel pack his gear, but Per saw through her scheme, and he began a chorus of whining and teasing. He made big smacking sounds with his lips and pretended to hug and kiss one of the slender trees, then flopped onto the ground as if he were in a fit of passion.

"Who taught this kid about sex?" Spiegel asked.

"He watches too much TV," Monika said.

"Did he see our great debate?"

Monika laughed at that and shook her head. Spiegel didn't want to prolong the scene. He felt sorry for Monika, having to listen to Per's blabbing all the way home. "Come here, little guy," he said, and Per came running over to him. Spiegel kneeled and reached out his hand to Per to say good-bye in a soul handshake. To his surprise, Per grabbed him around the shoulders and hugged him, a quick and startling embrace, and then he turned and ran off to the boat, singing.

"I think he will miss you," Monika said.

They stood by the shore as Per rattled rocks against the ribs of the rowboat. Monika turned to watch Per, and Spiegel felt the strands of her hair brush against his face. He whispered something to her. She tilted her head back, looked up at him and smiled, and she touched his lips with a quick but sensuous kiss.

"Good-bye, love," she said. "I'll be here for you."

As he set off up the trail, he knew in his heart that she would. It was as if her love was a light that clarified all the disorder of his life, a filter that purified an unsettled mixture so that it became clear and bright. Since he had opened his heart to Monika, he was beginning to see that everything that he had once thought of as love had been the fulfillment of a baser need, not a sexual drive, but a defense against loneliness, insecurity, and the tar pits of depressive gloom. He had fallen for Iris because she had rescued him from the clutches of the law, and he thought that he could prove something to her by coming to Sweden, that he could demonstrate his worthiness and valor, like a knight on a Crusade. And he had proved himself, yet in doing so he had moved beyond his need for Iris's approval. He lost her, and then he found Tracy. And what drew him to her? He feared that he had loved Tracy, or thought he had, only to fill an absence, the absence created by the disappearance of Aaronson. To win Tracy's heart was also a way to become someone that he was not. But Spiegel wondered whether he was ever the one that Tracy loved or whether she had always loved the image of Aaronson that she saw behind the mask of Spiegel. Perhaps Tracy had been using him—even to get back at Iris for some obscure past rivalry—as much as he was using her. They never talked about this, as if to do so would have placed the whole construct of their relationship in jeopardy, and he was beginning to recognize these silences as a great chasm that had opened up between them. To talk about their feelings for each other and their future together would have stripped away the surface sheen of their relationship, forcing them to realize that what they thought was love had been an illusion that had taken root in the rich mixture of their needs and their fears.

As Monika had explained, the spur trail took Spiegel north through modest hills, a steady climb toward the iron-rich mountains of Lapland where he would reach the Kungsled, a rugged climbing trail that traversed the highest ranges along the remote stretches of the Norwegian border. There were shelters at regular intervals along the trails, she told him, and it was fine to stay there, although often one had to share the lodgings with other hikers.

At this time of year, however, the trails were little used. For the first mile or so, footing was slippery from the spring rains and the late snowmelt. Frequently, Spiegel had to cut into the brush at the trailside to skirt a mud pit. After a time, he decided to brave the oozing ground. He stayed on the trail, cautiously seeking the most secure footing, but this slowed his progress and forced him to keep his eyes focused downward. He grew intimate with the tops of his boots.

Eventually, though, the trail began to climb, and the footing improved. The ground was soft and dry, though uneven. The trail itself might have been a streambed during the early spring, a channel for the runoff from the melting snow of the highlands. The swift water had left bare many rocks and roots, and from time to time Spiegel came upon a natural wall of branches that had washed up into an interstice where the trail narrowed or where a log had fallen. Spiegel kicked through most of these barriers. It pleased him that he was the first of the season to pass this way.

He noticed, as the trail climbed, that the forest was changing from spruce to birch. In the lowlands he had walked in almost constant shade. But on the higher ground, where birch was predominant, the light began to cut through, at first in streaks that shot to the ground through breaks in the overhead leaves. Then, as he climbed and the growth became less thick and the trees themselves were sparsely foliated, the beams of light widened to patches and the forest opened to daylight. At higher altitudes, the birch trees looked withered, sick, their bark a dusty gray. On many, the trunks and branches were swollen into great, bulbous tumors that choked the life from the trees. The upper branches reached into the air, frail and brittle and black, like dead fingers.

Spiegel stopped to drink from his canteen. Though the light was weak, the sun was surprisingly hot. He had been hiking for several hours. He planned to push on to the first shelter, where he would spend the night. It was strange, he thought, that the views backward, toward the lake and Monika's village and the Baltic and the highway to the south, had never materialized. On the lower ground, the thick forest had concealed the view, yet now that his field of vision had opened he had already crossed or rounded several promontories, so it was impossible to turn about and survey the course of his journey. Behind him, the trail seemed to curl off into a valley and then disappear into the bluish hills, like a ribbon of smoke vanishing in a windy sky. Ahead of him was a great expanse, a long, flint-strewn slope that tilted down toward a meadow and a rocky stream. In bad weather, a hiker might lose the trail as it crossed the open ground, but in the good light Spiegel could see the markings, small cairns of broken rock, that guided him along the field to the banks of the stream. Blue butterflies scribbled, like a child's pencil across colored paper, just above the tips of grass as he followed the trail along the streambed. The only sound was the rush of the water along the rocks. The water looked clear. The rocks at the bottom were red like iron.

The trail crossed the stream on a bridge of rock and led Spiegel across a long flatland of spongy ground toward the base of a steep ascent, the first of the real mountains. Far ahead, Spiegel could see forms moving at the margin of the level ground. At first he thought he was seeing grazing cattle or even a pack of large dogs. He hesitated, concerned about approaching too suddenly and startling the animals. But he had no choice except to move forward, cautiously. As he neared the herd he could see what he had come upon: wild reindeer. He hadn't known that they roamed the south face of the mountains. The trail took him right through the center of the herd. Some reindeer nuzzled their noses into the damp ground, foraging for lichen or berries. Others stared ahead, on the lookout. Despite the vast open space of the field, the reindeer huddled close together, almost flank to flank. Passing right next to them, Spiegel was tempted to scratch one behind the ears, as if it were a big dog, but he was worried about disease carried by Arctic ticks and he thought it would be safer to pass through the pack without attracting the attention of the leader. The reindeer seemed so docile, peaceful. But they were large and strong, each the size of a Great Dane. One kick with a cloven black hoof sharp as a stiletto could be crippling, and the herd, if it should panic, could easily knock him to the ground and drag him or stomp him, maybe not to death, though who would find him here if he were knocked unconscious and disabled? But the reindeer were oblivious. He passed through the herd like a jet passing through a cloud.

As the trail climbed, Spiegel looked down to the flats through an opening in the birch trees and saw the deer still grazing. He sensed that an army could have marched through the herd and the deer would not have broken the rhythm of their eternal ruminations. They live on a different plane from us, he thought, different even from most animals, which flee in fright at our approach. The deer were more like the climate itself, grandly indifferent to human presence.

The hike up the mountain put a strain on Spiegel's legs, and he broke into a light sweat. He paused several times to rest and to drink. For the first time, he thought it might be good to stop. He wondered if he should eat his light supper or press on to the

first shelter. He was hungry, but concerned that he would be too
tired to continue if he paused for dinner. The weather was good;
could he sleep by the trailside if he didn't reach the hut? But he
had heard about sudden Arctic storms, and he didn't want to risk
exposure. On the higher ground, the trees were too sparse to
offer any protection, and the land was rocky and uneven. So he
decided to continue to climb for as long as his strength held. In
the unchanging light, he had no idea how long he had been hiking—several hours at least, but maybe more. It was possible that
he had hiked into the evening or even into the night.

As Spiegel neared the treeline, the trail gradually hardened
into rock, and Spiegel found that he was walking along a ridge of
shale that spiraled up toward the summit. Above him, he could
see long fingers of snow reaching down from the upper ledges.
At the higher elevations, there was no sign of life. If the trail went
up there, Spiegel could easily lose his footing on the crusts of ice
or miss a marking that had been buried beneath a drift. He began
to realize how ill-equipped he was for this excursion, what a fool
he had been. Again, he thought of turning back and camping for
the night by the valley stream. But he could see ahead that the
trail wound to the north side of the mountain before making its
ascent to the peak, so he decided to push on a little farther, to
see the range from the northern perspective. He hoped that the
trail might descend from the north slope, bypassing the barren
summit with its treacherous spans of summer ice.

The trail rounded a column of rock and then was bisected by
a swift stream, spring runoff from the heights. Spiegel had to
scramble a hundred feet or so off the trail to find a safe crossing,
then step gingerly down the opposite bank, mossy and wet, to
recover the trail. But from the new vantage, he saw that the trail
did in fact angle down toward lower ground. The air before him
was misty, as if a fog had settled in on the less exposed northern
side of the range. Through the damp air he could see ahead of
him the outline of the roof of the first shelter, a rude structure in
a grove of withered birch.

Spiegel was greatly relieved at the sight. The wind off the
summit brought a wet chill to the mountain face. Despite the

good light, he could tell that it must be quite late. As he worked his way down the trail toward the shelter, with each step he imagined what he would do when he could lay down his pack. He would strip off his socks, build a fire in an iron stove, eat a quick dinner at a pine table, unroll his bag, and curl up for the night, like a fox in a den, to sleep without dreams. Too tired even to reach for the door handle, he kicked the door open with the toe of his boot. He turned as he stepped inside, letting his pack slip off his shoulders. It hit the wood floor with a thud, and Spiegel felt so light he thought he would float like a balloon. He didn't. He sank to his knees, then sat on the mud-specked floor and leaned against the doorjamb, shaking from exhaustion.

He drooped his head and closed his eyes and made a conscious effort to breathe slowly and evenly, to regain his composure and his strength. He should not have pushed so hard his first day on the trail. But he would be okay if he could get some water and eat a little dinner before collapsing into sleep. Just being inside was good. His hands steadied, and he could feel the blood moving back to his toes, his face. He imagined that he must have looked white as paper when he stepped, or practically fell, into the shelter.

He wondered if he would have the stamina to push on to the railroad junction after only one night's rest. His hands fumbled with the knots at the top of his pack. He had set aside some candy bars in a zipped pouch. That would do for dinner, he thought. In the morning he would see about a hot breakfast. There was the stove, just as he had imagined it, an iron potbelly with a flat cooking griddle. Beside it, firewood was neatly stacked. And, then, Spiegel felt a shock as if someone had touched his spine with wire. Behind the firewood, he saw a mess kit and a hand towel, hung from a peg on the wall and left to dry. Had someone else made camp in this lonely shelter? But who? How? Nobody had preceded him up the trail, at least not within the last several days. Spiegel would have seen footprints. Maybe the hiker had been living in the hut since the last storm or had approached the shelter from the north, or maybe the last visitor had packed in haste and left a few things behind to mark his passage.

A friend on the trail can be a good thing, Spiegel thought, a chance to trade stories and replenish provisions, like the whalers he had read about who would drop sail when they pulled in sight of one another on remote shipping lanes. But he felt that he couldn't keep up his end of the deal. He was too tired to talk. Maybe his cabinmate could speak no English. Or maybe he would be asleep by the time the fellow returned to the shelter.

Spiegel unrolled his bag and stripped off his shirt, delicately peeling the dirt-encrusted socks from his blistered feet. He bunched his sweatshirt to form a rudimentary pillow where he was about to lay his head when he heard a noise in the doorway. Shit, he thought. He was too beat to go through the civilities, and the extra effort of trying to do so in Swedish would be more than he could bear. He struggled to stay awake but, hearing no more disturbing sounds, he closed his eyes and gave in to the overpowering force of sleep.

His sleep was uneasy. Even at rest, his body could not cast off the fatigue of the arduous hike. He felt as if he were trudging through his dreams. His feet tingled, his legs twitched and he turned from side to side as if he were entangled, as if he were wrestling with a demon of the air. He woke, startled, several times, and could not tell if he had been asleep for hours or if he had just plunged deep into the pool of dreams from a great height and immediately bobbed back to the surface for a gasp of air.

He dreamed of the long day's events, the rowboat across the lake, Per tossing stones into the stream, Monika's tender kiss, the reindeer brushing its flanks against his shoulder, and through the night all the elements of his dreams converged and gained velocity: he was running across a field, with Per, with Monika, with the reindeer, chasing something or someone, the sky filled with the scream of birds, the sun blinding him, a great force pulling him backward, gripping his shoulders like pincers as Monika and her brother, running and laughing, slowly disappeared into the tall grasses at the farthest reaches of the open field. Spiegel tried to call to them, tried to pull himself free from the force that held him back, when he shot upright in bed.

A flashlight was shining into his eyes.

"Yes, I thought so," said a voice. A hand let go of his shoulder. There was a click. The light snapped off. The shelter, with the door latched and the windows shuttered, was cast into a penumbal darkness. Spiegel could not delimn the form that stood beside him. When he looked up, he saw only two bright rings, the retinal echo of the flashlight beam. "I hoped it would be you."

The voice was strangely familiar and almost seemed to be emanating from within Spiegel's own throat. It was as if he were hearing his own words spoken without having to utter them. Though it seemed that another person was in the room with him, he felt that he was alone, that he was conversing only with himself, as if his own words and thoughts were bouncing off a wall and returning a fraction later so that he misperceived the words as coming from another.

"How did you get here, man?" Spiegel asked, tentatively. He didn't want to let on how little he knew and understood.

"I've been watching you. We've got some things to settle."

As Spiegel sat up, the form stepped back toward the center of the room so that his face was illuminated by a band of light that passed through a slat in the wall. His hair was long and had grown into corkscrew curls that touched his bony shoulders. He had cultivated a thick beard, dull brown with blond highlights around the mouth, as if he had been kissed with gold. His eyes had become dark and hollow, tired. His aquiline nose looked pinched and drawn, white at the tip. He folded his arms across his chest. His hands were strong and graceful, his fingers flattened at the nub, like an artist's. Tall and lean, his shoulders held back in an almost military posture that seemed like a sly commentary on his otherwise disheveled and frayed-at-the-edges affect, he still had the commanding presence of a natural leader. Spiegel wondered how long he had been under Aaronson's scrutiny.

"Let me see you," Spiegel said. He swung his feet out of the bed and propped his elbow against a ledge notched into the wall.

"Let's get some light."

"It's okay," Aaronson said. "There's nothing to see."

"But how are you? Where the fuck have you been?"

"I've been here, waiting for you."

"That's not what I meant." As Spiegel's eyes grew accustomed to the dim light he got a better look at Aaronson's profile. Aaronson seemed to be trying to avoid meeting his gaze. Spiegel understood why. It was as if Aaronson, with his hair and beard grown out and his pallid, troubled demeanor, had become the Spiegel of six months ago. He wondered if Aaronson was having the same thoughts. Looking at Spiegel, trim and fit and nourished by six months of good food and regular sexual contact, did he see the ghost of the self that he had left behind?

"I knew you'd be coming this way," Aaronson said. "I didn't know exactly when. I wasn't even sure you'd stop here. I thought maybe you passed through along the trail in the night and I missed you. I was giving it one more night. If you didn't show up by tomorrow, I was going to leave."

"You were going back to Uppsala?"

"I was going after you. I was going to find you."

"But I turned up just in time," Spiegel said.

"Yes."

Spiegel felt as if he had opened a doorway and stepped into a dark house, only to find himself tumbling down a flight of stairs into the cellar. Spiegel realized how he had fallen into Aaronson's hands. He could no longer hide from the truth. Tracy had betrayed him and set him up, arranged to have him leave Monika and walk right into the trap.

Yet Spiegel was glad to have a final opportunity to set things straight with Aaronson. So many had vanished from his life without a word. With Aaronson, he felt, there was a need for closure, for healing. By chance at first, and then by their own volition, the skein of their lives had crisscrossed, entwined, entangled, and Spiegel sensed that wherever they went in the future, no matter how great their separation, neither would ever be wholly free from the influence of the other. Spiegel remembered that night long ago when Tracy had stood them back-to-back and taken their measure. It was as if, ever since that moment, they had been walking away from each other until they had come full circle, and at last here they stood, face-to-face.

"It's freezing in here," Spiegel said, as he shook himself out from his bag. "Maybe we could get a fire going and keep this place warm through the night. Or is it already morning? Who the hell knows? You have a watch?"

Aaronson shook his head. He had been living, like Spiegel, by an internal clock, which had been thrown hopelessly out of sync by the constant daylight and the stress of flight and dislocation.

"Then we're on our own." Spiegel got up and threw some kindling into the belly of the stove, and he busied himself getting a fire under way as Aaronson talked.

"You thought you could get away easy," Aaronson said. "You didn't expect to see me ever again, did you?"

"We were waiting for some word from you," Spiegel said. "We waited as long as we could."

"And did you enjoy the job? Of being me?"

"Look," Spiegel said. "I'm not sure how much you know about what's gone down while you were away, in regards to Tracy." As Spiegel spoke, he felt his throat clutch. He realized that the topic of Tracy was a dangerous vortex at the center of their conversation, like a black hole in a field of white ice.

Aaronson smiled and put his hand on Spiegel's shoulder. "You fooled them all, every last fucker," he said. "You never cracked, and you never let on. You gave me the chance I needed. Everybody thought you were me."

"I was your cover."

"The black cloak that concealed me from the eyes of the world. Well done."

"Thanks." Aaronson must have heard about the fracas on TV2, about the May Day riots, about the ARMS tribunal. Everything. "But what about you?" Spiegel said. "How come we never heard from you? You disappear and leave me to carry all that weight. Half the world's looking to find me: border patrols, army intelligence, the Uppsala police, religious fanatics, even the press. And the only thing I hear about you are these mysterious reports that you're back in Sweden, that you're drawing money out of the ARMS treasury. So did you even go to Germany? What were you doing all this time? Junior year abroad? Europe on five dollars a day? Where the fuck were you?"

"You should have been able to find me. You just looked in the wrong places or asked the wrong people."

"I didn't ask anyone," Spiegel said.

"You never asked the Uppsala police? You never talked to the press? You never had any contact with your father?"

"I never revealed anything to the cops about you," Spiegel said. "I never told that reporter my real name. In fact, he wrote a big story proving that I don't exist." Spiegel paused for a second before continuing. In the dim light, he tried to scrutinize Aaronson's face. But Aaronson's face showed nothing. The fringes of his unruly beard nearly covered his features, hiding his expressions from view. "And just what do you know," Spiegel asked, "about my father?"

"I know who he is," Aaronson said. "I suspect that he's been kept informed, that's all."

"Not by me," Spiegel said. "He doesn't even know that I'm in Sweden. I had someone in the States send him a bunch of postcards that I wrote before I left."

"Okay, so you never sent him reports," Aaronson said. "That's fine. But did you ever think that maybe somebody else . . ."

"Was watching me?"

Aaronson nodded. "You must know that your father's agency keeps a close eye on the resisters, on any American receiving support from a foreign government."

The kindling caught. Spiegel pushed two birch logs into the maw of the fire and slammed shut the stove door. Quickly, the room smelled of smoke and radiant iron. Spiegel sat on the floor, beside the stove. "And what about you?" he asked. "Is that how you received your support?"

"You mean from a foreign government?"

Spiegel remembered what Inspector Svenson had led him to believe: that Aaronson had been nourished on a diet of rubles. Maybe he had been right about the food but wrong about the source of the supply. "I mean," Spiegel said, "were you getting support from my father's agency? Were you being paid for information?"

"You mean, am I a fucking spy?"

Spiegel didn't answer.

"I've cut my deals," Aaronson said. "That wasn't one of them."

"I didn't think so," Spiegel said.

"Now don't go making me out better than I am. After I busted up the draft office, I would've been willing to work for anyone who could have brought me and Tracy to safety. I would have worked for your father's agency if they had come through with an offer. They didn't, and I took the best deal I could get."

"What are you talking about?" Spiegel asked. "You make it sound like you were shopping for a used car."

"No, what I'm saying is that I didn't have a lot of time or a lot of choice. You've got to understand my situation," Aaronson said. "I couldn't stay in Canada, and I couldn't go back to the States. It wasn't easy getting to Sweden, believe me. I had a lot of help. But not for free, you dig? Not without cost."

Aaronson looked off in the middle distance as he told Spiegel more of his story. It was as if he had rehearsed the role for some time but had never had a chance to say his lines, an understudy behind a hale and durable lead.

"When they turned the heat up on me, and on Tracy, in Toronto, we began to look around for a way out of Canada. I'm sure she's told you. We thought about heading west to BC and trying to get lost somewhere in the Yukon or about buying a cheap ticket to Mexico or trading in her VW for two Harleys and taking our chances back in the States, on the road. Anyway, we heard about a cell in Montreal that specialized in cases like ours."

Aaronson described their journey to Montreal, their long nights in a transient hotel by the railroad, lying on a narrow bed beneath a dangling bulb, waiting for their contact. At last a message was left for them at the desk, and Aaronson set off for a workingman's café with long, bare wooden tables where men with coal-blackened hands ate sandwiches on thick bread and smoked hand-rolled cigarettes. He sat, he drank coffee, he pretended to read a newspaper in French, until a man tapped him on the shoulder and led him to a back alley where a rusted Renault was parked in idle. They drove on narrow streets to a dusty warehouse in the industrial flats by the St. Lawrence where, in a cloud of cigarette smoke and whiskey fumes, in air that sat still and dead beneath the huge blades of an immobile fan, a small brown man wearing thick plastic eyeglasses drew up a set of fresh documents. An old printing press clunked out some papers that smelled of cheap ink. A young girl, her face shrouded by a veil, her dark eyes averted, handed Aaronson a packet of tickets, which he stuffed into his jacket lining. They gave him pressed clothes and new shoes and money for a haircut and shave. He left the warehouse carrying a leather valise. He was told it was never to leave his sight until he handed it off in Copenhagen. Back at his hotel room in the city, a man was sitting on the iron-frame bed. Tracy was gone. The man held a gun casually in his right hand. He didn't flourish it or aim it. He just wanted to be sure that Aaronson knew the gun was there. He conveyed the information that Aaronson would not see Tracy again until the delivery had been successfully completed. On his way out, the man swung his fist at the dangling bulb, smashing it with the butt of the gun.

Aaronson flew to Frankfurt and took a series of trains north to Denmark. The journey went smoothly. Apparently, he was a clean marker and nobody picked up his trail. In Copenhagen, he made his delivery.

"But nothing is face-to-face," Aaronson said. "Everything's done through intermediaries, you know. There are so many steps and layers, so no one person can unravel the whole skein. The only people I saw were my two contacts on either side, the guy who gave me the valise and the one I handed it to in Denmark. From there, it entered a network where stuff can be moved very easily to all the Baltic ports. Do you know what I'm saying?"

"Yes, I think I do," Spiegel said. "You made your delivery to someone from the church." Everything became clear to Spiegel. The church must be a cover for a band of smugglers posing as proselytes. It was a perfect system. They lived on boats in the Scandinavian harbors, and they came ashore to preach among the lonely wanderers of the Western world, preferably ones whose wallets were bent like a bow around a bulge of traveler's checks. They set up their tables in airports and train stations, they worked their way through crowds, selling their pamphlets and artifacts, disciplined and ascetic, so visible that they were hardly noticed, at worst a public nuisance, living just below the horizon of official surveillance. Their internal network was intimate yet dark and complex, so a dollar handed to a threadbare prophet in Heathrow could be sucked into the system, flushed clean through any number of Swiss or German banks, then pumped back out into one of the clandestine passageways, the capillaries that connect the floating churches, the missions, the publishing houses, the schools, hospitals, academies. Nothing that entered the bloodstream of the church would bear a mark or a trace.

"I wasn't supposed to know much about what I was carrying," Aaronson said. "I was just the mule. But I was led to believe it was a sample case."

"You were crazy," Spiegel said. "If you'd been busted, they could have locked you away forever."

"It wasn't drugs, man. It was electrical stuff, wiring and diagrams, transistors for stereos, TV sets."

"Then why all the secrecy and the threats?"

"The trade embargo. This stuff was going to China, from an American manufacturer. The Canadian warehouse, the cash being moved through the church, the factory in Sweden where we held the ARMS meetings—it's all part of the screen to hide the source of the goods and to conceal the profits. These corporate pigs see an enormous consumer market developing in China, and they want their piece of it. They don't give a shit about the war, about politics, about the international Communist menace. They just want to be at the switch when Chairman Mao lets the masses turn on to the bourgeois decadence of rock'n'roll and Walt Disney."

"Power to the people."

"Right on."

Aaronson said nothing for a while.

"But when Tracy came to Uppsala," Spiegel said, "you could have quit the movement and walked away from the guys running the factory and all their demands. Why didn't you go back to school or go toss hay on a dairy farm?"

"Once you're in, it's hard to get out. I had access to all the money I'd need for ARMS—"

"—and for your way of life—"

"—but I knew that it wasn't like a contribution to United Way. There were strings, and obligations. I was supposed to keep a steady stream of money moving south to the church headquarters. Of course, eventually the stream became, shall we say, diverted."

"To your own little pool."

"Yes. I knew it was only a matter of time before they'd paddle up the stream to find its source."

"But they found me."

"Exactly. My plan worked."

"Did it? Maybe it worked for you. But not for everyone you left behind, you son of a bitch! Why didn't you get in touch with us? Why didn't you come back?"

"Easy, man," Aaronson said. "You've got to understand my situation. If the guys in the church found me, they'd have killed me—"

"Great. They'd have killed you. But you were willing to leave me there to take the heat, your heat. They'd have killed me instead!"

"But you were saved, right?"

That was true. But how did Aaronson know?

"The Uppsala police saved me. They knew I wasn't you. . . ."

"Not just them. The military police knew, too. They didn't want anything to happen to you on their watch. They wanted me. If they could get me, arrest me in Germany, and reveal the sources of the movement's financial support, it would be an enormous blow to ARMS. They had a trap all set to spring shut. They were just waiting for me to walk into it. They still are."

"Don't they know where you are now?" Spiegel asked.

"Their network is dismantled, thanks to you. Their lookout has abandoned her post."

"*Her* post?"

"Haven't you figured out that she was sending regular reports on you, on the whole movement?"

Spiegel's heart stuck in his throat. He felt sick suddenly, dizzy, as if the floor were spinning and the walls closing in on him. How could she do that? He couldn't believe Tracy could dissemble so convincingly, about her feelings, and her passion. But spies did that all the time, at least in the movies. Had she betrayed Aaronson as well? Had Aaronson vanished from Uppsala to get beyond the reach of her control?

"That's why you left Tracy," Spiegel said. "She was working for the other side, and you didn't care if I got involved with her. It left the road clear for you to make your getaway."

Aaronson laughed. "Not Tracy," he said. "Ms. Julie."

"Melissa? She was spying on me, all that time? And telling—"

"She was a better actor than you thought, right?" Aaronson said. "They cast her against type."

"They?"

"The military police. Criminal Intelligence Division. For all I know, she was on active duty. You didn't really think she was just an exchange student, did you?"

Of course, Spiegel thought. Melissa knew everything. And now she is gone, off to play another role. Her revels now are ended. He took a breath. How close he had come to the precipice, but he had not taken the plunge. Spiegel was glad he never fell for Melissa, despite her allure and her proximity. If he had, maybe he would have been the one to be shamed and defeated. Maybe his road would have dead-ended at the bottom of a pond. He felt a pang in his heart for Jorge.

Spiegel needed to move around, to shape his mind to all these revelations. He thought that if he were outside, in the fresh air, listening to the wind shaking the top branches of the trees, it would be easier to accept the truths he was learning from Aaronson: that everything is mutable, that each of us wears a mask to hide the shifting shapes of our allegiances and our longings.

"Aaronson," Spiegel said. He stood, to emphasize the gravity of what he was about to say, to show that he would back his words, if necessary, with force. "Tracy was supposed to send me some documents, papers that would allow me either to stay in the country legally or to move on safely. I think you knew all about her plan. Maybe she sent you with the papers, or maybe you were tipped off and you got to the drop-off first and lifted them."

"Hmm," Aaronson muttered. "You're very perceptive, very shrewd. Go on, I'm listening."

"I don't know what your game is, whether you're trying to get back at Tracy or whether you're trying to nail me for what went down between us when you split from Uppsala."

"Oh, well," Aaronson said, his voice crackling with sarcasm. "As they say, let bygones be bygones."

"If you give me the papers, I'm gone. I'm out of your life."

"And if I don't?" Aaronson said. "You have nobody to turn to for help. Everyone you trusted, everyone you thought you loved is dead or gone or turned against you. Go back and retrace your steps, man. You'll be walking down a lonely road. You'll be walking on the ashes of the dead."

"What are you saying?"

Aaronson looked Spiegel over, warily, assessing his strength, his condition. Spiegel felt exhausted, but he knew that he could summon whatever power he needed to fend off Aaronson, if it came to that.

"She'll turn you in. Maybe she has already. I don't know where you can go from here, but there's no way you can go back," he said. "You're still a wanted man, you know."

"You bastard," Spiegel said, and he leaped toward Aaronson, trying to grab him by the throat. He was fueled by fury. He didn't know what he would do if his hands reached Aaronson's flesh. But Aaronson was too quick and elusive. He dodged to the side. In a flash, he grabbed Spiegel by the wrists and swung him to the floor. Spiegel smashed his shoulder against the hot stove and knocked over the pile of kindling. He grabbed a stick and lifted it, trying to advance on Aaronson, but again Aaronson caught him off balance. Aaronson kicked, and the tip of his boot caught Spiegel on the elbow. The stick flew across the room and hit the far wall with a crack like a rifle shot. Spiegel's whole arm was on fire, as if a nerve had exploded. "Fuck, I think you broke it," he said. "Where'd you learn that?"

"So you had enough?" Aaronson shouted. "It's me should be coming after you, moving in with my old lady."

Spiegel sat on the floor, massaging his injured arm, hoping to get some feeling back in his hand and wrist. "I know," Spiegel said. "I was a shit. I can't explain it. Except, look, it's over between us." Why had he have been so quick to attack? It was as if his nerves were made of dry paper, and the slightest spark could set off a fire.

"I don't have your papers," Aaronson said. "Whatever Tracy sent is waiting for you at the railroad junction. We can hike there in the morning."

"Whenever the fuck that is."

"And you can decide what you want to do, whether you want to stay in Sweden and take your chances with the military police or cross the frontier."

"I think that depends on you," Spiegel said. "I think we know the truth. It's like a law of physics. The two of us can't occupy the same space at the same time."

"You don't have to worry about me," Aaronson said. "After tomorrow, you won't see me again."

In the morning, Aaronson explained, they would set out together down the trail toward the railroad line that ran through the valley. When they reached the junction, they would proceed along their separate ways.

"If you want," Aaronson said, "you can keep going north to the frontier. It would take you about another four hours—a pretty rugged hike. Or you could turn back and spend another night in this shelter," Aaronson said.

"And what happens to you?" Spiegel asked.

"I'm waiting at the junction for the next train. It's a really remote piece of track, mostly used for shipping iron from the Kiruna mines. Big flatcars rumble through there all the time, spilling rock dust on the valley floor. The trees there, you'll see them, they look red, like rust. But twice a day a passenger train comes through, once heading north, once heading south. It's a drop point for some forest rangers and for some of the mail that goes to the outlying mines. I'm going to pick up the northbound."

"The northbound? You're crazy. There's nothing north of here. You've reached the fucking top of the world. You've got no place left to run, man. You've run out of space."

"That's not true," Aaronson said. "Have you looked at a map?"

"Yeah, and there's nothing between us and the North Pole except Santa's reindeer."

"There's Norway."

"As I said . . ."

"There's fishing villages, and a pretty big port, called Narvik. I'm going to get myself on a boat, a whaleboat maybe, and work my way east. I've got the papers and a visa. . . ."

"If you're trying to get back to the States, I don't think a polar crossing is the way you want to go."

"That's not where I'm heading. Haven't you figured it out? I'm going to China."

Spiegel stared at Aaronson, amazed. He began to think that maybe Aaronson really was crazy, that the stress of the past year had stretched thin the filaments of his mind until the connections that should have held his thoughts together were left loose and loopy, dangling.

"China? You'll be the only American there, unless some missionaries are still holding out."

"We'll be heroes, vanguards of the Second American Revolution."

"We?" Spiegel said. "I ain't going."

"Me and Tracy. That's where she's headed, overland."

But the whole idea of going to China was preposterous. The country had been closed to the West for thirty years. There probably wasn't a person in a million who could speak a word of English. Aaronson the hero? More likely they would lock him away in a bamboo prison as a spy or, if he was lucky, ship him off to a rice paddy where he could shovel manure with the peasants. He would be better off almost anywhere—Israel, Moscow, Africa, even trying his chances with the justice system back in the States. No, Spiegel thought, there is nothing I can do anymore for Aaronson. Maybe all I can do is save Tracy—or myself.

17

Spiegel and Aaronson agreed to set out together on the trail during whatever felt to them like the morning. Their energy incinerated by the flash-fire fight, their senses dulled by the warm, smoky air inside the shelter, they had collapsed into sleep without coming to any understanding about Aaronson's needs and Spiegel's obligations. Spiegel slept fitfully, favoring his injured arm. When he woke, he lay still for as long as he could. He was in no rush to be under way. The shelter was a shambles. It looked like the cartoon image of a saloon after a gunfight, the furniture toppled and two cowboys splayed out on the dusty planks of the floor, snoring off their drunk. When at last Spiegel sat up, he put some weight on his arm, giving it a test. It was okay, he thought, not broken. Aaronson's steel-shanked toe must have caught him on the funny bone. He could still feel the tingling at the flat edge of his hand, but he could flex and grip and he would be able to shoulder his pack.

The fire was dead, but a thin film of soot seemed to cling to his skin, his clothes, everything he touched. The stove must have been poorly sealed or inadequately vented. That could have been a danger had not the shelter itself been of such rude construction. Spiegel could see daylight through numerous chinks in the walls, roof, and shutters. The dappled sunlight, filtered through the high birch trees, danced and flickered on the boot-scuffed floor.

Hot water would be nice, Spiegel thought, to wash away the grime and sweat of the night. But it wasn't worth struggling again with the stove. Instead, he slipped on his pants and his hiking boots and went outside. The sky was clear. The tops of the trees swayed gently in a light breeze. The ground was damp and soft, spongy against his step. He walked up the trail a couple of hundred feet to the last crossing he remembered, a swift stream where the water looked clear as glass. He hung his shirt on a branch and kneeled on the bank. He leaned forward, as if he were bowing before a god, and lowered his face into the stream. The coldness shocked him. He tilted his head and let his hair dangle in the rushing water, then cupped his hands and splashed his shoulders and chest with icy droplets that stung him and cleansed him. He shook his hair dry. He had forgotten a towel, so he sat on a stone to dry in the air. The sun was warm on his back, but he still felt a deep chill from his icy ablution.

He closed his eyes and tried to recall the events of the night, to piece them together and to make sense of all that he had heard. Each time he followed one of the lines of thought that Aaronson had laid out for him he smashed into a dead end, a brick wall of questions. So Tracy was leaving Uppsala, Aaronson said. In a way, that was a relief, for how could he have explained to her what had developed, so suddenly, between him and Monika? But why was she following Aaronson to China, and how could she possibly get there overland? Why had she bothered to send Aaronson to this remote outpost in the Arctic? Or had he split from Tracy and tracked Spiegel down on his own? Was Aaronson really planning to disappear across the frontier, another vanishing act, or had he come to the north on a mission of revenge?

Aaronson was sitting on the wooden step in front of the shelter when Spiegel returned. He was eating a candy bar, one square at a time.

"You know what I really miss?" Aaronson said.

"Almonds?"

"No, seriously." He offered Spiegel a square, but Spiegel shook his head no. The thought of a chocolate breakfast made his stomach a little unsteady.

"I miss the stars," Aaronson said. "I miss the black skies and the stars. I mean, it could be midnight right now, and the stars could be up there, behind the blue."

Spiegel looked up at the peak that loomed over them, a snowy summit with great, bare expanses of rocky ledge. The top of the mountain was obscured by a thin mist, like smoke. "That's true," he said. "But there are always stars overhead. During the daylight, we can't see them."

Aaronson thought about that for a second. "You feeling okay this morning?" he asked. "Maybe we should just hang out here for the day."

"I'm still a little banged up from last night," Spiegel said. He showed Aaronson his arm. There was a welt at the elbow and a solid bruise along the forearm. "But it would feel good to be on the move. I thought we could hike to the railroad station."

"Well, *station* might be the wrong word," Aaronson said. "It's like a siding."

"I wasn't expecting a shoeshine stand and a magazine kiosk," Spiegel said. "But you've got a train to catch."

"Except we have no idea what time it is," Aaronson said. "We don't know when the train's supposed to come through. So what's the point of hurrying? The quicker we get there, the longer I'll have to wait."

"I'm just eager to get moving again is all," Spiegel said.

"Don't you want anything to eat?"

"We can stop on the trail."

"Sure, at the first Howard Johnson's."

"Okay, some cereal maybe."

Perhaps Aaronson was right, Spiegel thought. There is a certain pointless futility in trying to hurry one's fate, like running down a track to meet an oncoming train. The train will arrive. You might as well walk. He decided to let Aaronson set the agenda, and the pace. They had a little to eat, they washed their dishes, they rolled up their gear and straightened the shelter so that the next hikers to come upon it would see no evidence of their encounter, of the violence that had roared through their blood in the night like a storm.

* * *

Spiegel guessed it was about noon when they set out together on the trail. The sky was still a watery blue, and a breeze tipped the outer branches of the dark spruce. But the peculiar silence of the summer night had yielded to the ambient notes of unseen birds that filled the great empty spaces of the mountainside with a chorus of riot and mimicry.

The hiking was much easier than the scramble up the south face that had left Spiegel so depleted the day before. They followed a steady but gradual descent along an open ledge to the upper crest of the valley forest. Once they entered the woods, the trail became soft, and the beams of sunlight that pierced the heavy filter of the overhead boughs sparkled on the mossy ground, like the spangled light cast across a ballroom by a revolving crystal chandelier. The air was cool, and they walked swiftly. They made no sound as they passed except for the occasional snapped twig or the swish of the pine needles they brushed aside where the forest began to close in and the trail narrowed.

Spiegel wanted to talk with Aaronson as they made their way along the trail, but Aaronson rebuffed his efforts to open conversation. He seemed distracted, as if he had withdrawn from the present and had already, in his mind, set forth on the next stage of his journey. That's all right, Spiegel thought. It was pleasant to walk through the woods in near silence, but he knew also that he could not let Aaronson depart without extracting the answers to his remaining questions. After all he had been through, all he had risked, Aaronson owed him that much.

They came to a fast stream, which they had to cross by a narrow spine of large, smooth rocks. "I think it's not too far," Aaronson said, breaking his silence. "I remember this crossing, hiking in."

"The station?" Spiegel couldn't imagine that they were anywhere near a railroad line. The woods were thick, with no signs of habitation. The earth was dark, the ground at a steep pitch. How could a track come through here? And why? He wondered, once again, if Aaronson was misleading him, or even if Aaronson was deluding himself.

"You'll see," Aaronson said, as he scrambled up the bank behind Spiegel, and they continued on their way.

Less than a mile along, Spiegel did see. The forest began to open up, and straight ahead he could make out through the gaps between the distant trees great stretches of blue sky, as if they had not hiked down into a valley but had somehow got their bearings wrong and climbed a summit. The woods ended abruptly at the head of a rock cliff, and the trail descended along a slice of ledge until it disappeared beyond an outcropping.

They had come to the brink of a chasm. The view was extraordinary. Ahead were the snowcapped mountains that rose to the Norwegian frontier. The valley floor far below them was blanketed with spruce, and a rising breeze lifted the scent of pitch to Spiegel as he stood on a small promontory jutting out above the precipice. Spiegel looked down, to see the red iron dust that Aaronson had described, but from above he could make out only a bluish green, as if the forest were reflecting the bright light of the clear sky and absorbing the summer air into its darker, more earthy hue. Ripping through the center of the wooded valley, like a long scar, was the seam that marked the clearing for the railroad track. "I see it," Spiegel said, tracing the line of the track with his finger. "But which way's it coming?"

"You see the train?" Aaronson said, with a touch of alarm. It occurred to Spiegel that Aaronson had no desire to sit on a rock, all by himself, waiting for the next northbound.

"No, just the track," Spiegel said. "From here, it looks empty, but it's hard to tell. There are spots where it's overgrown. But I think when the train comes you'd see smoke or steam, through the trees."

Aaronson said nothing. He set his pack down and untied the top flap. Spiegel continued to scrutinize the landscape.

"You'd probably hear it as well," he said. "Any noise from the valley would rattle off these cliffs like a drumbeat on steel. We're sort of at the lip of a bowl here, and I think—"

"Don't make a sound," Aaronson said. His voice was firm, cold, resolute. Spiegel felt something hard, like a metal rod, pressing into the back of his neck, right at the jugular. He picked up the faint scent of oil. He tried to twist around to get a look, but Aaronson grabbed his shoulder and pushed him down to the ground.

"Yes, it's a gun," Aaronson said. "Sit, here."

Spiegel sat on the outcrop, his feet at the edge of the cliff.

"Closer," Aaronson ordered, and Spiegel warily drew himself along the rock until his feet dangled over the drop. The barrel of the gun was pressed against the lobe of his ear.

"I'm sorry that it happened," Spiegel said. His throat felt parched, and his lips cracked like cellophane. "But it's over, between me and Tracy."

"Oh, yeah. I know that it's over," Aaronson said. "Tracy made that clear before she sent me up here to find you."

"And now that you've found me—"

"I've got some things to say to you."

Aaronson pulled the gun away from Spiegel's neck. Spiegel shuddered. He hunched his shoulders, a reflexive act of self-preservation, and anticipated the sound of a pistol shot. He braced himself against the forthcoming impact, the pain. But there was just a long stillness, and the soft sound of the wind touching the trees below.

"It's still on you, so don't try anything," Aaronson said.

Spiegel nodded.

"You must have figured out that I didn't leave Sweden to recruit deserters," Aaronson began. "That wasn't the plan. I needed your papers to make my escape."

"Your escape?"

"My idea was to use your passport as my ticket home. I was going home as you."

"Leaving me here—"

"You could have worked it out, proven your identity, applied for a temporary transit visa. By the time you returned to the States, I would be safe."

"And Tracy?"

Aaronson didn't answer. Spiegel understood that she must have been in on the scheme, too, all along.

"But of course I was being watched all the time. I knew that, once you told me about that thug from the church on the train from Paris. They were watching me the whole time I was gone, waiting to see what I would do, who I would contact. I disappointed them. I didn't do anything. When it looked like I was

heading back to Sweden, the border police had to grab me before
I left Danish soil. They turned me over to army intelligence."

"So they did arrest you," Spiegel said.

"Yes. They took your passport from me. The border police
put out an arrest warrant for you as well. At least that conveyed
a message to Tracy that they had me in custody."

After Aaronson had been held for several days, four guys barged
into his cell in the middle of the night. Aaronson found himself
hooded, shackled, shoved, and led blind into what he thought
must have been some sort of military jeep. It smelled of gasoline
and cigarettes. He shook with cold and fright as they drove out of
the city. He soon realized that they had taken him to an airport.
He heard the scream of planes overhead as he stood, frozen in
place, on the tarmac. He thought they might have left him alone,
to be crushed into the runway by the landing gear of an incoming
flight. He considered breaking away, but he had no idea in which
direction to run or how many people might be guarding him,
might even be standing right beside him. The whirlwind of surrounding noise made it impossible for him to take his bearings. At
last, too scared to stand still any longer, he started to move, and
hands grabbed him. He was led toward the furnace roar of a jet
engine. He tried to pull his hands free, to shield his face from the
heat, his ears from the monstrous noise. He was guided up a ramp,
and suddenly he heard a door slam shut.

Someone yanked the hood from his head. He was left shackled,
however, chained to the armrest of his jump seat. He was in the
vast hold of a cargo jet. Yellow bulbs overhead cast a dim, spooky
light. He could see the ribs of the fuselage, the pocked metal
skin of the old plane. Across from him, on canvas seats folded
out from the wall, sat four soldiers. Small clouds obscured their
faces. At first Aaronson thought that the men were smoking, but
soon he realized that it was frost from their breath. There was no
heat. Aaronson started to speak, to ask where they were heading,
but one of the soldiers cut him off with a string of expletives.
Another soldier, the officer in charge, Aaronson figured, ordered
the hothead to give it a rest, and Aaronson understood that none
of them was to speak for the duration of the flight. Each soldier

carried a large pistol strapped to his chest, to make a point. They wore the crisp khakis and black boots of the military police.

They held Aaronson in the brig, isolated from the common soldiers, the guys picked up for taking a swing at an officer or passing out drunk in the bathroom of a German whorehouse, then waking up two days after their leave had expired. They treated him okay, hot meals and clean work clothes, and they gave him a cell with a working toilet and a reading lamp by the cot. The interrogations were polite, formal, crisp. Aaronson got the message. They were trying to break his allegiance to the movement, to bring him around, to mold him, simply by wearing him down, into a pliable tool that would fit nicely in their hands. Yet behind their treatment lay the implicit threat that they might turn up the heat, throw him into the open wards of the psych unit where he would have to survive among the GIs trying to prove that they were too demented and violent even for service in Vietnam.

They questioned him about the movement in Sweden, about Zeke and the Worm, about the leadership insurgencies that had stirred the community since he had departed. They fed him information and misinformation, led him to believe that ARMS was in a shambles, that the group had splintered into warring factions. They explained that the rift had widened between those who considered themselves Swedish immigrants and those who thought of themselves as political exiles waiting for amnesty and redemption and triumphal return to their homeland. They said that the animosity between the hard-core soldiers who had risked their lives in battle and the guys who had deserted from the European theater or from boot camp or, worse, even before enlistment, had so intensified that the once egalitarian community had developed a calcified hierarchy, a status ladder more rigid and insurmountable than any system ever dreamed of by the minds in the Pentagon. In short, they alternately harassed him, tried to break him, and flattered him into thinking that the movement he had established had disintegrated because of his absence.

"And you believed them?" Spiegel said.

"Eventually."

Spiegel heard a metallic *click*, as if Aaronson had cocked the trigger of the pistol. He imagined that the barrel was only inches from his ear, but he decided he had better not try to verify that assumption. He had been trying to edge forward toward the brink of the cliff. He could see a ledge about ten feet below the crest. He thought if he could shift his balance forward, ever so slightly, and then distract Aaronson for a moment, he could safely make the drop. If his luck held and he didn't injure himself in the fall, he could gain the trail and escape into the valley. Of course, it was possible that the ledge was an isolated protrusion and he would be marooned there, in Aaronson's sights.

Aaronson didn't seem to notice Spiegel's incremental advance. He went on with his story.

"I'd set up a line of communication to Uppsala before I left, of course, but once they locked me up that line was cut. So I really had no clear idea. I thought they were bullshitting me, but, still, over time, they wear you down."

"So you're telling me that you gave in and agreed to tell them everything you knew about the movement in Uppsala?"

"No, that's not the point," Aaronson said. He seemed annoyed that Spiegel didn't get it, couldn't see the whole picture. "They're already telling me that they knew everything going on in Uppsala, right? Why would they need me to go back there and spy for them?"

"I don't know. Why?"

"They wanted me to go back to Uppsala to get busted."

Spiegel didn't say anything. He was truly puzzled.

"They gave me the same valise I'd carried into Denmark, or it looked like the same one, and they packed it full of plastics and switches. They told me not to look through the bag, that they'd make sure I got across the borders and through customs and all. And they gave me back my own passport. I mean a copy of it."

"But you must have looked anyway," Spiegel said. "In the bag."

"It was filled with East German banknotes, worthless shit, zipped into the inside flaps. It was a setup. The plan was, I was to carry the bag to a checkpoint at the Djurpark in Stockholm. It was all arranged, a bust that would link me and the ARMS

movement to Third World terrorists with Communist backing. I'd give depositions, make a public statement about how I
came to Sweden, about the shipments we'd handled, the money
that had gone into the ARMS treasury. They figured that would
destroy the deserter community and discredit its supporters in
the Swedish government."

"So the government would be forced to ban social services
for American deserters or else face a challenge from the Sweden
First Party," Spiegel concluded.

"Yes. The deserters would starve, or leave."

"And you agreed—"

"In exchange for protection, a pardon, passage home."

"But . . . you would have had to leave Tracy behind," Spiegel
said.

"Would she have come with me, if she could?"

Spiegel didn't even have to pause to think. "Yes," he said. "I
know now that she would have. She was waiting for you all the
time."

"But that wasn't so clear to me," Aaronson said, his voice rising. "When I came back and found out—"

"Don't try to put the blame on me," Spiegel cried. "Where
the fuck were you? You say you set up communications with
Uppsala before you left. Great. How come we never heard a
fucking thing from you? And then you come sneaking back,
with a plan to betray the whole movement so you can get
your freedom, your passport, your new identity, leaving all
the other Americans to fry. To hell with them—the guys who
risked their lives deserting the army in time of war. All hail
Aaronson, the hero!"

"And what about you? A guy I thought I could really trust, a
brother. It took you all of about two weeks to get into Tracy's
pants—"

"So go ahead," Spiegel yelled. He turned, and Aaronson
pushed the barrel of the gun into his rib cage. Spiegel raised his
arms, a gesture of submission. He could feel the ring of steel kiss-
ing his chest, imprinting a target on the soft flesh and the plank
of bone that shielded his racing heart. "Shoot me. Do it!"

"No," Aaronson said. "You've got to know—I didn't go through with the deal. I never made the handoff. I'm not going to."

"So instead," Spiegel said, "I'm the handoff. You're going to kill me."

Aaronson raised the gun slightly higher so that Spiegel was practically looking down the barrel. "Why would I want to kill you?" Aaronson said. "It's been in the papers already. Remember? Leonard Spiegel does not exist."

A chill shook Spiegel's whole body. Maybe Aaronson had really gone insane. Perhaps the physical exertion and the emotional turmoil of the past few days had broken him so that he was seeing things, hearing voices from within, and he could no longer distinguish reality from illusion.

"If I don't exist," Spiegel said cautiously, measuring each word, "I can't hurt you. Why don't you just let me go? I'll hike back toward the shelter, and you can go on your way. I won't tell anyone about our encounter. You can cross the frontier, move on to China, vanish."

"Yes," Aaronson said. "That's what I want to do." Spiegel let out a thin breath, through his clenched teeth. "But first," Aaronson continued, "I've got to die."

Aaronson tilted the gun before Spiegel's face. Sunlight glinted off the barrel, blinding Spiegel for a second.

"I understand," Spiegel said. "You brought me here to stand in for you one last time, to take one more dive for you. You're going to send me out there . . ." He gestured at the open space that lay before them, the still air of the wooded valley.

"Yes, over the wall—"

"—off the edge. And then what? In a few days, Monika reports that a hiker is missing, they send out a search party. They find my body at the base of the cliff and they figure—a tragic climbing accident, a death on the trail. But it won't be me who's reported dead. It will be you. So the search for you is off. The church, the military police, everyone figures you tried to run away and you died. And meanwhile you're safe in China, or somewhere else, living with Tracy, living as . . . me."

"Well figured," Aaronson said. "Well reasoned! If I weren't

holding this gun, I would applaud you. Consider it done, though. Imagine that you have heard my applause."

"But there's something you forgot," Spiegel said. "The only way my dead body's good to you is if I fall over the edge. If you shoot me, your plan is ruined. When they find my body, they'll know it wasn't a hiking accident. They'll know it was murder."

"So what?"

"So the gun doesn't scare me is what." He crouched, as if to leap forward, onto Aaronson, right into the range of the pistol. But Aaronson jumped to his feet and backed away, keeping the barrel trained on Spiegel.

"Now hold it, Lenny. Don't force me to use this," Aaronson said. "I have more—"

"You won't use it," Spiegel said, slowly advancing. "You can't shoot me."

Spiegel reached out his hand. "Here," he said. "Give me that gun."

Aaronson hung his head. His shoulders were shaking as if he were sobbing, but Spiegel could hear no sound. Slowly, Aaronson raised the gun, and Spiegel stepped forward to take it from him. But Aaronson kept lifting the weapon, to eye level. He cocked his elbow, flexed his wrist, twisted his neck, and pointed the gun at his own right temple. He froze, and Spiegel stood by helpless, powerless. Spiegel tried to call, but his words were strangled into a whisper. "Don't do it," he said.

As Spiegel spoke, Aaronson raised his right arm, straight up into the air, and Spiegel heard the crack of an explosion, he heard a bullet whistle up through the trees. A small branch fell as if it were shot from the sky, and it landed on the patch of ground between them. Spiegel smelled burning powder, and he could see a little puff of smoke, a tiny cloud, dissipating in the still air. Before Spiegel could say another word, a second shot rang out, and a third, as Aaronson, his face locked in a grimace, kept squeezing the trigger. The noise from the volley of shots ricocheted off the cliffs and off the face of the mountain, and birds wheeled in the air, screaming. At last Aaronson let his arm drop to his side, and the dying noises seemed to drift away, floating down the valley, like summer wind.

"I was going to do it," Aaronson said at last. "But I couldn't. I guess I'm not brave enough."

"It's not such a brave thing," Spiegel said. "To shoot yourself."

"Not me," he answered. "You. You had it figured out. I was going to kill you. But I can't do it. I can't."

"I guess I should say—thanks," Spiegel said. But he was wary about approaching Aaronson. He sensed that there could still be a trap. There might be another bullet in the chamber. Because of the echoes, the reverberations, Spiegel had been unable to keep count of the rounds Aaronson had fired.

"No," Aaronson said. "Don't say anything. I'm just a shit. We were both shits, to each other."

"And now we're even?"

"No. You still owe me."

"I'm not going to pay with my life," Spiegel said.

"You can pay with my death."

"No!" Spiegel cried. "I can't do that to you. I won't!"

"Oh, fuck the gun," Aaronson said, and he reared back and heaved the pistol off the edge of the cliff. It seemed to take a minute before Spiegel heard the clatter of the weapon landing on a base of loose rock. "There. You satisfied?"

"Then what is it you want from me?" Spiegel asked.

"I want you," Aaronson said, "to make it look like I died. I want you to let me live by making me dead. Will you do this for me? It's the last thing I'll ask of you."

Thoughts raced through Spiegel's mind, brief images, passing before his mind's eye like flip cards, of all he had done for Aaronson and of all the troubles he had endured—the fracas in the TV studio and the fight in the underground café, the May Day riot and the police interrogation. He thought of death and betrayal and loss, of his expulsion from ARMS and of Melissa's duplicity and of the lonely death of Jorge. He thought of friends in the movement who had disappeared, of Zeke and the Worm, of Iris somewhere back at home—he no longer even knew where—and Tracy back in Uppsala or maybe already on her way to Asia, and now Aaronson himself, the last one to go, the last to seek his help.

No good had come of his efforts to help Aaronson. All he had brought about was the death of a friend and the dissolution of the movement that Aaronson had created. Spiegel had been like a bit of celestial debris, floating through space, drawn into the orbit of the nearest dominant star. Not for long, he thought. He would free himself from Aaronson's field of gravity by helping him one last time, by sending Aaronson on his final passage and cloaking his disappearance behind a mask of death.

"Yes," Spiegel said.

"You will?" Aaronson said. His voice seemed to tremble, to melt in relief.

"Listen." Spiegel raised his hand and pointed off to a distant reach of the valley. Carried above the wind was an intermittent whistling sound and the steady hum of an engine. At the horizon, a wisp of smoke rose above the trees.

"Yes, that's it," Aaronson said.

"Can we make it?" Spiegel asked.

"Shit, I don't know," Aaronson said. "Let's go." He slipped his arms through the straps of his pack, and in what seemed like a single fluid motion, he was bounding along the cliffside trail. Spiegel had to scramble to catch up. His legs were still shaky and his movements clumsy after the standoff. He stepped awkwardly and unsteadily, breaking twigs and stumbling over rocks, struggling to keep pace.

The trail crossed the lip of the cliff and zigzagged down a series of steeply inclined ledges. Spiegel and Aaronson moved at a reckless clip, kicking up dust and rock. Stones rolled off the edge of the trail and rained on the valley floor. At every turn, their boots crunched into the dry, hard soil. The footing was loose, and sometimes they slipped and had to reach out blindly for balance. Once Spiegel teetered over the edge, and for a second he entertained the idea of letting himself drop into the welcoming blanket of spruce far below. "Come on," Aaronson yelled from ahead, and his call echoed through the valley, the reverberant words crashing against one another as they rose in a crescendo toward the sky.

At last the trail leveled to a gentle slope along a rockfall at the base of the cliff. When Spiegel caught up to him, Aaronson was kneeling at a streambed, drinking water he had cupped in his hands.

Spiegel was out of breath. "Can you still hear the train?" he asked. He strained to listen for the chug of the engine or the hiss of steel on steel, but he heard nothing. "Maybe it was headed away from us."

"No, you can hear much better from the summit," Aaronson said. "Down here, the sound gets swallowed by the trees. But it's coming."

"How do you know?"

"Put your hand to the ground. You'll feel the vibrations."

"Then we ought to pick up the pace," Spiegel said.

"The station's just there," Aaronson said, pointing into the woods. "A couple hundred yards."

The narrow trail followed the upper bank of the stream. They walked in silence beneath the thick spruce boughs. The long needles brushed their sleeves and their skin, staining them with pitch and with traces of iron dust. The ground was soft and resilient. Spiegel kicked a small log in the path, and it broke apart into splinters of punk. He knocked aside a rock with his boot and saw the damp ground in the exposed hollow swarming with insect life.

In a short distance they came into a small clearing where a shack of weathered barn board stood beside the railroad track. An old woman was sweeping the wooden platform with a straw broom. Across the tracks, the trail led to a cluster of cabins shaded by a tall stand of old forest.

"The station," Aaronson announced. "The village is up there."

"Who would live here?" Spiegel wondered.

"The railroad owns it," Aaronson said. "Train crews use it, when they're repairing track. And a watchman, who tends the station."

"What a lonely life."

"Yes, it kind of gives you the creeps. But you don't have to stay. You could hike north, to the Kungsled."

"I think I'm going to head back, after we say good-bye."

"I guess despite everything I owe you thanks," Aaronson said.

"For letting you spare my life?"

"For lending me your—everything."

The woman on the platform set her broom aside. She was the first to pick up the sound of the approaching train.

"Once I get where I'm going, I'll get to choose who I am," Aaronson said.

The ground shook as the train cut through the woods toward the small landing. The woman on the platform waved a flag to signal the train to stop. Aaronson's words were barely audible over the hiss of steam and the metallic ringing of the breaks.

"Will you?" Spiegel shouted. "Or will they choose for you?"

"They?"

"Whoever you're meeting. Whoever's setting you up."

Aaronson opened his arms and pulled Spiegel to him. They held each other in a firm embrace, as Aaronson said his last words to Spiegel.

"I'm not working for anyone, anymore," Aaronson said. "I guess I'm no longer part of the solution. I've become part of the problem. And what about you, brother? You know? You must choose."

Aaronson held Spiegel's face before his and gave him a hard kiss on both cheeks, a rough and masculine gesture. The woman tending the platform shouted something to them, words lost beneath the beating of the diesel engine. Aaronson leaned back to get a last look at Spiegel's face, worn and tired and the mirror of his own. He reached his hand to Spiegel and handed him some papers, then turned and bounded up the folding steps and boarded the train. In a flash, the whistle blew again. A man in uniform drew the folding steps up into the car. The woman waved her flag once more, and the train pulled out of the station. Spiegel strained to see Aaronson through the cloudy windows, but he had taken a seat on the far side, looking north. His eyes stinging from the oily smoke, Spiegel watched, waving his hand farewell, until the train, with its strand of freight cars in tow,

rattling like an iron chain and spitting lines of gravel, had passed
out of sight around a distant notch of trees. The woman on the
platform was walking up the hill toward the dark cabins. Only
when he reached up to brush the cinders and dust from his face
did Spiegel realize that he had been clutching a small white envelope with no address. He ripped it open. Inside, he found Jorge
Ramos's passport.

18

Responding to a tip from an anonymous caller, the Uppsala police yesterday recovered the body of an American war resister and leader of the American community in Uppsala. . . .

. . . Aaronson's body was found in a late-model Volvo that had been submerged for several weeks in an irrigation pond on a dairy farm in the village of Ekby, about fifteen kilometers west of the city.

The police are calling the death an accident.

"He drove into the pond," said police detective Anders Svenson, the department's liaison to the American community in Uppsala. "It appears Mr. Aaronson was trying to drive across a field, probably at night, and perhaps he didn't see the water."

There was no evidence that Aaronson was using alcohol or drugs at the time of his death, according to a preliminary report from a medical examiner. The report said that due to the prolonged submersion the identification and examination of Aaronson's body would be difficult. Tentative identification was made on the basis of Aaronson's passport and other documents found in the vehicle.

Officials at the American embassy have been notified of Aaronson's death and will make arrangements for burial.

Aaronson, twenty-two, came to Sweden last year, apparently from Canada. He had never served in the American armed forces, but he was wanted in the United States for damaging a draft office in New York State early last year.

In Sweden, he settled in Uppsala where he established the local chapter of the American Resisters Movement—Sweden (ARMS), an activist group for the American war resisters and military deserters. He headed the organization and was its spokesman at public assemblies, before government agencies, and in media forums. He gained some notoriety when his appearance earlier this year on a TV2 debate program led to a fistfight inside the studio between Aaronson and the right-wing Swedish politician Erik Edström.

Edström, chairman of the Sweden First Party, called the report of Aaronson's death "a shame," but he added: "It is to be expected when we let people into this country who have no respect for our traditions and ways of life."

Aaronson's whereabouts had been somewhat of a mystery of late. After his celebrated television appearance, he went into seclusion and apparently ceded control of the ARMS group to two of his deputies.

His last public appearance was at the city's May Day rally, where his presence in the crowd caused a serious disruption in which another American resister was knocked off the Drottninggatan Bridge and injured in his fall into the river. Aaronson was detained at the time by the Uppsala police for his role in creating the disturbance, but he was released without charges.

"He was a great leader, and his death shall not go unavenged," said ARMS chairman James Hyde, who calls himself the movement's general-in-chief. "We hold the American imperial military machine responsible for Aaronson's untimely death. This is what happens to men who challenge the establishment in a pig culture."

"His death is a tragic loss for all of us in the movement," said Ezekial Al-Shabazz, the ARMS deputy general. "Along with our brothers and sisters at Jackson State and Kent State, Aaronson is another casualty of the American imperialist war in Southeast Asia."

American officials in Sweden released a statement

expressing regret that "Mr. Aaronson and others like him fail to perceive the consequences of their flouting of national and international law."

The Uppsala police declined to speculate on how Aaronson came to be in possession of the car in which he drowned. The car's owner, a university student who lived in the housing complex at Flogsta, reported the vehicle stolen last month. She told the police that she believed the car had been taken by a student at the Swedish Language Institute with whom she had lived at one time. Based on her report, the police had issued an arrest warrant for Jorge Ramos, whose current whereabouts is unknown. The police have now cleared Mr. Ramos of all charges.

—from a front-page news article in
Svenska Dagbladet

The tragic death last week of an American war resister should lead all of us to reconsider our attitude toward the secret heroes who live among us. For Mr. Aaronson was just that—a hero. He was willing to give up everything, all the comforts and privileges of his homeland, in order to stand for his beliefs. He came to Sweden in hopes of making a better world. Who knows why he died? Perhaps the frustration and sadness of watching the war in Vietnam drag on, month after month, to no purpose. Perhaps the escalation of the war into Cambodia and the attack in his homeland on American students. His hopes were crushed, and with them his life.

How can we not think that, had he lived, he would have devoted his life to causes of justice and peace? Is this not the kind of young man we should welcome, with open arms, into our culture and our society? Let us, instead, reach out our hands and bid welcome to his American brothers.

—from an editorial by
Gunnar Mendelsohn in the *Uppsala Tidskrift*

Let others mourn the death of Aaronson, or whoever it was they dredged up from the bottom of that pond, but I say—good riddance. The only thing that saddened me was the destruction of a perfectly good Volvo. What a horrid waste!

Under the weepy eyes of the socialist government, our country has enough problems already. Rising unemployment, high taxes, crime in the cities—before you know it, we will become another America! So what do we do? Open our doors to the worst of the Americans, the ones too sick, perverse, lazy, or ungrateful to fight for the causes of their own nation. Oh, sure, we say. Come to Sweden. We will not only welcome you. We will feed you, house you, give you schools, jobs, lovers, and wives. Take from us. We are guilty. We are Swedes.

I tell you—we are a joke. Around the world, people laugh at us, they shake their heads in disbelief. Fellow Swedes, wake up! The foreigners are eating away at our culture like worms in the bud. Reject them, before it is too late. Before we all find ourselves drowning in the mud at the bottom of a frozen pond.

—from a speech delivered at a Sweden First forum by
Erik Edström

Dear Iris,

I write this to you on what I expect will be my last night in Sweden. It's nearly midnight, and there is a touch of gray in the sky. Already, the long summer nights are beginning to ebb and the darkness is lapping at the edges of the day. I'm sitting at a writing desk by a window that looks out on the tall hedges at the border of the Uppsala botanical gardens. I am with a woman named Monika. This is our last night in her house.

I don't know what you have heard regarding news from Sweden. Monika has translated for you three recent news clippings that report on Aaronson's death. There are things, however, that have never been in the newspapers and never will be, and I must explain them to you before I leave the country.

The body found in the Volvo that had sunk in the muddy pond was not that of Aaronson. It was that of my friend Jorge Ramos, who took his life in despair, mistakenly thinking he had shot another man to death. Although I never suspected this while Jorge was alive, I have come to accept that Jorge had been recruited by the CIA to provide information about the international community in Uppsala. He was giving them reports on me, on Aaronson, on others he met among the resisters and deserters, even on another spy who had been planted in the university by the military police. I suspect that my exchange of identities with Aaronson was well-known to all government agencies, military and otherwise. Perhaps through Jorge's reports even my father was kept informed about my time in Sweden, about what I have done here.

As to where Aaronson has gone, I just can't say. When I last saw him, he was bound for Norway. He said that from there he was going to ship out aboard a whaling boat and then try to make his way to safety in Asia, where he would rendezvous with Tracy. She left the country without a word to me. Perhaps she has told you more about their plans.

Before leaving, Aaronson asked me to do one thing for him—to make it appear, somehow, that he had died. I was able to do that, with Monika's help. She knows a local newspaper editor who has extensive ties both to the left and to the local police. She gave them the "tip" that Aaronson's body was entombed in a Volvo in a remote irrigation pond. The story appeared in the press, the police went to drag the pond, and they did find the body, along with Aaronson's passport and other papers that Jorge must have been carrying. Whether the police had any doubts about the correct identification of the body, I really don't know. The CIA, trying to protect its sources, may have asked the Uppsala police to suppress the true identity of

the corpse. So the Uppsala police put out the story that
the dead man was Aaronson, and his death by drowning
has developed into a great public morality play. The newspapers, and then the politicians, have kept the story alive,
exploiting the tragedy for their own purposes.

Meanwhile, I had been left with Jorge's Portuguese
passport, which you might think would do me no good.
But Monika's newspaper friend, a Danish Jew who years
ago fled to Sweden to escape the Nazi invasion, has an
amazing print shop in his plant, and his engravers can
perform wonders with official documents. They stripped
out Jorge's photograph, bleached off his name and date of
birth, dissolved the last vestiges of his identity into a puddle of ink and some scrapings of pulp. In their place, like
a photographic image slowly emerging from its chemical
pool, appeared a signature and a snapshot and a name in
black. Here, said the old man, the foreman of the works,
as he handed me the new passport, still warm like fresh
bread, it's you. But it was not me. As I stared at the unfa-
miliar picture and at the words that I couldn't understand,
I wondered—had my appearance changed so much that I
no longer recognized my face, or was I looking not at my
face but at another's, some silent partner who was saying:
This is the way. This is the man you must become.

So I will be traveling, too. Monika and I leave tomorrow by train for Holland, and then by boat for England. I
don't know where we will stay. She has dreams of a cottage
on the Irish coast. Perhaps when we settle I will be able to
reflect on all that has happened since I left America.

I came here to help the antiwar movement, I thought,
and it seems that my presence has caused nothing but
havoc and destruction. The movement would have been
much stronger had Aaronson stayed in Uppsala and
worked at building his political base. Once I realized he
was not coming back, I should have applied for a new
passport and gone home. But I didn't—not because I was
in love with Tracy or committed to the cause or loyal to

Aaronson or afraid to face the consequences of what I'd done. No. I was no longer playing a role because there was no longer a Lenny Spiegel. I dived so deep into Aaronson's identity that I nearly lost hold of my own. It was as if I had come to Sweden to enable Aaronson to disappear, but I had disappeared instead. And now, writing to say good-bye to you from the other side, I feel like a voice without a language, a face without a name.

Spiegel set aside the letter and laid it on the writing desk. He took a last look around the house. Months ago, he had arrived in Sweden carrying only a backpack and a canvas duffel. That was all he would need, it seemed, to take everything he owned back out, for he had accumulated nothing, nothing tangible, that is. As for Monika, there was much that she would have to leave behind. She had done her best to pack all she would take with her into two cases. The rest of her belongings she had stowed in packing boxes. She had stacked them in neat rows beneath the eaves and had labeled each box with black marker. At some point, she said, she would write to her friends and ask them to ship some of the boxes ahead and to divide the rest among themselves. She wanted part of her material life to remain behind in Uppsala.

Monika was asleep. The air was still and quiet. It was a time for thinking, or more precisely for clearing the mind. Over the next few days, Spiegel imagined, he would be consumed with the rigors of hard travel and then with adapting to the ways of life in a new land.

His one regret on leaving Uppsala was that he had not been able to say good-bye to Tracy. Whether she had loved him for himself or as a kind of artificial Aaronson no longer mattered. They had loved each other at the time, until each had found the right person with whom to move onward. He wished that he could have told her so. But, as Aaronson had warned him, by the time he returned to Uppsala, Tracy had vanished.

One evening, Spiegel decided to look for her. He walked to their old apartment, saw the Volkswagen parked at the curb, saw lights on in the bay window, but when he tried the door he was barred by a huge dark man in a black leather jacket who spoke through broken teeth. "Tracy?" he said. "Never heard of the bitch." Behind him, through the crack of light in the doorway, Spiegel could see forms sprawled, stupefied, on the bare wooden floor. He could hear the sound of clattering dishes beneath the wail of a Hendrix guitar riff. "Now fuck off," the man said, as he shoved a hand the size of a dinner plate against Spiegel's chest. Spiegel had seen enough. He turned and walked off into the warm summer night.

He asked Monika what she knew about Tracy's escape, and Monika told him that she and Tracy had long ago reached an agreement about him and Aaronson. Concerned about Aaronson's safety once he returned to Sweden, Monika said that they could work out a plan to get him across the frontier, but they must choose their course of action and see it through to the end.

I understand, Spiegel said. You told her she had to choose between Aaronson and me, and she chose Aaronson.

No, Monika said. That's not it at all. The fact is I chose you.

Yet Monika could not explain why Aaronson had gone to see Jorge at Flogsta, and how he had convinced Jorge to exchange passports. Spiegel had an idea. Perhaps Jorge had not been the only line from Uppsala to the CIA. Perhaps Jorge and Aaronson had been playing on the same side, so to speak. Had the CIA been using Aaronson and Jorge, the underground network of the church, the ARMS chapter and its clandestine financial arrangements to create a link to China, a back channel that could somehow lead America down a secret path to peace?

Spiegel wished there was someone he could speak to about all that was racing through his mind. But these were ideas too dangerous to put into writing. That will have to be enough, he thought, for tonight. He signed his letter to Iris, folded it, sealed it in an envelope, and put the envelope in his pack. He would carry it with him to remind him of Iris and of the others he had left behind.

It may be that I will never send Iris this letter, Spiegel thought. But someday I will see her and we will talk about these things, and then she will know.

ACKNOWLEDGMENTS

For background information on American exiles in Sweden in the Vietnam era, I consulted *American Deserters in Sweden: The Men and Their Challenges*, by Thomas Lee Hayes (Association Press, N.Y., 1971). My friends Ron and Christina Krouk were my guides to the Swedish language. *Tack så mycket!*

I am most grateful to Laura Hruska of the Soho Press, for her faith in this book and for her excellent editing of the manuscript. For their encouragement and advice, I would like to thank M.J. Andersen, Alan Feldman, Bob Kerr, Peter Phipps, Bill Reynolds, Lowell Rubin, Alex Smithline, Andy Wolk, and the members of the former Providence Area Writers (PAWs). Most of all, I would like to thank Marge, Anna, and Josie Krieger, for their love and support.